T0359915

MODERN

Glamour. Power. Passion.

MILLS & BOON

HOW TO WIN A PRINCE
© 2023 by Juliette Hyland
Philippine Copyright 2023
Australian Copyright 2023
New Zealand Copyright 2023

First Published 2023
Second Australian Paperback Edition 2024
ISBN 978 1 038 94456 6

HOW TO TAME A KING
© 2023 by Juliette Hyland
Philippine Copyright 2023
Australian Copyright 2023
New Zealand Copyright 2023

First Published 2023
Second Australian Paperback Edition 2024
ISBN 978 1 038 94456 6

MIX
Paper | Supporting
responsible forestry
FSC® C001695

Published by
Harlequin Mills & Boon
An imprint of Harlequin Enterprises (Australia) Pty Limited
(ABN 47 001 180 918), a subsidiary of HarperCollins
Publishers Australia Pty Limited
(ABN 36 009 913 517)
Level 19, 201 Elizabeth Street
SYDNEY NSW 2000 AUSTRALIA

Cover art used by arrangement with Harlequin Books S.A.. All rights reserved.

Printed and bound in Australia by McPherson's Printing Group

How To Win A Prince

MILLS & BOON

Juliette Hyland believes in strong coffee, hot drinks and happily-ever-afters! She lives in Ohio, USA, with her Prince Charming, who has patiently listened to many rants regarding characters failing to follow their outline. When not working on fun and flirty happily-ever-afters, Juliette can be found spending time with her beautiful daughters and giant dogs, or sewing uneven stitches with her sewing machine.

Also by Juliette Hyland

Rules of Their Fake Florida Fling
Redeeming Her Hot-Shot Vet
Tempted by Her Royal Best Friend

Boston Christmas Miracles miniseries

A Puppy on the 34th Ward

Discover more at millsandboon.com.au.

For my editor, Laurie, who helped take this long-held story dream and make it a reality!

CHAPTER ONE

BRIELLA AILIONO SNAPPED another photo of herself, hoping the angle highlighted the long dark gown her best friend had designed for this final engagement. The image was about the dress, not her, but if she'd learned anything, it was that appearances were always scrutinized. If her mother was still talking to her, Brie might thank her for the multitude of lessons she'd taught on the subject.

She scrunched her nose as she examined the image. She wasn't as bubbly as the other potential brides here, wasn't bouncy and excited for the tiny possibility she'd win the "prize" in a few minutes. She only had one princess ticket in the giant glass spinning lotto wheel up on the palace's balcony. One shot to become a princess. One shot to wear a crown.

One shot too many!

Prince Alessio's Princess Lottery was all the country of Celiana had talked about for the last year. Throughout each week, potential brides had purchased tickets and then deposited them on Sunday while cameras watched. It was a year of spectacle.

If she could have devised any other way to launch Ophelia's bridal gown and specialty dress shop so quickly, Brie would have. A standard rollout with a mixture of graphics across social media platforms, booths at bridal fairs, a well-placed billboard or sponsored "news article" were options.

Success lay down that path, in two or three years. This way, this scheme, with her standing next to all the brides in a new wedding dress designed by Ophelia as she rattled off comments about the gown and the spectacle... Well, it meant success was at Ophelia's door year one. And wild success, too, not just keep-the-doors-open, scrape-by success.

And her own business was rocketing out of the gate, too.

Her marketing firm; her "little" business, the one her parents refused to acknowledge—it had a phone that never stopped ringing. An overflowing email inbox. Even buyout offers. There were possibilities at every corner.

Built from the ground up with no help from her family, it was Brie's achievement. All hers. She was making the choices—finally in charge of her own life.

The cost was a ticket in the Princess Lottery. The winner got a crown, and Prince Alessio as a husband.

Blowing out a breath, she looked at the image on her phone. It was good, and the dark dress was highlighted nicely against the wall of white and cream behind her. She stood out.

Which was the point of this marketing campaign.

"If my name comes out, I think I might just faint!"

"Me too!" the women squealed, then looked at Brie.

She raised a hand and winked as their eyes widened. Her dress's dark hue gave off a less hopeful vibe. Though like all Ophelia's designs, it was gorgeous.

"Good luck, ladies." Brie smiled as they walked away. She didn't really mean the words. No one should "win" their groom.

But the palace hadn't asked her thoughts on this marketing campaign. If they had, she'd have at least pointed out that requiring attendance on the palace grounds, if you'd placed your name in the lottery, was a terrible plan. There was exactly one lucky winner, and over a hundred unhappy losers.

Not great optics, which was unusual for an entity whose whole role one could label "optics."

"This is so exciting! So exciting!" The squeals echoed behind her.

It felt like she was the lone person here who didn't want to wear a crown.

You are!

If she didn't need to be here for the final splash of Ophelia's wedding dress line, she'd have watched this play out on her small television screen in yoga pants, a T-shirt, messy bun and with a giant bowl of popcorn.

Instead, she was the standout in a sea of princess hopefuls dressed in bright cream.

"If my name comes out of that monstrosity, I suspect I'll do more than faint," she murmured, keeping her eye on the balcony where Prince Alessio would appear any minute.

"Not excited about the possibility of becoming a princess?" Nate, one of the local reporters who hadn't gotten the plum press pass the palace gave international media, asked as he sidled up next to her. "People consider Prince Alessio the most handsome prince."

There is one prince in this country—not much of a competition.

Though even before his brother, Sebastian, was crowned king, Alessio would have won that title. The spare had become the superhot heir.

Whoever ended up with Alessio would never have a hard time looking at him. He was tall and blond with brilliant green eyes, muscular shoulders and full lips. The handsome prince was not the issue she had with this public relations stunt.

The palace swore the reformed rebel was excited for this. The man who'd left Celiana for almost three years, only returning following his father's stroke, was happy. That was the story they needed. Easier to sell to the masses.

The real story was about ledgers. This modern fairy tale was the quickest way to remind the world that Celiana was once the honeymoon capital of Europe. It had already boosted the country's tourism and aided shops and attractions struggling since the global tourism economy crashed a few years ago.

In each press release and interview, Alessio dutifully discussed the woman he'd meet at the altar as though he already loved her—like that was even possible. He reminded everyone that his parents had had a marriage of convenience that turned to a great love. Then he worked back to the benefits for the country, reminding anyone watching that Celiana was the most romantic place to start your union.

A bride to right the country's travel economy...who wouldn't want to fill that role?

She couldn't fault Alessio for caring about the people of this country. Their elected leaders were more concerned with retaining power. And Alessio seemed far more concerned with the kingdom's day-to-day running than his brother.

The once dutiful Prince Sebastian, now King, was missing engagements and generally acting like a playboy, and the previously rebellious spare was stepping in for the benefit of Celiana. The role reversal for the men since their father passed was an epic story.

Or it would be, if the palace commented on it.

There were other ways, better options, to jump-start the tourism industry.

"My dreams don't involve a crown."

Her dreams had already cost her the aristocratic life she'd been born into. Cost her the family that "loved" her only when she performed the script they'd drafted from the moment of her birth. She wanted to be more than a trophy wife to some man her father wanted to do business with. She was carving her own path.

Brie's dreams were going to carry her from the small, rented office to a penthouse with a view. No one else was writing the story of her life. Nope. Briella Ailiono controlled all her publicity statements—not that she actually planned to make any about her personal life.

"Since my name is only in there once, the odds are very good I will have to fight with everyone else for a place on public transportation following this fiasco."

She shook her head and looked to the balcony again.

Where was Alessio?

He was meant to pick his bride at the top of the hour, and it was three minutes past. Maybe he was having second thoughts.

Marriage was a commitment, one that should involve love. A promise of forever between two people who cared for each other, rooted each other on.

The opposite of her parents' union.

Her best friend, Ophelia, and her husband, Rafael, had the kind of union Brie would have.

If she ever met someone at the altar.

After watching them cheer each other on, love one another in sickness, health and business ventures, she would not settle for less.

She'd spent her teen years surrounded by people who only cared about her family's wealth. It was better to be alone than to marry for power and connections.

"Care to make a comment for the press?" Nate grinned as he held up his notebook.

There were many comments she wanted to make. She wanted to call this whole thing out for what it was: a PR stunt that made the heir to the throne a prize for whoever's name got picked. The prince was a commodity instead of a man worthy of having a partner who chose him.

And it wasn't like this was a true game of chance. The lottery had gone on all year, with the press corps gleefully showing up weekly to watch women put the tickets they'd purchased into the huge crystal ball specially made for this occasion.

Each "bride" could put her name in once a week for fifty-two weeks. The first week the entry was free...a stunt to show that anyone could be the next princess of Celiana—and the reason more than a thousand women had entered the first week.

But with each week, the cost of entry rose by ten euros—donated to the arts fund Prince Alessio championed. It was a good cause, but the price was steep for a year's worth of tickets. Thirteen thousand euros was needed for a genuine chance at the crown.

That meant there were very few women who could expect to step onto the balcony today. All were from wealthy families. In fact, the final week Brie had watched less than twenty women put their names in. Those were the ones most likely to stand on Alessio's arm today. All "real" princess material.

"No one wants to hear my thoughts on this, Nate."

"It's just as well," the reporter huffed. "I doubt anything I write will make the cut anyway. The actual story is the women up there." He pointed to the front of the group—where those with fifty-two entries stood.

"So true. They look beautiful. Several are wearing Ophelia's gowns."

She grinned as she looked to Anastasia and Breanna. She'd been in the same class in school as the identical twins, though not close friends. Even as girls, their parents had made little secret of their plan to marry their daughters to the crown. Her parents had thought the plan to marry Breanna to Alessio and Anastasia to Sebastian was crass and had discouraged Brie from forming any close attachment.

It was horrible of her parents, though when the twins' mother had mentioned being fine about interchanging the girls if one was pulled as the lotto bride, Brie had cringed. The words were horrible, and the fact that the girls were picking bridal outfits for today made it so much worse.

Not that the twins had reacted. Neither had commented as Ophelia fitted them. Their silence broke Brie's heart. They deserved more than a scheming family. But the price of breaking with your powerful family, the price Brie had paid, was high. She couldn't judge others for not choosing it.

"The wedding gown thing is weird." Nate chuckled as he looked at the women all around. "It's not like the marriage is happening today."

"Agreed."

She looked at the sea of white. The contract they'd all signed when entering this fiasco had required their attendance today and the wearing of a gown fit for a bride. What were women supposed to do with the gowns after today?

It was unlikely they'd want to wear them when they met

their true love, but she supposed the royal family didn't think of such minor details.

"Black is an interesting choice."

This she was willing to put on the record. "You can print this. My dress is technically dark green, Nate." She held up the small train, letting the light hit it just right. "At Ophelia's there is a wide variety of gowns, including a selection of dresses with a modern flair."

"It certainly stands out. Though I'm not sure my editor will print that."

The green stood out. That was the purpose, but it was also her own personal statement.

"Dark colors are best when love dies."

"Ouch!" Nate bent over, pretending to take the hit to the gut, then laughed. "Guess you won't cry if your name doesn't come out today."

"I'll cry if it does!"

The last thing she wanted was a marriage of convenience, particularly one trying to save the kingdom. That was too much pressure. It was a burden even the now-dutiful prince shouldn't have on his shoulders.

"The prince!"

The cry went up from the gathered and Brie took another photo. The whole point of this was to make Ophelia's shop shine.

Going live on her social media site, Brie waved and smiled as people started joining the live stream. Sure, the national and international media were here, but Brie was an actual potential bride who'd been at the crystal entry ball every week this year. Her following had reached two million last week as people waited for today's outcome.

"Prince Alessio just stepped to the balcony. He's wearing a dark suit..."

Mourning the loss of love for himself?

Brie didn't know why that thought bothered her. After all, he seemed the ever-willing participant in this game.

She was too far away to see his face, but his walk seemed stilted. It was a hitch that she wasn't sure the cheering crowd noticed.

"We offer a wide range of suits for the suit lover in your life, too." Brie's voice was bright as she flipped the screen back to her. "He's reaching into the vat of tickets! Who will be our new princess?"

Cries of excitement echoed around her as she waved for the camera. This was finally almost over, and she'd done a good job. Ophelia's shop was on the international market now. Her appointment books were full for the next six months! Brie's baby company was entering the international stage, too.

It meant the Ailiono family would never control her life again.

"Briella Ailiono." The call echoed across the field.

Time slowed as she watched the phone fall from her fingers. No. No. *No.*

"Briella Ailiono!" Alessio called again, hoping his voice sounded steady. Every bit of today would be monitored, filmed, dissected. Those looking for a love story would swoon; those thinking this was nothing more than a charade would look for any sign that Alessio wasn't sure of the plan.

He was sure...sure that this plan would revive Celiana's wedding and honeymoon tourism industry. He was certain that the people would benefit from it, and equally certain that he owed his father's memory more than being known as the rebellious prince who'd fought with him just before the stroke that ultimately stole him away.

Marriages of convenience were the way of the royal life. And there were benefits to wearing a crown... Hopefully they outweighed the thorns for Briella.

Where was his bride? Shouldn't she be running to the front...brimming with excitement?

He knew she was here; attendance at the lottery was mandatory.

In a wedding dress.

That was an instance of dark humor gone wrong. From his brother, King Sebastian, whose word was now taken far more seriously. He was a man Alessio hadn't thought capable of cracking a joke before their father died. But Sebastian wasn't the same since the crown of Celiana had landed on his head. The dutiful son, the heir to the throne, the one who'd always known his place in the family, seemed lost as destiny finally gave him what he'd been trained for.

And that left Alessio in the role of dutiful heir. It was not a position he coveted…but if not for his fight, his rebellion, perhaps his father's blood pressure wouldn't have spiked. Maybe this wasn't the role Alessio wanted, but it was the one he owed.

"Where is she?" Alessio looked over the balcony. The crowd was dispersing, and no one looked like the happy winner.

"She was live on her social media page just as you called her name," his mother, Genevieve, said. The queen mother offered an encouraging smile, something he'd rarely seen in private after his father's untimely death.

Not that Queen Genevieve had ever smiled much. The love story between King Cedric and his queen was well scripted. Everything about it perpetuated the island's fairy tale. But like most fairy tales, the proper story lacked luster.

His mother and father had never loved each other. They respected one another, but it wasn't love. Alessio doubted his father was capable of loving anything besides the country he'd served.

It was King Cedric who'd mentioned how well the island flourished after his union with Queen Genevieve. His father had contacted Alessio, asking him to marry. That was in the "before times," when he was in his little glass shop in Scotland, working, acting, as just a man. It was the happiest he'd ever been.

His father had told him he owed it to the people of Celiana. Alessio had countered that he didn't owe anyone anything, that the future king should do it.

King Cedric said no one would believe a queen lottery. That as the heir the expectations for Sebastian were different. His father was looking for a foreign match, one worthy of the title of queen. Alessio's match was far less important since he'd never sit on the throne. It was a pointed reminder that Alessio was second in his father's eyes, heart and plans—in all things.

They'd screamed at each other. He'd said some terrible things. Things he couldn't take back now.

His father's stroke happened less than an hour after Alessio hung up the phone. The king had never regained consciousness. He'd never realized Alessio had returned home, embraced his father's plans and followed through. This world was his prison, but he would do his best to make sure Briella was content.

Somehow.

At least the stunt was working. The shops were busy. The island's hotels and hostels were booked solid. Many of the residents had opened their guest bedrooms for people wanting to visit...for a fee.

His father's final idea was saving Celiana.

And nearly a year of wedding planning would cement the country's place again.

Celiana—the home of your love story.

Becoming engaged to a stranger was unnerving. There was no way to sugarcoat that. However, for centuries royals had signed documents, wed strangers and then spent years betrothed. At least he and Briella had time to get to know each other before setting an actual date. His lottery was unique, but the idea of a union for business or the greater good of a country was ancient.

That reminder did little to calm his racing nerves as he looked over the departing crowd. There was still no sign of Briella.

He knew her. Or rather, knew *of* her as the outcast of the Ailiono family. They owned more land than anyone else on the island. Their businesses touched nearly every aspect of life on

Celiana. Not that they'd done much to help the country. The family only focused on adding to their already endless coffers.

And their daughter had done something to get disowned, something they refused to discuss. He didn't understand why she would willingly step back into this world, but maybe she'd not wanted to leave. Most aristocrats clung to power, hating even the thought that they might lose the thing they felt made them better than others.

Ridiculous.

"Her live ended as soon as you said her name." His mother's words pulled his mind away from his worries—mostly.

"Live?" He looked over the departing sea of white, again trying to imagine where Briella was and why she wasn't racing to where the royal guard was waiting for her.

"She's the marketing manager for a dress shop. She's stunning and she talks about the shop, highlighting why one should get their wedding day attire from Ophelia's. It's a brilliant campaign."

That his mother would know that was only a little surprising. Through social media, she'd followed the eighteen brides with fifty-two entries as closely as Alessio had followed the economic progress. She was in her own way vetting potential daughters-in-law. If Briella was marketing through the lotto, the queen mother would have seen her.

"Your father would have enjoyed the ingenuity. That was something he respected." The queen mother tipped her head, looking at the departing "brides."

He thought his mother missed his father, but it was like one missed a confidant, not a great love. Stepping away from the balcony, he patted her arm. Affection was not something the royal family did well.

"He'd have been proud of you focusing on Celiana's future." *No, he wouldn't.*

Alessio was doing what was expected of him. That did not earn a place of pride in the royal family. His father gave everything to Celiana. Doing anything less than that was unacceptable, even if the palace walls felt like they were always closing in.

"I know he thought a royal wedding was a good idea. Ours worked...mostly." She bit her lip and offered a smile, but there was something in her voice. The unstated hesitancy sent his stomach spinning.

Briella would have adjustments to make. Life as a royal was not the glamorous stuff of magazines or the fantasy of movies. The royals of Celiana served the country and its people. The sacrifices that came with that—well, the sacrifices of a few for the many—were the bedrock of royal service. He'd run from his duties once, but not again.

"This way, Princess."

"I am not a princess." Her tone was sharp, carrying around the corner as security led her to him.

His stomach, already unsettled from the day's activities, tumbled on the sound. She didn't sound happy or excited. He'd counted on the winner being thrilled, happily standing beside him for the rest of the day's activities with a giant smile. The blushing bride-to-be. He'd selfishly even hoped her excitement would quell his anxiety that had grown stronger as today crept ever closer on the calendar.

They needed to present a united front. It was necessary to quiet the naysayers, who claimed this was nothing more than a short-term publicity stunt.

There were whispers floating through social media and a few regular news channels. The rumors, if proved true, could impact the entire country. A royal wedding brought tourism and prosperity. A royal scandal... That could undo everything.

"She was trying to flee," Henri, head of security, stated as he deposited Briella in the small alcove.

Flee?

"A runaway bride... That is quite the headline. Though not the one we're aiming for," Alessio quipped as he stepped forward.

Briella let out a soft chuckle as her bright blue eyes met

his. She was gorgeous; her long blond hair was wrapped in an intricate braid, and a near-black dress hugged her curves in all the right places.

The few times he'd seen her at court, she'd been reserved. Not a slip of laughter or hair out of place, she was the perfect Ailiono daughter. Until she wasn't. Rumors swirled about the reasons, but there'd been no concrete answers.

"Running away would be easier in tennis shoes... I might have even made it." She glared at the fancy heels poking out from under the gorgeous dress.

"One often overlooks the power of footwear." Alessio shrugged, not quite sure what to make of this conversation. The idea of running was intoxicating. During the three years he'd lived abroad, he'd felt freer than he ever expected to feel again.

"I should have considered it, apparently." She crossed her arms as her ice-blue eyes caught his.

Any words he might say evaporated as he met her gaze. He'd planned to bow to his bride-to-be, exchange a few pleasantries, bask in her excitement. He'd focus on the spectacle as he tried to make it through the next steps.

Now...now he couldn't quite find any kind of response.

Briella bit her lip then shook herself. "My apologies, Your Majesties... Your Highness." Dipping into a low curtsy, she let out a soft noise he feared was a caught sob.

That broke his heart. He might not be sure of this plan, but there were no monsters in this castle. Well, not really.

"Mother, could you give Briella and me a few minutes?"

The queen mother looked at Briella, still bent in her curtsy, and nodded. "I'll have the king delay the formal announcement and pictures a few minutes."

It was still weird to think of Sebastian as the king.

"Thank you." He slid down to the ground, catching the shock of surprise in Briella's face before she smoothed it over and joined him on the floor.

That was an ability the royal family excelled at, too. He instantly recognized the ability to conceal all feelings. And he hated that she'd learned the trick. Hated that she was using it on him.

Why wouldn't she?

"Briella—" He crossed his legs and leaned forward, making it clear that he was paying attention but giving her a little space.

"Brie." She coughed, clearing the sobs from her throat as she looked at him. "I prefer Brie. We're sitting like kids in a gym class."

"It's comfortable." Honestly, he'd sat without thinking. The position was hardly regal.

It was something he'd once have done to anger his father.

"Though before we go out, I'll have to ask you to look at my pants and make sure I have no dust on them. Pictures and all...we wouldn't want dust to take center stage in today's narrative."

"Of course not." Brie shook her head. "Dust is such an important factor for the press."

"Royalty is all about the show."

It was the first lesson princes and princesses learned. Everything is documented, speculated on, gossiped over.

"What the heck is this conversation?" Brie put her fingers on her forehead, rubbing at the line between her brows.

"The first lesson in your new life. Things that seem meaningless matter."

"This isn't a life I want."

Her cheeks darkened as she rolled her eyes. Her voice was soft, but the hint of terror came through clearly. He reached across and took her hand, squeezing it, trying to ground her.

Grounding himself.

It wasn't one he wanted, either, but that hardly mattered. She'd signed a contract. For all legal matters, she was basically a princess.

Her hand in his was warm. It felt...right? That was a weird descriptor; after all, they didn't know each other. Not really. She was to be his bride, but today, today was an unknown.

"Brie."

He offered what he hoped was a comforting smile as she broke the connection between them. The empty feeling in his palm echoed through his soul. He wanted to reach back out to her.

If you didn't want this, you shouldn't have put your name in the contest.

Saying those words wouldn't help now.

"Brie," he started over. "We have guests we need to see to. Expectations to meet."

"Expectations."

She propped her hands on her knees. In another time or place, they might have been sitting in the schoolyard waiting for their turn on the tennis or basketball court. Instead, they were in fancy clothes on the floor of his father's office—a room his brother still refused to convert to his.

"How can you possibly think of expectations? We don't even know each other. What, we just go out and role-play happily-ever-after?"

Role-playing was the name of the game. Hell, he'd expected his bride to be so excited. That way people might not notice his own discomfort. Instead, he was trying to convince her to go along with the day's duty.

"We have our whole lives to get to know one another." Not exactly comforting, but true.

"Our whole lives!" Brie stood, her dress swooshing with the quick movement. She walked past him and started pacing. "Our whole lives, Your Royal Highness—"

"Alessio," he interrupted as he stood. "It is only right that you call me by my first name, too. At least in private."

"In private. This can't be happening."

He'd felt the same many times. Yet it didn't change what had to be done. "But it is."

"I don't want to marry you." Brie planted her feet, preparing for battle.

This was not in the day's script. His mind raced; what was he supposed to say to that? The rebel buried in his soul shouted with joy before he reminded himself to keep calm. Duty was his life now.

Alessio sucked in a deep breath. That bought him seconds but didn't stop the pounding of his heartbeat in his ears. He'd spent a year figuring out how to make his father's goal a reality—a royal wedding for the country to rally around. Then another year prepping for today. It couldn't unravel. It simply couldn't.

There was no other plan. If this imploded today, Celiana's name would be in papers globally for days, maybe weeks.

For all the wrong reasons.

He could already see the headline: Princess Lottery Bust!

The success Celiana had gained would evaporate overnight. And coming home after his father's stroke, taking up the mantle of duty he'd sworn off, being the face of Celiana's resurgence…it would all have been for nothing. That couldn't happen.

"If you didn't want to be a princess, why was your name in the lottery?"

It wasn't like they'd forced people to put their names in. It was a choice. One that more than a thousand women had chosen.

She'd chosen this…just like he had. And with that came a responsibility to the people depending on them.

"To help Ophelia!" Brie rocked back on her feet as she looked toward the balcony. "To help her get her wedding dress business off the ground. It was a marketing stunt to help my friend. My name was in there once.

"Once," she whispered the word again.

One lucky ticket was what the lottery was all about. He'd parroted that line in many interviews. Alessio hadn't actually counted on someone with one free entry winning. But her reasoning was perfect.

Dutiful…but in a different way.

"That was kind of you." Alessio stepped to her side, grateful when she didn't step away. Helping her friend was admirable. And it was what she'd be doing as a princess.

Except instead of one friend, she'd help the entire kingdom.

"Kind?" Brie's sapphire gaze met his. "It was a marketing strategy, Alessio." Her body shifted and for a moment, he thought she might lean toward him.

"So is the lottery. A marketing strategy to jump-start the tourism industry. One that is working."

"And the only cost is *our* futures."

A tear slipped down her cheek and his hand rose without him thinking. His thumb rubbed away the drop, and Brie let out a sigh as he cupped her face.

"You signed a contract. Duty is why you put your name in. Duty is why you continue. We'll make it work."

"Make it work." Brie's hand rose, taking his and pulling it away from her face. She squeezed his fingers, her mouth opening as her eyes darted to their joined hands, before she let him go. "Make it work... Such romantic words."

Romance wasn't in the cards. The *idea* of romance was...but *actual* romance? That was not what royal marriages really were.

"According to the movies, Prince Charming and his bride always live happily ever after."

He wasn't Prince Charming. That ideal didn't exist. At least Brie knew that already. He wouldn't have to watch the light dim from his lottery bride as the realization struck.

"This isn't a joke."

The old Alessio would have said that this whole thing was a joke, a giant prank that was over-the-top. Unfortunately, the die was cast.

"You're right," Alessio agreed. "It's our duty to Celiana."

Brie looked at the door. Voices were mixing on the other side of it. A host of events was scheduled for today.

"What if I make you a deal?"

"A deal?" He needed to shut this down, they needed to get moving...but curiosity, and a hint of the rebel he'd been, kept him in place.

"Yes. This was a publicity stunt, and I am a marketing manager now. What if I can get tourism moving in areas not revolving around this? In six to eight weeks, if the focus is on something besides just us, we part ways."

"How would we even measure that?" As the question fell from his lips, he realized there was hope in it, hope that she might actually know a way. Hope he couldn't afford.

"The same way any business measures success." Brie rolled her eyes, gesturing into the air at nothing. Her thoughts on the Princess Lottery were quite clear. "We measure hotel bookings. The bookings need to increase in the next eight weeks— let's say by at least five percent—and tourism at our major sites needs a ten percent bump. That is doable in eight weeks or less."

Was it doable? If so… No. He needed to shut this down now.

"The contract for entry was binding. We've entered into a royal marriage contract and there's no going back."

The contract was similar to the one his parents had signed.

"I'm aware of what I signed. But if the royal family finds me an inappropriate match, you can void the contract."

She'd read the fine print.

"If I show you that I can get the tourism industry back to what it was without the need for a royal wedding, then you can find me inappropriate and end the contract."

The word *no* was on the tip of his tongue, and he knew that was the right answer, but the idea of fulfilling his end of this devil's bargain, while not having to go through with a royal wedding… It was intoxicating.

What if he could make good on the argument he'd had the night his father died without giving up everything?

But what did that mean for Celiana? If the tourists didn't come back for the royal wedding, would they come back at all?

"What if I convince you that there are benefits to royal life? That yes, the trade-off can be steep, but you can find rewarding things in service?"

Those dutiful words had been parroted so often to him when

he'd complained that he'd had no choice in the position of his birth. They were the words he should have said immediately when she offered the deal.

"So rewarding you ran away."

Touché.

"I came back."

She raised an eyebrow and shifted, like she wanted to call out the statement, poke at it.

"I can show you another way. A better way." Brie crossed her arms.

He saw so much of the man he used to be in her. Trapping that energy felt wrong, but duty still came first. It had to... didn't it?

"Without a scandal that destroys the kingdom or my brother's reign." His fight had led to so much damage already; he would not add to it. He couldn't.

Brie bit her lip before nodding. "If we can't do it without those things, then I guess I meet you at the altar." She held out a hand. "Deal?"

"Deal." For the first time since returning to Celiana, Alessio thought there might be a way to earn his freedom. Maybe.

"All right, first steps." She pulled out her phone and took a deep breath. "Do I look like I've been crying?"

"No. Your cheeks are a little flushed, but that's all. Why?"

"We have to tell our followers what we're doing. Rule one of marketing, don't miss prime opportunities. And flushed works. People can think you swept me off my feet."

She held up her phone and looked at him.

"Do you blush when you're swept off your feet?" he asked.

"No one's ever tried."

That was a shame. A woman who stepped in for a friend, who was so determined to chart her own course, deserved someone who'd sweep her off her feet. If her plan worked, then she'd get that chance.

Why did that give him an uncomfortable feeling?

"All right, Prince Charming, here we go." She pressed a few buttons. "Smile!"

He wasn't sure if the order was for him or her.

"Surprise!" She waved at the camera. "Guess who's here with me."

Brie stepped beside him, and he wrapped a hand around her waist. Her hip brushed his, but she didn't remove his hand.

"I guess you all get to follow me on my path to being a princess now!" Her voice was too bright. Too happy. "It's going to be a blast." She waved and disconnected the live.

"We'll get better." Brie blew out a breath as she glared at the phone.

"I thought that was fine."

She stepped away, just out of arm's reach. "That's why I'm the marketing manager. We came off stilted. *I* came off stilted. I'll make a post later about nerves and seeing royalty. It will be okay."

He suspected the *It will be okay* was meant for herself. Still, it was time for the next stage.

"We can practice with the guests here." He offered her his hand.

"Right." Brie slid her hand into his.

She looked up at him. Her full pink lips were so close, so perfect. Her hips shifted, pressing against him. It was an odd moment, one that his former self would enjoy too much. The old Alessio might even have joked that one sealed such deals with kisses.

Kissing Brie… His mind tumbled through the thoughts as the air in the room seemed to guide them together.

The crowd let out a cheer on the other side of the study door, breaking whatever magic was spinning between them.

Brie breathed out. "Ready or not."

"Ready or not." Alessio squeezed her hand, grateful that it was this woman standing beside him. Grateful that fate might have given him another chance at freedom.

CHAPTER TWO

HOW HAD THE day gone so off course? She was meant to be home, not reminding herself to not flinch as camera flashes popped off. Brie's feet were ice blocks, and the idea that she had to step into the room, pretend to be a happy princess-to-be, made her stomach twist. This wasn't the plan.

This evening was supposed to be about celebrating Ophelia's successes and planning the next steps of her future. She needed to focus, find the next steps. That was what Brie did well.

Yes, she was standing next to Alessio. After making a deal with him and nearly kissing him. Kissing... Her mind wanted to wander back to that moment. Even with all the calls and camera flashes, it was that moment her brain wanted to replay. He'd nearly kissed her.

At least she thought he was going to kiss her. Brie had very little experience with that. Well, none actually. She'd not lied when she told Alessio no one had ever tried to sweep her off her feet.

Her family had kept her sheltered, which was a fancy word for controlled her. The few men who'd asked her out after her escape had wanted access to the Ailiono family. She'd gone on exactly three second dates and no third.

The romance books she devoured described the moment before lips connected. The light touch of his fingers. The scent of sandalwood and cedar. The hesitation and excitement.

All those things were present. Except Alessio smelled like the ocean, fresh and free.

The prince, who'd joked about shoes and runaway brides, was rigid now. It was the dutiful Alessio beside her. The one who'd returned from overseas, never discussing what he'd done, assuming the burden of expectation.

Except she'd seen the hint of resignation in his eyes. It was a look she'd worn so often in her family's home. It was that look that made her ask for the deal, which he'd agreed to far quicker than she'd expected.

Maybe he acted like the dutiful prince, but she thought the rebel was still there. He yearned for freedom as much as she did.

Alessio leaned his head against hers. "Take a breath, Brie." The words were barely audible, but his arm slipped around her waist.

Her lungs screamed as she inhaled fresh oxygen.

"It's role-playing, remember."

His soft voice insinuated itself to her soul, reminding her of what was at stake. They needed to look happy today. In a few weeks, they could start pulling away in preparation for ending the engagement, but today... Today they needed to look happy.

His fingers gripped her waist, comfort washing over her as he held her tightly.

She'd never liked men to touch her like this. It felt possessive... It was possessive, at least when her father did it to her mother.

But Alessio's grip, his hand placement, felt more like protection, security in the storm. It was peaceful.

Protection? Security?

Brie didn't need protection or security. She took care of herself. She'd learned quickly that the world didn't care for rich kids. Even if they'd been cast out. She'd been on her own for years.

It was difficult, but she'd found her way. She'd graduated,

opened a marketing company, found her own footing. She was an independent woman.

Still, Alessio's touch felt nice. Too nice. It reminded her of his fingers on her cheek and the gentle touch of his thumb on her wrist.

She should reclaim her space, but she couldn't make herself do it. In fact, she had to fight the urge to lean her head against his shoulder as the barrage of questions started. That would be too much. It would look overdone, even if it was a natural action.

"Are you excited?"

No. She knew her smile wasn't enough to respond to the reporter's question.

"Any thought to the royal patronages you'll support?" Another question popped off before she could answer the last.

Thank goodness.

"Not yet." She'd never considered the fact that Alessio might call her name. She'd refused to think of the possibility she might be a princess. The odds were not in her favor...and that was the way she'd wanted it.

"Do you think your family position played any role in your selection?" The reporter's smile wasn't quite a smirk, but she felt Alessio's hand tighten on her waist.

"It was a fair drawing. Are you suggesting otherwise?" Alessio's voice was casual, but she heard the bite behind it.

Which was good, because she knew the answer to that question was that if her family had had their wish, she'd have married at nineteen. It was a choice they'd not even bothered to run past her before making.

"Will your wedding dress be by Ophelia or a royal designer?"

Finally, a reporter's question she could answer...sort of.

"I'm positive that I will wear one of Ophelia's dresses when I marry."

Alessio's fingers tightened on her waist. It wasn't a lie. If she ever married, and Brie was far from sold on the institution, she'd wear one of Ophelia's designs. However, Ophelia's designs would not grace the royal chapel.

At least not on Brie.

A twinge of sadness pressed into her chest. Ophelia's work deserved to be in the royal wedding. If Breanna or her twin sister had won the prize, Ophelia would at least be in the running to design the gown of the decade.

But when Brie didn't wed Prince Alessio, when the ruse was over... She doubted the next royal bride would choose the best friend of the woman who refused to play the part of the lotto bride.

The idea of another woman meeting Alessio at the altar sent a mixture of emotions through her soul. She couldn't quite determine the mixture. It should be relief...should be acceptance. Those were present, but the sadness lingering in the recesses of her body shocked her. Alessio deserved more than a royal union focused on what it brought Celiana.

Would they let him marry for love? Probably not. But at least it wouldn't be the spectacle of a lottery bride. That would be some consolation, right?

"Prince Alessio, do you think your father would be happy with your lotto bride?"

He shifted. Not much. Not enough that she thought anyone in the room noticed. If his arm wasn't around her waist, she wasn't sure she'd have noticed, either.

"I'm sure King Cedric would have been pleased."

They were words. That was the best she could say. It was his interview tone, the one she'd heard so often over the last year. But there was a hint of uncertainty, too. Maybe it was the camera flashes or the casual mention of the man Alessio had called King rather than Father.

Brie slipped her arm around his waist. He was providing her comfort in this sea of uncertainty; she could do the same. And it would look good for the cameras.

His eyes locked with hers and she smiled.

"We forgot to examine you for dirt," he said.

The words were quiet, but she saw a flash of the playful Alessio. That was the magic they needed to tap into.

"If that is the story of the day, remind me to say I told you so." He winked.

If that was the story of the day, the first episode in this marketing adventure was a loss. But he was smiling, and she was looser, too. So she winked back.

"Fair."

For a moment, it was easy to pretend they were a genuine couple. A few minutes of comradery in the storm of whatever this fever dream was.

"How about a kiss for the camera? A proper kiss?"

Her mouth fell open before she clasped it tight and forced a smile back on her face. Kiss. Of course the cameras wanted a kiss. This was a spectacle, after all.

And what was a romantic spectacle without a kiss?

Her fingers shook as she tried to prepare. The idea of kissing Alessio didn't bother her. If he'd dropped his lips to hers a few minutes ago, she might even have swooned a bit. The man was handsome, funny and more relaxed behind closed doors.

She wanted to know how the man beside her, who'd wiped a tear from her cheek, who'd joked about dust and looked like he might like to run away from all this, kissed.

That curiosity was something she'd need to deal with later, without an audience.

But kissing Alessio for the camera, letting the world see her first kiss, felt wrong. A first kiss held power. It contained so much possibility.

Except there wasn't any possibility in their situation.

"I think my future bride has had enough excitement for the day." Alessio's formal tone hung in the room.

What if he doesn't want to kiss me?

Why was that thought banging in her head? This was a charade. A charade. She needed to remember that.

"Are you saying that kissing her Prince Charming would be too exciting?" Lev, a royal commentator who spent most of his time finding fault, however minor, with the royal family, raised a brow.

Prince Charming.

How did the title sound so different when it fell from Lev's mouth?

Lev had spent the last year calling the bride lottery a stunt. He was even hosting an informal betting pool on his website for people to wager how long the royal engagement lasted. The largest bet was placed for three months from today.

The fact that Lev was here was a signal. The royal family wanted to smother his suggestions. Rather than exclude him, they'd made a point of inviting him. If she'd marketed this union, she'd have made the same suggestion.

Media was a game and it was one she was quite skilled at, one that was going to grant her freedom from this trap.

Still, she hated that when she won, it would prove the man right.

"I am quite the kisser. My bride-to-be will certainly swoon the first time our lips connect." The words were said with an over-the-top flair.

Anticipation coated her skin, but she could play into the moment, too. "So sure of yourself."

The audience chuckled, smiles draping everywhere as they clapped for the couple. Good, they were back in control of the narrative. Those that controlled the media narrative won.

Only Lev frowned as he typed something into his phone.

This wasn't real. She knew that, but she hated the look on the gossip reporter's face. She hated that, even unintentionally, they were playing into his expectations.

Brie lifted on her toes, pressing her lips to Alessio's cheek. The connection was brief, over before she could really think it through.

More than a few calls echoed throughout the crowd for her to do it again, but it was Alessio's reaction that fascinated her.

His jade eyes held hers. The questions and camera flashes

evaporated. For a moment, they were the only two people in the crowded room.

"Alessio." His name escaped before she leaned her head against his shoulder.

The day was too much, just as he'd said. The questions, the spotlight, the way the life she'd known had shifted in the space of seconds when Alessio pulled her name.

She was reacting to the day, to the hope of a way out...not to him.

"Shall we get a drink?"

"Please."

Alessio held up a hand. "Briella and I are going to seek refreshments. Enjoy the party. There will be plenty of time for questions during our courtship."

Alessio didn't release her as they walked away from the journalists. His arm was light on her waist. It was a reminder of the role they were playing, and that if she stepped away, everyone would comment.

First lesson—things that seemed meaningless mattered.

She took a deep breath, all hopes of calming herself evaporating as Alessio's scent invaded her senses again. The man was gorgeous, a literal prince... Did he have to smell like heaven, too?

Brie had never allowed herself to fall in lust—not that there'd been many options. Just because she was horrified that her name came out of the giant glass tumbling ball didn't mean she couldn't acknowledge the man beside her was hot.

Right?

Alessio was tall, attractive, kind. There were worse men to play pretend with. Her mouth was dry as she looked at him. His jade gaze met hers and her belly flipped. The man was the definition of *gorgeous*.

A table layered with treats came into view. The decadence reminded her that she was in the palace, next to Alessio as his bride-to-be. She shouldn't need the reminder. She needed to focus, start thinking of her plans and their next steps.

She'd spent her youth looking attentive at boring family functions while drifting away to her own mental space. Even in this ruckus, she should be able to do it. But as his fingers stroked her side, it was impossible to focus on more than his touch.

"This is lovely."

Hints of sugar, lemon and a host of other flavors skipped through her senses. So many sweets finally overtook the delicious scent that was Alessio.

Pastries overloaded the table. Rather than hiring one caterer, Alessio had asked each bakery to deliver a few dozen of their best desserts. That way, everyone got to claim a piece of the day. It was a marketing coup.

"It is." He smiled and looked at the table. "What kind of dessert do you like best?"

"I don't know." She laughed as she looked at the sweets, hoping to cover her uncertainty as she stared at the table. She'd not run in aristocratic circles in years, but she knew the game. Smile, look attentive, even when you feel like falling apart. Muscle memory had been reinforced by years of Ailiono training.

Her mother had not permitted Brie to have sweets as a child or teen. Her family raised her to be...to be exactly where she was, actually. However, her parents would never have attempted to marry her to one of Celiana's princes. Alessio and Sebastian had crowns, but the man her family had wanted her to wed had power. He was a business partner of her father's, a scion of industry with no regard for the women who stood by his side.

Her father's arrangement was for Brie to be his third wife. His third wife and nearly thirty years his junior, she would be the definition of a trophy bride—a young woman he could mold into his "perfect" wife. Only, she wouldn't gain her freedom like the other two had.

Rationally, she knew her mother no longer controlled the

food she ate. That just like the outfits she wore, Brie could now choose her food. She was allowed to make her own choices.

She'd not graced her parents' impressive doorstep in almost seven years, but this action... She'd tried so many things since being disowned, but never sweets. Each time she looked at one, considered it, she'd heard her mother's screaming voice, and the urge to taste something had died away.

She didn't have to stay in this restrictive world. Brie had a path out. She could do this.

"I prefer lemon and lavender treats," Alessio said as he handed her a plate, then started putting things on his while making small talk with the person in line before them.

The plate was tiny, embossed with the royal crest at the top and the bottom. Brie knew it only weighed a few ounces, but it was lead in her hand.

She'd overcome so much. This shouldn't be that hard. But still her finger gripped the plate like it might fly from her hands. Her ears buzzed, and she knew people were watching. The longer she stood here, the more likely someone would make this a moment out of their control.

Alessio put a chocolate petit four, a lemon bar and a lavender cookie on his plate, then turned. His eyebrows pulled together as his gaze fell to her empty plate.

"Brie?"

"I don't know what dessert I like." It was such an inconsequential thing, something that wouldn't bother her if she wasn't surrounded by dozens of cameras, in the palace, suddenly engaged to a prince.

She might even make a joke about being a twenty-six-year-old sweet virgin. And she would laugh to cover the past and how it made her different from her peers. She would joke so she didn't have to remember that her family only wanted her if she played by their rigged rules.

"These are my favorite. Try one." He put the cookie on her plate, his fingers tracing along her wrist.

Her breath caught on the connection. Heat raced up her arm as his touch grounded her. She wasn't alone.

"And I do not know what this is, but it's lovely." He set another treat on her plate, leaning forward and pushing a piece of hair behind her ears.

He leaned close, ocean breeze coming with him. Her nerves were still racing, but now they focused on the handsome man's lips brushing her ear.

"You don't have to eat them. Or you can."

She knew the touches, the small talk, even the refreshment table, were designed for the day. It was all a perfect marketing tool for the country and the royal family. If she'd overseen the event, there were a few changes she'd have made, but whoever had planned the occasion was an artist.

And yet, part of her wanted to believe he was caring for her, that the concern sweeping his features was meant only for her. Truly for her. She wanted to believe that if the participants all fell away, if the fancy dresses disappeared and he was in lounge pants and she was in comfy pants no one should see, he'd still care.

Brie smiled. "Thank you. You don't have to hold my hand through all this."

But it's nice.

"You are my bride-to-be." He leaned a little closer. "And the cameras are watching."

Cameras.

The cameras would be focused on the caring prince performing actions for others…not for her.

The press corps surrounding Brie's apartment didn't surprise Alessio. The swarm must have descended as soon as he announced her name. He knew the families with fifty-two entries for their daughters had scheduled security for today, anticipating such an occurrence.

Actually, all the families that could afford the high cost of a year's worth of entries had security. Brie's neighbors were undoubtedly unhappy...and worried.

They needed to fix this. Maybe she could spin this into a "move into the palace with me" post. Yet the public didn't have access to the royal quarters, so there wasn't much of a tourism trap there.

"What the hell!" Brie leaned against him as camera flashes assaulted the tinted windows.

"You won the Princess Lottery." Had she really not expected people to be here?

Brie somehow got closer to him. Her body was warm against his. Maybe it was silly to be so happy with the simple action. But she felt nice against him. They were partners in their goal, two souls from powerful families that craved freedom.

And if it didn't work...if they had to wed to protect Celiana...they'd find a way to make do. Maybe his parents hadn't loved each other, but respect was more than many got.

If there was another way to aid the generations of bakers, shop owners, bistro and hotel operators who based their businesses around honeymooners, reaching for it wasn't selfish. Right?

Alessio had been the rebel. He'd been the runaway unhappy with his role as second fiddle. Stepping in as the dutiful one felt weird, and he wasn't quite sure he was doing it right.

"This is...this is..."

He understood her being at a loss for words. Alessio had grown up in this life, and it was still a game he felt like he was failing at most days.

"It's royal life. The start of it at least. And the role you agreed to play."

Brie's blue eyes flashed. She was gorgeous, and the day was long. The blend of emotions sent desire through his soul. And he ached to protect someone from the world that had finally beaten him.

After all, she hadn't chosen this. Not really. She'd submitted one entry, one tiny slip in a sea of hopefuls, one chance for the crown that would sit on her head forever.

"Only until I get a plan in place that brings more than honeymooners." Brie sighed as the driver pulled as close to her place as the crowd allowed.

"If you can make that happen, then yes. It's temporary. But it might be a good idea to at least consider that it's forever." He paused before adding, "Trust me. If it doesn't work and we meet at the altar, you'll feel better having at least considered it."

If he'd made himself believe his little glass shop was temporary, maybe closing it wouldn't have broken him as much.

"I refuse to think of that until it's absolutely necessary." She pushed away from him, her top teeth digging into her lip.

"Fine. But for now, you're a princess-in-waiting. And the world needs to believe that you believe that." The flash of anger turned to frustration as her bright eyes found his.

"Right. Control the narrative." Brie pulled the bottom of her dress to the side, readying herself to step out.

His life was a series of narratives. Some of them were so well spun, even Alessio wondered what was real and what was the official palace line. It shouldn't bother him that she was speaking in the same tone, but frustration pooled in his soul.

"It's not just about narratives. It's about the country and duty and making sure everyone is safe, even if it means giving up something of yourself."

It was like his father's ghost had spit the words out. They were words the old Alessio would never have spoken.

"Soon you'll have a plan for this country that will bring it more than just honeymooners. And I'll be a blip in the royal family's memory."

Not in my memory.

No matter how long he lived, he wouldn't forget the woman who had marched in after being offered a crown and made a deal to get out of it. How often had he craved the same thing? If her plan worked, he might get back the life he'd had. The life he craved.

Most people only saw the glamour of the crown, not the pain behind it. And now he had the beauty beside him.

"So, what are we going to do?" Fine lines appeared around her eyes. Her lips tipped down before she plastered on a smile. "Move me into the palace?"

He hadn't expected her to suggest it, but he was glad she had, so he didn't have to.

"Yes. You move into the palace. You can make a video telling everyone."

"I was kidding, Your Royal Highness."

Your Royal Highness.

Her back was straight, and she was ready for battle. That was good. Celiana needed strong female role models. And even if they didn't meet at the altar, she'd impress people.

"Brie—" Alessio gestured to the crowd "—you won the Princess Lottery."

"We have a deal, Your Royal Highness."

"Do you plan to call me Your Royal Highness whenever you're frustrated? Not that I'm complaining... Well, not really. It will make it easy to determine when you are cross." He tapped his head. "Mental note made."

"This isn't a joke."

He agreed, but humor helped in difficult moments. It relaxed people. He'd been good at it once upon a time. That man seemed to want to emerge around Brie. He'd have to wrestle him back into the mental cage he thought he'd thrown away the key to.

The crowd was getting impatient.

"You can't stay here. It's not safe." He gestured to the sea of people.

Most of them just wanted a picture of the royal couple. They wanted to tell their friends and future grandkids where they'd been when Prince Alessio and Princess Briella arrived at her home.

But there were others. People who despised the monarchy and people who blamed the hard years on the royals.

It wasn't fair. Celiana was a constitutional monarchy. King Sebastian was little more than a figurehead. But the royals were the faces of the country. They were the attraction that drove tourism. Real-life fairy-tale creatures, they played a role with perceived, if little actual, power.

And the last few years had been hard. The economic downturn had hit nearly every sector and there were more than a few disgruntled citizens. And even if there weren't, that didn't mean that a future royal bride should live unprotected. Even one who never planned to wear the crown.

She sighed but didn't wilt. Her eyes roamed the crowd, and he saw acceptance register.

It was good, but it tore at him, too. Acceptance was part of the royal life. He and Sebastian had learned at an early age that their wills, their desires, all came at least second to the needs of the country. It was a lesson Brie would face again and again, too. Particularly if they wed.

His choices had evaporated the moment his father had his stroke. But hers... Until today they'd been wide open. The ease of life, the ability to just run to the store or go to work... all were gone for her, at least for a while.

"You're right. I can't stay here."

Brie's words pulled him away from his unsettled thoughts. He had to focus on the present. The past was lost, and the future was a reminder that his life was scripted now. *Focus on the here and now.*

"We'll pack up some of your stuff now, then I can send the staff to get the rest."

"Sure." Brie nodded. He could see that a fight was brewing in her eyes, but she was ceding the ground on this. A battle won.

"Princess! Princess!" The calls echoed as security opened the car door.

Brie raised a hand, smiling as she moved through the crowd, ignoring the questions and moving as quickly as security created the path for them.

She shut her apartment door behind them and crossed her arms. "This is too much."

"This is what winning the lottery looks like." The rules were clear. Each entry was a contract. By putting your name in the crystal ball you agreed that, if chosen, you became a princess.

"I'm aware of that, Alessio."

"She entered *for* me." A woman stepped from what had to be Brie's bedroom. "I am so sorry."

"Ophelia." Brie ran to her friend.

She held on tightly, and Alessio was grateful she had someone to pour herself into. And he was jealous there wasn't anyone who'd do the same for him. He glanced around the apartment, looking for a way to give them privacy, but it was too tiny.

"I shouldn't have agreed to the marketing strategy. This is a nightmare." Ophelia's voice shook as she looked to Alessio.

Before he could say anything, Brie squeezed her friend, then stepped back. "Not ideal, but at least this fiancé is cuter than the one my parents lined up."

"Closer to your age, too." Ophelia's laughter mingled with Brie's. "But this isn't the time for jokes."

She'd been engaged? That didn't make sense. The Ailionos made huge engagement announcements. Her parents' engagement party had cost more than his parents' wedding.

And she wasn't in contact with her family. Her family had disowned her...at least according to the not-so-quiet rumors.

Engaged.

The word tapped against his brain.

His life was a series of long days, but he was officially overloaded.

"Engaged?"

"Not important."

He wasn't aware he'd spoken until Brie waved it away. But he saw her shoulders tighten—so it wasn't unimportant. Another question for another day, then.

If there was a spurned ex waiting, well, he at least needed to make sure security knew. That was the reason for his curiosity. The only reason...

He almost believed that.

"I came to see if you wanted me to spirit you off the island. Not sure how, but Rafael and I planned to work that out later. Bringing *him* makes that harder."

Ophelia tilted her head as she looked at Alessio, sizing him up. He didn't shift under her judgment, but that didn't mean he didn't want to.

"Not impossible. Just harder." Ophelia raised a brow.

"No escape needed." Brie shook her head and moved to his side. She was close to him but careful not to touch him. There were no cameras here, no reason to pretend they were starting the journey of falling in love.

"I have a plan." Brie nodded to the door where the crowd was audible. "And my plans always work out."

Ophelia opened her mouth but said nothing.

But he could hear the concern. No one got everything. But this...this he wanted Brie to achieve. For her peace...and his.

"I'll get the dress back to you tomorrow, if that works?"

Her friend crossed her arms. "I assume the palace will purchase it. They often put high-profile outfits in the fashion museum." Ophelia's eyes held his, daring him to contradict her. "I think this one counts."

"Ophelia—"

"Send the bill." Alessio looked at Brie. "After all, it would be expected."

"Of course." There was a look in her eyes. Did she wish he'd said something else?

No. They were just tired.

"I will send the bill first thing in the morning, Your Royal Highness." Ophelia stepped to them and pulled Brie into her arms.

"I meant what I said," she said to Brie. "Say the word and

I will find a way to get you out of this." She kissed her cheek, then stepped back.

"Thank you." Brie took a deep breath. "Alessio, while I gather a few things, can you make sure security helps Ophelia get to her vehicle without being accosted by the crowd?"

"Of course."

Brie moved to her room.

Before he could open the door, Ophelia put her hand on his chest. "She's had a lifetime of hurt. You do not get to add to it. So, if you hurt her, crown or not, you *will* answer to me."

The threat wasn't needed, but he was glad Brie had someone in her corner.

"Understood."

"Good." Ophelia nodded then listened as he gave the security team directions for her safety.

As soon as Ophelia was out the door, he heard Brie shout from the other room.

"Alessio!"

He moved as quickly as his feet would carry him. Had someone broken in? Sebastian had once had a girlfriend who was stalked by individuals hoping to capture a picture to sell to the press. A few had even broken into her place, foolish hope of quick money outweighing rational thoughts of jail time.

Brie's apartment would be easy to get into, and the lotto bride picture would be worth thousands!

The small apartment was sparsely furnished. The only photos appeared to be of her, Ophelia and a man he guessed was Ophelia's husband. The apartment was close to public transportation, and was the kind of place university students and those just starting in their careers chose.

It was not a place one expected to find an Ailiono. Her room at the Ailiono mansion was likely larger than this space. What was she doing here?

"I made a mistake letting Ophelia leave." Brie's hands were on her chest, and her eyes were tired. The weight of everything seemed to press against her.

"Oh." Alessio wasn't sure what to say. "I thought you weren't escaping."

If she left immediately, would they ask him to draw another name? How selfish was he for considering that? When they broke up in a few weeks, he could pretend to be heartbroken. But today...

"I told you I could prove this stunt unnecessary."

"You did, but it's a lot. You know it and I know it." Alessio knew his voice was too tight, but while he wanted to believe in the possibility, reality was difficult to avoid for a royal.

"I meant that. I'm not running." The last sentence was tight, and he could see her shift slightly.

Not yet.

He'd run. He knew the look. But she was here now.

"Brie—"

"It's the dress," she interrupted, gesturing to herself. "The dress," she repeated as her eyes fell to the floor.

He wasn't sure what the issue was.

"It is gorgeous."

He marveled at the deep green, and the low neckline with a simple necklace. She was beautiful, but the dress turned her into a nymph, a mythical creature almost too beautiful to touch.

"Yes, it's beautiful. Some of Ophelia's best work, but I'm buttoned into it."

She turned, and he saw tiny buttons starting at the base of her neck, all the way to the top of her incredible butt.

He swallowed the burst of need pushing at him.

She looked over her shoulder, pulling her braid to the side. "Can you, please?"

"Of...course."

Stepping up, he lifted his hands and started undoing the delicate pearl buttons. Her skin appeared by centimeters. A tiny mole on her shoulder, a freckle in the middle of her back. He'd never been turned on by so little, but Alessio ached to run his finger along the edges of skin he was revealing.

He would not betray this moment. She'd asked him for aid so he would ignore the fact that he wanted to trail kisses across her back, wanted to strip the dress down. He cleared his throat as he refocused on the buttons. The rebel prince pushing against the dutiful man he needed to be.

"You all right?"

No.

"Fine." He breathed the word into being. He made it to the middle of her back and let out a sigh of relief.

"Is something on my back?"

"No." The word did nothing to stop the pulsating bead of need in his soul. It didn't clear the thoughts or the desire; if anything, the fuse seemed to speed up.

"You're perfection." Alessio's finger slipped, connecting with her bare skin. Desire blazed through him. What would she do if he kissed her? What would she taste like?

Fire? Passion?

"Think you can take it from here?" Alessio barely got the words out.

"No." Brie looked over her shoulder. "I mean…it's just, the pearls are sewn on by hand. It's so delicate. I can't see the buttons. I wore it to highlight her ability, given that you required a wedding dress."

"Actually, that was Sebastian." Alessio let out a sigh. This was a topic he could use to alleviate some of the need clawing through him.

Brie spun. Her hands clasped the top of the dress to keep it in place.

All hope of ignoring the desire evaporated. Her chest was pink…with frustration…or might she be pulsing with need, too?

His body ached as he made sure to keep his gaze focused on her face, when all he wanted to do was worship her with his lips. His tongue…

"Your brother?"

Focus, Alessio. Focus.

"He's still learning his words carry more weight. The Princess Lottery was my father's idea, the reason I came back." That was close to the truth.

"You came back for this. I might have stayed—" Her blue eyes caught his. "Where were you?"

"Not in Celiana." He didn't discuss those years. The happiness, the freedom...

"Right." He started to push his hands into his pockets before adjusting his stance. "Sebastian... Well, he thought the idea wild and hasn't kept his thoughts quiet."

"He's different." Brie looked at Alessio.

"The crown is heavy." That was another topic he wasn't going to discuss. Sebastian wasn't the same. He skipped duties. He seemed uninterested in the role he'd practiced for since birth.

"Good thing we aren't getting married... We might have to answer each other's questions." Brie pursed her lips.

Not necessarily.

That was a sad truth of royal life. As long as you looked happy to the outside, you could do almost anything behind the walls of the palace.

"Sebastian joked that I should have everyone arrive in wedding dresses, and before I knew what happened, they wrote it into the contract. Luckily, most people rented their gowns."

"Rented?" Brie's mouth fell open.

"Yes." He made a twirling motion with his finger, and she turned as he restarted his undressing mission. "I worked out a deal with one of the chain bridal gown places in America. The women could rent their gowns, then ship them back. If one of the women with a rented gown won, the chain would get to dress the princess on our wedding day."

"That was very kind." She bent her head, and his fingers slipped again.

The contact between his fingers and her bare skin lasted less than a second. It was no time at all and forever all at once.

"I think..." she started, but didn't continue for a moment. "I think I've got it from here."

"Of course." His feet screamed as he stepped away. "I'll…" Words were difficult to muster. "Should I pack anything in the living room or kitchen?"

"No."

He headed for the door.

"Alessio?" Her cheeks were pink; her lips pursed. Brie's hands clutched the bodice of her gown. She started toward him, then stopped.

"Yes?"

"Thank you." Her smile was soft. It wasn't a brilliant, excited grin or joyous beam, but it filled her eyes. "Today was a long day."

"Tomorrow is the start of the next chapter." Whether that ended in their freedom or at the altar was still too early for Alessio to know.

"I look forward to showing you how we save Celiana without sacrificing our own happiness."

"I hope you do." He stepped out of her room to give her space. Privacy was something in short supply within the palace walls where she'd be living—at least for a few weeks.

And maybe forever.

CHAPTER THREE

ALESSIO STOOD IN front of Briella's door. He needed to knock. It was nearly nine in the morning; time was moving fast. His bride-to-be was a stranger. They didn't need to know each other's secrets, but they needed to know enough to put on a good show.

That was all people really wanted. It was a sad truth he'd learned as soon as he was old enough to understand the news articles printed about his family. A smiling family was best. The press could translate any frown into a generational fight in an instant. Truth was only good if the gossip was boring.

And the gossip was never boring.

Brie was part of this now whether or not she wanted it—at least for a while.

The hint of his old self was rooting for Brie.

But the man standing in front of her door this morning was Prince Alessio, heir to the kingdom and man at the center of the Princess Lottery scheme.

The scheme could very well result in Briella Ailiono meeting him at the altar. The further he got away from her enthusiasm, the more he figured that would be the outcome. Maybe she was a marketing genius—he wanted to hope so because no matter how much he'd run through the deal last night, Alessio had found no ideas to help her.

Celiana was a kingdom built on honeymoon tourists. When they'd vanished, so had much of the prosperity. The tourism board had run a few ad campaigns, but none of them had resulted in much. The honeymooners had stayed away...until the Princess Lottery.

The morning was already slipping away, and he'd yet to greet her, yet to see the woman who might very well be his wife. In the palace, everything was scheduled. And on the schedule for the day was "Get to know the lotto bride."

His secretary had actually written those words. *Lotto bride.* It was a descriptor that would follow Brie for the rest of her days.

Unless she pulled off the unthinkable. Then she'd get her freedom...and so would he. Maybe he could go back to Scotland. He'd sold his shop, but he'd opened one once before and he could do it again. Except living incognito after being the international face of the Princess Lottery wouldn't work.

It had barely worked the first time. Every once in a while, people would recognize him, but he'd been able to play off the doppelgänger idea. After all, no one expected a prince in a glass shop.

It could work again—but he'd have to have security. It was something he probably should have had before. But his father had refused to provide it since he'd "walked out on duty."

Alessio squeezed his eyes closed. No. He couldn't give in to that fancy. Even if she had figured out a brilliant plan, there was no guarantee. He'd tasted freedom once. Giving it up had destroyed a sizable portion of his soul.

Brie could hope. Alessio couldn't afford it.

Today was about preparation, informing her what she should expect.

Everyone would snap pictures of her.

Language lacked descriptors for Brie's beauty. She was ethereal. Unbuttoning her gown last night was nearly a spiritual experience.

His subconscious had spun that moment into heated dreams. He was attracted to her. How could he not be? But it was her strength that echoed through his heart. How many women would challenge a prince the moment they met him?

He needed to knock, start the day's agenda by going over the rules, the expectations. He had to explain the bars of the gilded cage that was hers now.

How was he supposed to do that?

"You look weird hovering in front of her door, brother." Sebastian's tone was relaxed. Jokey...unbothered.

Unbothered.

That was once the descriptor applied by his father to Alessio. Sebastian was dutiful. The obedient son. The one who did what was expected...until his father passed.

Now the man was unbothered by everything. Despite the crown on his head. It was infuriating. But given that the last argument Alessio had had with the king of Celiana resulted in his brother's coronation, Alessio had sworn not to argue.

Bury the emotions. Deal with it privately.

"Good observation, Sebastian." Alessio turned, wondering what would happen if Brie opened the door to find the king and her fiancé facing off.

"Aren't your rooms connected?" Sebastian leaned against the wall.

"Yes." His brother knew that; he was just pointing out that Alessio didn't have to be out here. But he did. He was trying to make Brie feel less trapped.

"Trying to work up courage?"

He wanted to deny it, but what was the point? He'd been caught. And he needed courage. Though that wasn't all he needed.

Part of him, the rebel prince who cried out in her presence, wanted to open the door, pull Brie into his arms and see if the heat burning between them last night was still there.

"Did you need something?"

"I'd like to remind you that no one forced you to follow through with the king's plan." Sebastian looked at his fingers then back at Alessio.

The king's plan.

"You're the king and you didn't have any better ideas." Alessio didn't like the hint of bitterness in his tone.

The royal family's only actual power was influence, but it was influence his brother seemed inclined to ignore for as long as possible. Their father was gone; if they didn't step up, who would?

"Maybe you should have worn the crown."

Alessio laughed. "King Cedric is rolling in his fancy tomb hearing that."

His father had spent his life pointing out Alessio's flaws. Getting away had been so healing. It was ironic that he'd finally become the prince his father wanted.

If King Cedric was here, I'd still be free.

"You wear the crown well." It wasn't the truth, but maybe one day it would be.

"We both know that's a lie." Sebastian knocked on Brie's door.

"Wai—" Alessio's mouth froze as his brother rapped his knuckles again.

They waited a moment, but Brie didn't answer. His stomach hit the floor. Surely, she hadn't fled…

"Rattling you is fun. Hard since you came back. But fun." His brother winked. "Your bride-to-be was in the kitchen at four thirty. She's now installed in the media room in the east wing."

"We only have one media room," Alessio grumbled as he started toward where his fiancée was hiding.

Four thirty.

He was an early riser by necessity. If he wanted any time to himself, he took it before the world woke. He'd go for a run or a swim a little after five thirty and have breakfast by six fifteen.

However, when he owned his life, Alessio regularly waited until eight or nine to begin his day.

Stop thinking of that.

It was the past. Focus on Brie. On the here and now.

"She's under your skin."

"She's…"

Alessio pushed his hands into his pockets then pulled them out as words refused to come to mind. Brie wasn't under his skin; it was the thought that her idea, her plan, whatever she'd figured out, might actually work. There was the rush freedom brought, the hint that maybe the life he'd had could be his again.

Still, he did not get ruffled, not anymore. That was Sebastian's role.

Alessio was cool, calm and dutiful. The prince everyone expected…the one the island needed.

"There is one thing we should discuss before you greet Briella *Ailiono.*"

The inflection on her last name gave away the issue. "Her family."

"So you've thought of it, too?"

Not really. Not in the way that seemed to echo off his brother. He'd seen her panic yesterday at the dessert table. Heard the jokes that cut too close to her soul about an engagement to a man evidently many years her senior.

Her family had let Brie down. He understood that. She'd flown from her cage and landed in another. Just like him.

"She's estranged. The entire court knows that." The reasons for it were for Brie to acknowledge, not him.

Her panic at the dessert table yesterday had made Alessio see red. That she'd panic at such a thing implied the control she'd endured growing up.

Luckily, he'd kept his cool for the cameras.

"Do you know why she's estranged?"

"No. But it hardly matters. If the Ailiono family has issues with this union, they will go through me."

Brie was smart and kind—the woman had entered the bridal lottery solely to help her friend, and had protected Ophelia last night, too. Maybe those weren't qualities the Ailiono family valued, but they were ones he did.

Sebastian's head snapped back. "Going toe-to-toe with the Ailionos might not work. They have more power."

"More land, more money…power—they probably think so. But no one has ever really tested that." Alessio didn't wish to break that ground, but if Brie needed it… Well, the royal family would offer her protection. There had to be some bonus to wearing a crown.

"You'd challenge the Ailiono clan?"

"If necessary." Maybe it was weird to feel so protective of Briella. But it was the least he could do. She was under his protection for as long as she was his fiancée…and for forever if they met at the altar.

"You don't have to marry her."

"Good. Something we agree on." Brie was smiling as she held the door open.

For once Alessio wished the palace staff didn't keep the door hinges so well oiled.

"Brie. You look lovely this morning."

Alessio dipped his head, unable to keep the smile from his lips. She was gorgeous and so sure of herself. Once more his heart swelled with the idea of freedom. Of escaping…with Brie.

Except that if they escaped, it wouldn't be together. His happiness deflated a little on that realization.

"I've breakfast in here for you, Alessio. There is enough, if you'd like to come to the presentation, too, Your Majesty."

"Sebastian." The king tilted his head. "You are to be my sister-in-law after all."

"We'll see about that."

"I *like* her." Sebastian nodded to Brie, then turned to Alessio. His brother didn't hide his chuckle as he walked away. It was still weird to hear Sebastian laugh.

"A presentation?" Alessio stepped into the media room and felt his mouth fall open.

One side of the room looked like a miniature studio with a ring light, green screen and laptop set up. The other side indicated she'd found the library and carted what looked like dozens of books.

How long had she been awake?

"Did you get any sleep, Brie?"

"I did." She smiled, hesitating before adding, "Thank you for asking."

The hesitation before her thanks nearly broke his heart. It was a simple question. A kind one. And he could tell that no one usually asked.

No one asked him, either. How he wished they shared more in common than family trauma.

"How?" He blew out a breath as he surveyed the media room.

"I slept here." Brie grinned. "The couch is surprisingly comfortable."

Alessio shook his head. "I haven't slept on a couch since I was a teen trying to make King Cedric mad."

He couldn't even remember the argument now. There'd been so many with his father. But the result was Alessio sleeping on the same couch Brie had for almost a month until he had finally relented on whatever the fight was about. Which was why he didn't remember the reason. He only remembered the fight his father had won.

Though since he was back in Celiana, his father had won that one, too. Not that he'd ever known it.

"Why do you call him King Cedric?"

Alessio took the coffee from Brie's hand, her fingers brushing his. The lightening he'd experienced at her touch last night reappeared immediately.

He took a long sip, before asking, "What else would I call him?"

Brie's eyes widened.

"I fear I said a princely thing."

"A princely thing?" Brie moved to the small table where fruits, scones and breakfast meats were laid out. "What does that mean?"

Alessio made up his own plate then followed her to the couch. "Oh. It's a thing that makes people realize Sebastian and I aren't normal. That our upbringing was...unique."

Unique was as good a word as any.

"I called him King Cedric because that was his title."

In his mind it made sense. He knew others viewed their parents differently. He cared for his mother, loved her. His father, on the other hand... He'd respected his devotion to Celiana. If a little of it was ever directed toward him— Alessio shut the thought down.

His father had done the best he could for the country, but he'd seen Alessio and Sebastian as extensions of his duty more than as sons.

"Alessio..."

Brie's eyes held a look he knew was pity. He didn't need it. Didn't want it—particularly from her.

"Presentation time." Alessio clapped his hands. "We have a wedding to stop!"

A wedding to stop.

Those were words Brie desperately wanted to hear, so why did they turn her skin cold?

Alessio, the rebel turned dutiful heir to the throne, was a mystery. He'd spent his teen years avoiding royal duties, arriving almost late to events and ducking out early. It was typical teen behavior—but as a prince the press had labeled him a rebel. And he'd seemed to lean in to the role.

Brie mentally shook herself. This wasn't a mystery she needed to crack. She needed his support, which he seemed willing to give. But he'd dodged every deep question she'd asked.

That didn't matter. It didn't.

A yawn gathered at the back of her throat, and Brie forced it away. There wasn't time for exhaustion. She'd worked through the night. Literally. She'd taken catnaps on the couch, woken and restarted.

Brie had pulled all-nighters at university. Her parents had cut her off just after her first semester, when she'd made it clear she had no intention of marrying her father's business contact. From that moment, the payments for school all fell to her.

But for the first time in her life, she could make her own choices. So she'd taken out a loan and made it her goal to graduate in three years instead of four. Working as a barista on campus, studying on every break and going on less than five hours of sleep most nights nearly broke her.

Her family had hoped she'd break, that she'd come crawling back and do what they wanted. Follow their plans. But doing that meant never getting a say in the choices of her own life.

Was that what had happened to Alessio? Why he was back? He'd spent three years abroad, and the royal family had said nothing of his whereabouts. It was like he'd vanished to another dimension, only to reappear when his father, the man he only called King Cedric, suffered his stroke.

The royal family had welcomed him back. They'd pretended like the years away never occurred. Her family would do the same if she bowed the knee and agreed to marry a business contact or foreign heir, if she added value to the family firm. It wasn't as if the Ailionos needed more.

Part of her did wonder about the conversation, if there was any, around the dinner table last night. Her mother had made her thoughts on the Princess Lottery clear when a reporter asked her about it at a ladies' charity event. It was an event Brie knew her mother didn't want to be at, but appearances were what mattered.

According to her mother, the lottery was gauche and in poor taste for the royal family. She'd said that no one would treat the lotto winner like a real princess and that she thought the whole thing ridiculous. She'd not commented when asked about Brie's participation.

"What was your favorite dress Ophelia made?" His question broke through her tired brain.

"The one I wore yesterday." Brie grinned as she pulled up

the presentation slides. "I know white is tradition, for some pretty horrid reasons in my mind. Purity." She made a face. If that was important to a person, then fine, but it wasn't important to her, and that should be fine, too.

"A little old-fashioned, true. The color of a gown should be a bride's choice, for whatever reason she likes. Of course, it needs to be coordinated with the groom."

"So he gets a say?" Brie raised a brow. She had no plans to meet Alessio at the altar, so the argument was pointless, but she couldn't seem to stop herself. "I thought the day was about the bride?"

"But what if she wears orange, and he's in blue? A color clash in their photos! Forever, Brie. Think of the pictures!"

Brie shook her head as the laughter bubbled up. The silly Alessio was here. The one that sat on the floor with her yesterday. The one she needed beside her for this campaign to work.

"That is ridiculous!"

"It is." Alessio leaned toward her, and her eyes fell to his lips. Round, full...so close. "But it made you laugh."

A joke. It was perfect. He'd not questioned her statement on bridal purity. Instead, he'd made a joke about color theory. It was silly and there was no judgment in his voice.

Not that there was much to tell about her love life. Brie had never been with a man, and at twenty-six it made her feel awkward sometimes. But that was better than the alternatives.

She was an Ailiono, which meant everyone who'd asked her out wanted her because of her family. No one wanted her for her, and she wasn't willing to give her heart away for less.

Maybe once she made her own way, found her own path. But deep down she worried she couldn't run far enough to be free of the Ailiono name.

"I love the deep green, the buttons. I obviously can't wear it for my wedding day, though." She saw his lips twitch on the words *wedding day*. The giant white elephant in the room.

"If we marry, you can wear any color on our wedding day. The jade highlights your eyes, gives you a fairylike appearance. And acknowledges your strength, your ability to step away from tradition. But I must know the color so my tie coordinates."

A lump pressed against her throat. What was she to say to that? He'd told her to prepare in case they married, in case she couldn't pull it off. And for just a moment, she let herself visualize marrying Alessio.

He'd be so much better than any man her family would choose. But he wasn't her choice. Not really.

It was just years of loneliness reacting to his silliness and an acknowledgment of a kindred soul. He was a man caught in the same storm of family expectations.

The memory of him unbuttoning her dress flared in her mind. Her body had ached for release. Her brain had screamed for his lips to trail the path of the buttons. Her body had shuddered as his fingers brushed her skin. If he'd asked to kiss her…

She cleared her throat. Time to put away intrusive thoughts about the man before her. The prince. Her fiancé.

Her fake fiancé.

"Let's get the show started."

Alessio turned his focus to the smart board she had hooked up to the laptop. "All right. Show me what you've got."

Brie saw the hint of hope and the moment he cleared it from his face. He wanted to believe this was possible, but he wasn't willing to fully give in to the thought. Would that hurt her plans?

She wasn't sure.

"All right, so you ran the bride lottery to rejuvenate tourism, correct?"

"My father pointed out, just before his stroke—" Alessio paused, made a clicking noise with his tongue, then started again. "We were once the honeymoon capital of the world, Brie. Many of our shops, our bakeries, rely on the tourist traffic."

"You're right," Brie conceded.

It was an issue she'd acknowledged in her research last night. The number of families that relied on revenue from honeymoon tourists was far larger than she'd realized.

And the tourism bounce the Princess Lottery had brought was real. In fact, she'd spent a solid hour last night running numbers and trying to control the panic building in her soul. The country clearly needed the fairy tale.

But that reliance was also a weakness.

"I might have looked for another option, maybe. But then the Ocean Falls Hotel—"

"Closed last year," she interrupted.

This was her presentation. Focusing on failures was a recipe for disaster. She'd listened to more than one professor drum on the need to focus briefly on the past then force the client to look at the future, at the bright picture you wanted them to see.

She continued, "The upgrades needed to bring the historic building into the twenty-first century were too much for the current owners. I've heard rumors of a corporation stepping in. So it might reopen."

She hoped it did, even if she'd never stayed there. The Ailionos did not stay in regular hotels, and once she'd been cut off, she couldn't afford a night. But she'd listened to tourists in the bistro talk about the murals and salt baths. The closure was a devastating blow to the local economy.

"Your family are buying it?"

Could they still be called her family? She supposed she carried their last name. Their DNA created her. Her mother had spent her entire childhood using knife-edged compliments to sculpt her into the perfect Ailiono bride: submissive, willing to do whatever the family asked.

Her father was never home. His life was spent at the office or with one of his many mistresses. She was only a thing to be bartered for his power.

The only thing her parents had agreed on in the last decade was her dismissal from the family firm.

"I'm not privy to the inner choices of the Ailiono firm, but if I had to guess...yes." She shrugged.

According to reports, the hotel needed extensive renovations. The historical beauty was crumbling from the inside. Her family was one of the few with the resources to accomplish such a task.

"Tourists—"

"Do not need to be honeymooners," Brie interrupted again. "We've limited ourselves by catering only to them. All the efforts the tourism board made were to court honeymooners, not tourists in general. The island revolves around love, but it doesn't need to."

She waited, but he didn't offer anything, so she moved to the next slide. "The Falls of Oneiros, the market stalls stuffed with goods from around the world, the Ruins of Epiales, the hiking trails, the art scene, which is world-class, cuisine that is spectacular—a place foodies should flock to—we have it all here."

Brie sucked in a breath, nerves making her rush. "In short, we've got something for most kinds of tourists, and we're limiting ourselves by focusing our efforts on honeymooners. Marriages fail, even if they don't end in divorce, and return trips are few and far between."

"Such a dismal statement." Alessio crossed his arms.

"I know King Cedric and Queen Genevieve's union was the stuff of legends."

Alessio made a face but didn't add anything. Her parents' union was the stuff crafted from the worst nightmares.

"Not every marriage is a success story. And there are people who never wish to marry. They have had bad marriages and won't want to travel to an island of love. They are people who could bring their money to this kingdom but won't if we are only a honeymoon destination. That is the mistake we have made so many times. We can be more. The country *needs* to be more."

Alessio's stance loosened as he leaned forward, his hands resting on his thighs as he looked at her screen. "How?"

The urge to clap nearly consumed her. She knew this moment. She'd seen it in meetings, when a client who'd been uncertain saw her pitch and knew it had possibilities. That was when the momentum shifted her way.

She was going to gain her freedom.

Hidden under the joy was a pinch of something, a pain that shouldn't be there. She didn't want to marry Alessio. She didn't. So why was there anything besides joy?

"We—" she pointed to him, then herself, ignoring the bite of discomfort in her belly "—do all the things." She flipped to the next slide, focusing on the joy winning brought. "We use the bride lottery and our 'impending nuptials'—" she put the words in air quotes "—as the marketing. Everyone will follow us anyway, so we become tourists in our kingdom. While the world looks at us, we market everything Celiana offers. We use my social media platform and engage with people, but talk about everything but the wedding."

"Everything but the wedding?"

"Yes. We'll refer to each other as fiancé and act the part some."

"All part of the show." Alessio nodded.

Show.

It was the right word, but Brie hated it. Still, those were the roles they were playing.

He stood, stepping toward her. Her heart picked up, the annoying organ steadfastly ignoring her brain's commands to stay calm. Alessio smelled divine this morning, the smile on his lips, the twinkle in his green eyes for her...

"This might work." His hand reached for hers, the connection blasting through her.

Her tongue was stuck to the roof of her mouth. Once more her brain issued the orders to say yes. One did not fall in love fast. In lust, however... Well, that box was already checked. But who wouldn't lust after the Adonis standing before her?

"It will work." It didn't sound as confident as she'd like. "And we can start today." She moved to pull up her plans to hike the trail, but Alessio's fingers tightened on her wrist before he let her go.

She looked at him. The prince stood here now. The silly rebel was gone. This was the man she'd seen on television. It was a subtle shift: a tightening in the shoulders, a tip of the lips, a coolness in the eyes. Here stood Alessio the dutiful.

"We are not starting today."

If her breath was thready and uncertain, his was firm. There was no hint that the touch between them was driving lustful thoughts through every inch of his body.

"Alessio," she began, thinking maybe she wasn't the dutiful daughter of the Ailiono family now, but it was the role her family had groomed her for. It was a mask she could slide back on. "This is a good plan."

"It has promise."

Promise!

Before she could argue, he reached for her wrist again. Once more her body betrayed her. Her chest loosened, her skin heated and an ache to lean closer poured through her. There was a pull she'd never felt before, one she needed to ignore, no matter how much her body might yearn to explore it.

"But tomorrow is an early enough start date. You've been up all night." His fingers ran along her palm.

Pulling herself together, she stepped away from his touch. She needed to focus. "I'm used to it."

"Just because you are used to it doesn't mean that you should be." His voice was velvet. A calm water. That was what he felt like.

There was the urge to relax that pulled at her. She'd never given in to that impulse when her life was overwhelming. And if she'd given in, if she'd returned to her family, she'd have lost everything.

Brie couldn't give in now, either.

She raised her chin. "I'm not weak."

That was the word her mother had thrown at her over and over. Eat too much: she was weak. Get anything less than an A-plus on homework: weak. Rebel against family plans: weak.

"I hate that you feel the need to defend rest."

Who was he to say that? Since returning to the island, Alessio had worked tirelessly. It was all he did.

"How often do you rest? You and your brother have reversed roles. He plays and you—" She cut herself off. This was not an argument they needed to have.

Alessio raised a brow. "Don't hold back. I can take it."

My feelings never matter, so say it.

That was the underlying statement. Why was it so easy to read him?

Because they were two sides of the same coin.

"What does everyone say about me, Brie?"

"That you work yourself to the bone for Celiana. That you've changed. That maybe you should have been king."

Alessio shuddered. "I am not the king. Just a prince serving his country." He closed his eyes for a second, then opened them and offered a smile. "It's a good plan, but starting tomorrow is good enough. Rest today. You will be on the go for as long as you are in the palace."

Maybe forever. He didn't say those words, but she heard them in the quiet.

Fine. She could rest today, but there was still something else, something she'd thought about too much since her name left his lips yesterday.

Her insides quaked. She could do this…she had to.

"There is one other thing." Her voice shook, and his eyes softened.

He read people well. That was good, but it also meant he paid attention, and no one had ever paid attention to her. Not really.

"Brie?"

Say the words, Brie.

Her mind was screaming; blood pounded in her ears.

"We should kiss." She swallowed the lump in her throat before pointing to the ring light. "For the camera."

"For the camera?" Alessio looked at the setup. "Is that necessary?"

"We need to put something out today. Control the narrative. And people wanted to see us kiss yesterday. This will be a good teaser for tomorrow."

"Teaser?" Alessio blew out a breath. Maybe he didn't want to kiss her, but it needed to happen.

"There's more." He raised an eyebrow but didn't interrupt. Which was good, because if she didn't rush this next part, she might not get it out. "I want to kiss before we do it for the camera. I don't want my first kiss to be for an audience…even one we are controlling."

"First kiss?"

There was no way to miss his shock. What was she to say? The truth.

Brie did her best not to drop his gaze.

"Yes."

The word shook as it exited her mouth, and she clenched her fingers. This wasn't a big deal… Well, a first kiss might be. She'd hoped it would be—once—but those girlish dreams had died years ago.

At least she thought they had. Last night she'd nearly turned and kissed him. Kissing Alessio didn't frighten her; in fact, she wanted it. More than she'd wanted something in a long time.

And yet he just stood there, his green eyes boring through her.

"My engagement was arranged and not for long." Brie cleared her throat, not wanting to travel that road right now. "And the Ailiono name means the few dates I've been on in the last few years were epic failures."

She didn't owe him an explanation but once she started it the words tumbled forth.

"Relax." Alessio's arm wrapped around her waist, the weight of it heavy against her back. "Breathe."

She took a deep breath, looked at him, and still nothing. "If you don't want..."

He placed a finger over her lips and dropped his forehead to hers. "I want to kiss you, Brie."

The words were soft, and hard, and her body tightened. Flutters of excitement raced across her skin. His scent wrapped around her.

"But I'm not going to kiss you."

That stung. In the softest, gooiest part of her soul. A place she never let anyone in.

"This moment deserves to be yours. As special as I can make it. So, you're going to kiss me." He opened his eyes, his lips so close. "This moment is yours, Briella. All yours."

She waited only a moment before brushing her lips against his. The touch was so light—so unsatisfying.

Closing the tiny distance between them, she wrapped her arms around his neck. If this was her first kiss, she was making it memorable. Her nerves vanished as she grazed his lips again.

His hand trailed along her back, each flick adding more heat to the internal inferno he'd awoken. His other hand lingered on her cheek, his thumb rubbing against her jaw.

Brie let her body lead as she opened her mouth. His tongue met hers and her world exploded. She pulled him closer, though she wasn't sure how it was physically possible.

He tasted of coffee and scones and life. *Life.* It was a weird description, but it felt so true. She had plans, goals, but much of her life was lived in stasis, waiting to really begin. Here, now, it felt like something so much more.

Finally, she released him. The nerves that had vanished in his arms roared back immediately. What was one to say after they'd kissed a prince? After acknowledging their lack of experience? When their entire body seemed to sing?

Silence hung between them.

"Maybe we should have videoed that." Brie let out a nervous laugh. In the realm of good things to say after a first kiss that was at the bottom of any list.

She straightened her shoulders and pointed to the media setup. "Round two?"

"This is your show." A look passed over Alessio's features, but whatever it was disappeared before she could decipher it.

"Now for the camera?" Alessio gestured toward the media gear.

Brie opened her mouth. Of course the moment wasn't momentous for him. It was only her first kiss after all, a prep for the real show.

"Now for the camera." Brie smiled, hoping it looked real.

CHAPTER FOUR

BRIE'S HEAD WAS buried in her phone as she lifted what he suspected was at least her second cup of coffee. She made a few notes on the small notebook beside her, a frown crossing her lips.

"What's wrong?"

Brie looked up, her eyes widening as she met his gaze. "When did you get here?"

"Not long ago, but you were focused."

When he was in his glass shop, people had been able to sneak up on him. He'd get lost in the moment, in the creative juices that flowed when he was working on a piece.

"You frowned. So I repeat, what's wrong?"

"Our second kiss looked too stilted. The feedback on the story I put up is less than stellar. There are comments that we look like robots."

"Oh." Alessio slid into the chair next to her. "I take it that is bad." He'd known that the second kiss was lacking, especially compared to the first.

The first. The feel of her lips on his, her body molding to his. It was magic, a kiss like he'd never experienced. He'd wanted to melt into her, spend the rest of the night worshipping her lips. Then she'd joked that they should have filmed that one.

A nervous joke. He'd understood that immediately, but it had stolen the illusion from the moment. Their second kiss,

the one she'd uploaded, felt much more like two strangers—
which they were.

"Yes. It's bad." Brie downed the rest of her coffee, hopped
off the chair and filled her cup again. "But we're marketing
Celiana. Not us." Brie blew out a breath. "Love is boring."

"Really?" Everything about the Princess Lottery seemed
to indicate otherwise.

"Yes." Brie sighed like it should be obvious. "It's why your
parents' love story never really made headlines."

Love story.

It was weird to hear that knowing it was false. "Their wedding kept the honeymoon industry going. That is the legacy
of their love."

"No." Brie slid back into her seat. Her jeweled gaze caught
his.

His breath skipped. She was so close, the aroma of her coffee and the sweet scent that was just Brie reminded him of
their kiss. Their first one.

"Their legacy is the wedding." Brie shrugged, like she
wasn't just dismissing the mythos of the great love the palace
carefully sculpted.

Before he could add to that, she continued, "Your father
had no identified mistresses."

Only the country.

"Your mother was faithful, too. Delivering an heir and…"

A blush invaded her cheeks as she looked away.

"And a spare."

The word didn't matter to him. He'd heard it his entire life.
He was the spare. The one that really only mattered if something happened to his brother. It was a scenario Alessio never
wanted to happen.

Brie's hand closed over his. "The point I'm trying to
make—" she squeezed him and for a moment he thought she'd
let him go, but instead she kept holding his hand "—is that
gossip is more fun. Love—true love—is boring. Aka your
parents."

She blew out a breath. "I don't know how we fake that, though. We need to be boring so they focus in on the locations."

"I do." Alessio lifted her hand, kissing the center. It was a sweet gesture, one he'd seen his father do a million times with his mother.

"That is a Prince Charming move." Brie sighed. "But I am serious."

"I know." Alessio took a deep breath. "You can't tell anyone what I am about to say."

Brie nodded.

"My parents weren't in love."

Her mouth fell open, but he didn't wait for the exclamation he saw building.

"It was an act. A well-scripted one. They cared for each other, but it wasn't love—not really." Alessio knew he was rambling, but he wanted her to understand. "They caressed a lot in front of reporters when they were first wed—at least that's what I've heard. Once the story was set, they lessened the touches, but people just figured it was normal longtime married-couple things."

Alessio ran his thumb along her palm, grateful she was still holding him. It was weird to talk with an outsider about this. "I know it sounds bad. And I know they respected each other, but behind the palace walls, they lived independent lives."

"That is perfect!"

Perfect. Not exactly the response Alessio expected. Or wanted.

"So we pattern ourselves after your parents. We act like they did. Happy is not fun to discuss."

He understood that. At the heart of the show, he'd always heard not to frown, not to make a face. A face could be interpreted, and the interpretation was always the thing that sold the story.

"So for our hike up the falls today—" Alessio looked at her hands, ones he'd need to hold, to kiss, to touch "—we act like we are falling in love."

The path to freedom wouldn't be difficult to walk. But the idea of role-playing love with Brie sent an uncomfortable arrow through his heart.

"And in the palace, we can lead separate lives for the next few weeks." She looked down and ran her hand along the back of her neck.

Then she grabbed her phone. That thing was an extension of her. "Shall we try a little live? It's early still, so we won't have as many viewers, which might make us looser."

"Sure." Alessio shrugged. "But what are we going to talk about?"

Brie bit her lip, then shook her head. "Let's run it without a script. A 'get to know you live' kind of thing. My family is off-limits. So is yours. Any other questions unwelcome?"

"I don't discuss the years I was away."

Brie nodded. "Understood. Though I'll admit that I am a little desperate to know. The only trips I took out of the kingdom were with my family, and I spent far too much of those vacations with a book in a boardroom while Dad had a meeting he couldn't—or didn't want to—reschedule. Not information I'd planned to share. And that right there is why we put things off the table."

Brie laughed and let her hand graze his knee. She set up the phone on a stack of books she must have carted down from the media room, and he watched her slide into "on" mode. Her shoulders were just a little straighter, her smile a little too full. But then he had an "on" side, too. One he needed to get into.

"Good morning, Celiana." Brie waved before holding up her coffee cup. "Alessio and I are in the kitchen, having coffee, and thought we'd spend a little time with you."

She leaned closer, making sure they were both in the frame. His arm slid around the back of her chair, and he could tell it pleased her.

After all, it looked good for the camera, though he'd done it to make sure she didn't tumble out of the tall chair. It was an unrealistic fear, but his body had acted without thinking.

She lifted the coffee cup again.

"How many cups of coffee have you had this morning?" Alessio winked before making eye contact with the phone. Was he supposed to talk to her or them? That was a question he should have asked.

"More than one, less than—" Brie put a finger on her chin "—less than six."

"Five cups, Brie!"

She grinned and her look was so infectious he nearly forgot about the camera.

"In my defense, your cups are small." She held up what looked like a regular coffee cup to him.

"If you think about it, it's unfair to judge by this tiny thing." She set it down and leaned on the counter. "I should have thought to grab one of my coffee mugs."

"I fail to see how the size of the mug impacts the amount of coffee you drink." He reached his hands across the island, letting his fingers wrap with hers.

Touching her was intoxicating, and they'd agreed that they needed to look affectionate. It should feel like acting...at least a little. Yet...it felt so natural as her fingers linked with his.

"It's the same amount by volume." She made a silly face, then stuck her tongue out at the "tiny" mug. "But then I can say that I drank two cups, and it sounds less horrendous."

"How big is your mug?"

Brie threw her free hand over her face, the drama making him chuckle. "There is no mug big enough. But mine holds basically half a pot." She beamed, then looked at the phone. "Next topic. Are you ready for our hike?"

"Sure."

He'd hiked the Falls of Oneiros several times as a child. The area was beautiful, but he hadn't visited in years.

"The Falls of Dreams." Brie sighed and pulled her hand away. "My brother, Beau, and I used to stand at the top, think of our dreams and throw a petal over the falls."

She bit her lip then lifted the cup. Family was supposed to

be off-limits. Beau Ailiono was a business scion, the heir to
the Ailiono fortune, but he and Brie had been close enough
once to hike and wish for something at the falls.

It was the standard routine at the falls. Oneiros, Greek for
dreams, was where the locals came to cast wishes. Few tourists found their way there.

That would change once they visited—hopefully. The tourism industry had not courted the outdoorsy types. She was
right; they had restricted their focus, and opening that up was
a good thing.

Though he wasn't sure it would be enough.

"What were your dreams?"

He and his brother had never participated in making wishes
when they'd hiked the falls. Their lives were planned out. The
expectations known. What good were dreams when the path
was already set in stone before you?

What had she thought was possible? What had she wanted
more than anything?

"Freedom." She cleared her throat.

He did not know what to say to that. Freedom.

His heart clenched as he stared at her wavering smile. Freedom. One word, with so much meaning.

Freedom was something royal life did not allow.

"What were yours?"

The question interrupted his worries. At least he had an
easy answer. "I never made a wish."

He felt the weight of her stare, but what was there to say?
His role was determined from the moment of his birth. To
wish for more... Well, that had led to the greatest heartbreak
of his life: closing his shop and returning home.

"Well. That changes today!" Brie waved at the camera.
"Who wants to see Alessio toss a petal?"

A ton of hearts and comments saying "Yes!" flooded the
chat screen.

"All right, stay tuned." Brie leaned over and kissed his
cheek, then shut the live stream off.

"Was that better?"

"Yes." Brie tilted her head, thoughts clearly evident in her eyes.

Sadness or pity? He wasn't sure, but he didn't like either option.

"You are more than the title prince."

Whatever he'd expected her to say, that wasn't it.

"Not really." He finished his cup of coffee and left the chair. Once upon a time he'd been more than the spare. More than a prince. He wanted to believe it was possible for it to happen again, but the odds... He didn't even want to calculate them.

Freedom.

The word echoed in his mind.

"You are more than your title, Alessio."

"Well." He stepped around the kitchen island and pulled her into his arms. "I am a fiancé now, too."

"I'm serious, Alessio." Brie's hands cupped the sides of his face.

He could tell she'd done it impulsively, but he enjoyed her touch. A little too much.

This didn't feel like living separate lives when her phone's camera wasn't on—when no one was looking. It felt real, and far more terrifying.

"Fine. I'm more than my title."

"Good." Brie released him, her gaze following her hands before she crossed her arms. "Now...um..." She looked over her shoulder. "I need to get ready for the hike. Good job this morning."

He playfully offered a military salute. If she saw the humor in his movements, she didn't react. And then she was gone.

"I guess people got the message..."

Brie stared out the window of the SUV. The crowd was at least three people deep even though they'd blocked the hiking path off and they had a three-hour window to hike on their own. She'd pushed for an open hike; the palace security team hadn't laughed in her face, but they'd squashed the idea with exceptional speed.

However, she didn't mind spending time alone with Alessio as she should. This morning they'd said they needed to look happy, like they were falling in love. That was the method his parents had used—so successfully that she'd had no idea. But her touches for the camera were the ones that felt off, unlike touching his knee over coffee or when she'd put her hands on either side of his face; those felt so real.

And for a moment today, she'd seen herself, felt the connection between them that was more than the lottery. She'd worn the same look as him once.

The Ailiono daughter. A piece on her family's chessboard. She'd seen the same despair when he said he wasn't more than his title. She'd still have that feeling if she hadn't left her family.

If she married Alessio, would she experience the same desperation again? Yes. It was why she needed her freedom. But after seeing his look this morning, she needed freedom for him, too. Alessio was far more than his title. He wasn't the spare, the heir only until his brother married and had children. From this point forward she'd focus on the man, not the title.

"The message you broadcast?" Alessio's hand tapped her knee. "Yes, I think that message got out."

He pulled his hand away. Technically no one could see them yet, but part of her wished he'd left it.

"True." Brie knew the crowd was here for the lottery princess, here for the story, but it was weird to see so many people. People normally avoided the Ailiono family—unless they were hoping to make money with them.

No one would describe the Ailiono family as easy to be around. Beau had been, *once*. Then he became their father's mini-me, the man set to take over the Ailiono family dynasty.

He'd abandoned her. She'd hoped he might ride to her rescue when she was unceremoniously kicked out. She'd held out hope for far too long that he might show up.

She shook the memory from her head. Beau was the perfect Ailiono family member. She wasn't. So their paths had parted.

Had Alessio and Sebastian had a good relationship growing up? What happened when Alessio left? Those were questions she couldn't ask him, though Brie was curious. Deep down, she knew they'd experienced some of the same trauma. And they craved the same thing.

He kissed the top of her head. They'd agreed they needed to touch, needed to make it look real for the camera. Her plan wouldn't work unless people focused on the recreational sites Celiana offered. That meant they couldn't give the likes of journalists like Lev things to feed into rumors of unhappiness.

People liked a love story…they loved a disaster. That was the real public relations rule. If they looked unhappy, it wouldn't matter where they went. All the world would see were the frowns.

But she didn't want him to kiss her forehead. She wanted him to kiss her lips. Their first kiss had poured through her far longer than the few minutes her lips had touched his. It was an ugly reminder of how much the second kiss was lacking.

She'd thought about that first kiss far too much, which was acceptable if she was a blushing schoolgirl. But as a twenty-six-year-old woman…

"Let's do this. Your smile ready?"

This needed to look good. Tourists were on vacation. Vacation was happy time.

"I can always find a smile." Alessio grinned, but it was the prince smile, one she might not have fully pegged as fake until she'd spent time with him. But now it was easy to see; if she could see it, so might others, too.

"We need authentic smiles."

Alessio's brows rose before he pursed his lips. "It is a real smile."

"No." Brie shook her head. "It's Prince Charming out for an outing. It's not real."

"Prince Charming is a fantasy. I am no fantasy." Alessio leaned closer to her, his lips spreading into a convincing smile.

Brie held up her hands, pretending they were a camera. "Click." She laughed as his head tilted, his grin growing even bigger. "That was a genuine smile. Focus on whatever brought that out."

"You brought it out." Alessio pulled on the back of his neck as he turned his attention to the crowd.

She knew those words had slipped out unintentionally, but her insides warmed as she watched the smile on his lips. She'd done that. It was silly to care about, but still...

"Luckily for you, I will be on the trail beside you the whole time." Brie blew out a breath and grabbed the door handle. "Showtime!"

"Briella! Princess Briella!"

"Princess!"

"Briella!"

The calls rose around her. Flashes from cameras and held-up cell phones, which she knew were recording, greeted them on the side of the path. There were makeshift barriers with lots of people stood behind them.

She'd wanted an audience; her plan depended on it. But it was still a lot to take in.

Alessio squeezed her hand as they wandered to the barrier. His smile looked genuine, full, and it eased her as she stepped into the role, too.

Alessio started shaking hands, and Brie smiled at a young girl.

"You're such a pretty princess." The girl held up a sunflower.

Brie bent down so she could meet the girl's eyes. "I'm not a princess...not yet. Just Brie. What's your name?"

"Ella. Like the end of your name. My mom owns a bakery. It's always busy now. She said last night that it was because of you."

A woman standing behind Ella let out a soft groan. "I've

told you not to eavesdrop on Daddy and I. Give her the flower, honey."

Ella looked at her mother and made a face. "But I want her to know the rest."

"Know what?" Brie asked, making sure she kept a serious face. Ella was serious, and Brie could be serious, too, though a laugh was bubbling in her chest.

"I like to play Cinderella, but now I can play Princess Briella." Her smile was so wide, so open.

Brie looked to Ella's mother. The woman had taken time out of her bakery to come with her daughter today. The country needed the tourists; family bakeries thrived on them. But the hope in Ella's and her mother's eyes sent fear tumbling through her. What if Brie's plan failed?

Ella and her mother weren't the only regular people here. Yes, the press was here, but so were many regular folks whose livelihoods were riding on Prince Alessio and Princess Briella.

Brie looked at Alessio. His gaze met hers, and he grinned before turning back to the gathered crowd. She'd sworn to meet him at the altar if her plan failed, but she'd refused to think of the possibility. And she couldn't focus on it now.

"Thank you for the flower, Ella."

Alessio placed a hand on her shoulder, and she rose. "If we want to hike the trail before the day gets too warm, we should get moving."

"Agreed." Brie smiled at the crowd, though now she suspected it was her smile looking forced instead of Alessio's.

She took his hand, her body relaxing a little with the touch, waved with the sunflower, then followed him down the path.

"I think we did pretty well there." Alessio adjusted his backpack as they started up the trailhead.

"I think so, too."

At the very least, it was a good start. The actual test happened with the video they did at the falls. Could they successfully turn the attention to the falls and not them?

"And now we hike." Alessio pulled one arm in front of him, stretching his shoulder, then did the other.

"Now we hike," Brie conceded. The trip to the falls would take about an hour. In silence it would seem like forever. "So maybe we should play twenty questions."

"Twenty questions? What is that?"

Brie shook her head. "Seriously, Prince Charming? It's exactly what it sounds like. You ask each other twenty questions, 'get to know you' style. I'll start. Favorite color?"

"Green. You?"

"Light blue. Like the water over the falls. Favorite season?"

"Summer."

They continued the questions as they walked the path. The questions were getting a little deeper but carefully avoiding anything too deep.

"Who was your first fiancé?"

She lost her footing, and Alessio's hand caught her elbow. His eyes locked with hers as he steadied her.

"Brie?"

That was not a question she'd expected.

"Sorry. Maybe I shouldn't have asked, but I assume he is not a security threat. Or is it possible he is?"

Security was important for the royal family, but she didn't think that was why Alessio was asking.

The fiancé... That was the night she'd broken with her family forever after refusing to play the role they'd carefully planned out for her. The role her mother played for her father, despite how unhappy it made her.

Kate Ailiono was the "perfect wife."

In public. Behind closed doors, *shrew* was the kindest word one could say. She was jealous of the mistresses and time spent away from the family home. The screaming matches were epic.

The only problem was Brie, and that she wasn't willing to follow in her mother's footsteps.

Time slowed as they stood together on the path. Alessio wrapped an arm around her waist as they looked over a mountain pass. Her past and the future were slamming together. Except he wasn't her future.

She never talked about Milo Friollo. Ophelia only knew because she'd helped Brie escape the Ailiono compound the night her father announced the union.

She could still visualize the man sitting beside her at the table. Milo had smiled and reached out to hold her hand. No notice had been given to her. There was no expectation that she'd do anything other than follow.

"Forget I asked. What was the last book you read?" His tone was sweet, but she could hear the bead of worry under it.

Her most recent read was on marketing to different Enneagram types. She could tell him that and ignore the other question. That was the simple answer, but she couldn't quite find the words.

Brie reached for Alessio's hand and started back up the trail.

"I never talk about him."

The sentence slipped into the open. His name burned the back of her throat, but she didn't say it. Alessio walked beside her but said nothing. No questions, no pressure.

Pressure was an Ailiono family specialty. No one could make silence hurt like her family.

And yet, she'd nearly gone back—so many times. When her feet were bleeding from standing for hours as a barista with burns on her hands, and her eyes were so heavy from exhaustion as she tried to study and keep a tiny roof over her head, she'd thought of it. On her birthday, when no card, no phone call, no acknowledgment from her family came, the desire to belong again had nearly driven her home. When her rent was due and she was short... When everyone was out at bars, having fun, and she was skipping meals...

"Milo was older." That was a kind statement. The man was three times her age, a lifetime of lived experiences to her teenage self.

"Milo Friollo?"

That Alessio could guess at the man her parents had arranged for her wasn't surprising. Milo walked down the aisle more than most. And each wife was younger than the last. He'd married six months after that dinner. And there'd been another last year—wife four was nineteen…just like Brie had been.

"My father and he are business partners. Or they were. I'm not sure their professional relationship survived my flight. Though it probably did. Money is what matters after all."

Once the words were out, her brain refused to stop. "They ambushed me at a family dinner. Announced that we'd marry in six months." Her fingers flexed as the memory of Milo's touch echoed in her brain. "He married another on our wedding date. Though that union lasted less than a year."

"Ambushed?" Alessio let out a grunt.

"It's not that different from the countless other marriages made for prestige, family alliances or money. People like to pretend that we are so different from our historical counterparts, but the truth is the wealthy and privileged rarely marry for love.

"Hell, we are trying to get out of a nearly ironclad marriage contract." Brie laughed. There had to be humor, or she'd cry. "They disowned me for refusing to follow my parents' demands and somehow I ended up back in an arranged marriage." The laughter died away.

"I hope you get out." His words were barely audible.

"You hope I get out. What about you? If you could be anywhere, where would it be?"

"I don't know."

"I think you do." The heat in Brie's cheeks had nothing to do with the hike. She'd answered the one personal question he'd asked, but it appeared that he would not do the same.

They hiked the rest of the trail in silence.

"The falls!" She raised her hand, pointing to the crystal blue water cascading over the mountain's edge. The Falls of Oneiros.

The Falls of Dreams.

"It's gorgeous." Alessio let out a breath as he followed her gaze.

His lack of response to her question frustrated her, but she also wanted him to have this moment, a real one, before she turned on the camera. She grabbed two petals and pressed one into his hand as they moved to stand as close to the edge as possible.

"Do you need to get the phone out?" Alessio looked at the petal like it might bite.

"No. Not for your first wish. We'll film another, but this one… I don't know, it's tradition. You should get to do it the way everyone else does."

"Sebastian and I always knew our roles. Heir and spare—what good were wishes?"

The words broke her heart. Family expectations were hard, but he'd had expectations from the country, too.

"Make a wish. There has to be something you crave."

A look passed over his eyes and Brie lifted up on her toes. It wasn't planned, and there was still frustration bubbling in her. But she was drawn to him. She pressed her lips to his. His arms wrapped around her waist. Alessio deepened the kiss.

The mountain hummed in sync with the racing falls. The world seemed to cheer their connection.

Here and now, there was only her and Alessio. The security team had cleared the falls before they arrived and was standing down the trail, around a bend. In this moment it would be easy to pretend this was a regular date. He was a man who just wanted to spend time with Brie.

It would be easy to pretend they'd met somewhere and were regular people with regular expectations.

But pretending wouldn't get her what she wanted, the freedom she craved. Pulling back, she held up her petal.

"Ready?" She winked and gestured for him to hold up his, too.

He looked at his petal and she could see words tumbling in his eyes. A want, something buried so deep.

"Here, I'll show you how." She held the petal to her chest.

Freedom. It was the word she'd always thought when she stood here. *Freedom.*

She let the petal loose and opened her eyes to watch it float over the falls.

"Your turn." She reached for his free hand. "Close your eyes."

Alessio looked at her, then closed his eyes.

"Lift the petal to your chest and think about what you want. What you really want, Alessio."

He did as she said, taking a deep breath.

"Now let it go."

He opened his palm, and the petal floated into the falls. He opened his eyes and wrapped his arm around her waist. She didn't think as she laid her head against his shoulder.

"See, that wasn't so hard, was it?"

His lips brushed her head. "Thank you for the experience, Brie."

Again they stood in silence. Finally, he squeezed her. "Scotland. If I could go anywhere, it would be Scotland."

Before she could ask any follow-ups, Alessio grabbed two more petals. "Now, showtime."

"Right." She'd nearly forgotten. She'd been lost in the moments of his kiss, in him.

It was good that he'd reminded her… It didn't sting. Not even a little bit.

CHAPTER FIVE

ALESSIO LOOKED AT his watch. He'd gotten a quick swim in after dinner and had the rest of the evening to himself. Brie would be in the media room. It was where she spent any free time. And today there'd been quite a lot of freedom.

Which meant he'd not seen her much.

They'd enjoyed a quick outing at a local bakery. The small trip was designed to give the illusion of dating while highlighting a local establishment. They'd stayed less than an hour, and talked to the baker and her son. He'd eaten a few cookies. Brie had—

Alessio closed his eyes. He'd been so focused on the discussion that he wasn't sure she'd sampled anything. He stopped, his mind flashing to the first day—how was that less than a week ago? She'd looked like a deer in headlights by the dessert plate.

Her mother was notorious for controlling what food passed her lips. The comments Brie's mother made to the ladies and men of the court were often downright rude. If that was what she was willing to say in public, what vitriol had Brie heard behind closed doors?

It wasn't hard to imagine. His father had leveled complaints against him at every chance. Though never about food.

It was nearly seven. That meant that if she'd grabbed dinner, she was bent over spreadsheets and crunching data that seemed to appear from nowhere.

She wouldn't look for him for the rest of the night. They

were in the palace. That meant separate spheres. She hadn't wanted to put up a video about them this evening. Instead, she was tracking what people were saying about the visit to the Falls of Oneiros two days ago and the bakery this morning.

They each wanted this to succeed, but she needed a break, too. And he had an idea that might just work. It would only take a few minutes to put it together.

He knocked on the door, waited for her call to enter, then swept the door open and pushed in the cart the kitchen staff had helped him prepare.

"What?" Brie's hair was falling out of her bun and there were smudges on the glasses she wore when working at the computer. Her oversize sweater easily fit over her knees, which she had pulled up in her chair.

"Good evening, Brie."

She looked at the tray he was pushing and raised a brow. "Good evening. I...um... I already ate."

He knew that. The kitchen staff had told him she'd gotten a chicken salad sandwich and some veggies. But no dessert.

Alessio walked over to the desk and nearly leaned in to kiss her cheek. They were in the palace. The little touches weren't needed, but that didn't stop him from wanting them.

Brie's gaze focused on his lips. Had she wanted him to kiss her?

Kissing was not the purpose of this encounter. He honestly wasn't entirely sure what this was about, but he'd wanted to spend time with her.

"I know you ate, but this isn't dinner." Her brow raised again. "Figure you gave me something special the other day, so I'm hoping to return the favor."

"Something special?" A frown touched her lips, and he wanted to wipe it away. "A wish isn't something special, Alessio."

"Why?" He walked to the cart and pushed it by the little table she used for meals before gesturing for her to join him.

This wasn't a grand affair, but he wanted her to enjoy it away from spreadsheets and numbers.

She bit her lip as she walked over and looked at the covered trays.

"Because mine was staged. I think it is important that you made a wish. You are more than a prince. You get to have your own dreams and wishes, but…"

Brie hesitated and looked at her feet. She sucked in a deep breath, then looked back at him. "But mine was for the show."

"Not the first one." He squeezed her hand, then lifted it to his lips.

"Yes, but—"

"But nothing. My first wish was mine. So little in my life is." The wish was a moment, one he got to hold deep in his soul even if he doubted it could come true.

"But now…" He pulled off the covers of the two trays with what he hoped was a flourish.

"Cookies and pie." She let out a laugh. "Not sure what I expected, but somehow sweets wasn't it."

His stomach twisted. What else might be under such a display? The Ailiono family was notorious for controlling business dealings, but it was clear Brie had been controlled in other ways. And she'd escaped.

She'd made her own way, only to find herself behind the bars of another cage.

"I know your mother doesn't like sweets."

Her laughter was bitter as it echoed against the walls. "My mother abhors treats. Anything that might add a pinch of weight to her waistline."

"Her waistline…" Alessio leaned forward on his hands. "And yours?"

"Ailiono children are extensions of their parents. Beau is my father, even if once upon a time I thought he might break away. Thought he might come with me, but…well…he didn't."

There was more to that story. But Brie cleared her throat as she picked up a cookie. Her eyes didn't move from the raspberry lemon one.

"I was my mother."

"Was." Alessio reached for her hand. "You *were*, but now you are Brie, Princess of Celiana, eater of whatever sweets she chooses!"

"Princess?" Brie pushed at his shoulder. "Alessio. I know you're joking, but it is so weird to hear 'Princess Brie.' Even after crowds have shouted it for days."

She was stalling. So he grabbed the other raspberry lemon cookie. He popped the tiny pastry in his mouth. The flavors were divine.

"Your turn."

Brie looked at the cookie, then up at him. If she pushed back, he'd stop, but he wanted her to try. She squeezed his hand then took a small bite. A tiny bite in a tiny cookie, but a bite.

"Thoughts?"

"It's tart. Fine."

"*Fine* is not what we are looking for!" He grabbed a dark chocolate bar and passed it to her. Chocolate was his mother's favorite. He preferred fruit flavors.

She took a bite and then another. "All right. That *is* good."

Chocolate made her smile. Good to know!

She lifted the lavender cookie from the tin. "This looks too pretty to eat." Turning the cookie, she pointed to the small lavender outline the baker had created in the center.

"A work of art." He grabbed its twin. "That is designed to be eaten."

"Art shouldn't be eaten."

"No. This art should. Art is designed to give the person near it a feeling, an experience. A painting might bring out happiness or sorrow. A sculpture may remind you of a loved one who passed or a brilliant childhood memory. And cookies, pastries, they are designed to evoke the majesty of the flavors. It does the baker a disservice to think it too pretty to eat."

"Wow. What is your creative outlet?"

Brie's jeweled gaze captured him. Expectation and happiness were bright as she guessed at what was truly in his soul.

"What?"

Brie set the cookie down. "What is your thing? Painting? Sculpture? Did you make the cookie?"

"No." He'd not meant to let so much out, but the words could be of an art aficionado, not an artist. He was a patron of Celiana's art scene. Even the Princess Lottery was a fundraiser for it.

Her hands wrapped around his waist, her sweet scent lighting through him. "Come on, Alessio. No one talks that passionately about art without doing something."

"Lots of people talk about art passionately."

They did. He'd stood in many a gallery with people who'd never picked up a brush but waxed on about the meaning of a piece.

"I'm sure they do. But not with the feeling you had in your voice or the twinkle in their eye. Are you a mime?"

"A mime?"

Brie pulled back, a giggle in her eyes. "Sure. That's an art form. What's yours?"

No one had ever just asked him what his creative outlet was. No one had even guessed the prince had one. In his glass studio, covered in sweat from the fires and dust from the shop, he'd looked less than regal. But he'd been happy.

"Glasswork."

"Oh. Like melting glass and bending it." Brie tilted her head, and he could see all the questions building.

Alessio nodded. "It's a little more but yes, at its base, it's melting and bending."

At his height in the shop, he'd made a few pieces a day. Most of them sold, and he had a few in his suite that he couldn't part with.

"You have to show me."

"Can't. I gave it up. Princely duties and all." There was a workshop on the palace grounds. It was his workshop. But the glass ball he'd made for the lottery was his final piece, his goodbye to the art as he stepped into the role he'd been born to play.

"That's a shame." She stuck her bottom lip out, then opened her mouth but closed it without saying whatever had come to her mind.

She put the whole tiny cookie in her mouth, closed her eyes and let out the softest sigh. He wasn't sure exactly what Brie was experiencing, but watching her was magical.

"That is divine."

"You're divine." The words slipped out, but he didn't want to pull them back. She was perfection.

Brie looked at him, and he nearly shifted as she seemed to stare right into his soul.

The world with its requirements, its worries, the concerns for the kingdom and Brie's plans—it all vanished as she dropped a quick kiss on his cheek.

"Um…" She looked at him, and he could see the shock running through her face.

She'd not planned to kiss him. It wasn't on the schedule after all.

His hands moved without thinking, pulling her back into his arms. She sighed, like there was no other place she'd rather be, then lifted her head. Their lips met and once more the world seemed to stand still.

She tasted like chocolate and freedom, and he craved every piece of her. Her fingers moved along his back, her body pressing against his. Every sense was tuned to Brie.

Brie stepped back and he let her go, even though the urge to deepen the kiss, to run his fingers over her bare skin, was crying out within him.

Her cheeks were a delicate rose as she pointed to the trays. "Chocolate. I like chocolate. The lavender is good, too. I mean, even the lemon raspberry was good."

They were shifting topics. That was probably for the best. "You don't have to lie. You didn't like it."

Brie pursed her lips and pushed a piece of hair behind her ear. "It was all right…nothing like chocolate, though."

"So we start trying out different chocolates for dessert."

If she wanted to shift the conversation away from kisses, he'd go with the flow. She'd lacked control before. There were parts of their lives that would always be out of their control, but Alessio would give her as much as possible.

"Chocolate flavors? How many flavors are there?"

"More than I can count." He wrapped an arm around her shoulder, not really intending to, but his heart skipped as she laid her head on his shoulder.

"Dessert is nice. No wonder my mother wanted me to avoid it." Brie sat up, the past breaking through the illusion of the treats.

"I wanted to show you the metrics I have. The falls have seen a large booking, and the bakery sold out. Of course, we won't have all the metrics for several more weeks. Still, the focus of the first few adventures has stayed on the location after brief mentions of us…touching."

The hesitation caught his attention, but she was already throwing things up on the smart board. Tables, charts, growth exports—all were very impressive, he thought.

He'd done his time in economics and stats classes, getting through on pure grit with a barely passing grade. Most of the time he'd spent in those classes was daydreaming ways to sculpt whatever creation was burning through his mind.

King Cedric hadn't allowed Alessio to major in art or art history. That was not a proper "princely" topic, according to the king. That hadn't stopped Alessio from spending all of his free time with the art teacher and master glassworker.

"Do you ever tire of it? Of the cameras? The questions?" Brie's questions roused his mind from trying to make sense of the numbers before him.

"No."

She spun around, horror clear on her face. "Come on, Alessio. Never? You were the rebel once upon a time. The skipper of as many engagements as possible. The royal who stuck his tongue out instead of answering pointed questions. You really never tire of it now? Of the lack of privacy? Of the rules? The regulations? The stares...the..."

He caught her fingers, holding them tightly, grounding himself in the present. Once upon a time, he'd rebelled against everything. He'd hated the cameras, the lack of privacy. Giving in to those emotions again might be cathartic, but if this effort failed... Alessio wasn't willing to hope yet.

"When I returned, I pledged myself to Celiana."

A look passed across her features. It sent a shiver through his soul. It would be her life, too, should they meet at the altar.

"It's not a horror show, Brie." He squeezed her fingers.

"It's not *not* a horror show."

That was hard to argue with. "I guess I just see it as part of the duty. Just an extension of the crown."

"Dutiful Alessio. Why the change?"

"It was time to grow up."

She pulled her fingers back, and he watched the wall crash back down between them. The openness was closing as she flipped back to her spreadsheets.

Brie could tell when he wasn't fully honest. She was the only one bothered by his surface-level answers. She was also the only one that paid close enough attention to tell the difference. Brie deserved the answer, but he couldn't give it.

It was cowardly, but that was a story he wasn't going to share with anyone. Even Sebastian didn't know the real reason he'd returned. That secret was buried with his father and that was where it was staying.

CHAPTER SIX

Brie bit her lip as she looked at the email, then looked to the door. Alessio would be here any moment for breakfast. Despite saying they wouldn't spend time together in the palace, they took all their meals together now. And if he saw her frowning, he'd worry and ask why. And she'd probably tell him.

That wouldn't be a big deal if he was telling her personal things. Like what was in Scotland—or who. Or why he'd come home to stay. He could have come for the funeral and then headed back—right?

Brie let out a sigh. She wasn't actually clear on what the rules were for the heir. Maybe he'd had to return and stay. But that didn't mean he had to give up glassworking.

She'd wanted an answer but he'd refused to discuss it or give a full explanation. He was holding back. And if Alessio wasn't opening up fully, then neither was she.

Her business was precious, and this was the second possible cancellation this week for a job she'd scheduled before her name had echoed across the kingdom two weeks ago.

Fourteen days and a lifetime all at once.

The first week, two cancellations had come in saying they wished her well on this endeavor, but understood that her new duties would mean diminished time for their accounts. The email on Monday had asked if she planned to complete the jobs scheduled. It was polite, but they'd included all the account information to return their retainer.

And now this email was here. Yes, no princess in the history of Celiana had worked outside the palace. But she didn't plan to be a princess.

The stats were still up, though not as much as she was hoping to see. It had only been two weeks. That was a blip in marketing time. But with the viral marketing campaign she'd developed, she'd expected more. Or maybe she was just hoping for more. And there were pockets of dissent already, comments that they'd done nothing "wedding" related.

No bridal gown shopping. No cake testing. No venue discussions.

Two weeks. They'd been "engaged" two weeks. It wasn't like all couples immediately hopped to planning. Still, a rumor could tank this whole thing, so she'd scheduled a wedding outing to calm the waters before the ripple fully developed.

Tapping her fingers, she tried to bring her focus back to this problem. If she sent back the retainer for this job, that would mean she'd lost four jobs—so far. She blinked back the tears that were threatening. She'd built her business from nothing once. Brie could do it again.

If she had to.

Taking a deep breath, she typed out the reply thanking them for reaching out and offering to return the retainer, then deleted it. Instead, she sent a quick line saying that, while she was busy, she fully intended to fulfill all her contracts. She'd planned to take a few weeks off following the bride lottery anyway, so nothing was disrupted. She'd be in touch at the beginning of next month and let them know they were at the top of her calendar.

By then she and Alessio would be laying the groundwork for the breakup anyway.

The thought tore through her. Breakup.

This isn't real, Brie. It's not a breakup. Not really.

So why did the thought of not seeing him again bother her so?

Her mind drifted to how he kissed, how his lips felt as they brushed hers, how he tasted when she deepened the kiss.

Then her mind took it a step further. She dreamed of how his fingers tracing down her skin might feel, dreamed of his lips finding far more than her mouth.

Pushing away from the computer, she wandered to the smart board and looked at the graphs she'd developed for the latest outings. She needed to focus on those, not on the handsome prince always by her side, despite their initial pledge to not spend time together inside the palace.

The door opened, and she couldn't stop the smile as Alessio stepped in—juggling two cups of coffee.

"Good morning." He handed her a cup, and she saw his eyes flit to the pot in the corner. "Not sure I should aid in your caffeine intake."

Over the last week, he'd told her that a walk outside or a swim in the pool would be just as good a way to wake herself up. She'd visited him at the pool once. And him in a bathing suit had definitely woken something in her.

"I've only had one...no, two." She thought hard. "Yes, only two so far."

"Only." Alessio shook his head before dropping a kiss on her cheek. "You all right? You look a little off this morning."

Little got past him. It was sweet and unnerving.

Her family had never noticed little things about her. And her coffee habit was not a little thing. She'd used caffeine to keep herself up since she was in high school. It was a habit her parents hadn't minded.

Her parents felt the same way about work as Alessio did now about duty. It was what you did. To question that was unthinkable.

"Breakfast for the princess and prince. Celiana's lovers," Sebastian sang as he strolled through the door with a bag of something he tossed to Alessio.

"Muffins?"

"Homemade!" He winked as he slid onto the couch.

Alessio looked at the bag and frowned. "In other words, you

slipped your security team, spent the night with a woman and left before she woke?"

"Alessio—" Brie's voice was soft as she stepped to his side.

"No need to fret, Princess." Sebastian let out a soft laugh. "This is a common refrain we share. Unlike my brother, I waited until dear old Dad passed to learn how to slip my security detail. You should try it again, brother."

Alessio's body went rigid beside her, and she heard the bag crumple in his fingers before he handed it to her, the top of it nearly mangled.

"You are the king."

The words slipped from her lips before she'd thought them through. This wasn't her fight, but Alessio's brow was furrowed. He'd clenched and unclenched his palm three times and was fighting to keep from shifting on his feet.

How quickly she'd learned his little tells over the last weeks. She wanted to wipe away the worry. But she also understood Sebastian's need for freedom.

She'd craved it for so long, come so close to it. Surely Alessio understood, too.

"Thank you. Exactly." Alessio wrapped his arm around her waist, grounding himself as he stood just a hair taller.

"Wow, the lovers are teaming up. Interesting."

"Don't change the subject, Sebastian. What happens if something happens to you?"

Alessio shifted his feet and Brie thought he wanted to stomp them but was resisting. Was that a hint of the rebel pushing out?

"You have security for a reason," Alessio stated.

"If something happens, you can handle it. The man that returned to the island is quite dutiful." Sebastian closed his eyes and leaned his head against the couch's back. "Perhaps that is a win for everyone."

"No." Alessio's voice echoed through the room.

"Because you don't want the damn throne, either. Don't want everyone wanting you for the crown."

"Because I don't want to lose you." Alessio was vibrating.

"Weird statement, considering you were the one that abandoned the family. Didn't care if we lived or died then."

"Damn it, Sebastian. That is not—" His eyes flicked to Brie. She saw him bite back whatever it was he planned to say.

Brie reached for him as he stepped away from her. "Alessio—"

"Excuse me, sweetheart. I need a moment. I'll see you shortly." He turned, closing the door softly.

"It would have been more dramatic to slam the door." Sebastian clicked his tongue. "Not that my brother would ever do such a thing. At least not now. He used to do it as an art form. When he ran away to Scotland, the door he slammed nearly came off its hinge."

Maybe Alessio slammed doors once, but now he held the hard emotions inside. The worries, the anger—those emotions were buried under the princely cover. Happiness, joy, excitement—things that brought out smiles for others—seemed easier for him.

Brie had learned that in the little time she'd been with him. His brother, his king, knew it and was using it against him. Sebastian was dumping his own issues on the man who was doing his best for the country, for his brother.

"You shouldn't have said that." Brie's words were quiet as she stared at the closed door, willing Alessio to walk back through it.

Brie bit her lip, then turned her full attention to the king. "You shouldn't joke about him not having you in his life. My brother isn't in mine, and…" Her throat tightened as Beau's face danced in her mind. "You shouldn't wish for such things even if you don't want the crown."

Sebastian's eyes opened and color coated his cheeks. *Good.* He should think of his words and what they really meant.

She missed Beau. Their lives had separated. Or more accurately, their parents had separated them. It hurt to think that he'd not reached out to her. But he was still in their world.

Even if he'd never reached out for her, she'd never wish Beau gone. And if she found out he'd said it, she'd scream at him, demand he understood how much she needed him in the world, if not her life.

She opened the bag of muffins, mostly to give herself something to do. The tops were perfect, and she wanted to chuck one at the king. "These are store-bought."

"No." Sebastian looked at her. "Homemade."

"Nope. They're from Lissa's Bakery downtown. Ophelia loves their orange ones. I always brought her one when she was having a bad week."

Brie lifted the muffin from the bag and showed the bottom of the confection, sugar and sweet wafting up from the pastry. "The little heart made with a C&D is her signature. It represents her children, Charlotte and Delia."

Sebastian cocked his head. "Quite the detective, Princess."

"Not a princess."

"Not yet."

He was trying to rile her up. She wasn't sure why, but Brie wasn't going to fall for it.

"Your brother loves you and he worries about you. You shouldn't toss that in his face."

"Even if he would be a better king?" Sebastian raised an eyebrow as he stood up from the couch. "The man that came back is exactly who father wanted on the throne. Ironic that it's him and not me."

"Especially for that reason. You grew up the heir." She held up her hand when he went to interrupt. "I'm not saying that was easy. I am sure it wasn't. But he grew up the spare, the replacement for you, a role no sibling should have to play."

When one thought about it, the ancient idea was quite sick.

"You are both more than the crowns on your heads. He is your brother. Don't let whatever personal issue made you lie about muffins get in between that."

"Careful, Princess." He took the muffin from her hand, taking a big bite out of it. He tilted his head, like he was trying to act brave or just redirect her focus. "You seem to be falling for him."

"I don't have to be falling for him to want to see him treated with care."

That was true. But it didn't change the fact that the words *falling for him* sent a wave of butterflies through her belly.

"If you say so." Sebastian took another bite of his muffin and wandered out of the media room. Brie looked at the marketing notes she had on the board. There was work to be done.

There is always work to be done.

Grabbing his forgotten coffee, and her own, she went in search of the man she most certainly wasn't falling for.

Alessio flipped and kept his body moving. The cool water slipping over him as he skimmed through the pool calmed him. At least it usually did. His fingers were wrinkling, but he didn't care as he flipped and pushed off the wall again. Move. Just move.

Usually twenty minutes was enough to burn off any unpleasant emotions. He wasn't sure how long he'd been gliding through the water, but the fury of his brother's words still wouldn't dissipate.

How could Sebastian have said such a thing? How could he have voiced such awful thoughts?

His brother was struggling with the crown, and Alessio was the reason for that. His argument—Alessio's rebellion. Even if Brie's scheme worked, it wasn't freedom he'd get. It wasn't freedom he deserved.

Sebastian needed him, even if he wouldn't say it directly. So the palace was where Alessio would stay.

Without Brie.

He pushed off the wall as sadness overtook him. Brie didn't deserve this gilded cage; he did. Losing his brother was not an option.

This is my place.

He shook his head in the water, wishing there was a way

to wipe the pain of staying from his soul. He was his brother's helper. That was the way his father had always worded it.

Wanting to be more, his selfishness and his desire for freedom, had cost his family.

His shoulders burned as he reached the wall, but he didn't stop. He'd told the lifeguard to let him know when thirty minutes passed. It felt like that call should have come a while ago, but perhaps he was just tied up in his emotions.

That wasn't something he could let happen today. He and Brie had a full schedule, wedding dress shopping. It was an event she'd scheduled to cool the comments about them not wedding planning. It shouldn't be something he was looking forward to.

But part of him—the selfish part—wanted her with him. His partner in the life his choices forced on him.

He wanted to watch her walk down the aisle. He wanted to dance with her. Wanted to see her cut a chocolate wedding cake and eat lavender cookies. Wanted to see her smile. Wanted her beside him.

Brie made him laugh, she made him smile and she challenged him. She was fun to be around. With her he felt like the Alessio he'd once been. Not number two. Not the spare. Not the rebel that disappeared. With her he felt nothing more than a man. It was intoxicating.

Despite their unique situation, he felt like they were connected, meant to be.

Rationally he knew that was because they'd spent so much time together and because they were united in their quest for freedom.

But he wanted to believe she felt the connection, too.

Two legs appeared at the end of the lane, dangling in the water. She'd found him.

He didn't change the speed of his stroke, but his heartbeat picked up. He'd left Brie with his brother, an upset and pouty king. He'd wandered off and just left her.

Heat that had nothing to do with exercise flooded his

cheeks. Sebastian had been in the mood for a fight, but Alessio had walked away, afraid that if he gave in, all the hurt he had would spill into the open. The wounds created as the spare had driven him from Celiana...and then had driven him back. But Sebastian didn't deserve the pain King Cedric had laid on Alessio.

But that wasn't an excuse for leaving Brie. What had he been thinking?

Lifting out of the water, he felt his mouth slip open at the sight of her holding out his coffee cup.

"You left this, and it was getting cold." She leaned over and dropped a kiss on his nose. "So I drank it."

"Heaven forbid we let coffee go to waste." Brie's bloodstream must be at least 50 percent caffeine.

"So glad you agree." She beamed as she reached around behind her back and pulled out a bottle of water. "This is probably more what you're looking for after a swim, though."

She uncapped it without asking, then passed it to him as she kicked her legs in the water.

The water tasted perfect. It was what his body craved. His soul—it craved her.

"Thank you. And I am sorry. I shouldn't have left you with my brother. I was just..." His mind blanked on the right word.

"Angry. You were angry."

"He has a lot going on. The pressure of the crown. No one expected King Cedric's stroke. Despite being raised for it, I guess Sebastian thought he had more time before the weight of duty fell to him." The words slipped out, then he downed more of the water.

King Cedric's devotion was to Celiana. Everything else was second. It was that devotion Alessio tried to mimic with the Princess Lottery. It was that devotion that Sebastian continued to fail to meet.

Alessio was doing the best he could. But he wasn't the king.

Alessio swallowed and choked on the thoughts. He was number two. He'd always been number two.

"Sebastian does have a lot going on." Brie kicked her legs, water splashing up onto the T-shirt she wore. "But that doesn't mean you can't be angry about him joking about his demise. Or be angry that you have to step up. You are allowed to be angry."

Anger was emotion and emotions were normal, but if he gave in to them, he wasn't sure he'd stop.

"Sebastian expresses enough emotions for the both of us."

Leaning over, Brie cupped some water then splashed it in his face. "Nope. One person does not get to express the emotions for another. Try again." The water splashed in his face, again, but this time he was ready.

"Brie, it's all right."

More water. "Seriously—"

More water.

"Say 'I was angry.'" She dumped more water on his head.

"I'm already wet!"

More water dropped on his head. It was coming quickly now.

"Fine. I was angry."

Brie beamed. "Why was that so hard?"

"I don't know." Except he did. He'd let his emotions rule once, and the consequences were catastrophic.

"Ugh. You're lying." Brie shook her head and let out a soft sigh. "If you don't want to tell me, just say it's not up for discussion. So much is not up for discussion with you anyway. I don't get it but…fine." She crossed her arms, tears hovering in her blue eyes. "See, anger. It's an emotion and you can give in to it."

He hated causing her tears and the acknowledgment that he was holding back. "I show emotions."

"The easy ones." Brie gripped the edge of the pool. "Joy, happiness or excitement. Fear, anger, hurt…those emotions are just as valid."

"I know." The words felt wrong on his tongue. Since returning, he made sure no one saw his anger or his hurt.

How he'd yearned for something he could never have. He was a prince, born with a literal silver spoon in his mouth. How could he want more?

What kind of person did that make him?

Brie's brow furrowed, but she didn't call out the lie or splash him again.

"Do you need to swim more laps, work off the emotions I caused?"

There was no way to work off the feelings she brought out in him. In the two weeks she'd been at the palace, his world had shifted.

He'd expected that. You didn't get a lottery bride without everything changing, but he'd expected to still feel in control of himself.

He'd expected it would take time to know her, to be comfortable in her presence. Instead, his soul was dancing to a new and unknown rhythm.

"I killed my father." The words slipped into the open in the pool. They were words he'd never voiced, not even alone.

"No, you didn't." Brie slipped into the pool.

"You don't have on a swimsuit."

"Don't care." She wrapped her arms around him. "You didn't kill your father."

"I did, though." Alessio pinched his eyes closed, "King Cedric's plan for Sebastian's foreign bride fell through. So he dreamed up the Princess Lottery—for me. He was sure it would fix tourism. And he called me in Scotland, demanded I come home. Do the duty I'd refused for so long. I said..." His voice trailed off. He couldn't say the words. Couldn't give them voice.

"I said something I can't take back. Then he had his stroke. He never woke up. Never saw that I'd come home to do my duty."

"Alessio—"

"I am sorry that you got caught in the royal cage. Though with luck, you won't have to stay in it."

"We don't have to stay in it. You can still be whatever you want. Go back to Scotland."

There was a hesitation in her voice on the word *Scotland*. Or maybe he just hoped there was.

Sebastian needed him. He'd known that since before his brother's coronation. He'd seen it the first time everyone in the hospital room bowed to the new king as the old one was pronounced gone from the mortal plane. Alessio wasn't going anywhere. It was best to simply accept that.

"Enough about me. We have to get to Ophelia's. You're trying on wedding dresses and 'choosing' my suit."

Alessio made air quotes on the word *choosing*. He planned to enjoy the make-believe time. He might never see Brie in a wedding gown, but for today, today he could almost believe she'd be his.

"Nope." Brie kissed the tip of his nose, then swam away from him and started floating on her back.

"This morning was a lot, so I shifted the schedule. There are benefits to being best friends with the shop owner."

"What about the rumors? The articles. Do we need to take a photo of us in the pool? It will look sweet."

She floated over to him, her gaze locked on his. "What if today is just for us? And we don't think about the show part of it. We splash each other in the pool and have breakfast and watch a movie or take a walk where no one can see us. What if today we're just Alessio and Brie?"

Brie was so close to him, her eyes bright with an emotion he wanted to believe was hope that he'd say yes.

Like he'd ever say no to this.

"That sounds like heaven." It would be a little slice of perfection. Then he cupped a hand and splashed some water at her.

"You call that a splash?" She pushed an enormous wall of water toward him.

"Really, really, Princess. Is that how you want to play?"

Her giggle echoed behind another huge splash, and his heart exploded as she smiled at him.

Pulling her close, he was very aware of her body next to his.

"It's hard to splash you when you're holding me." Brie's cheeks were pink, but she didn't pull away from him.

"You want me to let go?"

"No." Brie captured his mouth.

Her fingers tangled in his wet hair, and he tightened his grip.

"Alessio."

His name on her sweet lips anchored him. Nothing mattered in this moment but her touch, her heat, her presence.

"Brie."

His fingers flirted with the edge of her wet shirt. He'd been her first kiss. They'd kissed so many times in the last fourteen days. It brought him joy each time.

But now, in this moment, his body ached to lift her from the pool, carry her to his rooms and forget everything else.

Her breasts pressed against him. She only had to say the words, and he'd do it. Lose himself in her.

She pulled back, desire blazing in her eyes, but the hint of hesitation was there, too. She pulled farther, and he didn't try to hold her. He wanted her desperately, but not before she was ready.

Alessio blew out a breath, then ran a thumb along her cheek. "Thank you for finding me."

"Anytime, Prince Charming."

She splashed more water, her laughter echoing around the pool, and he joined in the fun.

CHAPTER SEVEN

"Princess! Princess!"

It was weird to hear the title called out. The first time she'd heard it, Brie had nearly cried. Every other time, she'd used it as her focal point to make sure she kept her ideas on point. Today, though…today it felt different.

Her gaze flitted to Alessio, clearly getting into his role of dutiful heir to the throne. She understood now the reason the rebel returned the ever-dutiful heir to the throne. It was tragic.

But knowing it made her feel closer to the man beside her.

"Princess! Princess!" They were calling out for her. It should make her nervous. It always had before. That title symbolized the loss of everything she'd gained.

But it also meant Alessio. What if she could work and be a princess? What if the connection she'd believed was just the aftereffects of the lottery high was real? What if he was her match?

No. No. She wasn't traveling that path. This was a show. And they were getting far too good at the optics. That was all.

That didn't explain the pool or the meals they shared. No one was watching them then.

"So many people. I still have a hard time believing they're showing up."

"Everyone believes we're prepping for the wedding of the century, Brie. Trying on gowns—that's a can't-miss event. Our union is a big deal today. Tomorrow, we focus on some other tourist location." He held up his hands. "I know you sent me the schedule. I think it's an art gallery."

It was. And she knew he was playing with her. Alessio knew their schedule down to the minute.

"Right." It was the only word her tongue seemed capable of forming.

Our union.

Why had those words felt so right to hear, even when he was joking? This wasn't the life she'd planned for...the life she'd fought for.

If she turned her head, the flashing lights she could see in her periphery were all the reminder she needed. This life was the opposite of freedom.

Alessio would look delectable in a wedding suit. A wedding suit he'd wear when he pledged his heart to another.

Her heart raced and her stomach turned. He'd meet another at the altar, maybe in Scotland. Someone he chose, hopefully. And she'd be working in her downtown office, proving to her parents and everyone else that she didn't need them to accomplish her dreams.

Each was getting what they wanted...

There was no need for jealousy. This was a show. A roleplay. A marketing campaign for the best Celiana offered. Nothing more.

Morning coffee...and kisses.

And why wasn't he saying anything! He was just staring at her, his deep green eyes holding hers.

Lifting a hand, he caressed her cheek. "You all right? You look as though you've seen a ghost."

Tiny bolts of electricity slipped along her skin. His mouth was so close to hers. They needed to pull apart, to get the show started. But she couldn't make herself move.

"Fine." Her voice quavered, and her breath seemed caught in her throat. "Just having a think on the agenda."

"Your brain is always spinning with ideas." He brushed his lips to hers.

The touch was so light, nothing like the passionate kisses they'd shared in the pool. Yet somehow it felt deeper.

The door to their car opened. She could hear the click of cameras, photographers capturing the perfect moment.

Except it hadn't been for the cameras. She saw the frown form on Alessio's face before he wiped it away. It was good they'd been caught in an organic kiss. But part of her wished the moment was just for them, too.

There is no us, Brie!

"Time to go, Prince Charming." She plastered on a smile as he leaned closer.

"You got this." Alessio's words were soft against her ear. Sweet and kind, but the worry wasn't for the crowd.

No. The crowd she could deal with. Her feelings for Alessio... She wasn't quite sure how to handle those.

"A kiss for the camera." Lev's voice was haughty and the first thing she heard upon exiting the car.

"We are engaged, Lev." Alessio smiled. It wasn't the full, beaming one that caused crinkles to show on the sides of his eyes, which was the smile that made her heart and soul dance when he showed it to her.

She squeezed his hand, then slid her arm around his waist. "Do you have an actual question?"

Lev's eyes lighted on hers. "You're supporting your best friend's shop. Do you plan to stay at your brother's new hotel for your honeymoon when it opens? Will any of Celiana's citizens not tied to you personally reap benefits from this—" Lev gestured to their joined hands "—union?"

Beau had a new hotel? So the rumor was true. It didn't surprise her. Their father had extolled the virtues of owning land, buildings and businesses at the dinner table. No time was spent on the children's days, other than admonishments if they'd fallen short of expectations. And they'd fallen short so often.

Still, she'd hoped that Beau would find his own way.

"I haven't spoken to my brother in years."

Each word felt like a tiny knife against her tongue as she

voiced publicly what she'd barely admitted in the privacy of her own home.

Alessio's hand tightened on her waist. Not much, just a touch tighter to remind her that she wasn't alone.

When they stopped this charade, she would be solo again. And the knife the question created cut even deeper.

"I wasn't aware that he was opening a hotel. As far as my dress goes, yes, Ophelia will design my wedding dress, but Alessio and I have plans for as many citizens as possible to participate in our wedding."

Our wedding.

She'd not actually meant to say that. In fact, Brie had carefully scripted her words to ensure she never actually said *wedding*. She hinted at it with marketing euphemisms designed to highlight where they were, not the nuptials they didn't plan to have.

"Will the press get that list?" Lev was calling her bluff.

"Of course." Alessio kissed the top of Brie's head. "I'll have it sent over this evening. Now, my fiancée and I have an appointment to get to."

Alessio nodded to the crowd, raising his hand to wave as they made their way to Ophelia's door.

"Why is the shop so dark?" Alessio's question echoed in the empty room. "Did Ophelia run off?"

"Without me?" Brie chuckled, though she was as surprised as him to find the lights off and the blinds drawn. Usually the room was bright with natural light. "She better not have."

"I didn't," Ophelia called from the back. "I typically use natural light for these fittings. However, with all the camera flashes and such..." she offered as she came into the main room. "I've set up the back for you two. I told the press when they asked that the dress was a state secret."

Her friend beamed, clearly enjoying being in on the actual state secret.

Brie stepped into the back room and knew her mouth was

hanging open. The storeroom was transformed. How much work had Ophelia put into this subterfuge?

The plan was to try on dresses and suits. That way they looked rumpled when leaving. Not disheveled but clearly tousled from trying on outfits. But the room looked like a real bridal setup.

Gauze hung over walls she knew were a dull gray. The boxes of materials usually stacked back here had vanished. The soft sofa she'd seen many brides' mothers sit on was back here, too.

She looked at the bright purple couch. The vibrant color popped against the gold gauze on the walls. Her mother would never sit there. No aunties would watch her try on dresses.

The walls seemed to close as she looked at the couch. What a silly thing to care about. Her mother hadn't been in her life in years. She'd not even reached out since Brie's name was drawn in the lottery. Maybe Lev asking about Beau had triggered the memories.

In her family's world, Brie no longer existed. If she crawled back, they'd take her. But the strong woman she was...that woman wasn't welcome. As she looked at the empty couch, the reality that this was just one more experience she'd lost hammered through her.

"Brie," Alessio and Ophelia spoke in unison.

Her eyes darted to her friend, then to Alessio.

"My family isn't here."

He stepped to her side, pulling her into his arms, holding her. It felt perfect and it also reminded her of the illusion. Still, she couldn't step away.

"I'm sorry, Brie," Ophelia said. "The mothers, aunties, the family usually sit there. I didn't think when I pulled it back here."

"Why would you?" Brie let out a laugh that was far too close to a sob as Alessio stroked her back. "It's a couch. This shouldn't matter. It's just a couch."

His lips pressed into her forehead. "It represents what

you've lost through no fault of your own. You are allowed to be upset by that. Even angry."

"Now anger is acceptable." Brie swallowed the lump in her throat.

"I thought you pointed out that it was always acceptable."

"Using my words against me, Prince Charming?"

"No." His lips brushed her forehead again as she looked up at him. "Just trying to help."

"Thank you." Stepping from his arms, Brie shook herself. "Well, that was quite the dramatic bridal moment!" She wiped a stray tear from her cheek. "But now we have a fashion show for the prince!"

"Yes." Ophelia looked from Brie to Alessio, a thought passing over her friend's face as she met her gaze.

Brie tilted her head, waiting for Ophelia to say whatever she was thinking.

Instead, she nodded to Alessio. "A fashion show for a prince. In my shop."

Brie smiled as Alessio sat on the couch and she followed her friend into the dressing area… She'd talked to Ophelia about finding her most outrageous dresses, the ones she'd designed because the idea just wouldn't leave her but she knew might never leave her racks.

Ophelia was an artist. Most of her designs were meant to sell, which meant they followed similar patterns: mermaid dresses, tight on the waist but flaring at the bottom, poufy princess ball gowns, sleek A-lines in shades meant for a bride.

But there were other dresses: over-the-top creations that fit on a runway or a magazine shoot. Those were dresses that Ophelia loved but doubted would ever sell. Brie had made Ophelia promise to pull as many of them as possible for this escapade.

The first dress did not disappoint. It was an actual mermaid theme, the blue bodice fading to sea green as it spilled past her feet.

"You are a dream in that gown. A mythical being. I swear,

if your hair was wet, it would look like you just stepped out of the ocean."

Alessio grinned as she stood before him, but there was the hint of something in his eyes.

Disappointment.

She struck a pose, trying to bring out his real smile. The one she craved.

The dress hugged her in all the right places. It was beautiful, but there was no place for Brie to wear it. And it certainly wasn't a wedding dress.

And he'd expected to see one, expected to see her playing the part. She'd not counted on that. Her plans, her expectations for today, all vanished.

"Next one!" She dipped from the room and met Ophelia. "Can we put a few wedding dresses, like actual ones, in the rotation? Alessio—"

Brie cleared her throat as Ophelia raised a brow. "Like a dress you might wear down the aisle?"

"I mean, I'm not walking down the aisle, but he..." Again her throat closed as she looked at the closed door of the dressing room.

She could picture Alessio sitting on the couch. Picture him waiting, hoping that she'd step out in a wedding dress, even for a fashion show he knew was fake.

The fact that she wasn't, the look on his face, the acceptance hiding hurt...

"I set aside a few earlier. I'll grab them."

Brie nodded, ready for the next few hours of dress-up.

After an hour of trying on dresses, playing princess, Brie couldn't take her eyes off herself. The image in the mirror *was* a princess, a woman she could see walking toward Alessio.

The soft gold glimmered on her skin. The scalloped bodice hugged her breasts as the A-line dress slipped over her hips. The simple cut contrasted with the delicate flowers embroidered from the bodice to the train. They were the flowers of Celiana.

This dress…

His mouth would fall open. He'd smile, a real one, dimples, creases around his eyes. He'd beam as she walked toward him.

It was easy to imagine. Easy to see.

"I can't show him this one." The whispered words hung in the dressing room.

Ophelia wrapped her arms around Brie. "I've seen this moment many times before with my brides."

"This moment?" Brie placed her hands on her stomach, staring at the image in the mirror.

"When they find the one. This is your wedding dress."

Except she didn't need a dress. Even one as perfect as this, which she could see herself wearing while standing next to him. His hands were reaching for her over the altar as they promised forever.

"I'm not marrying Alessio. I'm not." The words were soft, barely audible. Brie wasn't even sure she'd managed to push them out.

"Who are you trying to convince? Me? Or yourself?" Ophelia squeezed her shoulders.

"I have my company."

"Maybe you could have both…" Ophelia met her gaze in the mirror.

"Princesses don't have careers." Brie hiccuped as she looked at the gown. "This isn't my gown. It's beautiful, but it isn't mine."

"Brie—"

"This isn't real. I'm not the protagonist in a fairy tale. Alessio and I have a deal and a goal to *not* meet at the altar. We aren't in love."

Aren't in love. Why did saying that out loud hurt so much? It was a marketing scheme—her best plan ever. But it wasn't real.

Apparently her heart would need her brain to remind her of that more often.

"Honey." Ophelia's gaze was full of questions Brie didn't want to answer.

"Time for Alessio to try on suits. My turn on the couch." The words were rushed, and her emotions were spilling everywhere as she looked at the gown in the mirror one last time.

This was a dream.

Alessio and she got on well. He was sweet, and he was kind. And his kisses awoke places in her body…

In another time, another place, maybe they'd have found each other. Found happiness.

But that wasn't this time. It wasn't this place. And her heart felt like it was cracking as Ophelia helped her out of the wedding dress.

"You look like you stepped from a fairy tale." Brie clapped as Alessio stepped from the dressing room.

"You've said that about the last three suits." Alessio playfully crossed his arms. "I know there isn't as much difference in these as your dresses, but still…"

Brie laughed and he moved toward her, dropping a kiss on her lips. "Do you like this one more or less than the last two?"

"Can I be honest?"

His heart pounded against his ribs as he looked at her. She'd not shown him the last dress. He didn't know why. She'd said that it hadn't fit right. A lie, he suspected, but something had shifted.

She was laughing at all the right moments, clapping and having a good time—she'd even posted a picture of him in the first suit and asked people to weigh in—but there was a look in her eye, like she was assessing him each time he walked out. It was like she was actually looking for a suit.

Of course she wasn't. And he shouldn't want her to. Though that didn't stop the rebel from wishing that maybe she was thinking of staying no matter what the marketing scheme produced.

He tried pushing those selfish thoughts away.

"So what is your honest feeling on these suits, Briella?"

"That you looked delectable in each of them, but they are very similar. Each of my dresses was different. The mermaid gown to the last…"

The last.

She'd hesitated. What was the last dress, the one she'd refused to show him?

Brie looked away, so he focused on the other part of her sentence.

"Delectable?"

Her cheeks darkened but she met his gaze, desire burning in his eyes. "You know you're attractive, Prince Charming." She shook a finger at him playfully. "Searching out compliments? Really?"

He knew he was conventionally attractive, that he met society's definition of handsome.

It wasn't society's definition he wanted, though.

"It's still nice to hear." He kissed her again. Since opening up in the pool, they'd kissed so freely. It was a gift he didn't deserve, but he couldn't stop worshipping her lips. "Ophelia has one more option. Though it sounds like you could pick any of these options and be happy with the outcome."

"Alessio—"

He captured her lips before she could argue that there was no need to pick out wedding attire. He knew that. It was a slip of the tongue, a wishful thought. But he didn't want the reminder right now.

"Go!" Brie pushed at his shoulders after he broke the connection. "Maybe the next suit will be magic."

He stood and headed back to the dressing area. The suit he'd seen on the rack was gone. Alessio looked in the dressing room. Nothing.

"Ophelia?"

She rounded the corner, a dress bag slung over her arm. "I don't think the final suit I picked before is a good fit."

"Oh." Alessio didn't quite know how to respond. He didn't

think of his clothes that much. It was a statement of privilege, he knew, as was the fact that he had a personal shopper who knew his tastes and the clothes appeared when he needed them.

His mother thought more about her outfits. He'd heard her argue that people were going to talk about what she wore, how she wore it and when she wore it, so she might as well make the statement she wanted with the clothes on her body.

"The suits seem fine." He pulled a hand over his face. Those were not the words to give a designer, but what else was there to say?

"*Fine* is not what we are going for." Ophelia sucked in a breath, then looked at the closed door. He knew she was seeing beyond it to the woman on the other side.

The best friend she'd offered aid to flee the island.

"*Fine* is not what one wears to a royal wedding, Your Royal Highness."

He shook his head. "Ophelia?" She knew this wasn't real. Knew they were here only because the hints of rumors were bothering Brie. Hell, the only reason they were trying on outfits was because Brie was worried if they came out looking too perfect, people might suspect they'd only sat and chatted with Ophelia.

That was a worry that would never have crossed his mind. Her brain saw all the patterns, the questions people might ask, like his saw the potential in glass.

"Just humor me." Ophelia pushed past him into the dressing room and hung the bag on the wall hanger.

Alessio waited in the hall, not wanting to crowd the woman. Brie's family was gone—not from the mortal world, but from her life. Ophelia was her sister, not by blood, but in all the ways that mattered.

Ophelia nodded as she stepped from the room. "If you can give her choices, then maybe there will be a royal wedding."

Choices.

The word hung in the silent hallway. Choices were not what

royals got. The country came first. What royals wanted came in a distant second.

Brie deserved more than that. Still, Ophelia's words hung in his soul.

Brie deserved all the choices. He could give her that, behind the palace's closed walls. In public, they'd be supporters of his brother, beholden to the people of Celiana. In the palace… His brain ceased the conversation as his heart screamed that it wasn't enough.

But what if it was?

Rather than try to voice anything, Alessio stepped into the room and quickly donned the suit.

It was a charcoal gray, with a gold tie. The cut was similar to the other suits, highlighting his broad shoulders and slim waist.

It wasn't all that different from the black and navy suits Ophelia had shown him, but it felt right. That was a weird feeling for a suit.

He stepped into the hallway, and Ophelia raised a hand, covering her mouth.

"I take it you think this is the one, too." Alessio chuckled and reached for the door handle. "Shall we see what my Brie thinks?"

He stepped into the room and saw Brie's mouth open, then shut. Her eyes flicked behind him. He wasn't sure what the silent communication was, but he didn't stop looking at her.

"What do we think of gray and gold?"

"Perfect." Brie pursed her lips, tilted her head, took a step toward him, then stopped. "It's a perfect wedding look."

"Brie?" He closed the distance between them. She looked happy, but also terrified. Two emotions he'd never seen together. "What's wrong?"

"Nothing." She shook her head against his shoulder. "Nothing is wrong. Why is nothing wrong?" Her nervous laugh echoed in the back room.

He looked to Ophelia and then back, unsure what to say. "You want something to be wrong?"

"We're picking out wedding outfits."

"Not really." He pressed a kiss to the top of her head. "We're playing dress-up." That was such a bitter truth.

"We're weeks into this charade."

Charade.

His soul rioted against that word. It was a charade. And he hated that. This wasn't what she'd planned, but they were having fun together.

Her kisses were not what he should be focusing on in this moment.

"We're picking out a gown and a suit and it should feel *wrong.* This isn't supposed to make me—"

Her words cut off and Ophelia's words echoed in his mind. *If you can give her choices...* Could he keep her? Could he actually have her as a partner in the life he hadn't wanted? Would she stay?

"Brie." He pulled her into his arms, unsure what to say but needing her with him. Her body relaxed into his. He rested his head on hers, soaking in the moment.

CHAPTER EIGHT

"BRIE!"

"Briella!"

"Princess!"

Calls echoed from around the market stalls. Everyone wanted to see Celiana's future princess.

Brie was doing great. She'd waved when they'd exited the vehicle. Then she'd answered a few questions and taken so many floral offerings he suspected their vehicle would smell of pollen, sweetness and leaves on the way back to the palace.

People were snapping photos, and he'd heard more than one person mention how they'd never have thought to come to the markets if Brie wasn't here.

She was a hit. And her idea was working. What would happen when she left? Would the excitement continue without her?

And would he be able to keep going?

Of course he would. He had to. Still, Alessio knew it would be fake smiles greeting the people then—even if they never realized it.

"Prince Alessio." Lev's voice echoed behind him. The royal tabloid reporter, despite his claims of hating everything about this "spectacle," was at each event.

His father had taken the position of answering Lev's questions in the past, granting him access like all other journalists. Sebastian had questioned the policy but left it in place.

Lev hated the royal family, even though they were the reason people clicked on his opinion pieces, the reason he made as much money as he did. Whether his antagonism was for website clicks or a true dislike, Alessio didn't know. Nor did it matter.

The man was going to write the articles he wanted; at least this way the palace got a little control.

"How does it feel to be third now?" Lev looked over Alessio's shoulder, clearly watching Brie with the crowd. "Always second fiddle to someone, huh?"

Second fiddle.

He felt his jaw twitch and he saw the gleam in Lev's eyes.

Second fiddle. Spare. Extra. Those were words his father used constantly. And they were words Alessio hated, words he never heard when he'd left.

"Briella is doing a lovely job. I'm proud that my fiancée is so loved by the people." The bite of jealousy in his heart had nothing to do with Brie.

She was a natural. But a lifetime of second fiddle, a lifetime of hearing the phrase, from those he loved and those he very much did not, still stung.

"People think this is more of a marketing stunt than a love story. Any comment?"

Alessio tilted his head and wanted to curse. Reacting to such a statement was a tell, one he was usually very good at controlling.

Technically, everything the palace did was a marketing stunt. They used their image for power, but Brie was elevating the game.

"I don't really think that needs a comment." Alessio smiled at a small boy who handed him a picture of him and Brie.

"What about people who say that Sebastian should be the one doing this? That you're stealing your brother's spotlight? The spare rising above his position."

"*King* Sebastian." Alessio emphasized the title the reporter had omitted, enjoying the hint of color invading Lev's cheeks. It was one thing to disparage the royals at the keyboard, another to do it to their faces.

"King Sebastian is busy taking over from King Cedric. He didn't plan to take the crown so suddenly." So suddenly. The stroke, brought on by Alessio's argument. Or at least elevated by it. No matter what Brie thought.

Sebastian seemed to wilt as the crown he'd been raised to wear landed on his head. Alessio wasn't sure what had happened, and the few times he'd brought it up, Sebastian had changed the subject or just walked away.

Sebastian was the one their father loved, the one he'd doted on. Of course his grief would take a different course from Alessio's.

So he'd done what he hadn't before. He'd stepped into his duties. It was as simple—and complicated—as that.

"You didn't answer my question." Lev raised a brow.

"What question?" Brie's sweet voice was tinged with fire, though he doubted Lev realized it, as she slipped her fingers into his. "What question?" she repeated as she looked from Lev to Alessio.

"I asked if he had any comment on people saying that Alessio was overshadowing *King* Sebastian."

"Are people saying that or are you typing it and hoping they'll agree?" Brie's voice was steady as she squeezed Alessio's hand. Then she pointed to a stall. "I want to see that."

She pulled Alessio away without waiting for Lev to comment. He looked over his shoulder, unsurprised to see Lev make a note on his phone.

"He's going to stir that into some kind of rumor." Alessio made sure his words were only for her ears. To others it would look like he was whispering sweet nothings.

"Probably." Brie's bright blue eyes held his. "But we'll deal with it."

We. He loved that word when it was applied to them.

Brie leaned her head against his shoulder as they made their way through the crowded area, the security team a few feet behind and in front of them.

He kissed the top of her head; he loved touching her, getting close to her. The motions weren't for the cameras he knew were everywhere, not anymore.

"Brie!"

"Brie!"

"You're quite popular, my dear." He let the endearment run off his lips.

Brie's cheeks tinted pink, and he put his hand around her waist. "Popularity is easy. Keeping their focus on the important things is harder."

She kissed his cheek, then pulled him toward the stalls. "Come on."

"Of course." Brie was right. Today was supposed to be about highlighting the stalls, not them.

She leaned over a stall with a few handmade bags he was sure she'd pointed to randomly when she dismissed Lev. "These are lovely."

"Thank you, Princess. I'm glad I came this weekend. I almost didn't with prices for travel—" The seller cut off her words. "Anyway..."

"You've struggled?" Brie's voice was even, and Alessio looked over a few bags in the stall to give them at least the appearance of privacy.

"Who hasn't?" The woman sighed. "I mean, I guess you—"

"My parents disowned me a few years ago. I spent days living off coffee and stress as rent came due. My upbringing was very privileged—I can't deny that—but I've also known what it feels like to be terrified that I'd lose my tiny studio apartment."

The woman reached over and gripped Brie's hand. "My parents passed two years ago. I've taken over the care of my teen sister. I started making bags to sell to supplement the income as tourist visits dipped at our family restaurant.

"But since the lottery," the woman continued, her tone instantly brightening, "it's been quite full. I don't need to be here, but these—" She looked at the bags. "My mother always called it a hobby. But it..."

"It makes you feel whole." Brie grinned.

She really was in her element here. Alessio saw the young woman relax, Brie's calming presence giving her something he couldn't describe. If she stayed, married him, she'd be such an asset to the royal family.

And that was exactly why she should leave.

No one should be an asset.

"They're just bags." The woman bit her lip as she looked over her wares.

"No." Brie picked up a small white leather bag that looked big enough to carry a cell phone and maybe a tube of lipstick. It wasn't practical, but Alessio could see the craftsmanship.

"That's part of my bridal collection—guess you're drawn to it."

"I guess I am." Brie grinned. "I'll take it."

"Oh. No, it's my gift to you, Princess."

Brie shook her head. "I appreciate the kindness, but lesson one in business—don't turn away paying customers. Even if they wear a crown."

She laughed, then looked to Alessio. "Except, who has our money?" Her cheeks darkened as she looked from the purse to the woman behind the small counter.

By rule, the royal family didn't carry wallets or cash on them. People sent their bills to the palace. Or they did just as the woman suggested and offered things as a gift.

Alessio handed the woman a card. "Send the bill here, and the palace will make sure you're compensated."

"Thank you."

"And I'll check," Brie added. "Send the bill!"

"Yes, Princess."

Alessio wrapped an arm around her waist as they left the stall. "You are amazing. Just so you know."

Brie hit his hip with hers. "I am. But the reason her hobby has a chance to become a business is because her restaurant is thriving again."

He heard the hesitation in her voice. "The lottery did what

I intended. Your marketing..." He paused, barely catching himself before the word *scheme*. Her marketing was more than a scheme, and there were ears and cameras all around. "It's working."

"If we don't meet at the altar..." The whispered words vanished into the commotion of the crowd.

But he didn't need to hear the end of the sentence. If they didn't meet at the altar, would the kingdom continue to thrive? Brie's plan was brilliant. It should have been instituted years ago. But was it sustainable without the wedding? He wasn't sure. When they separated, shattered the illusion, would the kingdom suffer?

All were questions to consider, but his brain was focusing on one word. *If.*

If we don't meet.

Not when. It shouldn't bring him so much pleasure, but damn. His heart felt like it wanted to jump out of his chest.

"Oh!" Brie brightened as a glasswork stall came into view. The light struck the handblown glass; it was a sight to see.

"Did you make this?" Brie stepped into the stall, her mouth hanging open as she looked at the art on the shelves.

The man's weathered hands had held the tools for molding liquid glass into the most beautiful pieces for over forty years. Emilio taught a class at the college Alessio had attended. And Alessio had been fascinated from the moment he'd shaped his first piece.

He'd learned everything possible from the master glassworker.

"Emilio is the island's only master glassblower." Alessio looked over the art, amazed, as always, at his friend's ability. The glass pieces molded in his tools, whether dinnerware cups or ornamental works, were masterpieces.

"Not true. You are here, too." Emilio stepped from the booth and reached for Alessio's hand. "What have you made recently?"

It was his standard question. Not *How are you?* or *What's new?* but *What have you made?*

"I've been a bit busy."

"You said you were a glassworker but..." Brie's eyes were bright as she looked at Emilio's art. "You blow glass? Like this?"

"Not anymore." Alessio bit the inside of his cheek, fighting the urge to ask Emilio if he'd seen the recent exhibit in Paris. The images Alessio had looked at on his computer made his hands itch to craft something. But he'd put that world behind him.

"Alessio?" Her voice pulled him back.

"Let me introduce you to my fiancée, Brie Ailiono." He smiled, ignoring the questions he didn't want to answer in Brie's eyes.

Emilio reached for her hand, but Alessio saw more than a hint of reservation in his eyes.

"I was at your family estate last week," Emilio said to Brie.

Brie's body shifted as she leaned toward Alessio—reaching for him, seeking him.

"I'm not in contact with my family."

"They said as much." Emilio pursed his lips, then clicked his tongue.

Alessio knew he was weighing his words. He'd heard the click so many times in the man's workshop. It was a tell Emilio knew about but was unable to stop. Except there wasn't a piece of artwork needing critique.

"Emilio—" Alessio wrapped his arm around Brie's waist. If his friend had heard something important, they needed to know. The Ailiono family was powerful; anyone who doubted that found out at their peril.

"What am I missing?" Brie's gaze met his.

"Emilio clicked his tongue. I was his student for years. It means he's weighing a tough set of words." Alessio squeezed her. "What aren't you saying, Emilio?"

"Your family hired me for a big piece of art. In your old

room. Told me to throw everything out. Not what I was paid for, but some clients..." He cleared his throat.

Some clients were entitled. Alessio had run into more than one during the three years he'd run his own shop. One client screamed that the art he'd commissioned was too big. When Alessio reminded him that it was the exact measurements he'd requested, the man had become apoplectic.

"I'm surprised my stuff was even still there." Brie smiled but her eyes didn't light up. The bouncy spirit she'd had with the woman in the previous stall was absent.

"They said marrying the prince in a lottery was beneath an Ailiono." Emilio's words were direct.

Beneath an Ailiono. Only that family would think having a royal bride was beneath them. Sure, the lottery was different, but it wasn't like the Ailionos' unions weren't also arranged. That was why Brie had fled.

"Your mother said that if you followed through with it, there was no hope for you."

Brie's breath hitched but she didn't say anything. Was she mourning that loss or realizing a door she thought closed forever had a crack? At least it had, until her name rose from the lottery drawing.

Until this moment, Alessio had never understood the phrase *I saw red*. The color danced across his eyes. He was mad at the Ailionos, mad at Emilio, mad at the situation as a whole.

"Emilio—" His voice was harder than intended. It was the tone he used as Prince Alessio in the rare cases where a strong royal persona was necessary. Brie wrapped an arm around him, squeezing his side just like he'd done for her.

Emilio held up a hand. "I do not say this to hurt you, but I wanted to explain why—" he looked over his shoulder "—why I brought something to the market this weekend."

He turned and went behind the bench that served as his checkout stand. "Your campaign to showcase the island makes it easy to know where you'll be."

Campaign.

He saw Brie shift. The rumors were still there, not as squashed as she'd hoped. But that was a worry for another day.

Emilio pulled out a box overflowing with pictures and trinkets. "I managed..." He cleared his throat. "I'm sure I didn't get everything important to you, Princess, but these things looked loved."

Brie took one step toward the box, paused, then quickly closed the distance.

Her fingers reached for the box, her shoulders shaking as she looked over the trinkets of her girlhood. She'd mentioned leaving, but this box meant she'd truly fled. She'd left behind nearly everything.

She lifted pictures, holding them up to show him. Some people in the images he recognized, while others were acquaintances that moved in similar circles. She flipped through a few notebooks and journals, laughing to herself.

"These were my secret dream journals. I had to hide them under my bed."

Emilio nodded.

And her parents were throwing everything out, all the things she might have cherished.

Brie ran a hand over one of the journals. Her face was so full of excitement over a secret dream journal.

It was a secret because she couldn't be Brie. Until she'd left their home, she'd been Briella, the daughter of the wealthiest man in the nation, but not a loved child. She'd been an object for gain. It was only when she left that she became herself.

Freedom.

Worry pressed against his chest. He didn't want to steal that from her. But he also didn't want to give her up. If he gave her choices, perhaps he could find a way to make her want to stay.

Brie was so much more than a pretend lottery bride. She was the woman who listened to his darkest secret, comforted him, then splashed him with water. She was the woman who could take a simple outing and turn it into a viral marketing campaign. She was the one he was falling for. Truly falling for.

A small bumblebee stuffie rose and she let out a sob. Alessio pulled her to him without thinking. If she was upset, then her place was in his arms.

"My brother gave this to me when I was five or six. He used to joke that I was always buzzing around him. When I left, I was so alone, no one to bother. I always wondered if Beau missed me. Or if he was grateful the annoying sister was finally gone."

He kissed the top of her head, holding her tightly, reminding her that she wasn't alone. Not as long as she was with him.

He held her for several minutes, letting her gather herself.

Finally, Brie pulled back and walked around the bench, pulling Emilio into her arms. "Thank you. Thank you so much."

"Consider it an early wedding present." Emilio hugged her.

"No one will be able to top it, Emilio." Alessio winked. This was a gift Brie would remember for forever.

Brie stepped back and wiped a tear from her cheek.

"Make me a promise, Princess." Emilio tilted his head as he looked at Alessio. "Make him show you his studio. Don't let him give up his gift."

"I plan to see it. As soon as we return to the palace." Brie nodded, determination clear in her features.

"Wow!"

Brie couldn't believe the "small" studio she was standing in was Alessio's glassworks studio. It was organized chaos. Designs covered the walls, sketches that were gorgeous on their own but that he could craft in glass in their image. The man was a master.

"Alessio." She whispered his name as she walked past the drawings and then saw a completed piece on the table. Twisted flames licked up at an indistinguishable human figure. Whether the man was beating the flames or consumed by them was up for interpretation.

"That was the second-to-last piece I created." His eyes hovered on the piece, a frown hinting at the edge of his lips. "I haven't been in the shop as much this year."

Consumed by the flames.

He'd put all his efforts into saving Celiana through the bride lottery. And it was working. She'd heard that throughout the market stalls today.

People were seeing improvements. They were smiling and happy to have the prince and future princess in their places. And just like in Ophelia's shop last week, it felt natural. It felt like where she was supposed to be.

It's because I've been doing it for over a month. I've been living and breathing this life. That's all.

And maybe fear. She'd lost nearly all the jobs she'd lined up during the bride lottery. No matter what line she gave, no matter the hints she dropped, they all assumed when she wed that the princess wouldn't work. And she couldn't come right out and say she was planning to leave Alessio. Not yet.

The idea of walking away from him, from the man that understood her need for freedom, understood the craving, grew more painful with the passing days. This was a fake relationship; it was. And it was impacting the company she'd built.

If she didn't have her business…what did she have?

Alessio. She had Alessio. If she wanted him. If she was willing to step into this life, hold his hand and walk this path.

So many ifs…and yet none of them felt insurmountable. They felt…they felt perfect. And that was terrifying.

They could continue as they were, marketing Celiana. It was different and not a traditional job. There'd be no penthouse suite…but the success might be more meaningful.

He was grinning as he walked to his furnace, his hands running along pipe-looking fixtures next to it. This was his happy place. This was the place the real Alessio loved most.

The pool was where he worked off unsettled emotions. This…this was his sanctuary.

"You should have seen my shop in Scotland. It was this

tiny cottage. I sold my wares in the front and the back was my workshop."

"Scotland. You had a shop there?"

Alessio turned, his face lit with happiness. "It was the best place. Mine. I was a glassworker. No one even knew I was a prince of Celiana. Three years I got to take orders and live as a creative."

"You could do it again."

Alessio shook his head. "No. My place is by Sebastian. I might get to play in here more—after all your plan is working. But my own shop full-time—that dream is over."

He reached for her hand, squeezing it before stepping away. "The glass ball everyone put their lottery tickets in was my last major piece. I knew that when I made it."

"You made that?" It had been large, so large. She took her phone from her back pocket and pulled up her social media page. She scrolled back and found an image she'd taken in front of the entry post.

The large ball was on spinners. She'd joked on more than one occasion that the intricate hearts traced in the ball were over-the-top, but she'd privately admitted that ball was lovely. On sunny days, rainbows formed in the glass. Press releases had talked about how it was a sign of good fortune.

And she'd have never guessed that it was sculpted by Prince Alessio.

"Why didn't you tell everyone? That is a story the press would have eaten up!" The marketeer in her wanted to scream at the lost opportunity. The stories she'd have spun in Ophelia's dresses...

Plus, it added depth to Alessio. It let the world see the man she saw.

"Because." He wrapped her in his arms. Time froze as his green eyes held hers. The urge to tickle him, to make him laugh, nearly overwhelmed her, but she wanted to hear his answer. "Then they would have wanted to see my workshop. There'd be pressure to film me creating something."

"True."

Everyone would want to see it. Would that be so bad? Prince Alessio had a secret creative side. The dutiful prince was so much more than just the image he projected. More than the interviews projected, more than the crown. More than the re-formed rebel.

Alessio was funny, kind, silly. He was a full person, but the rest of the country didn't get to see that man. Why?

"Heaven forbid that the world should learn that you are a master glassworker."

Her fingers brushed along his jaw, enjoying the feel of his beard.

Alessio leaned his head against hers. "This is mine. I didn't want to share it. But if you want to post about it, I can strike a pose."

It would be the perfect story. But she knew she'd never post a single image in here. As long as he wanted this to be only his, that was how it would stay. He'd given so much up for Celiana already; she could give him this space.

"It can be our little secret, Alessio."

He kissed the top of her head. "Want to make something?"

"Make something? How would I even do that?"

Alessio pulled back and pushed a few buttons on the wall. The furnace made a few loud noises that must be normal since he didn't blink an eye at them, then it kicked to life.

"I taught classes in Scotland on the side. Taught others the craft. My shop was the one place in the world I was number one."

Brie's heart turned on his words. "Alessio."

He held up a hand. "I didn't mean anything bad, Brie. Want to give it a go?"

She was torn. She wanted to see him in this place, witness the true artist emerge. But she wanted to touch the hurt spot in his heart, too. That was the place that claimed he was only the spare, the man caring for the new king, the one who felt responsible for his father's demise.

He was so much more.

"Yes."

He flipped a few more switches and grabbed supplies from around the shop. She watched his face relax and the stiffness leave his shoulders. She watched him come into himself. His face was open, free of duty.

"All right, come here."

She moved to the furnace, letting him guide her. He handed her safety goggles, then directed her behind a small metal-and-wood table beside the furnace. His hands were firm on her hips as he shifted her slightly.

"Relax, Brie."

That might be possible if his hands weren't resting on her hips.

"Trying."

Alessio grabbed a blowpipe and fitted it against the hole in the furnace before coming back with the molten glass.

"Whoa." It was one thing to know he did this with such skill, another to see the red-orange glass.

"I got you." He placed the pipe on the table, the glass hanging off, and wrapped her hands around the pipe. Then he stepped behind her again, pressing his body against hers.

He whispered instructions in her ears. Brie did her best to follow them, but all her mind could think of was the man behind her, the feel of him against her, the promise of what might be.

Her life had changed, altered completely. The idea of leaving, escaping, no longer felt like an absolute necessity. If she was honest, the thought of leaving hurt.

Together they molded the glass, turned it, twisted it, made it into something new.

That was what this relationship was. Her heart rate pulsed in her ears; she felt her face flush and it had nothing to do with the heat of the room. It was him, the man whose body made her sing with promises she'd never sought.

The man she was falling for.

Her brain had tried to ignore the attachment.

"See?"

She blew out a breath. As she looked at the molten blob he'd pulled from the furnace, it transformed into a heart. It was weird how one second it was nothing, but now it was something.

Just like us.

They were something now.

But what did that mean for the future? Brie wasn't sure, but for tonight, she wanted to pretend they weren't the prince and his lotto bride. Just Brie and Alessio.

"Ta-da!" Alessio's lips skimmed her neck before he took the pipe from her hands. It was a glass heart with a yellow one inside. Beautiful.

"Nice work, Brie." He dropped a kiss on her cheek before taking the heart to a little box in the corner. "Needs to cool."

"Alessio—" she walked toward him "—I did very little of that. It was all you."

"It was us." His eyes glittered.

She couldn't stop herself from moving. She wrapped her arms around him, capturing his lips. Tomorrow she'd start to figure out the conflict between what her heart felt and her mind wanted. Tonight, all she needed was the man before her.

Need, desperate to make him hers, completely wrapped through her.

"Take me to bed, Alessio."

Take me to bed.

Alessio lifted Brie in his arms, the weight of her body a thrill on his already warm skin. Standing behind her, holding her hands as they molded the glass, had been as blissful as Alessio ever thought to get. But her words and her lips, they dragged him even further toward heaven.

Her lips pressed against his neck, her fingers ran along his chest, and it took every ounce of attention to ignore the flames licking at him to ensure they made it to his bedroom as smoothly as possible.

Brie laughed as he kicked open the door. "I swear that is a movie move, Alessio."

"Maybe." His mouth lowered, drinking her in, savoring the moment.

He laid her on the bed and her hands immediately flattened, her face changing.

"Brie…" Her whispered name burned on his lips. "If you've changed your mind—"

"No, but—" she pursed her lips and he saw her swallow "—what if I'm bad at this?"

"Not possible." Alessio lifted her fingers, placing a soft kiss against each one before dropping her hand. "Tonight is yours, Briella." He opened his arms and saw his words register.

"Just like my first kiss." Brie sat up on her knees, her hands threading under his shirt.

This would be the most blissful torture. But Alessio would not deny her the moment.

Her hands explored him. She lifted his shirt over his head, a smile radiating across her lips. "You are so magnificent."

Alessio's fingers found the edge of her top and his body quivered as she raised her hands. Her red lace bra nearly brought him to his knees.

"You are the magnificent one, Brie."

His lips trailed along her collarbone, and she reached behind herself to unhook her bra.

They explored each other, and he made a mental note at every breath change, every sigh. Bringing her pleasure and driving her to wonder were the only thoughts in his brain.

When she lay beneath him, Alessio dragged his lips across her thighs before finding her inner core. Brie bucked under his dancing mouth as he devoured her. She was sweet and fire and everything he needed.

"Alessio!"

Her cry as he felt her body tighten turned him on even

more. He'd not thought it possible. He stroked her with his fingers, bringing her to bliss again. Then he pulled the condom down his length.

The urge to drive himself to the hilt pulsed against every nerve, but he held himself steady as he pressed into her folds.

Brie wrapped her legs around him, pulling him deeper. She took a long breath.

"You are so beautiful," Alessio whispered against her ear, holding himself steady until she started moving against him.

They found their rhythm and he lost all thoughts of anything besides the woman with him. This was as close to heaven as he'd ever get and he was savoring every moment.

CHAPTER NINE

BLOND HAIR SPILLED over his chest, and Alessio gently stroked Brie's back. The urge to touch her, to convince himself that she was here, that he'd spent last night worshipping her body and was not trapped in one of his dreams, cruised through him.

He'd once heard a friend say the afterglow of being with his girlfriend, now wife, was the best feeling in the world. It was how he knew he wanted to propose, to ensure he spent the rest of his life with a person who made him feel so whole.

Alessio, like many of the guys in attendance, had laughed. The stereotype that women enjoyed snuggling, but men moved on, ran deep in their youthful subconscious.

Now though, as he held Brie in the early hours, he knew what his friend had meant. He knew how deep the feeling was, and the rightness of being exactly where you belonged.

But what did belonging to a prince mean for her?

"What time is it?" Brie mumbled as she lifted her head. The hair spilled over her eyes, and her lips were luscious and calling to be kissed.

"Just after six. I found a way to keep you in bed." He grinned, then brushed his lips over hers. "How are you this morning?"

He'd been gentle and made sure she reached the heights of making love, but that didn't shift that last night had been her first time. Mentally, and physically, that was a big deal. And it was the only reason he hadn't woken her this morning with kisses trailing along her magnificent body.

"Deliriously happy." Her fingers danced along his chest. Pink rose in her cheeks and her smile radiated straight to his heart.

"Deliriously happy." He kissed the tip of her nose, unable to keep from kissing her. "I love the sound of that."

He loved her.

The words hovered in the back of his mind. It hadn't been intentional, and suddenly all the things she'd have to give up by his side hit even harder. But her marketing plan was working. She could get her freedom...and what would that mean for his heart?

"We need to get breakfast." Brie rolled over and sighed.

"And you want coffee," Alessio teased.

"How well you know me." Brie laughed. "I'm going to head to my room. I'll see you soon." She dropped a kiss to his lips, then slid from the bed, grabbed her clothes and headed through the connecting door to her room.

It was the first time she'd used it, and he couldn't describe the burst of happiness that floated through him to see it open now.

Alessio rose from the bed and grabbed his phone. The text from his assistant, Jack, made him smile. They had a state function tonight. It would be his brother's first; he was welcoming a foreign dignitary from Europe. The staff had worked hard on the function, but it wasn't his concern.

Brie and Alessio were attending as ornamentation only. The spare and his future bride, they'd have the night mostly to themselves while everyone was focused on King Sebastian's first state dinner. But he had a surprise for her. And it had been delivered this morning.

He quickly donned some slacks and a comfortable shirt and went in search of Brie.

She was sitting on the bed, and he saw a tear slip down her cheek.

"Brie?" He moved to her side, sitting beside her and pulling her to him. "What's wrong?"

"Nothing. It's nothing, really." She hiccuped back a sob and shook her head. "I'll manage."

His stomach dropped. "What will you manage?" *And why?*

"Another job I set up before the lottery draw just canceled. I've kept a few clients, but everyone believes that when I become a princess I won't work, so..." She laughed but there was no humor in the sound.

When I become a princess.

Those words shouldn't matter, but his heart wanted to cling to them.

"Royalty works all the time."

"I know. But not an actual job. I worked so hard on the floor of that tiny apartment and in the rented office I had. The life I'd planned for myself, the life that was supposed to keep me safe, that was supposed to build a life away from my family name—it's slipping through my fingers."

She sucked in a breath and pressed her hand to her chest. "It was my purpose. What I was good at. I can't draw or create beautiful dresses out of my imagination. I don't feel called to write or work in a glass studio. But I can see other's visions and I can make it a reality for them. Take their hopes and dreams and create the path to success for them. Princesses don't run businesses is all people can see."

"What if you did run it?" Alessio ran his hand along her back. "What if you had your marketing firm and the crown?"

"What?" Brie looked at him, her eyes bright with so many questions.

There was no reason she couldn't work. No law prevented a princess from running her own business. He should be telling her that she could end this experiment now, end the relationship, but he didn't want to let her go.

"I love you." The words danced from his mouth. "You are my other half. I never expected that. I don't know what you feel or..."

Brie's hand landed on his lips. "I love you, too. I'm not sure how it happened or when. But I love you, Alessio."

"What if we announce later this week that you plan to run your marketing business from one of the palace's office suites? It might not be as big an operation as you planned before. We'll still have royal duties, after all. But I guarantee you clients will flock to your inbox."

"You mean it?" Brie wrapped her arms around his waist, leaning her head against his shoulder.

"Yes. You are a royal, or you will be. But that doesn't mean you can't be your own person." It didn't. Not for her. He'd find a way to make that the truth.

"So if I wanted my first client to be a glassworker whose art is magnificent..."

She could have a different life inside the gilded cage of the palace. He couldn't, but he wasn't going to argue that point now.

"Your first client will be Ophelia and she would definitely agree with me."

"She would." Brie laughed.

A knock echoed at his door.

Brie looked through the open door between their rooms. "Someone is looking for us."

"Jack. He has coffee, and a surprise for you."

"A surprise?"

"Yep. Do you want that or coffee more?" He winked, hoping the joke would make her smile.

It did.

"I always want coffee."

"Want or need?" Alessio grabbed her hand and pulled her through the door.

"Good morning, Your Royal Highness. I have coffee and—" Jack looked up from the coffee cart, pausing as he saw Brie standing next to Alessio. "Good morning, Ms. Ailiono."

"Brie, Jack. Just call me Brie."

Jack nodded, and Alessio watched Brie roll her eyes. The man's family had served royalty in European courts for more than a century. When they married, he'd call her Princess or

Your Royal Highness. He was raised in old-school protocol and would never shift.

Jack stepped back out of the room, and Brie headed toward the coffee tray. She poured herself a cup, added two sugar cubes and a dash of milk, then took a deep sip.

Alessio watched her sink into the morning ritual, knowing it was grounding her. Coffee was a thing Brie claimed to live for, but he suspected it was really her liquid safety blanket. A routine she needed.

"All right, I have the dress here." Jack stepped back into the room, carrying a dress bag that he quickly hung on the door of Alessio's closet.

"Dress?" Brie's eyes flew from the bag to Alessio.

"For tonight, Ms. Ailiono." Jack stepped up to the dress, but Alessio waved him off.

This was his surprise. Maybe it was selfish, but he wanted to do the reveal. Jack took the hint, offered a quick bow and left them alone.

"I have a dress for tonight. A simple blue dress your mother found. She said it matched my eyes."

"And she wasn't wrong." Alessio stepped to the dress bag. "But this one was made for you. I knew that the moment I saw it."

Brie raised a brow as she set her coffee cup down. "Saw it…"

He unzipped the bag.

Brie's breath hitched.

This was the moment he'd wanted. The realization. The understanding.

"The mermaid dress." Her hand was over her mouth.

"My mother is right—blue is lovely on you." He looked at her. Her eyes were so full of emotion, so full of love.

"It's over-the-top. I might get more press than King Sebastian." Brie giggled as she moved toward the dress.

"I suspect Sebastian would enjoy that. But in truth, it is his first state dinner. We are mere ornaments to this play."

Brie wrapped her arms around him, holding him. "You are always more than an ornament, Alessio. At least to me."

"That's more than enough."

That's more than enough.

Brie had replayed Alessio's words all day while she was prepped for the state dinner. Today was the first time she felt like she was truly acting the role of princess.

It was the role she'd play for the rest of her life. And she'd get to keep her business, too. She would stand beside the man she loved and work the career she craved. Alessio was making dreams she'd never considered come true. She didn't mind being the lottery bride, helping the country, if she still got to be herself.

"Wow."

Alessio's voice echoed in her soul as she turned to look at him.

"You look—"

"Not like myself!" Brie's giggle was too high-pitched.

Her body was a work of art, but she was a ball of nerves. Tonight was the first night in the real role she'd play as Alessio's life partner. It needed to be perfect.

A beauty technician had worked on nearly every part of her today. Her toenails were bright blue in the peep-toe shoes. Her fingernails were a light green.

The makeup artist the palace had hired had looked at the dress and squealed with excitement. The woman had spent nearly an hour highlighting and contouring while palace staff went over protocols with her.

"You look mythical."

"Mythical."

She looked in the mirror one last time. Her hair wasn't wet. In fact the braid looked almost like a crown, though she wouldn't wear one of those until they were married.

Still, she looked like a mermaid. It was what the dress was designed to do. Ophelia was truly an artist.

"Protocol talked with you?"

Ad nauseam!

The woman had prefaced that this was King Sebastian's night so many times that Brie had almost asked if she and Alessio could just skip the thing altogether.

"Yes. I run a tight ship on the outings I plan, but when the palace is in control…" It was next level. Tonight was not about Brie and Alessio. That had been made clear. "I promise not to outshine King Sebastian."

The tips of his lips tilted down, and Brie wanted to yank her words back.

This was Alessio's lived experience. He'd grown up the spare, always walking behind his father and his brother. There was a protocol for who was highest in the family.

"I'm sorry." She stepped toward him, reaching for his hands.

"You don't need to apologize. I'm sure that is what the office said. Though perhaps more diplomatically."

"*Diplomatically* is cutting." The words were out before she could think them through. Again.

"I just mean…" She blew out a breath. If this was a movie, she'd have a loose piece of hair to push out of her face or blow away. Instead, she was literal perfection. "Their words are very sweet. Controlled, yet…" She shrugged, not sure why she was trying to describe how listening to the protocol officer felt.

"Yet biting. A reminder that you aren't supposed to shine too brightly."

It was this attitude that had chased him to Scotland, but she was not going to let it happen around her.

"Alessio." She squeezed his hand. Today was the first time she'd heard the words *be smaller* since she stood by his side. Everything about her marketing campaign for the country was about blending into the background—but that was for a different purpose.

"Are you all right?" His fingers ran along her chin.

"Careful, you'll get glitter on yourself." She looked beautiful, but was it too much? Protocol had told her the lotto bride was taking a back seat this evening.

Lotto bride.

It was what she was and was the title she'd used with everyone before she and Alessio agreed to make it real. Now that their relationship was a fact, the tag felt like a slight.

And not just to her. But to Alessio.

"I don't care about some glitter." His thumb traced her jaw.

"I'm fine." It was true, but anger was overtaking the nerves she'd had all day. "But we need to find our own place after the wedding. We can still serve the throne, without actually living next to it. And I'll have my business to handle."

And he'd have his glasswork. He'd deflected her comment this morning, but she was going to find a way to get him regular time in his shop.

His eyes brightened and his smile made her want to strip the suit from his shoulders and spend the night luxuriating in the warmth it drove through her soul.

"I think that can be arranged, Princess."

A knock nearly made her jump. This was really happening.

"Ready, Your Royal Highness and Ms. Ailiono?" Jack's voice echoed from the other side of the door.

"Showtime." Alessio dropped his lips to hers.

They needed to get going, but Brie wrapped her arms around him, deepening the kiss. The world could wait a few moments longer. Alessio's hands stroked her lower back as she drank him in.

The glittery world she was about to step into was just for show. Her and Alessio, and the life they built away from the cameras, from the palace, from duty—that was reality. The reality she craved.

He broke the kiss as another knock came. "Duty awaits."

"So it does. Stay by me." Brie's skin felt slick as she wrapped an arm through his. She'd been in front of the cameras for weeks. There was no reason for tonight to feel different.

It did, though.

Because I love him.

"You are going to do great. I won't leave your side."

He'd be by her side. Brie could do this, and royal events would get easier...right? The shine would leave the lotto bride, but Brie was still enough. She was. *Right?*

She smiled and fell into step beside him. "I'm holding you to that, Prince Charming."

The room was warm—like all crowded events—but Alessio was hyperaware tonight. All eyes had flown to Brie when she stepped into the room. His heart had nearly exploded watching everyone's heads turn as she walked in.

Brie, his princess.

"Your fiancée is quite lovely." One of the ambassador's entourage smiled as he looked toward where Brie was talking to a few other dignitaries.

She looked over at him and nodded. He made sure that he was never more than a few feet from her.

"She is beautiful inside and out, and brilliant."

Brie was the most beautiful woman he'd ever seen. And her family had hoped to capitalize on that beauty by marrying her to a business associate. That was only one piece of her. One tiny, tiny piece.

Alessio loved every part of her.

"She will be the talk of this evening. The gown is something—a show." The man's words were cool, but Alessio heard the statement in them. Brie was the star.

That was a problem.

Sebastian was hosting. Sebastian was meant to be the focus.

"I am surprised she didn't post it on your social media page. It has been less active lately."

The man's gaze focused on Brie and the direction of the conversation gave him pause. It wasn't that it was less active; it was that there was less of him and Brie. It hadn't been conscious, at least he didn't think so, but as they grew closer, sharing private moments, kisses, felt off.

That was a worry for another day. Right now he needed to find a way to refocus the evening on his brother's success. This was Sebastian's event. Alessio nodded to the dignitary, his eyes moving subtly around the room.

He'd lost track of his brother.

Once, it had been Alessio ducking out of these events and Sebastian covering for him when he said something flippant. Since his return, Alessio had protected his brother, offering a response when Sebastian froze or said something glib.

His role was to support his brother, a role he wouldn't have yet if Alessio had stayed in Celiana. Still, Sebastian knew how to play this game. He'd been good at it, too. Once upon a time.

Heat flashed up his neck and Alessio took a deep breath. It wouldn't do any good for people to see his frustration.

Where was the king?

"Everyone will be talking about the princess tomorrow."

The words struck him, and he looked again for Sebastian, still not finding him. Would he be in one of Alessio's old hiding spaces or someplace new?

"And her dress! I've never seen such a creation."

The conversation floated over him as he kept looking over the crowd. Where was the king?

"Will you excuse me for a moment?" Alessio waited for the dignitaries to offer a polite response, looked toward Brie and was relieved to see she was fine. It was Sebastian he needed to find.

Alessio moved through the crowd, searching for the tall, dark-haired king. He should be easy to find.

"Alessio." His mother's voice was soft but urgent as she captured his arm.

He saw the same panic in her eyes that he was feeling. Sebastian had slipped away. From his first state dinner. This was...this was a nightmare.

"Can you please tell the ambassador about Celiana's tourism goals? It's one of my youngest's pet projects." Queen Mother Genevieve smiled, but Alessio knew she was close to breaking.

"Pet project?" The ambassador raised a brow.

His mother had already wandered off. Alessio shrugged. "My mother downplays my interest a little."

It wasn't intentional. He just wasn't the king. As the heir, he helped, but there was no expectation that he'd sit on the throne. So his projects became "pet projects," even if they were literally the saving grace of the kingdom.

"My fiancée and I are heavily invested in ensuring Celiana's future." Alessio saw his mother disappear through a side door. "Let me tell you all we've accomplished."

"Where have you been?" Alessio strode to his brother's side as he saw him enter the ballroom from a side door.

"I had some business to attend to with the ambassador."

"Really?" Alessio wanted to shake him. The lie was preposterous, and Sebastian had to know that. "I've been with the ambassador for the last hour. He is interested in discussing trade options with parliament tomorrow."

"Then I wasn't really needed anyway, was I?" Sebastian nodded and started to walk off. "You and your bride-to-be had everything handled."

Brie.

Alessio's body went rigid. He'd been so focused on the ambassador and finding Sebastian, he'd wandered away from her. She'd been on her own for more than an hour now, all because he'd had to play the role that was meant to be Sebastian's.

"You're the king." Alessio's tone was harsh. "Act like it."

"Baby brother." Sebastian clicked his tongue. "What would our father say to that?"

It was a low blow. A consequence of boys who were close, at least once. They knew where to hurt each other. Which was why it was so easy to respond.

"What would he say about the man wearing the crown after him?"

Sebastian's face blanched but he didn't back down. "I suspect we'd both be disappointments."

The words were soft, but Alessio heard the hurt under them. He opened his mouth, but no words flowed.

"Enough of whatever this is," the queen mother said as she stepped toward them. "Sebastian, the ambassador is ready for dinner. And Alessio, Brie is handling herself well enough."

Well enough. Palace-speak for something was wrong, but they weren't going to speak of it here.

"This is Brie's first official function besides the day of the lottery. I think she's done exceptionally well." Alessio saw his mother's eyes widen. Since returning, he'd never pushed back. Never did anything more than fulfill his duty.

Which he'd done tonight to cover for the king's absence.

"Celiana comes first." The queen mother's words were tight. "You both need to remember that. Remember your father's expectations."

Sebastian made a noncommittal noise and wandered to the door leading to the dining room. A small bell rang, and the crowd turned to look at the king.

His father's expectations were the reason Alessio left…and the reason he was back.

"It is my pleasure to welcome Ambassador Ertel. If you will follow me, I know the staff has prepared a delicious dinner."

Alessio moved quickly to Brie's side. She linked her arm in his, but her face was devoid of the excitement he'd seen earlier. Her jaw was tense, her shoulders were tight and he was nearly certain that she'd rubbed some of the makeup off her face.

"Brie?"

"I'm fine."

The words were quick and an answer to a question he hadn't asked.

There were too many ears here, but as soon as he had her someplace more private, he was going to discover what had stolen the light from her eyes.

CHAPTER TEN

BRIE OPENED HER EYES, knowing there was still at least an hour before the sun rose. Alessio snored softly on the pillow next to her. They'd arrived back from the state dinner long after midnight.

Exhausted physically and mentally, she'd washed the remainder of her makeup off and they'd fallen into bed. Alessio had wrapped his arm around her, and she'd bit back her questions as he slipped into dream world.

The questions were pointless anyway. She knew the answers. That was the problem.

It was a problem the morning made even more difficult to ignore.

Slipping from the bed, she padded softly back to her room. She needed to get dressed, make coffee and settle her nerves.

He'd broken his promise last night. He'd left her. And the wolves had feasted.

Making it clear that the public might love the tourist uptick from the princess lottery but the aristocrats—the ones who'd spent a lot of money to try to make their daughters princesses—were not as pleased.

People had whispered, in just a loud enough tone to be overheard by her, about everything. How much makeup she was wearing—clearly too much. The dress she'd chosen—an obnoxious choice suited to her *social media*. The words were whispered with such viciousness they'd made her ill.

She'd not posted the dress or the process of getting ready.

She'd thought of it, but it seemed too personal. Alessio had gifted her the dress because of their private time in Ophelia's shop. She'd wanted to hold to herself all the emotions that brought out. Perhaps that was a ridiculous statement for a princess.

More than one person had mentioned that she looked like she'd been trying to overshadow the king's event. The upstart lotto bride.

They insinuated she was stepping out of her sanctioned palace role to make herself and Alessio bigger, grander than they should be. Like she wanted to upstage the king.

And the king had disappeared...making her wonder if somehow, despite knowing how ridiculous it was, the words were true. Of course they weren't, but that didn't stop the pain of hearing them.

Her dress, the beautiful piece of artwork, was the talk of the event. She'd heard more than a few whispers and seen people with cameras snap a few shots when they thought she wasn't looking.

She'd been asked more than once if the palace had paid for the dress. She assumed the answer was yes, or perhaps Alessio had asked Ophelia to borrow it.

Then there'd been the not-so-subtle insinuations that she was nothing more than a stunt for the royal family. Those statements had flowed far too freely with Alessio's notable absence from her side.

Because of his absence.

The problem was that there was no way to deflect the "jokes," not when they were the truth. The fact that they'd fallen in love didn't change the fact that he'd pulled her name from a glass ball in a princess lottery that she'd joined as a marketing manager. That was the role she'd played for weeks now—blasting herself and Alessio across multiple social media platforms.

Without the princess lottery she'd still be in her tiny apartment, in comfy clothes, the rebel daughter of the Ailiono family. She'd have grown Ophelia's business, and her own, in a slower fashion. Hopefully.

The coldhearted truth of business was that success was not guaranteed, particularly when the most powerful business family in the country refused to talk to you. That meant she had a limited pool to prove success. More than half of new businesses collapsed within two years. Ophelia's was stable because of the lottery.

The reason everyone talked about Brie today was the lottery. And the words were less than kind when Alessio wasn't around to soften their tongues.

She left her room and headed for the media room. There was coffee there, and she needed to run some business plans past the few customers who'd stuck by her after her name was drawn. In a week or two she could tell them the plan for her to work as a princess. And there were videos to review of her and Alessio dancing last night that would work well for the social media campaign. With any luck one of them was relaxed enough for her to upload.

People had left more than a few comments that they wanted more of the prince and princess-to-be. A few weeks ago, Brie would have easily uploaded a playful kiss, or a video of them laughing. But as she grew closer to Alessio, those images—and she had many—felt too personal to give up for gossip.

She needed to do some marketing, though, a way to highlight the Ruins of Epiales they were visiting at the end of the week.

Turning the corner, she nearly ran into Jack. The man was flushed and holding several papers. A lifetime of reading body language made the hairs on the back of her head stand up.

"Ms. Ailiono."

"Jack." She watched him look at the papers then purposely away from her. "What's wrong?"

"Nothing." He was lying, trying to protect her.

"My brother always looked away when he was hiding something." At least he'd been that way when she'd seen him years ago. Perhaps now…

Focus, Brie.

"Ms. Ailiono." Jack's voice was so soft. But he didn't say any more.

"What's in the papers?" Brie crossed her arms. "Alessio is still sleeping, so why don't you accompany me to the media room? I need coffee, then you can tell me what I did wrong last night."

Pink invaded his cheeks as he pursed his lips. The truth was radiating from him.

"You need to work on your tells, Jack."

He didn't offer a retort, but he did turn and follow her.

She entered the media room and immediately headed for the coffee bar. "I'll assume this is a 'strongest blend I have' kind of morning?"

"I suspect it is, Ms. Ailiono."

He waited as the pot brewed and she doctored the blend. Turning with the mug in her hand, she pointed at the papers that were still in his hand.

"What's the damage?"

Jack looked at his feet, then back at Brie. "The dress."

"Was lovely," Brie stated, hating that Alessio's gift, the mythical creation he'd chosen just for her, was causing problems.

"Yes." Jack moved to one of the tables and started laying out the papers. All online posts, from blogs, gossip sites…and finally the most reliable paper in the country.

Ailiono Family Taking over Palace!

Soon-to-Be Princess Spends over One Hundred Thousand to Outshine King!

Princess Briella—Royal Stunt Turned Royal Money Pit!

Jack had even printed the first slide of an online video breaking down Brie's sparkly makeup. It included commentary about how a princess did not sparkle, at least not more than the king. In one night, she'd gone from Alessio's beloved fiancée to an upstart.

The lottery bride turned villain.

Because of a dress.

It was ridiculous, but women had been torn down for so much less. A feel-good story earned hundreds of clicks, while a hit piece earned thousands, sometimes millions. As a marketeer she understood the dynamics.

As the focus of the stories, they stung. What would happen when they announced her plans to work outside the palace? Would that be seen as an upstart move?

She moved the papers and saw one other post under the others.

"Oh, I didn't mean to include—"

She read the headline.

Prince Alessio Already Tiring of His Lotto Bride?

The first paragraph of the article was direct.

Prince Alessio was noticeably absent from his fiancée's side last night. Our sources can confirm that the prince spent less than three minutes beside his future wife during the cocktail hour. One source remarked that Briella looked for him several times. No doubt she is learning that having her name drawn from a crystal ball does not actually make a princess.

The door to the library opened but Brie didn't look up. Tears coated her eyes, and she didn't want Alessio to see them. Today was already going to be hard. They needed a plan, a strategy to make sure that their plans for Celiana didn't unravel.

And to clear my name.

"Brie! I was hoping to—" His voice cut off, likely because he registered Jack in the room.

"Your Royal Highness. There were some reports about last night."

"The press noticed Sebastian's absence." Alessio's voice was tight. "I tried to cover."

"No." Brie wandered to the coffeepot, poured herself another cup and made one for Alessio, mostly to give herself something to do. To collect herself.

"The press didn't notice the king's absence."

Brie's fingers shook as she waited for Jack to finish his statement, to drop the hammer.

"The commentary is about Ms. Ailiono."

"Oh. Not Sebastian?"

"No. Not Sebastian." Brie's voice was tight as she turned to look at him. She knew he was his brother's keeper. Sebastian was the reason he was home, the one he felt responsible for.

But he'd given her his heart...or at least that was what he'd said.

"Brie..."

"The press is quite focused on the dress."

"I'm sorry. All of this is over a dress? I mean, that sounds like a win, considering what they could be printing."

"What!" Brie turned, pressing her hands behind her against the counter, mostly to keep herself in place.

Alessio raised his hand. "I just mean that if we have to choose between them running reports about a missing king or getting too focused on a dress, the choice is easy."

Brie walked to the table, grabbed the report about him tiring of her and one discussing how much she'd spent of the palace's coin. She marched toward him, slapped the papers against his chest, then left.

Rationally she knew that he'd not seen the articles. She knew he was reacting to what sounded like a silly idea. But he'd broken his promise. She'd been nervous. She'd asked him to stay by her side. If he'd been there...

This was what they'd printed over a dress. This was just the beginning, and he was blowing it off to protect his brother.

Because that was why he'd come home, why the rebel had become the dutiful.

But where did that leave Brie?

Prince Alessio was noticeably absent from his fiancée's side last night.

The first line of that article cratered his soul. He'd left her. That was true. The rest of it was absolute rubbish.

He wasn't tiring of Brie. The exact opposite. He looked forward to each moment, craved her touch. He loved her.

And the dress. He pushed his hand through his hair as he stepped into yet another room where Brie clearly wasn't. For a woman who'd rarely exited the media room over the last several weeks, she'd found a way to make herself remarkably scarce.

The dress was his gift. No citizen's funds had paid for it. Hell, Brie hadn't even planned to wear it. It was a surprise, his gift to her on what was her first true royal engagement—at least in her mind, even if the country never realized she'd planned to leave.

His surprise had blown up in their faces.

Another door, another empty room. Was she purposely hiding from him?

But what was he to do? If Alessio was honest, there was nothing he could have changed about last night. Sebastian's absence was a bigger problem than a dress and observations about them not standing together in the hour before dinner officially started.

"Brother."

"Have you seen Brie?" The question was out before he'd even turned around.

"Good morning to you, too." His brother's brow furrowed as he moved toward him.

"I'm in no mood to play games, Sebastian. Have you seen Brie?"

"Not since last night."

"Do you even recall seeing her?" Alessio's tone was sharp, but he couldn't stop the frustration filling him. "After all, you weren't in attendance for a sizable portion of *your* event."

Color coated Sebastian's cheeks.

He'd aimed his words and they'd landed. His brother should have been there. It was his responsibility. Whether he wanted it or not.

"You covered well." Sebastian crossed his arms.

Righteous anger seemed to boil in his soul. He tried taking a deep breath but that did nothing to stop the fury. The man he'd been warred with the man he'd become after his father passed—and the first won.

"Where the hell were you?"

"I needed a break." Sebastian shrugged as though it was nothing.

"A break. A *break*!" Stars exploded in his eyes. What the hell?

Sebastian rocked on his heels but didn't step away. "Don't you ever need a break, brother? A break from the pressure pushing against your chest, shaking fingers, each breath more ragged than the next."

"Not since I returned." Alessio heard the deep wounds in his brother's description, and maybe if he knew where Brie was, if he knew she was all right, if he knew she hadn't left him, he might feel more understanding.

"Well, I don't have the benefit of getting to run away!"

Run away, pushed away, left for nothing until the crown wanted something of him. All those were words the man he'd been wanted to scream at Sebastian. But none of that was his brother's fault.

"You were born to be the king." They were their father's words, which Alessio had heard him state so often to his brother. They were whispered with as close to affection as their father got.

"What a prize." Sebastian looked at his feet, then back at

Alessio. "If there was a path for abdication, the crown would be yours tomorrow. Then we'd see what you think of it." Then his brother turned on his heel and walked off.

"Sebastian!" Alessio understood the pressure. It wasn't the same for him, but he wasn't the person he wanted to be, either. Not anymore. At least he'd gotten a three-year reprieve. Sebastian would never get one.

"I'm sorry. I just need to find Brie. The press... I need to find her."

The king paused, and for a moment Alessio feared he wouldn't turn around.

"What did they say?" Sebastian started back toward him.

Rather than answer, Alessio held out the papers.

Sebastian read them, his brows rising at certain points. "These aren't nice, but—" He shrugged. "The palace's response is not to comment."

He knew that. The standard response was no response... unless it was about the king. The palace had squashed a few stories about their father, and more than one story about Sebastian's recent playboy lifestyle.

Alessio and Brie were not given the same treatment.

"I know. But Brie still needs comfort." She needed him this morning, and his mind had gone to where it always went since he returned home. The throne.

"Your bride is in the gardens. In tears," his mother said as she stepped from her rooms. Only her presence made him aware of where he was. He'd clearly been too focused on finding his fiancée to realize that he was so close to his mother's suite.

"Palace sources?" Sebastian sighed.

"Sources? Please, Sebastian. If you paid attention, gave anyone but the women you chase attention, people would tell you what you needed to hear, too." Genevieve had cultivated her staff well. She was their queen mother and employer, but she treated each member of the staff with absolute respect. It earned her their respect.

Alessio was trusted, too, but he was the spare, the one people bowed to but never paid as much attention to. It was the position he'd grown up in, the one he'd finally accepted when he came home.

"Which garden?" Alessio asked.

He didn't need to stay for whatever dressing-down his mother planned for his brother.

"Main courtyard."

"Thanks." He took off.

"No running in the halls."

He heard his mother's call but didn't slow his pace. He needed Brie.

Now.

He heard her sob before he saw her. She was sitting under a cherrywood tree, the stuffed animal Emilio had returned beside her. A set of notebooks was in front of her.

If she wasn't crying, the scene would be almost picture-perfect.

"Brie? Sweetheart?"

"Come to apologize?" Her voice wavered but the words were clearly a demand.

"Yes." He should have registered that she was upset, should have taken a few moments to comfort her before gently explaining that this was part of their role, too.

Sometimes he was the distraction—if it benefited the crown.

It was what he had to do. But by tying herself to him, she'd be expected to have the same role. The idea was a bitter pill as he slid to the ground, taking in her tearstained cheeks and red eyes.

"I'm so sorry, Brie."

She looked at him, her blue eyes still swimming with tears. Cocking an eyebrow, she raised her chin. "For…?"

"For not taking a moment to read the situation. For rushing to say that it was better that the press discusses a dress than Sebastian."

"Are you sorry for saying it, or sorry that it's true?"

"Brie—"

"I'm an Ailiono, whether my family wishes to claim me or not. I've been a sacrificial lamb before. How often will I have to do it here?"

Her words were daggers, sharpened weapons that struck with such precision.

"I don't know." Hiding that truth was not going to work.

"And what about when I'm working—will that be a host for gossip to redirect eyes from the palace?"

Working. Her company.

That was what this was really about, and there was more than a bit of jealousy in his chest that she'd asked about it. This wasn't really about them.

Maybe he should let her go, let her chase her dreams, relish the fact that he'd gotten more time than he deserved with a woman who made him feel whole.

The words to release her refused to appear. Instead, he said what was truly on his mind.

"You're my heart, Brie. All of it will work out. There will be hiccups and days that the barbs hurt. We just have to let the noise float away."

"Float away. Sticks and stones can break your bones, but words can never hurt you." She wrote something in the journal in front of her without looking at him.

"Words hurt. That schoolyard rhyme was made to make bullies feel better, not because it contains an ounce of truth." He leaned forward and put his hand on her knee. "Brie, look at me."

She raised her head. Shadows hovered under her eyes. She was clenching her teeth but there was a hint of something in her gaze. A hope.

"I can play games. I grew up in them." She held up a hand before he could say something to that sad statement.

"Some might even say that as a marketeer, I'm a professional game player, making people believe that they need something or that their life will be better with such and such product. It's a skill, and I am good at it."

"Brie…"

"What I will not accept is being second with you." Her bottom lip trembled. "With you, I need to be first. *Our* dreams and goals need to be first. I could have come with you last night. If the headlines were 'Prince Alessio and Briella Ailiono Taking Too Much of Ambassador's Time' or 'Spare and His Lotto Bride Stealing King's Show,' I'd shrug my shoulders."

She reached for his hand. It was warm as she squeezed him, grounding them in the garden.

"I spent my childhood as a pawn to my family's ambitions. I fell for you, Alessio. I want to be by your side, but we get to have our own dreams, too."

"We do. We do, Brie. I promise."

He should have pulled her with him last night. He should have stayed by her side. She was right; they could have talked to the ambassador together. The stories likely would have read exactly as she stated.

"We are a team. Promise."

"All right. Apology accepted." She pressed her lips to his. "Now we have to focus on the next problem."

"Next problem."

"Yep." She flipped the notebook around. "You were noticeably absent from my side."

"I read the article, Brie."

"Good. Then you know that in the first instance we had that wasn't controlled by us, you looked like you didn't want me. We'd posted less on my social media as…"

Her cheeks brightened.

He dropped a kiss to her lips. "As it became real?"

"Yeah." Brie ran her hand along his jaw. "So how do we shift the narrative back to the lovebirds, without throwing your brother under the well-deserved bus?"

* * *

"What is this I hear that Briella will work when she puts on the crown?"

His mother's words weren't harsh, but he could hear the steel in them. He wasn't sure which of the queen mother's staff had overheard and passed on the conversation, but it hardly mattered.

Alessio looked to the media room. He'd only just patched things over. She was planning their next steps and he was getting her coffee. This wasn't the time for the conversation, but one rarely got exactly what they wanted behind the palace walls.

Brie would, though. Somehow, he'd find a way to give her the choices she needed and the dreams she deserved.

"Brie plans to run the marketing firm she had before all this. It won't be for profit, though she plans to complete the work for the companies that have already contracted her."

Brie had told him that the few companies who'd taken a risk on her, and stayed on following the lotto bride announcement, deserved her to finish what they'd contracted. After that, her focus would be on the tourism industry and nonprofits.

It was a brilliant idea. One that would endear her to the country even more.

"That is not a good idea."

"Mother—"

She held up her hand and Alessio bit his tongue.

"Maybe in a few months. But right now, after last night, it will look like she is seeking freedom from the palace."

Freedom.

The thing Brie had craved her entire life. The thing she deserved.

"I fail to see how working during our union is seeking freedom from the palace."

Except he knew how the optics would look. Rather than doing "royal" duties, Brie would focus on her company. He could argue that the nonprofit work was an excellent royal duty, but it was different. And different was not something the royal family sought out.

"She will have too many duties. Your father took on too much. If you had stepped up sooner…"

Her words trailed off, but Alessio knew the ending. *Your father might still be here.*

The queen mother looked at the day calendar she carried, despite the staff switching to phones and tablets years ago.

"I have to see to some things. Let Brie know it won't work, Alessio. Your brother needs your help. It's not fair to give her dreams that cannot be delivered."

His mother turned and glided down the hall, the sweep of her shoulders just a hair off. *What dreams had she given up for Celiana?* That was a question she'd never answer.

But Brie was going to get her dream. It might take him longer to figure it out. A delay was necessary. That was all.

Or I could set her free.

The thought rocked his soul. Maybe it was the right answer. She could still have her dreams, outside the palace, without the royal life holding her back.

Alessio looked to the door of the media room and shook his head. No. There was a way for her to have it all. Maybe just not right away.

CHAPTER ELEVEN

"HERE WE GO!"

Brie waved to the camera as Alessio held her close. It should feel nice, should be lovely. Maybe it would, if it felt real. When the camera was off, they did fine—sort of. Alessio had pulled away since the state dinner earlier this week. It felt like there was an answer he wasn't giving. Or maybe she just hadn't asked the right question.

No matter what she tried, it felt like there was a wall between them, and she had no idea how to strip it down.

"Will that one work?" Alessio's sigh echoed in the car as they pulled up to the Ruins of Epiales.

They hadn't had as many redo moments since the first week. Brie looked at the video and knew it wouldn't work. They looked like robots, not two people in love. It would just fuel the conversations already running wild.

"No." She bit her lip and kissed him. He softened in her arms. The two of them were becoming as close to one as possible in the back of the car. This was the moment they needed to capture, but she also hated sharing it when it felt like the only time they were close was when the camera wasn't an option.

"How about you do one as we head to the moors?"

She nodded, kissed him again, knowing that wouldn't be best but it was better than the video they had. She stepped out of the car and shivered.

The Ruins of Epiales always felt chilly to Brie. The old palace and fortress of Celiana had been built around the same year as the Roman Colosseum. It was in worse shape than the giant structure in Italy, but there were still identifiable walls and a sanctuary.

Epiales, the personification of nightmares according to the Greeks, wasn't worshipped here, but according to legend, the ruler of Celiana had dreamed of invasion in the year AD 300. It was a nightmare he hadn't believed until it had come true.

"We're at the Ruins of Epiales today!" Brie waved to the camera, then panned to the ruins, making sure to capture a shot of Alessio while avoiding the security detail that was always just far enough away to give the illusion of aloneness.

The ruins' historical records were minimal, though archaeologists agreed that the area had been ransacked and burned. The place certainly harbored nightmare energy, but whether anyone had experienced nightmares before the area was destroyed, no person walking the earth for generations had known.

"This is an impressive site." Brie turned the camera back to herself and tried to ignore the unease. It *was* an impressive site, but its vibes always felt off to her. It wasn't something Brie could put into words. "Into archaeology? Or hikes in unique locations? Then this is the site for you." Brie smiled, then shut off the video and hit Upload.

That would have to work.

Whatever the general dread of this place was, it felt stronger today. She ached to wrap her arms around herself as she and Alessio followed the guide.

She had to pull away from the creeping dread that had followed her since the day after the state dinner three days ago.

The seismic shift had rattled the very foundation of her soul.

A week ago, she'd have stepped into Alessio's arms, walked hand in hand with him, joked about the icky feeling this place gave her or made some silly, or spicy, joke to lighten the creepy mood of the ruins.

Now, though...

She looked ahead. He was only a foot or so in front of her.

Brie could reach her hand out and touch him. The small physical distance was highlighting the chasm she felt growing between them.

The worst part was that Brie knew she should do it. That was the plan they'd hammered out in the garden: ignore the press and be as they were. She should reach for him, make the jokes, put the smile on. Play the game. After all, the papers were already running wild with speculation that the lottery stunt was coming to an end.

And once more the papers were focused on one thing. The mermaid dress was old news. Now all the press could talk about was the lack of a ring on her engagement finger.

Even now she absently rubbed the empty finger. Alessio had offered her a choice of rings when they'd started this stunt, but she'd not wanted one. Somehow that would have made this real.

Now that it was real, now that everyone was noticing, Brie couldn't help but feel the slight even if Alessio hadn't meant anything by leaving her without an engagement ring. In fact they'd discussed it last night. And he'd worried how it would look if they chose one while all of this was going on.

He was right.

But he'd also recommended holding off on announcing that she'd be keeping her marketing firm. Just until this blew over. There was no need to spin up more scandal.

They were the right words, too. She knew that, knew that it would be more illustration that their relationship was nothing more than a glorified marketing campaign for the country.

The irony that this was how it had started was far from lost on her.

Still, it felt like there was more to the story. There was something he wasn't telling her. Or maybe she was looking for cracks. Whatever it was, they weren't the same as they'd been.

And everyone was noticing. They'd not been acting before, not trying to tell a story. It had come naturally, a gift she'd not recognized until it was gone.

Now they needed to tell the story. They needed to quash the rumors, the cutting looks, the whispers. Now was the time to play the role of prince and future princess.

And it should be such an easy story to tell. They didn't have to pretend.

"This place is glorious." Alessio breathed in as they stepped to another section of the ruins. "Sad, but glorious."

"Yes." Brie nodded, happy to have some conversation other than the thoughts her mind was supplying.

"You can envision how beautiful it must have been just after it was completed." Her words were right, but they felt off. Stiff. Like she was talking to a tourist rather than the man she loved.

Alessio moved, and for a moment she thought he was reaching for her, looking for her hand.

But before he connected, the tour guide stated, "If you close your eyes, you might even feel the spirits."

Alessio turned and a chill slipped down Brie's back. As a rule she didn't put much credence in ghosts. However, she never quite ruled them out, either.

It would be nice to pretend it was the ghouls sending cool air racing across her skin, rather than the empty feeling of watching Alessio stuff his hands back in his pockets as he followed the guide's instructions.

Closing his eyes, he stood perfectly still. The wind blew his hair, and Brie drank him in. He was gorgeous, though the wear of the last few days was visible, too.

The lines around his eyes, the hint of darkness under them and the pinch of his jaw... The image he showed the world of the relaxed, dutiful prince was absent.

At least to her knowledgeable eyes.

Neither of them were sleeping well.

Her brain refused to turn off. It kept replaying the horrid headlines that graced websites and the few printed papers still around. It whispered terrible things, usually in the sound of her mother's voice.

She'd gone from the lotto princess bride to the interloper in one night. With one dress.

And the palace had said nothing. Alessio had said nothing. They didn't want to throw the king under the bus, though Brie wouldn't have minded doing it.

But couldn't Alessio have said that he bought her the dress as a gift? Couldn't they have issued some joint statement, been a team united instead of the quiet pair they'd become?

Their silence just fueled the questions she now heard peppered through crowds meeting them. The frowns she saw were difficult to ignore. And they seemed to chase slumber away.

As a result, Alessio was constantly shifting with her movements. She'd even mentioned moving back to her bed if her tossing was keeping him up. He'd declined each offer. That warmed her heart. He wanted her in his bed.

But that didn't chase the worries away that he was hiding something.

"I don't feel anything." He opened his eyes and grinned.

"Really?" Brie found that difficult to believe. Maybe he didn't feel ghosts, but the air felt...heavy, like the general vibe between them. There were so many things to feel.

"Do you?"

"I feel cold." The words came out before she could think them through. She bit her lip and tried to force a smile, tried to make things feel normal between them.

"The wind off the ocean is a bit biting."

Alessio tilted his head and looked at their guide, who'd given them a little space. It wasn't a lot, not enough privacy that they could have a real conversation. And the Ruins of Epiales were not the right place anyway.

He stepped closer and she waited for his arms to wrap around her. She waited to be pulled close...but the moment didn't come.

"We can leave. The press got a few pictures of us arriving, you put up the video and this is probably a pretty niche tourist location. Not sure anyone is visiting Celiana just for this place."

The ruins were interesting, if you were already on the island, but tourists seeking these kinds of places had far more exceptional locations to visit.

"Do you want to leave?" She buried her hands in her pockets. If he wasn't reaching for her, then she wouldn't reach for him.

"Brie—" Alessio shifted, opening his mouth and closing it before saying whatever was on his mind.

Then looked back at their guide. "The princess is a little chilly. I think we're going to cut this outing a bit short."

"Of course." The guide nodded, but Brie saw the hint of something in his eyes—a note of glee, or excitement. It was wiped away by a soft smile so fast she was sure she'd misread it.

Stop looking for worries, Brie!

If only her brain would listen.

The guide started back down the path to where their car was waiting. Alessio looked at her, his jade eyes seeming to bore into her soul, then he stepped to the side and started down the hill after the guide.

She sucked back a sob. Something needed to shift, needed to change; they couldn't continue like this. But what if asking the questions shattered her heart?

What if it's already shattered?

Brie looked out at the ruins one last time. The once beautiful location had been worn away by time and fire. She wrapped her arms around herself, then straightened her shoulders.

She was in charge of her life. That hadn't changed just because she'd fallen in love with Prince Alessio.

Turning, she followed the path Alessio had taken. Had he even noticed that she wasn't right behind him?

Alessio stared at the empty path and tried to determine if he needed to go after Brie. Or would that make the already uncomfortable divide between them larger?

He'd thought she was right behind him. After all, she'd said she was cold.

And rather than pull her close, I said we should leave.

Because pulling her close felt off, like it was for show. Behind closed doors they were better than in public, but not as good as they'd been. She'd agreed to delay announcing her plans to work, and he hated that he hadn't told her what his mother had said.

Alessio felt like he was acting. He felt like everything was for a show he no longer wanted to star in. He wanted Brie, not the drama, not the pain he suspected the palace would inflict on her someday.

And the guide was clearly planning to sell the story of today. Alessio had seen it in the man's eyes. He should have acted for the guide, should have pulled Brie close, but to do it just for the show... No, he hadn't wanted to give the guide anything.

Throughout his life, he'd gotten good at telling who was genuinely interested in talking with him, hanging out with him, and who was looking for a way to earn a few quick bucks selling royal stories. Maybe it wasn't fair to the tour guide, but from the second he and Brie had stepped onto the path, the man had watched them. And not in the friendly manner he'd seen on so many of their trips.

There'd been no questions and no friendly banter. Instead, it felt like the guide was memorizing the story he wanted to sell. And the Brie and Alessio that had been on display a few weeks ago had vanished. They needed to be the fun-loving couple they'd been, but the pressure to show it had sucked the joy from their love.

And that reminded him why he'd run from this place to begin with. The palace could start a narrative, could seed the story, but it was ultimately out of their hands how people received it. And by loving him, Brie was trapped in the same web he'd spun himself.

That wasn't fair.

"Prince Alessio, I thought Brie looked gorgeous in her gown last week."

The small voice in the crowd made him smile. Turning, he saw a teen leaning over the barrier.

"I thought she did, too."

A reporter stepped in front of the teen. "Do you think your father would have approved? Would he have been happy that your brother's first state dinner was refocused onto your lottery bride's fantastic expenditure?"

"My father always put Celiana first. I am sure he would be happy that his sons continue to do the same."

It was a stock answer. There was nothing Alessio and Sebastian could do to please their father. Or maybe they could have, if they'd done more. Sebastian might not have been able to do more, but his mother was right. Alessio could have stepped up sooner.

"We want a real answer, Prince Alessio. Would your father have approved of Princess Briella Ailiono?"

No. Brie wanted her business. He wanted that for her, but his father would not have understood. She wanted choices, and he was dreading how many the palace would strip away.

"Briella is *my* princess." It wasn't a lie and not an answer, either.

"Then where is she?"

She rounded the bend in the path, and he felt his body relax a little. Once again, he'd left her. And once more it wasn't intentional. He'd started walking and reached the car before realizing she hadn't followed. It wasn't nefarious. That didn't remove the shame, though.

"She was enjoying a few private moments in the ruins." Alessio pushed off the car and closed the distance between them.

He reached for her and saw her eyes widen as he took her in his arms. "You enjoy a few moments alone?" He dropped a kiss on her nose, then squeezed her tightly.

It was the first time that he'd held her in public in days. His soul was thirsty with need, but his heart was also raging at the injustice that their relationship had shifted.

Brie smiled but didn't answer as they walked back to the car. He moved to put his hand around her waist, but she stepped away. "Brie—"

She waved to the crowd, then opened the door and slid into the car.

Alessio offered another wave to the crowd before following his bride.

"Brie, I thought we were supposed to be trying to reignite the love story. Make them believe. People are asking hard questions…"

Were there worse words to speak?

"I am not a pawn. You reached for me because everyone was there—"

"No. I was worried."

"And yet you didn't come looking for me. Because then they would have asked about that, right?" She leaned her head against the headrest. "We get to decide our story, Alessio. Us!" Her blue eyes flew open as she gestured between the two of them. "Even if they misread it. It's our story. Ours!"

"I'm sorry, Brie. That was the worst way to say that. I just…" He paused, then decided to just go with the truth. "I'm lost."

"Lost." Brie repeated the word. "I guess that's as good a word as any for whatever is happening."

"So what do we do about it?"

"We talk." Brie laughed, though there was no trace of humor. "About real things. We stop worrying about the cameras…at least as much as we can."

"What do you want to talk about?"

She opened her mouth, then closed it.

He watched her shift, watched her battle back her discomfort.

"What aren't you telling me?" The words were soft, but her hands gripped his. "What are you holding back?"

Alessio took a deep breath. Of course she'd noticed. "My mother doesn't think you working, you keeping the company, is a good idea." The words were out. Now he waited for the anger, the frustration.

Brie nodded. "So the delay is more a not-happening if the queen mother has her way? Does your mother have that power?"

She didn't look angry, just concerned.

"Not directly."

"Does your brother?" Brie tilted her head. "After all, you left the island for years."

It wasn't that simple. Not anymore. He owed Sebastian. Royal duties took up time, and his brother didn't have a spouse to carry the load. He didn't want his brother to feel like he had to do everything. Maybe that wasn't fair, but it felt like a debt he needed to pay.

"I will find a way to make it work."

That was a promise he was keeping. He wasn't sure how yet. But Brie was going to work in marketing. She was. He loved her and she was great at this.

Maybe he'd gone into the bride lottery only looking for a bride willing to play the role, but he'd found a partner. He didn't want to lose that.

"I don't need a way to make it work, Alessio. We can make it work, just by saying it, if *we* say it—as a team."

"A team," Alessio repeated.

He wanted it to be that easy, but the palace...the duty he'd stepped back into... Alessio didn't control his own destiny. He never really had.

"Yes. As a team. But you must focus on the next thing. You deserve freedom, too. I know that doesn't look like Scotland anymore. But you have to be you. Your own person, not Sebastian's helper or the dutiful prince."

Brie raised a hand to his cheek. "What is your next thing? The thing that you choose when this is over? Your glass—"

He couldn't think of his glass studio. Not now. This was his life. It was what he owed his family, not the dream he'd had once upon a time. "That dream is over. I know you look for the next thing. Because you had to when your family threw you out."

"My family did not throw me out. I left. I chose a new adventure, and I am begging you to choose one, too. We can't be Prince Alessio and the lottery bride forever. So what's next, Alessio? What does our life look like for us?"

"I don't know."

"I know." Brie leaned over and kissed his cheek. "But you need to find your dream outside the title of Prince Alessio. The dutiful heir can only be one part of the story. We deserve to carve our own path. Together."

He raised his hand to her face, like he could magically force the touch to remain forever. Like he could chase loss and fear and everything else away.

CHAPTER TWELVE

ALESSIO ROLLED OVER, his hand brushing Brie's empty pillow. He stretched and looked around. Had she not slept here?

She'd been watching a reality television show when he'd yawned last night. She'd said she'd come in shortly, but...

Alessio slipped from their bed and started to head through the interconnecting door when a knock echoed through his room. He glared at the door. Early morning knocks never meant anything good.

He considered ignoring it. Finding Brie was all his heart wanted to do, but duty stayed his desires.

"Jack." Alessio wasn't surprised to see his assistant at the door. Nor did the mountains of papers the man was carrying shock him. The trip to the ruins had been a nightmare.

At least they'd lived up to their name. He wasn't a giant believer in prophecy, but perhaps that place truly was cursed.

"Where is Ms. Ailiono?"

"I don't know." Alessio pinched the bridge of his nose, hoping she might step through the door connecting their rooms. Or sprint in with a mug capable of carrying a full pot of coffee. Anything.

"The papers are all running some variation of the same story." Jack laid out several articles on Alessio's desk.

An image of Brie standing alone at the ruins was at the front of each story. Her hair was whipping in the wind, and it looked like a tear was falling across her cheek.

She looked lonely. Terribly lonely.

"Each article has the same statement from Ms. Ailiono."

"Statement from Brie?" Alessio grabbed one of the papers Jack had printed out, his heart sinking as he read.

On the day of the lottery draw Briella Ailiono intentionally chose a dark dress for the occasion, when most of the potential brides were wearing white, gold or cream. She was quoted as saying that "Dark colors are best when love dies."

When the reporter joked with the marketeer, "Guess you won't cry if your name doesn't come out today?" Ms. Ailiono stated, "I'll cry if it does."

The princess-to-be never wished to join the royal family. If this picture is any indication, the first weeks of the "romance" were a show.

Prince Alessio deserves a bride who wishes to be by his side. It's clear Briella Ailiono is not a good fit.

Something her estranged family found out years ago.

The last line was a low blow. Most of the island looked at the Ailiono family with a mixture of fear and disgust. The rich patriarch and matriarch cared little for the island, except for how to invest for their own benefit.

They'd thrown their daughter's stuff out without thought when redoing her room. Only Emilio's kindness had saved some of her precious things.

But the article was full of truth, too.

She'd never wanted to be his princess. Or anyone else's. She'd not hidden that fact from him. He'd been that person before.

He'd stood alone.

It would only get worse. He knew that. Brie was in love with the man who'd never sit on the throne, the one destined to be the spare as soon as his brother married and produced an heir. Then Alessio would slip further down the line of succession, but his duties would still be to the family.

He was not the prize the lottery had made him out to be. He'd unintentionally turned the woman he loved into a villain by focusing on his duty to Sebastian and the memory of his father. Brie deserved so much more than that.

I'll cry if it does.

He ran his finger over those words, then over the image of her crying. She'd not lied.

What's next?

Her question from yesterday had haunted his dreams and it seemed to echo from the paper.

It was time to respond. Forcefully. He had to demonstrate that the palace was behind her. Behind them.

There was another knock...or rather a pounding...at the door.

"Come in, Sebastian."

His brother entered, with their mother close on his heels.

"I used to knock like that. I thought you had more decorum, brother."

Sebastian stretched his arms. "I think you have enough decorum for us both now."

The joke fell flat as their mother crossed her arms. "This isn't the time for jests."

"Any time is a time for a joke." Sebastian yawned.

"That just wasn't a very good one." Alessio looked at his phone. There was no message from Brie.

"Boys."

Both Alessio and Sebastian straightened quickly. They might be grown men, but that didn't stop their inner child from responding.

"We need to draft a response. Brie can help craft it."

It would be a first. The palace would be responding to gossip, but it was time.

Alessio looked to his brother—the king of Celiana. Sebastian knew their father wouldn't have approved of commenting. He'd have ignored it completely or privately encouraged the discourse to distract from Sebastian's lackluster start to his rule.

But Sebastian sat on the throne now.

"I was married to your father for forty-three years." Their mother sucked in a deep breath. "He would have told you what a foolish statement that was."

She was right, but Alessio's eyes never left his brother. He was the king now. That didn't come with political power, but influence. Influence he could wield.

If he wanted.

"The lottery is being called a stunt, a scam, and now Briella is on record saying she never wanted to be the princess." Sebastian pulled his hand across his face, the same motion their father had made when frustrated. "We do need to issue a response. One that shuts all the narrative down."

Alessio could see the old Sebastian returning before his eyes, could see the man trying to finally step into their father's shoes. Why did it have to be this moment?

"You called it a stunt first. I seem to remember you being happy when Brie said she wouldn't marry me the day after the lottery."

"It was a stunt. If you two hadn't played the lovebirds so well, extracting yourselves would be easier. But hell, you made them believe the two of you were in love. Made them believe the story—either this is a lovers' fight or far worse. A scam on the island's goodwill."

We are in love.

Alessio kept those words buried.

"We move the marriage up." Sebastian pulled out his phone, typed a few things, then pulled up a calendar. "Does three weeks from tomorrow work?"

Alessio knew his mouth was hanging open. Those were words he'd never expected from Sebastian's mouth.

"No words, brother?"

His brain was full of words, but none that wanted to push their way into existence.

"We rush the wedding. Should anyone ask, it's because the two of you are tired of this kind of press. You just say you can't wait any longer to be man and wife."

"Husband." Alessio pulled his hand over his face.

"Excuse me?"

"It's husband and wife. Not man." Alessio didn't know why Sebastian's wording disturbed him so. But it wasn't just Brie taking on a new title. It was Alessio, too.

"Brie—" Alessio tried to find some words. "What if Brie doesn't want to rush the nuptials? She and I had a deal." Sebastian had laughed at their agreement when Alessio told him.

But that was his brother, the man uncertain of the role thrust upon him. And that man was no longer standing in front of him.

"She signed a contract. And you told me that the deal was off if it brought scandal to the island. We are dangerously close to that. Tourism is how our people survive. You didn't have to come back, but you did. You are the heir to the throne and sacrifices must be made."

"I came back for you. I came because I thought I owed Father."

"And you did. You owe a duty to the crown. Like it or not. You weren't here to help your father. He took on everything for this country." His mother's words were tight. The strain in her eyes ripped through him. Maybe she had loved him.

"You were born royal. That is who you are. The path you walk." Her fists were tight. "Your father gave you both as much time as he could. Step into the roles he wanted for you. For this kingdom."

The path he'd been born to—this was why Alessio didn't make wishes. His destiny had been laid out before he'd taken his first breath.

Sebastian straightened, raising his chin. Now it was his king before him. He was truly stepping into the role, and Alessio wished he wasn't. "If lovebirds can visit the Ruins of Epiales and break up, then we are a cursed island. You reawakened the imagery of an island of love—so if this fails, then we will watch parts of this island fail. Our people may have to emigrate. They might lose everything. Heaven knows her family will gobble up any property they can get."

Sebastian took a deep breath. "So, get her on board. Or come up with another brilliant plan to fix this."

With the final command, his brother stepped out of the room.

His mother looked at the door. Sebastian hadn't slammed it shut; instead, he'd closed it with cool effectiveness. Just like their father.

"He's right." The queen mother stepped to Alessio's side. "You chose this, and so did Brie. Maybe she didn't expect it, but the contract was nearly ironclad."

She kissed his cheek. "Your father and I made do. You two will, too."

"Celiana comes first."

She smiled as he repeated the mantra he'd heard from his earliest memories.

"I need to find Brie."

His mother nodded and stepped out of the room. Alessio looked to the pillow where she'd not rested last night, and his heart broke.

He wanted to meet Brie at the altar. He wanted her to be his wife, but this...

Perhaps a rushed wedding was right for Celiana—but that didn't mean it was right.

The best thing he could do for the woman he loved was set her free.

Brie sighed as another text came in from Ophelia.

Last night she'd fallen asleep in the chair while bingeing reality television. She'd been trying to relax and clear her brain—but it hadn't really worked. Ophelia's first text broke the barely there slumber she'd achieved.

It had a link—the first of many her friend sent. The reporter's words worried Ophelia, and she even offered to break Brie out of the palace.

The article didn't worry her. No, it was pure fury racing through Brie as she read each line. She'd sent a note to Nate, off the record, to let him know how low it was to sell her statements without at least reaching out for comment.

He'd reached out for comment then. Brie had laughed and hung up.

So far this morning, she'd gotten more than fifteen texts and three phone calls, and her email inbox was full. Several of the accounts that dropped her were letting her know that they'd be willing to renegotiate the contracts if the wedding was off.

In other words...you're going to be a big story and we can profit off it since it looks like you might have some free time coming.

As a marketing strategy, it wasn't half bad.

"Brie." Alessio's voice was strained, so he'd seen the articles.

It was cowardly to have hidden away, but she'd been trying to figure out a plan. Something to fix the blazing headlines. Something to help him figure out what was next. Something to let him see a path besides being the scapegoat for things he couldn't control. His father's death wasn't his fault. He'd returned and done a good job.

Alessio still needed something more than the crown. He needed his own thing. The lottery bride scheme would always be tied to what he felt he owed his father. And his life was bigger than that.

"So, it's been a morning, huh?" Her phone buzzed, and he looked at her pocket.

"Everybody and their brother seems to be reaching out this morning. I even had a company offer me a position, if I wasn't getting married." That email had been wild. The staffer had indicated that she could come on as soon as she liked.

We already have the press release written.

"Maybe you should take it."

Brie blinked; her mind was blanking on his response. He couldn't be serious. Yes, there were bad headlines, the image worse, but together they could fix it. Together.

"No." Brie was going to keep a calm head. She wasn't going to shout or scream or demand he take back that hopefully flippant statement. "We release a statement."

Her phone dinged again, and she grabbed it from her pocket. "Ophelia is texting every three minutes." Brie didn't plan to read the note, just silence the phone. But her eyes caught the words wedding in three weeks, followed by angry emojis.

She opened the text, read it, then looked at the man she loved. "Why is Ophelia asking if I am getting married in three weeks? She says the king reached out personally."

"Sebastian says that this is a scandal. That if lovers can visit the Ruins of Epiales and look as we did, then the island is cursed."

"That is a reach." However, given the headlines, she understood the king's concern. At least partly. It was why she'd been working all morning to find a solution.

Getting married in three weeks was not the solution.

"Well, since that isn't happening, what are we going to do?"

"I was born a prince."

No. His words pierced her soul. No. No. No. An *I* statement. When they were meant to be *we*.

"You are more than that. You are."

Alessio shook his head. "This is my thing, Brie." He gestured to the palace. "The role I play. There is no next for me."

"It doesn't have to be." Brie shook her head. "It can be part of it. But not all. We can figure this out. As a team."

"I read your comment." Alessio's words were soft, even, with almost no emotion to them.

"Words spoken the day of the lotto, before us." She'd meant them when she'd said them, but that didn't mean they were accurate today.

"So you are fine as the lotto bride? You want this?" He gestured to the palace.

That was a complicated question.

She looked at Alessio. She wanted him, wanted to be part of his next thing.

What's next?

She'd never considered that it wouldn't include her. She'd told him at the ruins that they made decisions. She got to have control. Her family had never allowed that, but Alessio had promised to make decisions with her.

"I want you."

"I am this." Alessio's smile was the formal one, the one he'd worn in so many interviews. The dutiful heir to the throne was standing before her.

"Are we a team?" They could weather this—as a team. They just had to choose a path together.

"I release you from the contract. I sent a note ahead of this discussion to a few news outlets, nothing fancy but just to beat Sebastian's press release of the wedding. I'll give a press conference in a few hours. I am giving you your freedom. You deserve it."

The words she craved hearing six weeks ago were knives to her soul now. "You released a statement? And organized a press conference, too."

Wow. He'd been busy. Her chest felt like it was caving in, like the air in the entire world had vanished. Stars danced in front of her eyes, but she was not going to crash—not here.

This wasn't a team discussion. He'd made the choices and she wasn't part of them. Just like her parents had decided everything. Alessio knew why she needed a say in the decisions. That didn't mean she wanted everything her way; there were always compromises. But she'd asked to be a teammate. A partner. And the most important choice—the one deciding her future—had been chosen for her. Again.

"All right." It was a chore just to get two syllables out. She could do a lot of things, but she couldn't be with a person who wouldn't even discuss such choices with her.

She looked at her hand, her ring finger empty. "I can't give

you back an engagement ring, since I never had one." A sob
pulled at the back of her throat, but she didn't let it out.

"So—" she stepped to him "—I'll just say that I hope you
get to be yourself. That you get what you really want. What
you truly deserve." She pressed her lips to his cheek. "Goodbye, Prince Alessio."

She turned and walked away, not sure where she was going.

"Brie." Alessio's call echoed at her back, but she didn't
turn around.

If she looked at him, she'd run to him, beg him to recon-
sider. And no woman wanted to beg a man to choose her.

CHAPTER THIRTEEN

ALESSIO STARED AT the smart board in the media room. Brie's block words outlining the plans, the expectations and how her marketing plan would benefit Celiana were all still in place. He'd held the eraser in his hands more times than he wanted to admit and hadn't erased a single word.

Her books, the coffee she liked, the way she'd arranged the pillows on the couch… He'd not changed a single thing. It was his homage to the woman he loved, the woman who deserved more than duty and a gilded cage. She deserved a world of choices, not select ones governed by security and history and duty and things that never seemed to be in a royal's control.

This was the life he'd been born to, the path he walked. He deserved this, not Brie.

"Alerting the press to your breakup was certainly one way to get around my suggestion of pushing the marriage up."

Suggestion.

Alessio let out a dark laugh. "It felt much more like an order."

His brother hadn't seen him in the last three days, though his presence was felt. He'd sent, or rather had his assistant send, Alessio's packed royal schedule to him every morning.

Alessio wasn't sure if Sebastian needed the help or was trying to distract him.

"It was." Sebastian's words were cool as he stepped beside him. "Imagine my surprise when my now oh-so-dutiful brother disobeyed."

"Since taking the crown you haven't been exactly the pinnacle of duty."

Alessio didn't feel like playing games. His duty was to the crown now, to his brother, but that didn't mean that Brie's life had to be that way.

The expectations, the sacrifices...

"I haven't." Sebastian sighed.

Alessio waited for him to expand on that, but instead his brother started toward the coffeepot and poured himself a cup. He took a deep sip, then returned his attention to Alessio.

"We did a one-eighty, you and I. The rebel king and dutiful returned heir."

"Do you have a point, Sebastian?"

"No." He crossed his arms. "But your former fiancée left her binder of ideas for the tourism board. Her company now takes the tourism board's phone calls whenever they have questions. The woman got right back to the work she loves. She is brilliant at it."

Alessio's soul wept for himself, but his heart soared. This was what he wanted for Brie. Her own life.

"She is brilliant." The words were barely audible, but Sebastian didn't press him.

"On to today's dealings. I have you slated to do an opening for the arts council tomorrow, and there is a board meeting for the tourism council this afternoon. Also, I was thinking of sending you as my representative to the UK for a state function at the end of the month. And there are two ribbon cuttings I need you to attend as the royal representative this evening—ribbon, not ideal, but the businesses didn't ask me. Still, we don't want anyone to think we are shirking the duties Father had."

Alessio didn't want to spend the rest of his life in council and board meetings, even for things he liked. He hadn't had a second to breathe while mourning the end of his engagement.

"No."

The word slipped out and Alessio waited for Sebastian to

argue. They didn't need to be King Cedric. Yes, some things were important, like the arts council. And someone should attend the state function, but they did not have to do everything King Cedric had.

His brother only tilted his head, a motion eerily like their father. "No to which part?"

"All of it." Alessio looked at the board with Brie's notes. Marketing was part of her, the thing that made her feel whole. "I mean, I can do some things, but I want my own life, too." That was something he should have realized when Brie asked him what was next.

Brie.

Her face floated in his mind. He needed her. And glasswork. Alessio didn't want half a life. He needed more.

Sebastian smiled. His brilliant grin spread across his face. "I was actually worried it was going to take at least three state trips, but I was prepared to sacrifice you." His brother clapped and looked around the room, his shoulders straightening.

"You don't owe the crown or the memory of our father a lifetime of sacrifice." Sebastian sighed. "The crown is mine and it is past time that I wore it fully."

"Sebastian—"

"Don't interrupt your king." He winked. "I am not our father. Your happiness, your choices, Brie's choices…they get to be yours. Your role is the one you decide."

"You couldn't have decided this before you ordered me to marry Brie immediately?" Alessio squeezed his brother's arm, color creeping up his cheeks.

"I'm still learning."

"You're going to wear the crown well."

His brother would find his way, and he'd be a good king.

"I'm getting there." Sebastian put his hands on Alessio's shoulders. "I release you. Not that I need to, but I do. From whatever role Father set for you. From whatever argument he had."

"Sebastian, we argued and then…"

"And then he had a stroke. I know." His brother held his gaze. "Or rather I suspected that was the reason you returned. But that was bad luck. If there was fault, it was his—not yours. He worked himself to death for the crown. You will always be my brother. But it's time that I took over the role I was raised to have."

He was his own person…if he wanted to be. A weight fell from his shoulders, and he looked at Sebastian.

"You kicking me out of the palace?"

"You will always be my brother. But yes, I am kicking you out. Find your path, Alessio."

Alessio looked at the smart board one more time, then at his brother. "Thank you."

He raced past him. There was only one place he wanted to be. Next to Briella—wherever that took him.

She was his next.

His last.

Brie looked at the art studio, and it was impossible not to think of Alessio. The tourism council had asked her to look at the place for an art exhibit and class space they thought they might be able to market. She'd nearly said no, but the proposal had taken over her plans for Celiana in the last week. Even adding to them.

Part of her hoped Alessio might be here. Such a foolish hope. The man was busy. It seemed he'd been at nearly every event since the press conference where he'd announced that their engagement was off.

The simple words had been given at a press conference that happened a few hours after she'd left the palace. He'd taken no questions, just thanked Brie for the time they'd spent together. He'd told the nation it was precious, and he'd hold it close for the rest of his life.

He'd said nothing else. So people had reached out to her. Her phone had rung off the hook for the first twenty-four hours. And she hadn't turned it off because she was hoping Alessio might call.

A foolish hope. She knew that, but the phone still buzzed at least once an hour and she still looked at it, hoping to see his name.

Instead, it was customers. Her marketing firm was booming. But she was taking on very few clients. Most of them were the nonprofit clients she'd planned to engage with as Princess Briella. She'd never sit in a fancy penthouse with that clientele. In fact, her business would likely only be a moderate success, if you only looked at the amount of coin it brought in.

It wasn't work that would make her family wish they hadn't thrown her away. But it was rewarding, more rewarding than just trying to prove she was more than the tossed-away Ailiono daughter. That was a label she hadn't realized she was fighting against until she relaunched her business. Like Alessio, she'd been chasing something she didn't actually want.

She loved marketing, but she'd proved herself to herself and that was all that was needed. At least the work kept her busy enough to only think of Alessio every other hour, instead of every minute.

She'd replayed the conversation after their visit to the ruins so many times. She'd thought of other ways to say she wanted him, wanted to be his next. Wanted to be a team.

When they were, they were unstoppable.

Hell, in her dream last night, she'd screamed "Choose us" when he'd told her to take the job. He'd done it, too. In her dream, he'd pulled her so close, held her tightly and told her they'd figure out everything together.

She'd woken in her small apartment and sobbed.

He'd sent her away, released her from the contract...without talking to her. That was the part that stung. But she also hadn't responded when he'd called her name.

She'd likely spend the rest of her life wondering if she should have turned around, told him she loved him, told him that she'd stand beside him at the press conference and set a wedding date. Not in three weeks, but in a few months. She should have offered him the chance to choose them.

Brie closed her eyes. She'd told him he needed to find something, but not offered her ideas. Not a great teammate there. She could have told him she thought he should focus on glasswork. If she could have a business outside the palace, so could he.

He could teach children or use it to encourage the arts. There were so many options, options she hadn't voiced because she wanted him to choose it himself.

What if I had? What if I'd asked why he was releasing me instead of just agreeing to what he thought I wanted?

Brie wiped tears from her cheeks. There was work to do. She had a lifetime to second-guess the choices she'd made with Alessio.

This building was out of the way for tourists. But locals could benefit from the classes. And a few artsy tourists might find their way here. She made several notes about brightening up the front of the building with a mural and flowers to make it more welcoming. Then she opened the front door.

Alessio stood in the middle of a large room. Boxes were strewed around the room and his furnace was already set up in the back corner.

"What—" Brie blinked as she looked at the large, nearly empty room and the prince. "I thought this was a marketing meeting."

"It is." His eyes found hers, and he started toward her. "Brie. I wasn't sure you'd answer if I called, but the tourism board said…" He let out a nervous chuckle. "This is my new studio."

Brie's hands moved to her chest. His new studio. She wanted to scream with joy and launch into his arms. But she kept her place. "It will be a perfect studio."

It felt like a lame statement, but all her other words seemed to have vanished now that he was in front of her.

Alessio pushed his hands in his pockets as he blew out a breath. "I had a whole speech, and it's flown from my brain.

So here's the main points. This is my next. And you are my next. You're my partner. I should have asked what you wanted instead of pushing you away. The palace was my prison for so long. I felt like I let my brother down by arguing with my father and that I deserved to stay. I didn't want you trapped with me. I wanted you to have the choices, but I didn't give you a say in those choices. I let my fear rule me, and I hurt you."

"You should've let me choose my path." Brie reached for his hand. "I never felt trapped when I was with you."

"I love you, Brie." He shook his head. "We are a team, period. If you still want to be. I am stepping back from my role with the palace but not away completely. There may be times we don't get to make all the choices, if Sebastian really needs—"

The world brightened. The pain in her chest, the ache in her heart, vanished as she stood before him.

"Shush." Brie put her finger on his lips. "I love you, too. But I let my fear of being controlled like I was at home rule me. Life means some choices are out of our hands. I should have pushed back the other day. I should have turned when you called instead of running. Us, us is what I choose. Even knowing there may be times when some choices are out of our control."

He closed the distance between them but still didn't reach for her. "I want you to be my wife. Meet me at the altar. As Brie and Alessio, nothing else."

He slipped to one knee and pulled a ring box from his pocket. "Marry me, Brie. Not for Celiana or tourists or anyone else. Just for me and you."

The ruby sparkled in the light.

"I love you. Yes!"

He pulled the ring from the box and slid it on her finger. A perfect fit.

EPILOGUE

ALESSIO LOOKED AT the twin-flame glass design. It was even more perfect than the image that refused to leave his brain for the last week. He'd made this in his mind so many times, shifting the glass design, but now that it was real, now that it was here…

"Alessio?" Brie called before she walked into the studio. The back half of the warehouse he'd proposed to her in was his studio, but the front was her office space. It was perfection.

He felt like he had in Scotland—like himself. Except even better than that, because he wasn't alone.

"I have a meeting to look over the marketing for the non-profit you set up, and Ophelia wants—" She stopped, her eyes falling on the glass.

Bright blue flames wrapped up through green flames.

"Alessio." Brie's blue eyes, the exact color of the blue flames, caught his. "That is…"

"Us."

"Us." Brie pulled up her phone and quickly tapped something out before looking back at his art.

"Our teamwork." Alessio stepped beside her. "Two flames, burning brightly on their own, but wrapped together, something magical." He kissed the top of her head.

"We are pretty perfect together." Brie leaned her head against his shoulder. Her hand reached out, touching the glass. "Emilio will want to see this."

"He'll want to put it in his gallery. It might fetch a decent price."

"It's priceless." Brie shook her head, turning in his arms. "And not for sale. It will be on display in *our* home." She brushed her lips against his.

Alessio deepened the kiss, pulling her tightly. "If you want to go see Ophelia, Princess, you need to pull back now."

Her eyes flashed with pure desire, and Alessio's heart exploded with the knowledge that Brie was his. Nothing in life would ever be more perfect than her by his side.

"That was Ophelia I was texting. Letting her know I'll be late." Her lips captured his.

"I love you." He breathed the words against her neck.

"I'm the luckiest woman in the world."

Brie's giggles echoed through his workshop. He was the lucky one. In a glass ball of hundreds of slips, he'd pulled the name of his soulmate. One lucky slip that led to her. Alessio wouldn't change anything.

* * * * *

How To Tame A King

MILLS & BOON

For Doreen.

Congrats on your retirement. Enjoy this next stage!

CHAPTER ONE

BREANNA GALANIS WAS glad she hadn't shared her doubts about her identical twin sister Anastasia's room design as she looked at the striped accent wall blurring into bright colors. It was striking. Not at all the gaudy image her mind had conjured when Annie had described it. Her sister's talent was wasted in the high walls of the Galanis family compound.

"This is gorgeous." Breanna clapped.

"I told you." Annie snapped a few pictures with her phone, then pulled the professional camera hanging around her neck to her eye. Her finger clicked over and over.

"You did." She wasn't sure their parents would approve, but then, she didn't know the last time they'd approved of anything the twins did. That didn't stop their mother from showing off the new designs to her friends.

They all assumed she'd found a hot new designer—and each had begged for their name. Her mother had refused to say it was Anastasia. Whether it was to make her friends jealous that she had access to something they craved or because she didn't want them to find out about Annie's gift, Breanna didn't know.

Probably both. Image mattered, after all. More than anything else in her parents' orbit.

Galanis women married well. They didn't have careers. Their job was to host parties, be armpieces and proof of the lavish wealth others coveted. In other words, showpieces in designer clothes, worn once and tossed away.

Aristocrats without titles—according to her father.

The view was outdated. After all, they were well into the twenty-first century. Breanna had wanted to run from their parents' control for years. She had her degree in early childhood education. She loved children, and would have been in the profession for years now if her parents hadn't intervened at every place she'd interviewed. She was also a skilled seamstress who thrifted and upcycled clothes, despite her parents' disgust of the "trade." She could sell clothes, teach classes, and Annie could open a design studio. Their life would be simple compared to the extravagant wealth they'd grown up with, but their lives would finally be theirs.

Anastasia wanted more of a plan. More concrete proof they'd be all right. She wanted a full portfolio of room decor designs before they left. So far, she'd remodeled ten rooms in the mansion, plus her and Breanna's bedrooms. This was the fourth "final" room.

"It's perfect." Breanna bit her lip, then forced her shoulders back. "And it's the last one, right?"

They could make a go of it. They just had to take the first step.

Annie's hands shook, and she lowered the camera. The happiness drained from her body as she looked at the colorful walls around her. Her gaze focused everywhere but on Breanna. "I was looking at my portfolio this morning. I don't have a kitchen yet."

"Annie…"

"I know. I know I said this was the last one. But we will have nothing. Mother and Father will cut us off completely. You tried to get a teaching position years ago. Father blocked it. He *will* do it again." Her voice caught, and she pinched her eyes closed. "People will balk at hiring me too, but design work… I can run my own business. Give us some income."

"I have my sewing. They can't take that. They can't control everything." Breanna said it with more certainty than she felt. What was the price of freedom?

"And we won't be alone. We'll have each other." Breanna was the younger sister by all of two minutes, but she'd always protected Anastasia. Annie was the one with the big dreams. The one who had plans...if she'd only start down the path.

Breanna was the extra. The interchangeable twin who asked too many questions but never pushed too far. Hell, she'd even accepted it when her parents gave large donations to the institutions she'd applied to not to hire her.

Breanna was determined that Annie got to have dreams outside the compound. She was too talented to stay. Too talented to only be someone's wife. Love, if it really existed, was wonderful—at least according to the storybooks.

Her parents treated their union like a chess game. A winner and loser, constantly making moves and trying to stay at least three steps ahead of each other. A winner and a loser and two daughters who looked identical for them to trade for the best offer.

Unless they left. "Annie—a kitchen?"

"Is a necessity in any portfolio. I have everything else. I should have seen it."

Breanna tilted her head and raised a brow. Annie had studied portfolios for months when coming up with the brilliant plan to ready her portfolio under her parents' careful watch.

Getting them to agree to redo their kitchen would be a lot of work. And a kitchen renovation...it would add months to the plan. Maybe even a year. They'd gotten lucky at Prince Alessio's Princess Lottery last year.

Prince Alessio had spent a year raising money for the arts by funding a princess lottery—with the prize to be his wife. Each week the price of the ticket had increased. The total cost for a year's entry was well over ten thousand pounds. Annie and Breanna were the only participants with a year's worth of entries. Statistically, one of their names should have popped out. Yet the universe had chosen another and given Prince Alessio and his new wife, Princess Brie, a happily-ever-after.

That kind of luck wouldn't last. Their parents would try again to find them a title. They needed to leave.

"Annie—we can—"

The door opened, and the twins snapped to attention as their father walked in. He was smiling. No. Their father routinely walked into rooms already halfway through an argument, but right now he was beaming. Glowing even. Whatever he was about to say would be bad news—for them.

It made her skin crawl. Lucas Galanis did not beam. His smiles were calculated to win a business deal. Whatever calculation he'd made, he planned to win today. Which meant she and Annie lost.

"Guess what, Anastasia?" The peppy words sounded congratulatory, but the authoritarian tone he used wasn't hidden. Her sister hated the use of her full name, but only Breanna ever called her Annie.

It wouldn't be hard for their parents to adopt the nickname, but in the Galanis family, everything was tinged with power. Annie preferred her nickname; therefore, the most powerful members of the family would refuse to use it.

Annie rocked a little and lowered her head. "What?"

"You're going to be the queen." His words were wrong. They had to be.

King Sebastian wasn't even looking for a bride. Though the press seemed to think every woman in his orbit was his future queen. One woman had even taken a job overseas just to stop the press from hounding her after an image of Sebastian smiling at her during a dinner function went viral.

The man was simply living his life. Except, *nothing to see here* did not sell ad space. Since Prince Alessio and Brie's happy union, the crown had been dull.

Sebastian had had a brief rebellious streak following his father's death. But most of those headlines were drowned out by Alessio's bride lottery. And the rebel Sebastian, whoever he'd been, had disappeared months ago. In his stead was the prince, turned king, she'd followed all her life.

The man was stoic. If the dictionary needed a picture of *duty* beside it, they could use King Sebastian. He never missed a meeting. Never stepped out of place at an event.

And never smiled.

"I can't be queen." Annie's words were barely a whisper, but their father heard them.

His smile slipped into the sneer Breanna knew so well. "King Sebastian chose you."

"He doesn't know her." Breanna's fingernails dug into her palms. There had to be a way out of this.

But if the king wanted one of them... The heat of the warm evening evaporated. Cold seeped through her body as she tried to piece together any plan. Breanna worked the system that was their family better than Annie. But in the chess game of her family, her father was the grand master.

Which was why all she had were *plans* to leave. Fancy ideas. A small bank account for a few months' rent. Thoughts. Discussion points. All of which were good. Until your bluff was called.

They needed to stand firm. The moment was here, and they had to rise to the occasion.

Now. Or never.

"He doesn't need to know her." What a sad, flippant statement. How could their father treat marriage, a lifelong commitment, supposedly, with so little concern? This was Annie's life.

But their parents didn't care about their daughters' lives. According to them, they'd been blessed with two identical beauties to give them access to a world that hadn't wanted them. Being rich beyond anyone's wildest dreams should have been enough. But Lucas and Matilda Galanis wanted titles. If they couldn't have them, then their daughters would.

Breanna looked to Annie, but her sister wouldn't meet her gaze. Her palm ached, but Breanna pressed on. She couldn't lose this round to her father. "He is marrying her. He needs to know her. To love…"

Red patches bloomed on her father's cheeks. She'd gone too far, but stopping wasn't an option. Not this time.

"Love is a childish game that gets you nowhere."

"Prince Alessio loves Princess Brie." Annie's head didn't lift as she pushed a tear away. At least she'd said something.

Their father's scoff carried in the beautiful room. "That isn't real. It's a media game. And even if it is real, what has he gotten from it? Outcast to a glass shop?"

Breanna personally thought Alessio and his "lotto bride," as everyone had initially called her, looked happier than ever. All the pictures were of them laughing or looking at each other like no one else's opinions mattered. Like the headlines that ran about them in the early days calling Brie all sorts of names were beneath their love.

Maybe that was staged, but it looked like Alessio had gotten freedom.

And it wasn't like they were thrown out of the royal family. Far from it, in fact. Alessio still regularly attended events. Brie was a constant presence on the tourism boards. He just had a life outside of the palace. A life of his own.

Something King Sebastian and his queen would never have.

Annie drew a deep breath, and Breanna knew what the resignation on her soft features meant. No. No. No.

The discussion of the room's design seemed so long ago now. In a place far away. The dream was floating away. It would be out of reach if Annie acquiesced.

"I'll do it." Breanna's voice was stronger than she expected. Stronger than she felt.

"Breanna."

She didn't look at Annie. If she did, she might let the tears pushing against her eyes fall. That could not happen. Breanna protected Annie. That was her role. She would not fail now that it truly mattered.

"If he doesn't need to know Anastasia, then he doesn't need to know me." Annie still had a chance for her dreams. She could make this happen, and if Breanna was queen, she could protect her twin.

As queen, she could ensure Annie's safety.

Their father tilted his head, weighing his options. A weird feeling as his daughter, but not the first time Breanna had stood under his hard gaze. "You are basically interchangeable."

She would not flinch. It was not the first time he'd looked at them as one person split into two bodies. Not the first time their parents boasted a "two for the price of one" statement.

"King Sebastian did not indicate he cared which of you met him at the altar. It's not like we can tell you apart anyways."

Really selling this, Father.

"Breanna. No."

"I had picked out a different spouse for you, Breanna." Her father's gaze shifted to Annie. "A lesser title, but…" Lucas considered his daughters his possessions, objects to be bartered for his own goals.

A future marriage partner had never been discussed. No consultations with the potential bride. Not in this family. She was only still under this roof because Annie was terrified of what leaving meant.

"But that union is not available until his divorce is finalized next year. So…"

So Annie has a year. A year to get out.

She could help in the lead-up to the royal wedding…and figure out how to get herself out of this predicament, too. She had at least a year, right? It wasn't like royal weddings happened fast.

Her father shrugged; one daughter for another hardly mattered. The outcome was the same. "Ready for me to meet the king?"

Breanna needed to move. Needed to get the next part over with before she lost the burst of courage. She walked over to Annie, pulling her close.

"I love you. This has to be the last room."

Her sister squeezed her tighter than ever. "I love you."

Her arms were lead as she dropped them and pulled away. "Time to meet a king."

King Sebastian wasn't surprised to see the guard hovering by the door. The security on the Galanis estate rivaled the palace's. At least his guards were better at remaining unobtrusive.

This level of security felt more like they were keeping him in, rather than guarding. He had no intention of running. After all, he was here for a bride.

One that wanted to be a queen.

And this house held two such women. The Galanis family had not been quiet regarding the twins' plans to marry into a title. It was rumored no one was even considered a viable match unless they were at least a viscount.

Anastasia and Breanna Galanis were the only two who'd had a year's worth of entries in his brother's princess lottery. More than twenty-six thousand pounds had been spent between them for a chance at the title.

They'd walked away unhappy that day, but today Anastasia would become a queen.

Anastasia…the name he'd drawn out of a hat this morning.

It seemed somehow poetic that Sebastian had given his brother, Prince Alessio, so much grief for his bridal lottery. In fact, on the day he'd pulled Brie's name from the lottery, Sebastian had urged him to cancel the charade.

That charade had turned tourism around, reinvigorated the local economy, and most importantly, resulted in true love for Alessio and Brie. Sebastian was under no illusion that today's twist of fate would grant him happiness.

He thought he'd found love once. Samantha, a woman chosen for him by his father. Beautiful, educated, the perfect queen. His father had planned to make the announcement of their union. Then a stroke had rendered him unconscious for weeks, before finally claiming his life.

He and Samantha had bonded during that stressful time. Hiding their growing affection away from the prying lights of the media. He'd selfishly let his brother and his lotto bride take all the heat to protect the woman he loved.

And then the illusion shattered. Sam refused to understand why the crown was so heavy. She'd wanted it…desperately. Not him.

The same was true for his new bride-to-be, but at least he was under no illusions this time. With no expectations of happily-ever-after for Sebastian.

He was the king. King—the only thing anyone saw. Hell, the moment his father died, the staff at his bedside had called the time of death. Then turned and bowed to him.

Only in death was the power of the title vanquished. The title his father had served with every waking breath—just passed to another. A fate he'd had no part in choosing and no way to break.

Celiana's throne held little more than ceremonial power, but every poll in the last decade showed that the vast majority of the population wanted to maintain their monarchy. His people wanted a king. A head of state that didn't rotate out like the politicians. A constant in a world of chaos.

And the poll was worthless anyway. There was nothing in the country's constitution or laws that allowed for abolishment of the crown. He'd spent a year looking, devastation seeping in when the truth hit him. If Sebastian stepped aside, Alessio would be crowned.

And with Alessio happily married, the pressure for marriage had been focused on him. Journalists, bloggers and random strangers hoped every woman he waved to or said hello to was his secret intended. One woman had fled the island after a photographer captured an innocent smile at a dinner outing. A simple interaction he couldn't recall the next day but that had altered her life forever.

Then a few weeks ago, he'd gone out for a stroll very early one morning, his guards at a close but not too close distance. A female jogger had raised her hand to him.

Someone had caught the interaction and uploaded it with sensational commentary that didn't match the moment. Social media had swiftly identified the single mother. It was like hounds descending on a target with no clue. It was cruel and unwarranted, and nothing he said seemed to make anyone listen.

At least after today those rumors would disappear.

He'd been raised to serve. This was what was expected of him. His and Anastasia's children would be next in line. But they'd know what was coming. Hopefully, he could find a way to prepare them better.

With time, he and Anastasia would become friends. That relationship had worked for his parents. Maybe not a great love, but peace in giving the kingdom the stability its residents craved was its own reward.

Wasn't it?

The door opened, and a striking young woman walked in.

Brown curls falling to her shoulders. A blue dress custom-fit to her hips. Soft caramel eyes that looked him over with more than a hint of hesitation.

"Anastasia." He bowed. This wasn't the way one planned to meet a forever partner. Except it was in many aristocratic circles. Luckily, the Galanis twins had been trained since birth to expect this.

"I'm Breanna." She let out a soft sigh, then curtseyed. "Your Highness."

"Breanna?" He cleared his throat. "I—I…" There was no diplomatic way to ask why she was here instead of Anastasia.

"I am to be your bride." She didn't lift her head, and she didn't elaborate.

There was no script for this. "I asked for Anastasia."

"Why?" Breanna lifted her head, the caramel eyes catching his gaze. A few freckles dotted her nose.

She was gorgeous. Fierce. Challenging a king within moments of agreeing she was to meet him at the altar.

"Why?"

"That is what I asked. Why Annie?"

Sebastian shrugged. "You both had a full year's worth of entries in the bridal lottery."

"For Prince Alessio." Breanna clenched her fists, and her stance wavered for just a moment, but she didn't break eye contact.

Not for you.

The words were unstated, but they echoed in the room. The pinch of pain that brought was not to be acknowledged. Alessio was the fun one. The one who got to have a life…and love. The one who broke the rules. The one allowed to break the rules.

Most of his childhood he'd spent annoyed that Alessio refused to follow the rules. That he questioned the life they'd been brought up in. Part of him was probably jealous that his brother had choices—not many—but more than Sebastian.

Then Alessio had stepped in for him when he'd fallen apart after the crown landed on his head. The bond they should have had as brothers growing up finally solidified. Better late than never. He would not subject Alessio to the crown, or any woman who didn't want it.

Anastasia and Breanna had wanted it a year ago. And she wanted it enough now to switch places with the woman he'd asked for.

"I promise a queen's crown is far prettier." He leaned a little closer, hoping his smile looked convincing. The press was waiting. This was the only plan he had.

The deep brown eyes ignored the comment on the crown, and she crossed her arms, then looked to the door and uncrossed them. "You still haven't told me why you chose Annie."

"I pulled her name out of a hat."

Silence hung in the room for a moment before Breanna hugged her stomach and let out a chuckle that soon turned into a belly laugh. "A hat. A hat. Our lives decided by what you plucked from a hat. What if you'd pulled a rabbit out, Your Highness? Would a bunny have met you at the altar?"

She wiped a tear from her cheek, but the laughs continued.

He couldn't help it. His own chuckle combined with hers. "If I'd pulled out a rabbit, I would have been honor-bound to at least offer it the crown. Luckily for Anastasia, or I guess you, I didn't pull a rabbit."

Breanna's laughs died abruptly. "Right. Lucky for me."

The tilt of her lips was perfect. Just enough teeth showing for a believable smile, but there was something about it that sent a knife through his heart. "If Anastasia would rather…"

"I won the crown, Your Highness. Fair and square."

Won. The air in the room shifted on those three little letters. Won. He was a prize. Nothing more. The Galanis twins wanted titles; everyone knew that. And she was getting the top one.

As she straightened her shoulders, the brief flash of pity, the question that maybe this was a misstep, disappeared. If Breanna wanted the crown more than Anastasia, then that was fine with him. Hopefully she wouldn't resent its weight too much after a few years.

"Your father was kind enough to let me use his office for a press conference. There are selected media there, and we will also broadcast the announcement of the engagement live."

"Now?" Breanna clutched her neck, a hint of pink creeping along it. "Press conference, now?"

"Yes. No time like the present. This is a marriage of convenience, after all. You get a crown. The country gets a queen. Everyone walks away happy."

Except me.

"And you get?" Breanna raised her brow, the challenge clear in her eyes.

If he believed in soulmates, he might get excited that it felt like she'd read his mind. Someone to share more than just the duty of it all. But wishing for love wouldn't make it appear. He was the king of Celiana. Nothing more.

"A partner to help me run Celiana." That was the truth. Most of it. He also got the press off his back and peace from constant rumors.

"Alessio and Brie love each other." Breanna swallowed, but she didn't break her gaze.

Another thing this union brought him. A way to crush the tiniest bit of hope that maybe he too could find love. That lightning could strike twice for the royal family of Celiana. But lightning wouldn't strike twice. He was the king. And this was his duty.

"They do. Which is good. Celiana has its royal love story. It doesn't need another."

"And what we need doesn't matter?" Breanna turned her head, her eyes widening as her father stepped into the room.

Lucas Galanis looked at his daughter, and his expression made Sebastian instinctively step closer to Breanna. He didn't touch her, but the urge to wrap an arm around her waist pulled at him. She was looking at her past, and he was her future. But he would not take an unwilling partner to the altar.

"If you do not want this—"

"Then Anastasia will be happy to meet King Sebastian at the altar." Her father didn't look at him. Some silent communication was seeping through the room.

This time he didn't hesitate. He wrapped an around her waist, surprised and pleased when she leaned into him.

"No. I am the choice. Not Annie." Breanna stepped out of his arms but pulled his hand into hers.

It was warm. Soft. A connection he wanted to lean into. Foolish dream, but at least they looked like a united front for the press. "Ready, Breanna?"

She didn't answer, but Lucas opened the door, and nodded to Sebastian—a far from friendly smile on his face. "After the royal couple." He bowed low, but somehow it felt almost mocking.

They started down the hall, her father a few steps in front of them. What was he supposed to say? What was the small talk etiquette of walking with your future bride less than ten minutes after you met her to announce a wedding? He'd had a lifetime of protocol training, and no one had covered this.

The buzz in the room was evident fifteen steps before they hit the door. The room was ready for whatever announcement was to come. Whether he and Breanna were was an irrelevant question.

He squeezed her hand as her father opened the door. Flashes of light hit them followed by a cacophony of questions. He'd promised them a statement, and the palace had said he would be taking no questions, but that didn't stop the determined lot from flinging them at the couple as he and Breanna stepped onto the podium.

"Good afternoon. I appreciate your patience as you waited for my bride and me." His fate... Breanna's fate...sealed in a single sentence.

The crowd seemed to lurch forward, and a wall of questions flooded them.

Sebastian raised a hand, the room quieting nearly instantly. "On Saturday, I will marry Breanna Galanis at the county offices at ten a.m. This will be a small affair, like many of the weddings our people have. We will hold a reception after at the palace for close family and friends. As I know many of our citizens are currently struggling with inflation and the cost of living, the amount that would have been spent on the royal wedding will be divided evenly between Celiana's food banks, and local shelters that help the unhoused find affordable housing."

He took a deep breath. "Breanna and I look forward to many years together in service to Celiana. Thank you."

Sebastian raised his free hand, very aware that he was fast losing feeling in the hand Breanna had a death grip on. He walked them both through the door they'd entered and back to the room where they'd met.

"Saturday. We are getting married on Saturday? How?"

"You already have a dress, the one you wore at the lottery result. You will move into the palace with me tonight. We will do the minimal planning we need to. Start the process of getting to know each other, and then we will marry on Saturday."

"Oh, just like that. Right. Of course." The laughter escaping her throat was nearly manic.

"If you're having second thoughts..." He wasn't sure where he was going with that statement. After all, the announcement was made. They were marrying.

"No. I just wasn't planning to pack tonight." She balled

her hands into fists and rocked on her heels. "So many things to put away."

That was an easy fix. Her father had ordered Anastasia's room packed up as soon as King Sebastian had arrived. The Galanis servants and the royal staff who'd traveled with him had certainly shifted the moment he'd learned it was Breanna who would be wearing the crown.

Given the efficiency of the team he'd brought, it was likely nearly done.

"My team started packing as soon as I arrived. I suspect most of the boxes are already loaded into the van. They are very good at their job."

"I'm sure they are." Breanna looked around the room, then nodded. "So, we get married."

Sebastian nodded, too. "We get married."

In three days.

CHAPTER TWO

THE ALARM'S INSULTING tone rocked the quiet room. Breanna reached for her phone, the shrill noise mocking the idea that she'd somehow found any rest after Sebastian showed her to her suite.

Between the exhaustion and brain fog following the announcement of their wedding, Breanna wasn't even sure of the path she'd taken to get here. She vaguely recalled something about him "fetching" her this morning. He'd probably even given her a time, but her brain hadn't absorbed the information.

Nope. All it knew was she was in the palace and marrying the king.

This weekend! How was this her life?

Her phone buzzed, the image of her sister popping up on the screen.

"Annie." Breanna sat up in bed, pushing her curls back. "Are you okay?"

That was one good thing. At least it was her in the palace. Not Annie. Their father hadn't won that round.

So why does it still feel like checkmate?

"I'm the one that should be asking that." Annie let out a soft cry. "Are you okay, Breanna?"

There was no good answer. She was dealing. That was probably the best she could manage. Particularly considering she didn't have a year to get out of this. Less than seventy-two hours stood between her and the throne.

"I'm handling it." Breanna sucked in a deep breath. "Now you."

"Not as well." She could picture Annie biting her lip on the other end of the phone, her eyes watering as she tried to sound brave for her twin. "Did they pack my portfolio in your boxes?"

Her portfolio.

My team started packing as soon as I arrived.

Sebastian had chosen Annie's name. They'd started packing up her sister's rooms. The portfolio she'd created. Their pathway out. Annie's pathway out.

It wasn't in Breanna's boxes. Because there were no boxes. Her room had been set up during her and Sebastian's dinner.

Breanna didn't remember any of the conversation. Maybe there hadn't been any. But when he deposited her at the door, she'd opened it to find the room exactly like hers at home, minus the cozy green walls Annie had chosen for her.

The laid-back beach house theme Annie selected was out of place against the royal ruby-red wall, but her bamboo chair was hanging from the ceiling. The houseplants she kept over her window were on the wire hanger she'd hung them from at home. The staff must have pulled it from the walls.

Even her sewing machine with the piece she'd been working on was set up in the corner of the room. The stitches not out of place at all. It was like her life had been picked up and moved across town.

Nothing to see here, just a complete change…and a wedding. Her chest tightened, but panicking was not going to do her any good.

The portfolio wasn't here. She was certain.

"Was your room tossed and messy?" She rubbed her free hand on her arm, trying to find some way to drive away the chill running through her. If the portfolio wasn't in Annie's room…if it was gone…

"No." Annie let out a sob. "I know they started packing, but they immediately stopped when you took my place. Everything is where it should be but the portfolio. I had it under my bed. The box it was in is there and empty."

Mother.

The woman was calculating. And she'd been conspicuously absent from the rest of the debacle with her daughters. A fact that was just now registering in Breanna's brain.

While their father was overseeing the announcement, she'd probably handled the packing. Going through their things. Recognizing that the hidden portfolio could only mean one thing.

"You need to leave, Annie." Her voice was strong. This had to happen now. Annie didn't have a year. Not if her parents considered her a flight risk. They had one soon-to-be-titled daughter, but two was better—at least to them.

"I can't. We will have less than nothing now. Without a portfolio, no one will employ me. And you as the former fiancée of..." Her sister's words died away, but Breanna could piece them together.

As the former fiancée of the king, no one would employ her either. They'd start from nothing. Less than nothing. Breanna might be willing to give it a go, but Annie wouldn't.

Her sister was the obedient first child. The one who never created waves. The one who bent and followed, even when it broke her spirit. Annie rarely said more than yes to her parents, hazarding a no only when she was sure that there'd be limited consequences.

To save her sister, there was only one choice.

Breanna looked around the room. Her room. Her forever. "And I am to be queen. So, you don't need our parents. You can redecorate the palace. Starting with my suite." She wasn't sure how to make that happen, but as queen, there had to be some perks, right?

"Breanna—"

"Leave, Annie. They can't come after the queen."

The queen. A marriage of convenience. There were worse situations. She'd never worry that her husband only wanted her because she was a Galanis.

She'd know forever that Sebastian hadn't plucked her name from a hat. She'd demanded the crown—and he'd decided she was good enough.

Story of her life. The second-born twin. The extra. The interchangeable bonus her parents got to use to their advantage.

The good news was it had trained to her to make the most of every bad situation. This was no different, and there were far worse situations to find yourself in.

Annie would get her dream. The one thing Breanna had always wanted was her sister's happiness. Annie's safety. And this was the best way to guarantee it.

She could be happy here. Or happy enough. It was all just a matter of mindset.

"Breanna."

"That's Queen Breanna to you." She giggled. It wasn't really funny. Or maybe it was. This was the universe's version of a joke. A pathetic one. But she'd make the most of it.

"Breanna…"

"I have a savings account. I started it years ago. There is more than enough in it for a few months' rental on a small apartment and some furniture. Pack, Annie. Promise me. I will send you the money as soon as you tell me you're gone."

"It's starting from nothing." Annie took a deep breath. "Nothing."

"Not nothing. Those are Father's words. Words designed to scare us. You are the sister of the queen."

A pause hung over the line. She wanted to pull the words out of her sister. But this had to be Annie's choice. Her decision. *Please.*

"You're right. Whatever is next has to be better than whatever this is. It has to be." Her sister said the final words more to herself than to Breanna.

Breanna looked at the ruby walls, so at odds with her tastes. Annie was leaving. It wasn't the way they'd planned, and they weren't together, but Annie would be safe. And in a few years, she'd be the country's top interior designer. Of that Breanna had no doubt.

"I'll send you a text."

"Great." Breanna's breaths were coming fast and hard, but hopefully her twin wouldn't hear the panic pushing all around her. "And as soon as you are a little settled, I need my room repainted. It's red. Ruby. Very royal."

"And very too much." Annie giggled. "Laughter, is that a good sign or a bad one? This is too much, Breanna."

It was. But they were on this path now. For better or worse. "Everything will be okay." Breanna said the words she always uttered when her sister was focused on the world falling apart.

"Or it won't." Annie let out her part of the phrase. "Those are the only two options."

"I choose." This was her choice. She was choosing Annie. "I am hanging up now. Pack and send me a text." Breanna swallowed the tears threatening. "I love you."

"Love you, too."

Then her sister was gone.

If she stood still, she'd give in to the wallow. The tears would flow, and she wouldn't be able to hold them back.

Walking into the suite next to her room, she looked at the overstuffed chairs and couch. Who would she host in here? No one.

"This is going to be my sewing room." Breanna put her hands on her hips, pretending this was a project that she wanted, rather than one forced upon her. Her twin was safe. Annie got her dreams. That was all that mattered.

* * *

The noises coming from the future queen's suite could be heard down the hallway. "What on earth is she doing?"

Away from the Galanis estate, Breanna had shut down. Whatever show she'd put on for the cameras had evaporated in private. He wasn't sure she even remembered the words he'd said on the ride to the palace. She'd sat through dinner, picking at the food, giving one-or two-word answers to everything.

The strong woman he'd met at the estate had wanted to be queen. The one across from him at dinner... He was less sure what this Breanna wanted.

She needed rest, and a good night's sleep. Sebastian had taken her to a suite not far from his. Technically the queen's quarters were connected to his, but his mother had never stayed in them.

His parents' relationship was one of cordial friendship, bound by respect. They'd done their duty with an heir and a spare. Put on a lovely show for the kingdom that made it appear they were ever so in love. In the palace, though, they'd lived separate lives.

Putting his soon-to-be wife in the queen's quarters felt like a step too far. And he'd already taken so many.

Standing at her door last night, he'd promised her that he'd pick her up today at nine, and they'd talk about next steps. If she was still in shock... Sebastian knew he'd offer her a way out. He wanted a willing queen. If she was having second thoughts, well, he'd cross that bridge when he had to.

He knocked, then opened the door to her suite. Sebastian stopped, his hand on the door handle as his mouth fell open.

Most of the furniture was gone. There was still a small couch and an overstuffed chair that he didn't recognize. The rest of the suite now looked like a fabric store.

"What...?"

"Good morning, Your Highness." Breanna turned, her

smile brighter than anything he'd seen yesterday. She looked happy. Ecstatic.

The perfect picture of a woman delighted to be in the palace. Good.

Her soft gaze held his. She was wearing what looking like old blue jeans and a flannel shirt, and her hair was pinned up in a polka-dot headscarf. Breanna was relaxed and busy.

And she was gorgeous.

"Good morning." He needed to say something else, but his mind seemed incapable of forming words.

Breanna tilted her head, then shrugged. "I hope you'd don't mind. But I figured I'd make this my sewing room. Give my bedroom a little more space."

"It's your suite." Sebastian cleared his throat. "I am glad the staff was directed to your sewing room." He'd given directions to make sure her room was packed and immediately unpacked. As little interruption to her life as possible.

There was already going to be so much change.

"I've never had a sewing room." Breanna crossed her arms, her eyes sparkling as they looked from the sewing machine in the corner to the cutting table in the center of the room.

Sebastian laughed. "Did you have a whole floor sewing suite? The palace is smaller than your estate, but there is plenty of room." If sewing made her happy, they'd clear all the space she wanted. Wearing the crown had some perks, after all.

Though he doubted she'd have a ton of free time for her hobby. A royal life was duty, meetings, events and then more duty.

"No, Your Highness."

"Sebastian. We are going to wed, after all." It was weird that moments ago he'd considered finding a way to grant her her freedom. But she'd been here less than twenty-four hours and was already redecorating. If she was happy to be queen, then he was content. Last night was simply overwhelming.

Understandable.

"Sebastian." Breanna hesitated for a moment. "Feels weird calling you Sebastian. Maybe after we've been married for a while."

"So, you didn't have a whole sewing floor? Was it more?" The Galanis compound could certainly hold more.

A small chuckle fell from her pink lips. "No, Sebastian." She tilted her head, like she was trying out his name for a second time. "I did not have a sewing room or a sewing floor or anything else. I had my room, which was large, but this—" she gestured to the craft table "—took up most of my free space."

There was more to that story. So much more. The way she parsed her words, weighing them. It was a strategy he recognized. One he'd used.

"I always assumed the Galanis twins would have their own palatial floors. To do with as they pleased. Any toy or hobby. Anything you chose."

Even a crown.

A curl slipped from her headscarf as she turned her attention to a yard of fabric. "You are the king, and before that you were the heir to the throne. Do you have a wing to do whatever you want with?"

There was something in her tone. A feeling of shared experience. A kindred spirit.

The Galanis twins were given the best of everything. Their parents' wealth granted access to places that were unimpressed by crowns. They were able to do anything they wanted.

And yet, neither had branched out from the family compound. Chosen their own path. They'd waited.

It had worked. She was to be a queen.

The thought cut him. She was getting a crown. That was worth holding out for...at least to some.

She placed a yard of fabric on a frame of some type. "Did you have a wing for your favorite activity?"

"Kings don't have times for hobbies." It was a line his father had stated more than once when journalists asked what he liked to do when he wasn't performing a royal duty. It wasn't a lie either. King Cedric had never had a hobby.

He'd given everything to crown and country. That didn't leave much for anyone else.

"That is not true, Your—Sebastian." Breanna put her hands on her hips. The action was protective, and her pink lips were set in such a way it seemed she wanted to battle.

For me.

"You are allowed a hobby, Sebastian." She reached for his hand, squeezing it.

Her skin was fire, and he craved the heat. When she dropped his hand a moment later, ice flooded his system.

Control.

No one did battle for Sebastian. He had a role. A duty. And he played the cards he was dealt.

Played them well. His body went through the motions even during the year his heart had rebelled. But Breanna smelled so sweet. Like cinnamon, apples, and allspice. And the way she looked at him made him want to believe in fairy tales.

Mentally he pulled that intrusive thought from his brain. It was just the hectic last couple of days. His heart refusing to fully accept what his mind already knew. This was a marriage of convenience between strangers.

She got a crown. He got a queen. Nothing more.

"I thought we should talk about our marriage. The union. The contract you signed for the princess lottery was a marriage contract. I had the lawyers look through it." They needed to discuss things other than hobbies. Or rather his lack of them. He woke early, worked until late, then repeated the process. That was all. Wishing for something different wouldn't bring changes. He knew his role.

"Lawyers. Right. I assume that means I've agreed to two

children and my full participation in the royal family until I die. After all, there is no divorce in the Celiana royal family. Some ancient law no one wants to overturn." Breanna walked back to her sewing table and started laying pattern pieces over the garment.

"I remember the words I signed. My degree may be in early childhood education, but one does not grow up a Galanis without knowing some legalese." She repositioned the pattern pieces.

He wasn't sure she was really seeing the pieces, or maybe this was all part of the process.

"That is the general agreement. Yes."

"So, you are here to talk about the heir part or the dutiful queen part?" She didn't stumble over the words. Said like they were nothing.

"The producing of an heir is part of the duty of a king and queen. An heir and a spare."

"No." Her curls bounced as she shot up. "No child of mine will be called a spare. Period. They are individuals. So, strike that word from your vocabulary, Your Highness."

Fire blazed in her dark eyes, and he nearly fell to his feet. He'd never been called a spare, but he knew the word had haunted his brother. The fact that Breanna was protective of their hypothetical children was the best sign he could think of.

"Consider it struck."

Her shoulders fell, and she bent over her table. He stepped beside her, rubbing her back. "Did you expect me to fight this?"

"Yes." Breanna stood, her body so close to his.

Emotions he hadn't let himself feel since his breakdown flooded his system. He wanted to laugh, to reach for her and bring out the chuckles he'd heard yesterday. Make her smile.

"I want my children to experience more than Alessio and I did. They deserve more."

"You do, too." Her hand brushed against his cheek.

The urge to lean into her, to say how much he hated the crown, was nearly overwhelming. But it wouldn't solve anything.

"We can conceive via IVF. The contract is for the marriage union, but you do not need to worry about sharing my bed." There were at least a dozen better ways to word that.

Breanna lowered her eyes and her hand dropped. "I see. Good to know."

"Breanna..."

A knock came, and his assistant stepped in before he could say anything else. A blessing since he had no idea what to say, and a curse given the tightening of her fists. At least one of the future queen's emotional tells was easy.

"Your Highness, Miss Galanis..." Raul bowed and then handed Sebastian a tablet. The bright words *Queen Bree!* radiated from the screen.

The headline was designed to draw attention to the similarities between Princess Briella and his Breanna. Briella and Alessio had an epic love story. The stuff of fairy tales.

And the exact opposite of this.

"Do you like the name Bree?"

"No." She stuck her tongue out, her nose scrunching as she shook her head.

So that was a definite no. They'd need to shut the press's nicknames down quickly. Once something stuck, it rarely unstuck.

"The press is likening you to Briella and the princess lottery."

"Princess Brie." Breanna cleared her throat. "I guess our names and situations being similar makes this a natural association. I mean, they don't know you pulled my sister's name out of a hat rather than the glass bowl your brother used for his wife. However, I do not like the nickname. I have always been Breanna."

"This isn't the same. Alessio and Brie love each other." They cared for each other. To each other they were everything. The whole world. If Alessio lost his title tomorrow, Brie would still love him.

Sam had confirmed what his father always said. Sebastian, without the crown, was nothing. Without the title, he had no place in this world. Everything about him revolved around a position he'd done nothing to earn.

"They didn't when he pulled her name from the glass bowl." Breanna tapped on the screen, making the text easier to read. "Looks like people enjoy your small wedding idea."

Shifting the topic was good. What was there to say? Neither expected the same to happen for them. "It makes a good statement. Makes us seem more regular when others have lost much in the last few years." The words felt off.

He wanted to acknowledge that many in the island nation were still suffering from the economic downturn. But the idea of having a giant celebration for such a union was unsavory. This was duty. Partnership. To spend Celiana's funds on such a thing would be unfair to the citizens.

"Royals caring. Always a good public relations call." Breanna stuck her hands in her pockets and rocked backwards. "So, umm... I don't think you just wanted to show us this." She paused. "Sorry, I don't think we've been introduced."

"Raul, my lady. The king's personal assistant." Raul bowed his head and held out his hand for the tablet. Once he had it, he tapped out several commands. "I wanted to go over a few things for the wedding. We got a list of your likes from your parents, but just checking. You want a bouquet of daisies and sunflowers?"

Breanna started to roll her eyes, then seemed to catch herself. "Only if you want me to sniff all the way down the aisle. Is there an aisle at the magistrate's? Or is it just a hallway?"

She shook her head. "Not the point. Focus, Breanna."

"Nice to know I am not the only one who talks to myself." Sebastian winked, wanting to overcome the negative feelings his early comments must have caused.

"A hard habit to break." Some of the tension leaked from her shoulders as she looked at him. "I am allergic to those. My parents tend to forget that Annie and I aren't exactly interchangeable. I am allergic to flowers; she can't get stung by bees. Anyways, I tolerate hydrangeas."

Interchangeable? They were identical in looks but still two different people. He couldn't focus on that now, though.

"Tolerate?" Sebastian shook his head. "No." She was marrying a stranger. The least he could do was give her flowers that didn't make her nose itch. "What flower can you be around easily?"

"Define *easily*." She looked at her feet, a hint of pink tracing her chin. "I can do ferns and pothos. I keep those in my room, but they aren't exactly royal wedding bouquet material."

Ferns and pothos. He knew the first. The second...surely a florist could figure something out?

"It's fine. It's not like I have to carry the bouquet for long. I can make do."

Make do. Words he was so familiar with. His whole life was concessions. Hers was now, too. Flowers for her bouquet were a choice that could be all hers.

"What about succulents?" Sebastian remembered seeing a beautiful design when Brie and Alessio were planning their union. Brie went with bright flowers for her bouquet, but the succulent option was stunning.

"Succulents? I mean, sure. I can also do cacti...they each have about the same amount of pollen. As close to zero as possible."

"Succulent bouquets are a thing. So, let's do that. Cacti would be a unique choice, but a little too prickly." Sebastian pointed to the tablet, happy when Raul picked up his cue to search for bouquet images. "Imagine the headlines if you carried cacti."

"Prickly queen! Touchy!" Her giggle was good, but those were just a few of the things the press might say.

He took the tablet and moved closer to her. She stepped closer, too. Not touching, but close. If this were a real relationship, he could put an arm around her. Instead, he swiped, showing off the different online options, watching her closely to see if any sparked her interest.

Breanna grabbed his hand as a small bouquet caught her eye. Her finger wrapped around his for an instant before she pulled back and cleared her throat. "These are pretty; let's do that."

Had she meant to touch him? Had she wanted more? Questions there was no easy way to ask a stranger, particularly in company.

"Anything else we should know?" Raul was poised, ready to take down any details.

Breanna seemed to purposefully step away from him. "I don't eat meat, and am not a huge fan of chocolate. Other than that, I am pretty easygoing. Promise."

"So, the steak and chocolate cake need to be canceled, too." Raul looked to Sebastian, the condemnation of her parents clear in his face.

Sebastian felt the same. This was not a traditional union, but Breanna deserved to make her own choices. "How about we go over everything and choose for ourselves?"

Breanna's shoulders relaxed, and she started to lean towards him before catching herself. "Thank you."

CHAPTER THREE

"YOU CAN STILL end this. You do not have to do this."

"I seem to remember saying something along the same lines, brother. You still pulled Brie's name out of the crystal bowl you made. It worked out." Sebastian didn't expect love for himself and Breanna. But they got along well enough, and she wanted the crown. This would be fine.

He straightened his tie for the hundredth time. "Why won't this damn tie stay where I put it?"

"Because you keep pulling at it." Alessio crossed his arms and looked towards the door, probably hoping that his wife, Brie, would make an appearance.

"Brie is with Breanna. She isn't going to come in here. It's royal custom for the princess to attend to the queen-to-be." Sebastian said the words with more conviction than he felt. He wasn't at all certain that Princess Brie would adhere to custom.

And it wouldn't be the worst thing if his sister-in-law arrived. Alessio could use the princess's calming effect. Though knowing Brie, she would have far more to say about today than his brother.

Alessio stalked to the mirror, pushing Sebastian's hands away from his tie. "Nothing about this is custom." His brother straightened the tie, then grabbed Sebastian's hands and pushed them into his pockets.

"Don't touch it!"

Sebastian wanted to pull his hands from his pockets on principle, but the tie was finally straight. "I think most of this actually is custom. I am just being honest about it. The fairy-tale stuff? The romance of royal unions—well, with present company excluded—we both know what it's really like."

"You can have more." Alessio threw his hands up, reaching for his own tie. "You deserve more. Just because you are the king. Sebastian—"

"Careful not to mess your tie." It was a pathetic joke, but what else was he supposed to say? Alessio got lucky.

Jealousy was pointless. He was genuinely happy for his brother. Brie was his match. But wanting it for himself wouldn't make it happen.

He was the king. That was all he was to almost everyone. Sure, his brother saw a different version, but the kingdom... even his own mother...saw only the crown.

The year he'd rebelled, he'd caused so much grief for Alessio. The fact that his brother had handled it perfectly didn't matter. Alessio had saved the kingdom. His and Brie's lottery had turned everything around. They deserved the happily-ever-after.

But Alessio should never have been put in that position. Sebastian had been raised for this role; he should have accepted it right away.

The frustration on his brother's face made it clear that Alessio had far more to add to this conversation. "Sebast—"

A knock echoed through the room, interrupting Alessio's next attempt. "Saved by the bell...or knock." He winked at his brother before walking over to the door. Sebastian pulled it open with flair, then stood there, not sure what to say.

Breanna was dressed in a floor-length white gown. The mermaid cut hugged her in all the right places. The scalloped top accentuated the swell of her breasts. Her dark hair was loose, curls wrapping her beautiful features, and her makeup looked natural. It was like she'd stepped from the pages of a bridal magazine.

In a few hours, she'd be his queen.

"Breanna."

"Well, hell." She crossed her arms, then looked around him and waved at Alessio. "Your wife was right, he's not in a tux."

"Umm…" Sebastian looked at his suit and waited for his brain to find any kind of statement. It was an afternoon wedding. At the magistrate's. A tux seemed out of place, but if she wanted him dressed in one, he had multiple.

Breanna hitched up her train and nodded to the interior. "Can I come in?"

"Isn't there a superstition about the groom seeing the bride in her dress before the wedding?" Sebastian wanted to reel the words back in as Breanna's face fell.

The hurt vanished in a flash. She shrugged and moved past him. "I think that curse only applies to those who aren't marrying out of duty."

Alessio made a noise and then started for the door. "I'll give you two a minute."

"No." Breanna held up a hand. "Brie said you should stay for this part."

This part?

His brother halted by the door. If Brie told him to stay, even through an intermediary, he'd do it. Until whatever *this part* was concluded.

"You are in a day suit. A lovely one. You're very attractive." A delicate rose coated her cheeks.

"I mean, you look nice. The suit. The suit looks nice." Breanna cleared her throat. "Wow. There really is no playbook for confronting the stranger you are marrying."

"Maybe we can write one." Sebastian playfully stroked his chin, trying to make his bride smile. *"No Big Life Decisions: Marrying a King in Three Days or Less."*

She tilted her head, "We need to workshop the title."

"Sure." Sebastian stuffed his hands in his pockets. "While we think of better titles, what is the problem with my suit?"

"I am in *this*." She frowned as she looked down at the exquisite gown, her fingers rustling over the beaded top.

"You look lovely." Such an understatement. Breanna sparkled as the light hit the jewels hand-sewn over the intricate gown.

"That is one of Ophelia's gowns, is it not? An original?" Sebastian knew most of the women from the princess lottery had rented their dresses. But the Galanis twins' gowns were specially made. With a year's worth of entries, the identical twins stood front and center as the odds of Alessio pulling out their names was high.

The twins were the focus of most of the early images on the day of the lottery, their bright, fancy dresses plastered everywhere. Commentators had discussed how their dresses even matched each other as Alessio drew the name, but he couldn't remember anyone saying if they looked upset not to hear their names.

"Yes. My and Annie's dresses were the most expensive gowns Ophelia has ever made."

"The price hardly matters." He doubted the price tag, even for two wedding dresses, had made a dent in the Galanis fortune.

"Except it does. People will talk." Breanna shook her head. "It is too fancy for this. Particularly with you dressed that way. The Galanis family upstaging the king."

The headline practically wrote itself.

"You want me to change?" He pointed to his closet. "My wardrobe is yours. Whatever you choose, I will put on. I have several tuxes." They weren't his first choice, but if that was what she chose, he'd put it on with a smile. "We can toss this offending day suit back in the depths where it belongs."

Breanna took a deep breath, her face softening. "You're very handsome, and the suit is lovely—as I said."

As compliments went, it was a tiny one. But coming from Breanna's sweet lips, it felt like he'd won a prize. "Handsome." He struck a pose, enjoying the giggle she let slip out.

She snapped her fingers. "Focus. This isn't the first time you've been told you're handsome."

"My future wife saying it feels different." He meant it. He didn't know why it made his insides gooey, but it did.

Breanna raised an eyebrow but didn't add anything else to that conversation. Instead, she pointed to her gown again.

"I can't wear this dress." Breanna took a deep breath. "We are having a small wedding. One similar to regular people, right?"

"Yes." Sebastian looked to Alessio, who'd remained painfully quiet during this exchange. But if his brother understood the issue, he wasn't giving anything away. Instead, he was looking at Breanna, a smile pulling at the corner of his lips. "I thought, given the cost of living crisis, smaller is better."

"Right. And this dress cost more than fifteen thousand pounds." Breanna sighed. "That is not a good look for that message, Your Highness."

He didn't like how the exasperated "Your Highness" fell from her lips.

"Breanna…"

She looked at the crystals lining the bodice. "I know you picked my name, or rather Annie's, because we had a dress, but this won't work."

What was the answer? They were heading to the magistrate's office in less than two hours. But she was right. If the cost leaked, and it would, the public relations team would be dealing with a nightmare.

"Do you have a plan to solve the issue?" Alessio had asked the right question. The one that should have popped from his mouth minutes ago.

Sebastian looked to Breanna, and nodded, hoping she had an idea.

"I have a dress. It's white—mostly. I made it from a dress I found at a thrift store a few years ago. It's simple, and I think it is the better choice. But if *you* want this…"

She had a simple gown. One she'd made. It wasn't exactly what people thought of when they imagined a royal wedding.

Though what about this was?

Breanna waited, then turned to Alessio. "Do you think I'm wrong?"

"No. And let me guess, Brie agrees with you." Alessio looked at his watch. "Brie's pretty good at estimating the press's response."

His fiancée's smile wasn't forced when Alessio mentioned his wife. Breanna sparkled, and it had nothing to do with the fancy dress. "She does. The princess is very kind."

"She is." Alessio nodded. "Do you need anything else from me?"

"No." Breanna shook her head, "You're free to go."

"Dismissed by the queen." Alessio bowed to the queen. This his gaze focused on Sebastian. "I like her." Then he was gone.

Sebastian had said the same thing about Brie to Alessio.

"Nothing about this is standard, but I figured you chose a couture gown for the lottery, and you won't get to wear it again." There was a law in place that kept the king and queen from divorcing. An ancient crusty script from a bygone era that parliament had never overruled.

The lyrical notes of her chuckle made him smile.

"I hate this dress. I didn't choose it. Mother did." She reached for his hands, then pulled back.

Mother did.

The words stuck in his head. That wasn't right. Breanna and Anastasia wanted titles. Everyone knew that. The press had followed their journeys for the princess lottery nearly as closely as they'd followed Alessio. A look inside the day of royal hopefuls.

Only after Briella's name bounced out did the Galanis twins' names fade from the press.

She wanted this. *But what if...*

"There was something else I wanted..." She looked at her feet, then straightened. "Kiss me." Breanna let out a nervous sound. "Wow, I probably could have stated that differently. Or maybe not at all, but too late now, so, yeah. We'll go with that. I want you to kiss me."

Her dark eyes flitted to the door, and color crept along her neck. "Breanna?" Kissing her wouldn't be hard. The woman was the definition of beauty. But her nervousness gave him pause.

"Have you ever kissed anyone?" The twins were waiting for a title, but surely she'd dated. She must have had suitors lined up around the family compound.

"Nope." Breanna bit her lip and let out a ragged breath. "I—I—I need to say something other than *I*, but my brain is overloaded."

Sebastian took her hand; the connection was firm but loose enough that if she wanted to pull back, it would take no effort. He was thrilled when she didn't. "Do you trust me?"

"I should say no. That is what makes sense."

Once more his soon-to-be bride was right. They were practically strangers, but he felt an odd sense of calm right now. Nerves should be popping; he should be fidgeting, but the only thing weighing on him was how to make this moment special for her.

"I trust you." She bit her lip, again. "Today is a lot, but I trust you. I do. Guess I am practicing for the vows." Her soft smile warmed his heart. "I do."

The phrase seemed to unlock part of his soul. The words

were sustenance on this day where everything felt more than a little surreal.

Using his free hand, he stroked her lip, pulling it from her teeth. "You are safe here." *With me.*

Yes, they were marrying. But he was not going to force anything on Breanna. They'd get to know each other. Learn to coexist and care for each other. It would take time, but she was safe. Always.

"Close your eyes." The words were barely above a whisper, but she did as he said.

A person only got one first kiss. Usually, it was fumbling and more than a little off as teens in the heady days of hormones figured out what the racing feelings meant. That was not the experience Breanna was going to get. But he could still make it memorable.

He squeezed her hand, trying to push as much reassurance through the touch as possible. "Breathe, honey." Sebastian let his free hand stroke her cheek.

Fire danced on the tips of his fingers. This was about Breanna. Giving her a memory. Still, his breath was picking up, and desire seemed to pulse on each breath.

Breanna.

So much of his life was out of his control. Even the woman before him wasn't his choice. But in this moment, it felt like the universe was granting something just for him.

"Sebastian."

His name. Just his name. Not his title, nothing else, fell from her sweet lips.

Finally, he pressed his lips to hers. He'd envisioned a short, nearly chaste kiss. A memory given to her, enjoyed by him.

Instead, the universe exploded. Breanna leaned into him, and his arms went around her waist without another thought, her hands wrapping around his neck.

Apples, lemons, sweetness divine filled his nostrils as his

soon-to-be wife's body fit against his. Time, space and everything in between vanished as he drank her in.

Then her mouth opened, and the taste of her nearly brought him to his knees. If the afterlife contained a paradise, the feeling of Breanna in his arms, lips pressed to his, would be the ultimate achievement possible.

"You cannot possibly wear that." Breanna's mother never raised her voice, but her tone right now was as close to hysterical as she could remember. "Your little hobby is cute when it is contained at home. But this is your wedding day. To the king."

"As though you wouldn't know what today is or who you are marrying." Princess Brie laughed and held up the champagne goblet. Her bright blue eyes sparkled as she met Breanna's gaze. "You are gorgeous."

Brie was saying all the things Breanna wanted to say to her parents but without a hint of bile or anger. Yet the daggers found purchase each time. The princess had skillfully put her mother in her place over and over again without ever raising her voice or getting testy. She was poised, confident and so sure that what she said would have the exact response she intended.

This was why Brie had broken from her powerful family. Started her own business. Created a name for herself. Even after marrying a prince, the patriarch and matriarch of the Alessio clan still didn't acknowledge the daughter, who outshone them all.

It was that willingness to take a leap that led Brie to carving her own path, while Breanna had made plans. But never followed through. Sure, she'd protected Annie, but she was still marrying a king she didn't know in less than an hour.

Sebastian. His name cascaded through her mind. Her hand reflexively found her lips where the ghost of the kiss remained.

Maybe first kisses were always like that. Maybe your body

felt like singing each time. It wasn't like she'd had any experience with it.

The boy she'd fancied at uni had stood her up for their first date. Later, she'd heard through the rumor mill that her father had paid the man quite handsomely to forget she existed. Whether it was true or not, and she suspected it was, all the men who'd asked her out afterwards seemed to be hoping they might also get the same fat check.

Life as a Galanis was privileged in many ways...but it did not come with freedom.

She hadn't expected his lips to feel so soft, so sweet, so refreshing. Kissing Sebastian felt like taking a sip from a fresh stream. Her body had nearly collapsed with want and need.

She'd pressed herself against him, lengthening the exchange. Desperate for another.

Focus!

Annie's hand pressed into hers, grounding her.

"I think she looks beautiful." Her sister cleared her throat, then continued, "That dress is gorgeous and looks nothing like the original dress you bought."

Her sister made a face. "It was hideous. I thought there was no way you could make it anything."

"I've thought that about your room ideas, too." Breanna pulled her sister close.

"You both have far too much faith in your abilities."

Annie straightened her shoulders, then looked at her mother. A week ago, those sharpened words would have bowed her spirit. Instead, she shrugged and twirled a finger through the curl by her cheek.

It was the only thing Matilda Galanis had said to Annie, and it was clear she wanted Annie to respond. Good for Annie that she was rewarding her mother with the same indifference she'd shown her.

The Galanis Trust had made it known that Annie was not

under their protection, and she'd been cut off. Which meant renting an apartment had been nearly impossible.

The only one they'd found was in a neighborhood people did their best to avoid. But the price was right, and the landlord had been willing to rent it on a month-by-month basis.

Breanna could have asked Sebastian for aid. But Annie had begged her not to. She claimed she'd needed to do as much of this on her own as possible. Breanna hadn't wanted to steal away any of her newfound confidence.

Breanna squeezed Annie's hand, then examined herself in the floor-length mirror. The dress was a vintage wedding gown she'd found at a local thrift store. The bottom had been stained, so Breanna cut it off, making this a tea-length gown. She'd added a crochet-like overlay, giving it a semiformal look. It was pretty, and handmade. It hung on her perfectly.

If she'd had a choice in the dresses she was allowed to pick for the princess lottery, she'd have chosen something like this. Light. Airy.

It didn't scream queen attire. Her mother was right about that. But it was perfect for her.

The sounds of the square's bell ringing echoed in the room. Time to go. Annie stepped to her side and kissed her cheek.

"You don't have to do this." Her sister's words were nearly silent, but the plea under them echoed into the universe.

Breanna put her hand on her sister's cheek. If she didn't there'd be no way for them to get Annie back up on her feet. Not for years...if ever. Her sister had goals and a plan, and the soon-to-be queen could protect her better than she'd ever hoped for. "I know."

Then she looked at her mother and Princess Briella. "I think that ringing is the sign that we are supposed to head to the magistrate's office." She'd not fumbled a single word. Pride and worry raced for first place in her mind.

Now, if I can manage not to stumble over my vows.

* * *

"You all right?" Sebastian's hand slid around her waist as she stood at the corner of the reception area. It was a light afternoon affair. Finger sandwiches, fruit, and for dessert, her favorite, lemon cake. It might be a normal reception. Except they were in the palace.

And a small gold crown was pinned to the top of her hair.

What a day. She started to lean into him, then pulled herself upright. He was her husband, checking on her. But they were still virtually strangers.

"Fine." The lie was easier than the truth. And it had nothing to do with the small crown Sebastian had placed on her head after she'd said *I do*.

No. Once more in her life, the upset was caused by the people who'd raised her. Or at least paid for the host of rotating nannies she and Annie loved and lost in their childhood.

Nothing about the day was right for them. The dress. The location. And now the reception.

They'd expected a huge party. Despite the press conference clearly outlining the fact that they were having a simple reception for close friends and family, they'd expected palace glamour. They'd wanted a queen for a daughter...but only if they could flash it to the world.

"This might as well be a pauper's reception. Where is the steak?" Her father's complaint carried across the room, and most of the heads turned in his direction.

Breanna started towards him, grateful that Sebastian moved with her.

"It's an afternoon reception, father." Breanna kept her voice low, hoping he might do the same.

Lucas Galanis got what he wanted. On the few occasions he didn't, hell tended to spill from its gates.

"Cucumber sandwiches, carrot and raisin sandwiches?

It's positively ghastly." Her mother huffed as she looked at the fare on her plate.

"There is smoked salmon, too." Breanna was a vegetarian. It was something she'd adopted after watching an online video when she was a teenager. Her father had called it a phase. A decade later, "the phase" was still intact. It infuriated him.

"And lemon cake," Sebastian offered, squeezing her side.

She'd never had anyone stand next to her while she tried to calm her parents. Annie had always avoided conflict.

Then she looked at her husband and felt her head snap back a bit. His eyes were boring into her father's. Fury matching her father's radiated in her husband's gaze.

Over what?

"Lemon cake." Her mother sniffed.

Sebastian's hand tightened on her waist.

Without thinking, she put her hand around his waist. They were a united front.

"Yes. Lemon cake." Sebastian's words were ice spikes, but neither of her parents appeared to pick up on the cool tones. "*Breanna's* favorite." The world seemed to shift, and the pressure on her chest evaporated. He was here. Choosing her side. Choosing Breanna. No one ever chose her.

Her mother let out a soft chuckle. "Chocolate is what *we* ordered."

Ordered. Like today was theirs. Their accomplishment. Their achievement. Not an irreversible life-changing moment for their daughter.

Before she could say anything, Sebastian offered, "It's *her* wedding day."

Her day. Hers. Such a simple statement that rocked her world. She leaned her head against his shoulder, enjoying having a partner for this exchange.

His lips brushed the top of her head, and she saw her mother's eyes narrow. They really didn't care if their daughter was happy. Maybe they didn't want that.

"Yes. But *we* are the ones that wanted to be here. Breanna didn't want the crown—" Her father looked at Sebastian, keeping his head tilted just enough for the king.

"Father—"

"He needs us, Breanna." He cut her off. "The country is a constitutional monarchy. They have no real power. He showed up on our doorstep for a bride, and we provided one."

And yet you wanted a daughter to wear the crown.

"Breanna, do you want your parents here?"

The soft question nearly made her laugh. Want her parents here? Of course not. She never wanted her parents around, but they were her parents.

Sending them away wasn't an option. Or it hadn't been before Sebastian put a crown on her head. "No?"

She hadn't really meant to say it as a question. It felt rebellious. Far more rebellious than anything else she'd ever done.

And liberating.

"Lovely. My wife, *your queen*, and I bid you farewell." Sebastian nodded towards the door. "Don't make me call the guard. In this palace, my word is final."

"Breanna, you don't mean to let him send us away." Her mother stepped towards her, but Breanna stepped back. Sebastian moved with her in unison.

"Where is Annie's portfolio?" It wasn't the answer to her mother's question, but Matilda Galanis was a smart woman. She knew the underlying question.

Her mother's eyes flitted to Annie, currently laughing with Prince Alessio and Princess Briella. She looked to her husband, then shrugged. "What portfolio?"

The lie was too much. Her mother knew what she meant. If the portfolio hadn't been burned, then it had been locked away. It didn't matter. The result was the same.

"Have a nice day." Breanna nodded to her parents, then turned attention to Sebastian. "Shall we dance?" A DJ had been quietly playing tunes, but no one had ventured onto the dance floor.

"Is that what you want?" Sebastian's gaze followed her parents' exit, then refocused on her.

No one, other than Annie, had ever asked her what she wanted. She was light. Happy. And she wanted to enjoy the moment.

"Yes. Let's dance!" She grabbed her husband's hand, trying to pretend that the king hadn't just kicked her parents out of their wedding reception. That this was just a fun afternoon get-together. The illusion would clear when Annie, Alessio and Brie all left. But until she was left alone with Sebastian—in the palace—Breanna could try to forget that she'd said *I do* to a king today.

A king. And a stranger.

Breanna hit her hip against his as the music bounced around them. His bride had kicked her shoes off five songs ago. Brie and Annie had followed suit. Only his mother still had her shoes on.

The dowager queen would leave her shoes on even if her toes were bleeding. But at least his mother was smiling. She'd even discreetly given him a thumbs-up when he'd told Breanna's parents to leave.

The fast song shifted to a slow tune. Briella and Alessio immediately went into each other's arms. A few other couples did the same while some of the singles exited the dance floor.

His wife stood still; her jeweled gaze watched him closely. Should he reach for her? They were married, but the fast dances let them be close without holding each other.

Did she want to dance in his arms? She'd put her arm around his when he was kicking her parents out. He'd kissed the top of her head, unable to resist. Breanna has pulled him onto the dance floor, but she hadn't touched him other than hip bumps and the occasional high-five since. And much of the dancing was in groups.

He was never more than a few inches from her. If she moved, he moved with her. And she'd done the same. He wanted to pull her close, hold her, but the day was already so much. They were husband and wife, but in title only.

The chords twanged on, and Breanna cleared her throat. "I am going to get a drink." She dipped her head to him, her eyes shielded.

Make a decision, Sebastian!

"I'll come with you."

Breanna nodded as she moved off the dance floor. There was nothing different in her posture, but he knew he'd hurt her feelings. It wasn't his intent, but the outcome was the same.

"Breanna." He said her name without knowing where he was going next. "Did you want to dance?"

"We've been dancing." His wife touched the crown he'd placed on her head after they'd said *I do*. "Your mother pinned this in perfectly. It hasn't moved with all the motion. She'll have to teach me how to do that."

"I am sure she'd be happy to." Sebastian grabbed two lemon drop mocktails, handed one to his wife and sipped his. The sugar on the rim blended with the tartness, but it didn't cut any of the awkwardness hovering between them now as they stood silently drinking the festive beverage.

The ease they'd had bouncing to the rhythms on the floor had evaporated. He wanted it back.

The slow song stopped, but the couples on the dance floor clung to each other for several moments after the final chords echoed. At most weddings, the bride and groom were center-stage.

But this wasn't a traditional reception in any sense of the

word, and the couples staring at each other with love were not the bride and groom.

His eyes again went to Alessio and Brie. They were whispering to each other as they moved to a beat no one else heard. No doubt saying the sweet nothings those in love spoke so easily. He looked to Breanna and barely caught the sigh in his throat.

A fast song kicked in. Good. They could get back on the dance floor.

"Breanna!" Brie bounced towards her sister-in-law. "This one is just for the girls." The princess stole the queen into the center of the floor with a host of giggles.

"Why did you stand there when your bride was looking at you, waiting for you to ask her to dance?" His mother's voice was quiet, but it carried an authority that made his back a little straighter.

The dowager queen looked at the dance floor. Her eyes rested on the queen and princess. "She wanted to dance with you. She is your wife."

"I froze." Sebastian finished the last of his drink. There was no use calling it anything else. The day was one for the record books. He was married to a woman whose parents insinuated she hadn't wanted the crown he'd thought she craved. It was enough to throw anyone off their game.

"Breanna wants you to show her how you pinned the crown so well. It hasn't moved." It was a bad segue but easier than anything else.

His mother sniffed but didn't offer anything else on that topic. "You will dance with her the next time a slow song comes on. Brie bought you a few minutes."

"Wha...?" He turned to see and caught Alessio's eyes as he waved to him from where he stood next to the DJ stand.

"He's helping you." His mother patted his arm. "He wants you and your queen to be happy."

"Do you think we can be?" He regretted the words as soon as they were out.

His mother looked to the dance floor again. "Happiness is much to ask for in a royal marriage. Contentedness. Maybe that will be in your reach."

Contentedness.

Was that what she and his father had had? Contentedness. Was that enough?

It would have to be.

The slow song began, and Alessio collected his wife. Sebastian started for the dance floor and met Breanna at the edge of it.

"May I have this dance?"

She looked over her shoulder, her eye following Alessio and Brie's rotations on the floor. Then she reached for his hand and squeezed it. "Only if you actually want it."

Of course his bride knew this wasn't by chance.

Not dropping her hand, he pulled her onto the dance floor and into his arms. "I very much do."

She slid her arms around his waist, gently swaying with him on the floor. After a moment she laid her head against his shoulder.

He breathed her in, holding her tight. Enjoying the moment a little too much.

"It's been a day." The whispered words were so soft he wasn't sure she'd meant to say them out loud.

His fingers stroked her back, and she melted against him a little more. They weren't so much dancing as holding on to each other as the storm of the day finally broke.

It didn't matter. They were together. Day one of a lifetime.

"We made it through the reception." She chuckled, "And our first family drama."

They had.

"What's next, Sebastian?"

"Next?" He looked over his shoulder at his mother, holding mini court with a few friends. She missed his father, but if he were still here, they would have stood near each other but never danced together. Two people who cared for each other but did not have a deep passion.

Two strangers who'd married.

Then his gaze fell on Brie and Alessio. They were holding each other, talking quietly, and laughing at a private joke. Two strangers who'd fallen desperately in love. A lightning strike.

Looking away brought more peace than it should. His brother and sister-in-law were happy. "We get to know each other." He smiled at his bride, seeing the uncertainty in her gaze. He and Breanna would be content. It would be enough.

It had to be.

CHAPTER FOUR

SEBASTIAN DOWNED THE cup of coffee, then poured himself another. He and Breanna had danced for hours last night. His legs burned with the memory of the exercise. But it was his heart that had kept him awake all night.

She'd held him tight through their final slow dance. Knowing the reception was nearly over. Today began the real story. Their life as king and queen.

But we are the ones who wanted to be here.

Her parents' words kept replaying in his mind. That couldn't be right. Breanna had won the crown from her sister. She'd wanted it more.

I think that curse only applies to those who aren't marrying out of duty.

So many phrases were burned into his brain from yesterday. As was the feel of her body against his. The soft scent of cinnamon apples in her hair seemed attached to his nose. Her downcast eyes as she'd quietly said I do in the magistrate's office.

The brush of her lips on his.

So many emotions to work through before the day had really even begun.

"I do hope you haven't drunk all the coffee." Breanna's voice was bright. No dark circles shadowed her eyes. She looked well-rested.

His mind couldn't seem to align the words her parents had

thrown at him yesterday and the bubbly woman pouring her own cup of coffee beside him.

"Not to complain, but is there any coffee syrup hiding anywhere?" Breanna looked to the cabinets like she was considering opening them but holding back.

"Not in this kitchen." Sebastian pulled up his phone, ready to text her order to the staff. The fact that she hadn't asked for syrup when she first arrived was frustrating. But she was asking now. "What do you want?"

"This kitchen? So how many kitchens are there?" Breanna went to the fridge, found some milk, poured it in, and then added more sugar than he'd ever seen someone put in such a small cup.

"Several." Take Breanna on a tour of the palace...today's task. "This is my, *our*, private kitchen. There isn't staff for this one, but it's always stocked with what I—we—want. I just need to know what that is."

"Do you cook?" Breanna slid onto one of the high stools.

"Yes, when I have time." Sebastian took a deep breath because part of him wanted to shake the phone in her face and demand the answer to the question he'd asked and she'd now dodged several times.

"What syrups do you like, Breanna?"

"It's no big deal." Breanna put her elbows on the counter, then rested her chin in her hands. It was adorable and infuriating at the same time. "So, what do you like to cook? Eggs? I swear that is what the movies always show. The man makes the girl scrambled eggs in the morning and everyone swoons—he can cook."

"I will answer that question when you tell me what syrups you want stocked in here. If you don't tell me, then I will have the staff order one of everything."

She laughed and gestured to the kitchen. "This kitchen is huge, and I still don't think you could fit one of everything."

"I guess we get to see then." Sebastian started typing.

Her hands were warm as they wrapped around his wrist. "It's not a big deal, Sebastian. And its early. Don't disturb the staff on my behalf, please."

Tears hovered in her eyes. "Please."

He set the phone down and walked to her without thinking of the next steps. Sebastian pulled her into his arms. She was still sitting on the stool, and her head barely came to his shoulder. "It's coffee syrup, Breanna. It's not earth-shattering, but it's something you want, so I will put in the order this afternoon. You will have it tomorrow."

She nodded against him and sniffed. "This is silly. I don't know why syrup is sending so many emotions through me."

It wasn't syrup. It was everything else coming through something that didn't matter in the universe's grand scheme. He'd had similar breakdowns when the crown got too heavy. Worrying over something minor was easier than addressing the elephant in the room.

"A lot has happened in four days." That was an understatement. He stroked her back, then leaned his head against hers.

No words. Just two people who fate had tossed together. He kissed the top of her head and took a breath. If the wedding orders her parents put in were any indications, the Galanis twins weren't allowed their own choices. But she could have them now. "What kinds of syrups, Breanna?"

"Your comment on filling the room isn't that far off. I love syrups, vanilla, mocha, chai, white chocolate, brown sugar cinnamon, seasonal favorites like pumpkin, peppermint, lavender."

"I know pumpkin and peppermint, but lavender?"

"More an add-in for tea. It's easiest to find in spring." She pulled back.

His arms ached to reach for her. To hold her again. To wipe away the hurt she hid too quickly in her eyes.

"Brown sugar cinnamon and chai are my favorites."

Then those would be here tomorrow. And a few others. He'd let the staff know to add a different new one each time a bottle was empty. That way she'd eventually have a nice stock without feeling like everything appeared all at once.

"All right. Was that so hard?"

"No." Breanna reached for the coffee mug.

"I have something for you." Sebastian had meant to wrap it, but the little box sitting on the cabinet would drive most of her days.

Breanna grinned. "A present?"

Yes. And no. "I thought this might come in handy." He pushed the box towards her.

"Handy. Interesting wording from a king." Breanna opened the box and nodded at the silver watch. It was delicate and well-made. But as her gaze roamed over it, he wished there'd been anything else in the box. A necklace or ring or…something.

Something that didn't scream *Sorry, but from now on the clock will rule your life. Time will be your enemy because there is never enough of it. Minutes will fly and hours evaporate.*

"Sebastian?" Breanna's hand was on his cheek. "It's a nice gift. I suspect I will need a good timepiece to make sure I am where I need to be."

Sebastian nodded, then looked at it. "Yes." What else was there to say?

"Thank you." Breanna brushed her lips against his cheek, then put the watch on her wrist.

"So." She held up her arms as she spun in their kitchen. "What do you cook?"

There was no quick answer to that. He cooked a little of everything. Sebastian loved trying new recipes, creating his own. He was skilled enough now that most of the creations tasted good. That had not always been the case.

"Anything. I can make a mean scrambled egg." Sebastian winked. "Since traveling to Japan last year, I've started some days with *gohan* and an egg."

"So cooking is your hobby?"

"No. Cooking is just cooking." Sebastian headed to the fridge. "Do you eat eggs? These were never fertilized." One of his university professors had gotten very upset during a lecture about the different kinds of vegetarians. He didn't remember what started the man's forty-minute off-topic discussion, but he remembered the type the professor outlined.

He looked over his shoulder, and she was smiling. "If they were never fertilized, yes. No one has ever asked."

Another punch in the gut. No one had asked his wife a basic question about her choices. He was used to that. As King, everyone assumed you got what you wanted. The reality was you got what others wanted for you.

Breanna hadn't worn a crown until yesterday. There was no reason for her not to be asked. Except for the Galanis family not caring what their daughters wanted.

"All right, well, I have rice in the steamer, and we can add the egg for protein. Then, time to get to know each other."

"Wonderful words to hear from your husband." She raised her coffee mug in a mock toast.

"So, you want to play twenty questions?" Breanna took a bite of the rice dish. It was savory and filling, but her stomach had no intention of settling. Get-to-know-you time was meant for dating. Meant for figuring out if you matched.

There was already a simple gold band on the ring finger of her left hand.

Sebastian's gaze was intense. The man's blue eyes seemed to say things that she suspected he had no intention of sharing.

"Let's think of it as more of a coffee date." Sebastian went to the machine and topped her mug off. Then he opened the sugar jar. "You tell me when."

He put one heaping spoon in. It looked just like what she'd done. He'd paid attention. Why did that make her want to cry?

"That's good." Breanna's voice, broke but Sebastian didn't acknowledge it.

Her husband was kind. That was a good thing. A brilliant silver lining.

"Did you want to be queen?" Sebastian passed her the mug.

It nearly slipped through her fingers. There was a simple answer. Two little letters that changed nothing. What was the point of answering it now?

"That is not a coffee date question, Your Highness." She took a sip of her coffee, set it aside, then leaned her hands on the table. "Though to be honest, I've never been on a coffee date."

Or any date.

"Still, I think it's supposed to start with hobbies or favorite colors or what you were like growing up." Breanna playfully wagged a finger at him. "You like cooking. Do you enjoy baking too?"

Sebastian made a face.

"Was that grimace about me shifting the topic or about baking?" She leaned forward, enjoying the grin that appeared anytime she got close. Did he know he was doing that?

The king reached out and took her free hand, loosely playing with her fingers. A simple motion that shouldn't send heat racing through her.

"Maybe both."

"I had a roommate in college who loved to bake. She made cookies, cakes, the most beautiful pastries. Ask her to cook pasta and she'd throw up her hands. No interest. You'd think we were torturing her with such a suggestion!" She wrapped her ring finger around his, their matching gold bands glinting.

Small lines appeared around his eyes as he laughed, again. It filled the kitchen, and her stomach let go of some of the tension that seemed to be her constant companion.

"I feel that way about baking. It really is more science than anything else. No thank you."

"So, you didn't make the lemon cake for our wedding reception?" Breanna laid a hand over her chest, mock surprise making him laugh harder. It was a nice sight. The king in public was so controlled. So dutiful.

In his own kitchen though, he could laugh. When they were alone, she wanted this man.

"If I made it, it would have looked more like a lemon mush than cake."

"Lemon mush... I bet it still would have tasted lovely." Brenna didn't care so much about what the cake looked like. Until he'd kicked her parents out, their reception was a horror show. After?

Well, after they'd danced and danced. It was fun. Then the slow songs had started. She'd waited for him to take her hand for the first one, then made a quick escape when it seemed he didn't want to.

The second song, and the third and fourth, she'd spent in his arms, a feeling of safety seeping through her. Clearly the long day had scrambled some of her senses.

"Your Highness?" Raul walked into the kitchen and stopped. "Sorry, Your Highnesses." He nodded to Breanna.

Your Highness. She doubted she'd ever get used to that.

"It's early for the look of concern, Raul." Breanna held up her coffee mug. "Want a cup of coffee before you spill whatever difficult thing is on the tip of your tongue?"

Raul and her husband both stared at her with open mouths. "Do you not normally get asked to join the king and queen for coffee, or are those looks for something else?"

"I know the schedule says get to know the queen. But we have a situation." Raul looked at King Sebastian.

The queen. Not Breanna. The queen. Anyone could have fit that description provided they had a dress and willingly signed a contract. She was just the one he'd picked—or the one he'd been forced to pick when she'd exchanged places with Annie.

Breanna blew out a breath, trying to focus on the comment from Raul.

"An emergency?" It wasn't. At least, not a real one. Raul was stressed but not bent in trauma. Sebastian, and now she, had duties as royals, but they also needed a life.

"Uh—"

"If you have to think on it, then it's not." It was day one of being queen. Maybe she shouldn't assert herself now, but if she didn't start right away, she might lose the gumption. Her husband needed a hobby and time to be Sebastian, not just the king.

And she refused to wear her crown, metaphorically or otherwise, before nine, unless it was absolutely necessary.

"So, coffee time. The king and I are not responding to business before nine a.m. or after eight p.m." She wasn't sure the times would stick, but whether they fluctuated or not, the idea was what mattered.

"Breanna," Sebastian's voice was soft, not quite a rebuke, but close enough.

Ignoring the twinge in her stomach, she went to the small mug stand and grabbed one for Raul. "We don't have syrups." She made a playful face at Sebastian, but he didn't react.

The king stood before her now. The duty-bound man who gave her a wristwatch the day after marrying her.

"So, cream and sugar or black?" Her voice wobbled, but she kept the smile on her face.

Raul looked to Sebastian, but the king didn't say anything. "Um…black, Your Highness."

"Breanna. Call me Breanna." She passed him the cup.

"We have a duty, Breanna." Sebastian was ramrod straight. The man who'd played with her fingers and kissed her head when she was panicking this morning was lost. But he was there, she'd seen him. He just had let go a little.

"We also have lives." She held up her hand before Sebastian could say anything else. Maybe she hadn't wanted this life. But she was making the best of it. Period.

"Raul, tell me about yourself." Color drained from the man's face, and she sighed. "All right, take a deep breath. We will start the actual work in an hour. Until then, we were talking hobbies. Sebastian claims he doesn't have any, but we both know it's cooking, right?"

This time Raul didn't look to the king. Instead, he laughed, and she saw Sebastian take a deep breath. Her husband was not used to putting off work.

Even the day after their wedding. She tried not to let that sting. This was a marriage of convenience. In the twenty-first century, it looked a little different, but that didn't change the truth. Her husband didn't want her.

He'd wanted a bride, and a queen. The person standing there didn't really matter. As exchangeable as pieces of paper placed in a hat.

But she needed to have some boundaries. Something to ground her.

"Yes. And I assume based on the sewing equipment the team brought to your room, you like creating new things."

It was more than that. She liked finding and repurposing old things. Rehabbing clothes that others thought were too outdated or damaged. Almost one hundred billion garments were made a year, and nearly ninety percent of materials ended up in landfills. Less than one percent was rehabbed or recycled, but she was trying to do her part.

It was a stance her parents refused to understand. Yes, her

closet could contain a new outfit every day. A couture item designed just for her never to be worn again. Her family's budget wouldn't even notice a dent.

But what was the purpose of that?

"Breanna, we really need to discuss the situation." Sebastian motioned for Raul to continue.

This time Raul didn't look to her for confirmation. Instead, he reached for the tablet next to him and started reciting off the "issues."

None of which sounded like they were more than the average headache. A frustration, but hardly something that had to be started right away.

In the passing moments, it had become clear that she wasn't needed. She looked at her new watch, then slid off the stool. She waited to see if her husband would say anything, then hoped to hear his voice as she walked to the door.

He never raised his head from the tablet.

A day after her wedding and already an afterthought...

CHAPTER FIVE

"WHAT DO YOU THINK, Breanna?" Sebastian lifted his head from the tablet and was shocked to find her gone. "Breanna?"

Color crept up Raul's neck. "She left."

"Left?" Sebastian shook his head and tried to remember if she'd said goodbye.

"About twenty minutes ago, Your Highness."

Twenty minutes.

He pushed his hands through his hair and looked at her coffee mug sitting in front of the stool where she'd sat joking with him about hobbies and setting a schedule. How could he have missed that?

Except he knew how. When he focused on duty, he drowned everything else out. It was a trick he'd learned as a child, that way his focus never drifted to things he'd rather do. Instead, his mind stayed in the present. Laser-focused on the responsibilities given him though a roll of the universal dice of fate.

It worked well when he was a child. Even as an adult—but as a husband it left more than a little to be desired.

"I think we are done for now. Reach out to Alessio. The art nonprofits usually like having him at their events. I agree that more notice would have been nice, but everyone gets busy, and things fall through the cracks. I am not surprised the requests for royal attendance came late."

Raul made a few notes. "If Prince Alessio and Princess Brie are unable to attend?"

"Then I will figure out how to be in three places at once." He and Breanna were already scheduled to make appearances at two other locations that day. A ribbon cutting and a speech given by a local celebrity on a topic he couldn't quite remember.

Breanna liked fiber arts. That was something she could highlight as the queen. Show off her pieces and work. Encourage others. Between her and Alessio, the royal family was quite artistic.

Sebastian pushed himself away from the counter. He needed to find Breanna. This was supposed to be their day together. Time to get to know each other.

And he'd let duty get in the way. It was necessary, but he could have explained better.

He quickly rinsed the mug, hung it back in its place, then went to find his bride. She'd be in her rooms. Mostly because he hadn't taken her on a tour of the palace yet.

There were many excuses he could give for that, but none of them mattered.

He raised his hand, knocked on her suite door. Her voice gave him entry, and he opened the door.

Breanna was bent over her large workbench. The ugliest dress he'd ever seen lay on top of it. He stood there waiting for her angry snap. He'd earned this one. Whatever she wanted to let out, he'd take it.

But the silence carried on, and his wife's eyes never left her project.

Finally, she grabbed some tool, and then started doing something to the garment on her bench. The sleeves fell away, but it didn't improve the garment's look all that much. "Did you need something, Sebastian?"

"It's all right if you want to yell at me." Maybe she wanted permission? His father often gave it to his mother when they had a spat. Sebastian didn't remember her ever raising her voice, but the option was there.

An option Samantha had never needed. When she'd felt like lashing out, she had not held back. She'd told him all the things she'd change when she was queen. How he'd not recognized that was all she wanted was beyond him now. *Love blinded you.*

The tool clattered to the table. "Why would I yell at you?" Breanna's dark eyes looked genuinely shocked.

"I ignored you." Heat stole along his collar. Married less than a day and he'd ignored the woman in front of him when they were supposed to be getting to know each other. Duty came first, but he should have noticed her leaving.

"An apology would be nice. But why yell? I know what this marriage is. What I am." There was no malice in the words. No emotion at all.

Just an acceptance that nearly sent him to his knees. Funny, he'd always thought anger was the worst emotion. But her quiet statement hurt more than any angry words Samantha had thrown at him.

"Breanna, I am so sorry. I got caught up in the emergency."

"No." She leaned against the table and crossed her arms. "I appreciate the apology, but that was not an emergency."

He didn't want to squabble, but he needed her to understand their roles.

"What might not look like an emergency to those not wearing crowns has to be treated as an emergency by those who are."

One of his father's favorite refrains.

"I know a gala event might not seem like an emergency."

"No." Breanna shook her head. "A gala event is *not* an emergency."

He smiled, but he knew the motion was tight. "It is to the nonprofit."

"No." Breanna laughed. "It is not."

"Everyone is struggling."

"No, they *are not*." Breanna pushed away from the table. "Princess Brie's tourism board has brought back all the tourists we lost during the recession, plus others who've never visited. Yes, there are those still struggling, but it is not the same situation the country was in a year ago. And *no one* throwing a gala is in danger."

"The nonprofit—"

Her hand pressed against his chest. "Would not be spending hard-earned coin on an expensive gala when they are in danger. That is something you do when you have money to spare and are looking for bigger donors. It is a *good* sign."

Her words struck him. He knew what was required of him as a prince, and a king, but Sebastian's life was as far from normal as possible. Attendance at events. Hosting diplomats. Staying politically neutral. It was a delicate balancing act.

But his day-to-day looked nothing like that of the people of Celiana.

"The last few years—"

"Were rough." Breanna ran her finger along his chin. "But that changed when your brother married Brie. The choice to have a small wedding for us was a good one." She swallowed, looking away for a moment.

He couldn't blame her. Brie and Alessio's wedding had been a giant party. Even though they'd made sure the cost was far from the weddings most expected of the crown. It could have been had in the smallest room on the island, with no music, and the happiness from his brother and sister-in-law would have carried the event.

The same couldn't be said for the affair they had. Even though he'd enjoyed dancing with Breanna most of the evening. There was no love in the air. No music created by two souls who never wished to be parted.

"People are still focused on replenishing savings, but they are not struggling like they were. So, it was a good idea." Whether his wife was trying to convince herself by repeating the idea or convince him didn't really matter.

Rationally, he knew that made sense. And he'd seen the metrics from the tourism industry, and others. It was good. But it wasn't the full story of the crown.

A life of service. Always. That was what the king and queen of Celiana owed the country.

"That doesn't change the fact that we need to be at events." It was their role. Draw attention to projects needing it—the power of influence.

"Which events do we pass along our regrets to?" Breanna raised her chin, her eyes brimming with challenge as she crossed her arms. He wanted her to touch him again, to comfort him.

"We don't." He hated the stress he saw fly through her eyes. But influence was a fickle beast. A cup overflowing could dry up with the wrong words or missed opportunity. He wore the crown, but the influence his father had cultivated, the embers his brother had kept warm when he'd floundered…it could disappear.

Sebastian didn't care about the influence for himself, but the nonprofits, the tourists, the people gained something from it. He would not strip that from them for his own selfish desires.

Breanna laughed, though the bell-like sound held no humor. "Seriously, Sebastian, you do get to have time off. You are just a man, after all."

"The crown does not rest."

Dear God, it was like his father's soul had just overtaken him.

The man's presence even a few years after his passing was still felt everywhere.

"That is nonsense."

Breanna wasn't used to a life of duty. The Galanis family had more money than nearly everyone on the island. Her family did not care what their influence brought for others. He doubted Lucas Galanis was capable of thinking of anything besides his own bank account.

Breanna and her sister had wanted for nothing.

Except affection.

His life had been similarly privileged, similarly lacking in affection from his father and to some extent his mother. But it was duty, not coin, that drove his father's ambitions. The deep knowledge ingrained in each royal that they worked for the people of Celiana.

He'd had one vacation. A few days skiing before his tenth birthday. A last hurrah before the real work of his life started. Was that unfair? Sure. But fairness was not what this world was built on.

During the year where he'd rebelled, he'd still attended the events required of him. Alessio had had to pick up most of the day duties, and he'd figured out a way to get the country out of the economic depression with his bride lotto. However, he'd arrived when he'd absolutely had to. Even the night when he and Samantha had broken up, he'd gone to the state dinner. Broken. Bitter. And late. But still in attendance.

"It can be fun. As queen, you can focus on specific charitable events." He pointed to the dress. "There are many arts functions that would love to display any of the garment talents you have."

Breanna shook her head. "No. This—" she gestured to the dress "—is just for me. Mine. Something no one can take from me."

He wasn't trying to take it. Just expand it. Use her knowledge and expertise to help others. She was queen now. She'd met him at the altar. Chosen this path. "You're the queen now. Nothing is just for you, anymore."

"We shall see about that."

He didn't argue. She'd come to understand the truth soon enough. "Would you like a tour of the palace?"

She closed her eyes for a moment, then turned a brilliant smile to him. "I suppose it is a good idea to know my away around my home."

"Home." He chuckled. "I don't think I've ever referred to the palace as home. It's not really mine, after all."

Once more the truth slipped out. He was typically very good at keeping his personal truths locked away. Sometimes he pushed them far enough away he almost forgot they were there.

Almost.

Breanna didn't push back though. Instead, she put her tools away, then looked at him. "Ready when you are."

CHAPTER SIX

THE TINY CROWN on her head didn't weigh much. Rationally she knew that. But it still felt like it was digging into her scalp as she greeted yet another guest at the fundraising event that she was more certain than ever was not an emergency.

"You are doing well." Sebastian's words were soft as he leaned over and pushed a hair that had fallen from the elaborate updo from her face. His fingers brushed her cheek, lingering for just a moment before turning back to the guests.

Well. A word her father had used to make sure she and Annie knew they could do better. Four letters that fell far short of best. And if you weren't the best, why bother?

Sebastian meant it that way, too. Not in the cruel manner, but in the "helpful" you-will-get-there way. The supportive king instructing his brand-new queen. There was no anger. No upset.

Because he'd expected his pick to struggle with the adjustment at first. This wasn't an issue with Breanna. It was an issue with "the queen."

An interchangeable bride the crown would sculpt. Anyone could be standing here and Sebastian would support them.

"You look tired." The woman's kind words were sweet as she squeezed Breanna's hand.

"I'm fine. But thank you."

The woman moved to Sebastian. Her statement not one

of a real concern, but a passing phrase. But it meant others could see her forced smile.

But how could she offer more? Her toes ached and her head pounded. She'd been on her feet for almost fifteen hours straight. Exhaustion had stopped nipping at her heels hours ago.

Now it was the pure force of pride keeping her upright. She was not going to collapse in public. With any luck, their commitment was over as soon as the receiving line ended. After all, the event had ended almost an hour ago.

Raul came up and offered Sebastian, and then her, water. "The receiving line just closed at the other end. It should be done in about an hour."

Breanna couldn't stop the harsh laugh escaping her lips. An hour. *An hour.* Sebastian stepped closer and put an arm around her. She leaned into him. Needing to give her feet some relief from the torture devices on her toes.

"It will be all right." His words were kind, but they did little to help her in the moment.

How did he manage this? They'd been on the go every moment since their wedding. She was maintaining some boundaries. Refusing to start her day before a certain hour might not seem like much, but in the palace, it was rebellion.

She wasn't sure Sebastian had any boundaries at all. The man said yes to everything.

"Take a deep breath." He shook the next person's hand. His arm on her waist tugged just slightly. He was offering to pull her close. Giving her some of his strength. Not pressuring, but the unspoken offer was clear.

She took it. Desperate times called for desperate measures. And standing close to her husband, enjoying the scent of him, the comfort he offered, was as far from desperate as possible. "I need different shoes."

Sebastian looked at her feet, then motioned with his free hand back to Raul. "Find the queen some flats."

"Oh." Raul was off before Breanna managed any other words. She'd meant the statement as a reminder to herself to wear flats for the next event. Like she'd have a choice. Her toes might rebel if she tried to put them in heels tomorrow.

She'd watched her husband swallow a yawn as he reached for the next guest's hand. The man was skilled at hiding exhaustion, but if you looked for it, it wasn't hard to see. He gave the country everything—he needed something for himself.

"The queen is stepping into her role quite nicely." Sebastian nodded to the gentleman, then turned to greet the next guest.

The queen. Not Breanna. Here she was the title. Nothing more. Anyone with the crown and the title could be here, and the line would form.

When the end of the line came into view, Breanna bounced, then winced. Wherever Raul had gone for flats, it was a futile effort now.

She started to lean her head against Sebastian's shoulder, then snapped it back up. Getting support from him was nice. And she needed it. That did not mean she needed to rest her head on his shoulder.

"Almost done." He squeezed her as the final two people came into view. "We helped raise a lot of money tonight. You've done wonderfully."

They'd done well. But money would have come in without them. Maybe not quite as much. People had purchased tickets to the fundraiser long before the king and queen's attendance was announced. So, the nonprofit would have made a hefty profit.

Then Sebastian had offered a reception line as a fundraiser. Now the pot was overflowing. Literally. A nice perk for a group that wouldn't have to fundraise much for the next year but hardly an emergency. If everything was an emergency, then nothing was.

Her husband needed some boundaries. If only for her own sanity.

Sebastian gave their goodbyes to the organizers as she smiled. The neurons not focused on the pain radiating down her feet were an exhausted mush too far gone to say much more than have a nice night. They waved and started towards the car.

She took two steps, then let out a sigh. "Hold up." She put a hand on her husband's shoulder and slipped one heel, then the other, off her feet.

The cold tile was heaven. "Ooh." Her toes rejoiced as they were finally allowed a little more freedom. Her hose refused to give them a full range of motion, but she'd take what she could get.

Breanna resolved to donate these torture heels. Those monstrosities were never going back on her feet. Never!

"We aren't at the car yet." Sebastian looked at her bare feet, then into the distance she had no plans on crossing in the heels.

"I know." She patted his arm, then started towards the car. "But I refuse to hobble my way there. I can't stand the way those things—" she glared at the offending shoes "—find every possible way to make my feet scream!"

"You'll tear your hose."

"Congratulations, Your Highness." Breanna giggled, exhaustion making her a little punchy. "I think you found the argument least likely to move me."

If she had her way, the hose in her top drawer would vanish. Flimsy material that was confining was the work of black magic—you would not convince her otherwise. Yet the dowager queen never set foot outside the palace without nude hose covering her legs.

It was expected of queens. For reasons no one could explain to her because hose weren't even technically invented until 1959. A fact she had not known until she was adding it to her arsenal of reasons why she had no intention of keeping up that tradition.

"The car isn't far." Sebastian took a breath. "What if you hurt your feet?"

She looked at him, really looked at him for the first time this evening. The lines under his eyes were darker, and worry lines were etched along his lips. Without thinking, she raised her free hand and ran her thumb along his chin.

His sigh echoed in the empty room, and his head leaned against her hand, like she was pulling a little of the exhaustion from his tired frame.

She took a breath and softened her tone. "I appreciate the concern. I do. But these heels will hurt my feet more than the pristine floors. And sometimes it is fun to be spontaneous. Take your shoes off, Your Highness."

Sebastian chuckled but shook his head. "A king is supposed to keep his shoes on."

"Says who?" Breanna stuck her bare feet out from under the full-length gown she had on. "Your queen is almost barefoot."

"She is." He stepped towards her, and the air in the room vanished as he smiled at her. He was close. So close.

"My queen is very cute almost barefoot." Huskiness coated his tone as he closed the bit of distance between them.

Was he going to kiss her? There was a glint in his eyes. A mischievousness.

She wanted him to. "Come on, Your Highness?" Was she daring him to take off his shoes? Or kiss her.

"Breanna." Sebastian paused then scooped her up.

"Ooh!" She instantly wrapped her arms around his shoulders. The relief in her digits sent a groan through her as she flexed her feet. He hadn't kissed her. That was fine. Picking her up was sweet. It was.

The tiny burst of disappointment was just from exhaustion.

"See." His lips were so close to hers. "You needed—" he pulled back, a yawn escaping his mouth "—the relief."

"Yes." She kissed his cheek. For a moment she could pretend this was a date. Or a fun night out. That they were just two people having a good time. Caring for each other.

Not a husband and wife…a king and queen…who barely knew each other.

"But you are exhausted, too. Who takes care of you?"

"I am the king." Sebastian nodded to the man opening the door and waited a moment as the other doorman rushed to the waiting car to open that door.

He slid her into her seat, and the relief in her aching back nearly brought tears to her eyes.

Sebastian climbed in next to her and told the driver they were ready. It would be easy to close her eyes and drift into sleep until they were at the palace. But she had so little alone time with the man she called husband.

"Who takes care of you?" Breanna pushed again.

"I told you." Sebastian closed his eyes and leaned his head back. It was like the final charge of his internal battery was gone.

"No." Breanna shook her head. "I am king."

His eyes popped open and he chuckled, his hand reaching for hers. "That sounds nothing like me."

"The words are an exact replica." Breanna squeezed his hand. "Who takes care of you?"

Sebastian pulled her hand to his lips, quickly brushing them across her knuckles. Her breath caught.

"I am the king." He let out a sigh so heavy it sounded like

it carried the weight of the country. "No one needs to take care of me."

He closed his eyes again.

All her words were trapped in her throat. What was she supposed to say to such nonsense?

"Everyone needs care."

The only response she got was soft snores, but his hand still cradled hers.

CHAPTER SEVEN

BREANNA REACHED FOR her toes, groaning as the muscles in her lower back cried out. She was active. She'd biked nearly every day and lifted light weights. The only trouble she had was heavy menstrual cycles, which were now well-controlled with an IUD. She was at peak physical condition according to her doctor at the appointment she'd had a month before Sebastian arrived at her door.

And the crown had worn her into the ground in weeks. Her feet had more blisters than toes, and no matter the amount of stretches she did in the morning and before bed, her body ached when she woke. How did Sebastian maintain this life?

He doesn't.

The thought pierced her mind as she looked over the schedule her assistant always forwarded just after midnight. A full day—like every day.

And like most days, she wasn't seeing her husband until a dinner engagement they were attending with Prince Alessio and Princess Brie. The man was gone before she woke.

Off to some meeting. Attending some function. Working on a task that didn't really need doing. How many things could a king really be expected to do before eight? Apparently far too many.

"Breanna?" That was her husband's voice. But according to his schedule, he was supposed to be handling personal correspondences this morning. A mountain of letters arrived with each post. He'd respond to so many that tonight he'd stretch his fingers when he thought no one looking. Bending them, flexing and balling them into a fist. Hurting but saying nothing.

She turned to look at the door to her work room. "Yes?"

Her husband stepped into her room, and she smiled. He was here. To spend some time with her. Since the morning after their wedding, they'd really only seen each other at events. In the car and in a few passing moments in the hall.

He was kind, asking after her needs. He'd never gotten close enough to make her think he was going to kiss her though. That night at the fundraiser was a one-off moment. Maybe she'd been so tired, her memory was playing tricks on her.

Her husband checked in on her. Far more than her parents had ever managed.

Part of her almost wished he didn't bother. If King Sebastian refused to acknowledge her, if it was clear that she was just a thing he needed to support his throne, to stop the constant wave of people harassing women even loosely attached to him, then she could adjust. Accept the life she had to protect Annie.

After all...filling a role was something she'd always done. Quiet daughter. Respectful daughter. Exchangeable daughter. If only the location had shifted, from the compound to the palace, she'd adjust easily.

But he cared for her when she was tired. Kicked her parents out of their wedding reception when it was clear that they were cruel. Got her coffee syrups and made veggie dishes that were clearly marked in the fridge—when—she had no idea.

It was the grounds for so much more than they had.

He was overburdened. If she found a way to give him peace, found a way to have him accept the need for boundaries, they had a chance to not spend the rest of their lives as strangers.

To give themselves a chance at more. Surely that chance was something they should reach for.

"Sebastian. Are you here to join me for coffee? I got my cup from our kitchen a few minutes ago. I can ring—" The words died on her lip as a woman who couldn't have been more than five feet tall stepped from behind him. Around her neck hung a measuring tape, and she had a box filled with tools Breanna didn't recognize.

"Where can I set this, Your Highness? It's heavy." Her thick accent accentuated each word.

"Of course." Breanna moved quickly folding her project but careful to make sure the pins holding the material in place stayed where they were meant to be. "You should have asked the king to carry your things."

She winked at her husband and immediately hated the joke as his shoulders stiffened.

"I offered Olga more than one chance to let me handle the box. She's as stubborn as my wife."

"Then we shall get along fine." Breanna clapped her hands, hoping this jest would remove some of the tension in his body.

Olga hmphed as she set the box down and then looked at the queen. The woman's eyes were sharp, but the assessment held no malice. After the weeks she'd had in the palace, it was refreshing.

"You are tallish."

Ish? Breanna wasn't sure what to make of that. She was a little over five foot seven. Average height. Though to a woman who had to look up at the world, she supposed most people qualified as tallish.

"Good feet." She pointed, then started pulling things from her box.

"They don't feel so good." Breanna glared at the sores on her toes, then made a silly face at her husband.

"Because your shoes don't fit." Sebastian stepped beside her. Not quite touching but close enough that if she moved even a little, they'd brush sides.

Except he didn't get any closer. It was silly to be upset by that. But the flicker she'd felt at the fundraiser had been snuffed out.

If it was ever there to begin with.

"They fit before I stood in them for hours on hours on hours on hours."

Her husband held up his hands. "I get it. I should have put a cap on the receiving line."

That was more than she'd expected him to acknowledge. "Yes. You should have." She bumped his hip with hers. Why did she want to touch him?

Sebastian wrapped his arm around her waist, just like he'd done the night they'd met, and that night in the receiving line. But unlike those times, he pulled away quickly. Like she'd burned him. Or more likely, because he didn't want to touch her.

Her chest burned as she sucked in a breath. Trying to focus on the task at hand.

"So I am here to fit you for shoes. Perfect ones. Ones that will not do that." Olga tsked as she pointed to the sores on Breanna's feet.

"They wouldn't if I wasn't standing so long."

"But you are queen." Olga said the words, but it was Sebastian's nod that tore through her.

This was the expectation. This was what she was supposed to do. She was supposed to stand all the time. Supposed to put everyone's needs before her own.

She'd done that her whole life. Breanna was good at it. But there'd been downtime, too. Time for herself. Filled with thread and bobbles, and laughter and rest.

Celiana was important. The royal family was important, but they were more than their positions. Weren't they?

Sebastian was more than the title. More than the king. The crown didn't have to be the only thing people saw.

"So, I need shoes that will let me stand for hours every day." She pointed to Olga's box. "What magic is in there to allow such a thing?"

Olga pulled a few things out and started gesturing for her to sit. A woman of few words, but the demands were clear.

"I need to see to my correspondence."

"Oh. I thought you'd stay?" If only there were a way to bite back that request. She'd hoped he'd adjusted his schedule. More than just to drop a shoemaker at her door and wish her good morning.

"Behind schedule. I'm going to have to skip lunch to get it all written up." He lifted a hand and headed for the door.

"Sebas—" But her husband was already gone.

She followed Olga's demands while plotting out her next move. One thing was certain. Sebastian was not skipping lunch.

Sebastian shook his hand, then rolled his wrists, even though he knew it wouldn't stop the pins-and-needles feeling trickling from his elbow to the tips of his fingers.

His schedule was off today, but the trip to see Breanna was worth it. The image of his wife popped into his head. He'd wanted to kiss her the night of the fundraiser. Wanted to pull her close, hold her and never let go.

But he'd promised her separate lives. A king and queen in title. Lives of their own. He couldn't ask for a change when she was a newly minted queen. She was overwhelmed. Finding her place.

He would not take advantage of that.

Sebastian stifled a yawn. No one was here to see the exhaustion, but the habit was ingrained in him. Only Breanna had seen him yawn in years.

"Kings do not get tired. They are perfection for their people."

Words his father had said during their early-morning

walks, back when he'd still complained about the exhaustion that was his constant companion.

He read the letter over, for the third time. Nothing seemed to stick this morning.

The door to the office opened, but he didn't look up. If he allowed himself to get distracted now, then he'd never get through all of this. Sebastian's schedule was already pushed to the extremes today.

"Sebastian?"

"Hello, Breanna. Did Olga finish your shoes?" He tried to read the letter in front of him and figure out a quick way to sign a response.

If only the letters on the page stayed still.

"Sebastian, I can hear your stomach gurgling from here." She stepped to the desk and took the letter from his hands. She looked at it, then leaned over him, taking the pen from his other hand.

Breanna's scent infiltrated his nose. His body tightened, then softened, like a strong breeze that suddenly shifts. He took a deep breath, letting himself settle. She was here. His wife.

"Now sign your name." Breanna pushed the pen back in his hand.

He blinked, then looked at the short note she'd written on the paper the staff had left for this letter's response.

Happy birthday, Serena. Sixteen is a wonderful time. We hope that your days are blessed with adventure and growth. Enjoy!

A birthday letter. A note that should have been so easy to push out. Yet he'd read the words multiple times without his mind clicking. Shame there wasn't time for a nap.

He quickly signed his name above Breanna's.

"Serena won't know it, but this is the first letter signed by the queen."

"Uh-huh." Breanna grabbed the rest of the correspondence.

"Wait. What are..." Sebastian stood as she started towards the office door. There were at least a dozen left to go. Probably more.

Breanna opened the door. "Come on. He needs to eat." She sighed then looked over her shoulder. "Raul wants you to know that I am forcing this issue and that he had nothing to do with it." She looked back through the door. "Does that cover it?"

It must have, because Raul marched in with a tray of food, set it on the table by the unlit fireplace, and vanished.

"You need to eat." Breanna grabbed his hand and pulled him towards the table.

"I *need* to—"

Her finger lay over his lips. "You need to eat. So that is what we are going to do, Your Highness."

"Your Highness...? Guess you're cross with me." Sebastian sat at the table, happy when she sat on the other side.

Breanna lifted the lid of the plate. "Not cross. Worried."

He opened his mouth, and she held up the finger that had pressed against his lips moments ago. "If you are about to do anything other than eat the veggies, hummus and egg salad, you can do it after."

She dipped a veggie in hummus took a bite, then motioned for him to do the same.

Tightness hovered in his throat. He was the king. No one looked after him. No one.

"Thank you."

"You are welcome. Now, eat." She pointed to his dish. "You look like hell."

"Only Alessio ever tells me that."

"Well, I am your queen, so…" Breanna huffed as she drove her fork into the salad.

They ate in a comfortable silence as he wolfed down the lunch she'd had prepared and let out a soft sigh. He felt better. "Thank you."

"You are welcome." Breanna smiled, then pointed to the desk. "How about I sort while you sign."

"Teamwork?" Sebastian started to reach for her hand, but stopped himself. "Umm, I don't want to hold you up. You don't have to help."

"I am offering. There is a difference." She looked at his hand, the one that had not reached for hers, then stood and grabbed the pile, sifting through the letters quickly.

He followed, very aware of his bride's presence at his side as she handed him one letter at a time.

"Birthday."

"Anniversary."

"Graduating with a master's degree in biochemistry. Wow."

He signed each one with a quick note, and the pile was nearly gone before he realized it.

"Wow." Breanna read the last one.

"Another graduation?"

Sebastian started to reach for it, but she shook her head. A look he couldn't quite interpret coming over her eyes.

"No. Anniversary. Fifty years. Fifty years. Their daughter requested the note. She gushes over how her parents are soulmates. How lucky she is to watch their love." She let out a breath. "Must be something special."

Something we don't have.

She didn't say the words but passed him the note.

He wrote a quick congratulations, aware of the shift in the room.

"Do you believe in soulmates?" The question was out, and he wished there was a way to pop it back in. That was a question to ask on a date. Or with a friend. It was not a question to lay at his wife's feet.

A wife he'd known for weeks. A wife he'd married days after a public announcement. A wife he rarely saw.

"No." There was no hesitation. "I am glad that others believe, but no. I do not feel like there is one perfect person in the world for me. Relationships take work. Good ones involve friendship and respect."

There was no way to ignore the pinch in his stomach that she didn't mention love or caring in her thoughts on marriage. Why should she? It wasn't what their marriage was built on. No, they didn't even have friendship. Though the respect was there. At least on his side.

Breanna sat on the desk, now clear of the notes he'd thought would take twice as long. "You have thirty minutes until your next appointment." She grinned as she tapped the watch on her wrist. The gift he'd given her the day after their wedding.

It was a nice watch, but he couldn't help but wish that he'd given her something more Breanna. Something that said he knew her.

Except outside of liking to sew and wanting to sleep in until seven, he knew very little about his wife.

"So what shall we do with the extra thirty minutes?" Breanna raised her brow as though she was asking something truly scandalous. "We could think of it as playing hooky."

"We could." He leaned closer. "The king and his queen."

"Or Sebastian and Breanna. There is no one here right now. No crowns." She patted her head, then patted his. "Nope. No crown."

"Had to check?" He laughed and put his hands on her hips. Heat, need and things he shouldn't want raced through him.

"It does seem like one might live on your head all the time."

"Very funny, *Your Highness.*" He laughed, pulling her into his lap. His touch was light. If she wanted to move, she could. This wasn't in the script of their separate lives' union. But then, neither was her showing up with lunch and making him eat.

What if they could have more?

Breanna poked his forehead. "You are lost in thought. Want me to move?"

"No." His arms wrapped around her.

Kiss her. Kiss her.

The mantra repeated in brain, screaming at him to take the next step.

Then phone on the desk buzzed, and he could tell by the instant fall of her face that she knew something else was popping in. He could ignore it. He could.

Except…this was the life of a king and queen. The call of duty for one who knew nothing else. If he failed in his duty, others got hurt.

This was his life. All he was.

Sebastian took a deep breath, pushed on the speaker, and heard Raul's out-of-breath sigh. "Any chance you can do a short video call with the director of Leaps for Launch?"

"Leaps for Launch?" Breanna asked as she slid off his lap. Whatever moment they'd been about to have was gone.

"A new nonprofit." Raul answered for him through the phone. "They are trying to set up micro loans for small businesses. A real leg up, but the idea is having some trouble gaining ground. Royal backing is good, but a businessperson would be better."

"Right now, all we have is royal backing." Sebastian reached for the pen he'd used to sign his name to dozens of letters. Now it was note-taking time.

"Not like royal backing is nothing." Breanna moved around the desk, resignation clear on her features.

"Raul." Sebastian looked at Breanna, smiled, then continued. "Give me five minutes to check in with my wife, then patch the call through."

He hung up the phone. "Thank you for your help with the letters and for lunch."

"Of course." Breanna crossed her arms, then uncrossed them, then crossed them again. The easiness they'd had before Raul's call vanished.

"If you need a businessperson, why not ask Brie to reach out to her brother? He's broken with their parents now. Beau might be willing to provide some backing."

"His break with the Ailiono is fairly recent. He and Brie haven't had much of a chance to get to know each other in their new relationship. He might not be up to it." But if he stepped in as a backer, it would send a powerful message to the island.

But would he?

Sebastian hadn't interacted with Beau Ailiono much. Beau was as much his father's protégé as Sebastian was his father's. Neither side was discussing the cause of the break, but given what Brie had experienced, he was inclined to side with Beau.

"The answer to every unasked question is no." Breanna shrugged. "What if I reach out to Brie and see what she thinks?"

A wave of appreciation washed through him. He didn't need to add anything to the mental list that seemed to run miles long through his soul. A to-do list that the king had no power to ever finish. All the checkmarks only vanished when another took his throne.

"That would be very helpful." Sebastian nodded. "Thank you." He looked at his watch. "We still have two minutes."

"Right." Breanna balled her fists and then looked over her shoulder at the door, "I will gift those to you, Your Highness. Spend them well."

The ache in his stomach now had nothing to do with hunger. He wanted to go after her. Ask her to stay with him for the day, chat, do fun things. Things that weren't on his schedule.

The phone rang, and reality slipped in. Duty called...literally.

CHAPTER EIGHT

"YOU LOOK LIKE HELL. I know no one else will say that. But it is still true." Alessio's muttered words were soft enough not to draw attention to them from other bystanders, but the bite was still strong.

"My wife said that exact thing this morning." Sebastian chuckled as his gaze found Breanna. She was dressed in a floor-length red beaded gown. One shoulder was bare while the other had a cap sleeve. It was elegant, queen-like. With a slit up the side that made his mouth water every time his eyes landed on her.

Alessio lifted his champagne flute in her general direction. "Then to our new queen."

Sebastian followed the motion. "To the new…queen." The word *queen* was heavy on his tongue. Breanna was more than that. So much more.

At least until he put the crown on her head.

"But you still look like hell." His brother blew out a breath. "You need to rest more."

"Said so simply." Sebastian tipped his head to one of the guests as they made eye contact. Tonight was more about the politicians and their goals for Celiana, but the royal family's attendance was still expected.

Expected. One of his father's favorites. Such a foul word. One that drove everything about his life. About Breanna's life.

He hated the word, but also knew that if he didn't play this role, then someone else would have to.

Someone else had.

The man beside him now. The man that it would fall to again if he failed.

"The crown—"

"Is heavy." Sebastian slapped his brother's shoulder as their wives walked up. He had no intention of continuing a conversation for which there was no resolution.

Brie slipped into Alessio's arms; he squeezed her tightly. While Breanna stepped close to him. A respectful distance between the two.

This afternoon she'd been on his lap. Laughing and joking. And looking oh, so kissable. For a moment it felt like the contract they had wasn't needed. Like maybe…

And he'd taken that phone call. Had to take a phone call.

He couldn't stop the sigh echoing from his lips. It would be so easy to want what Alessio and Brie had. To reach for Breanna and hope his queen wanted the same. But duty demanded he put the kingdom first. No one should settle for being second to that.

"Brie is going to reach out to Beau about Leaps for Launch." Breanna whispered as she waved to a guest who was walking their way.

"Do you know him?" Sebastian asked. The gentleman was a giant. A damn handsome giant. A well-known playboy strolling towards Breanna.

And his wife looked happier than he'd ever seen her.

"Yes. That is Hector Stevio. I thought everyone on the island knew Hector." She pushed on Sebastian's arm.

Knew of him was probably a better statement. And she was practically bouncing.

"Look at you!" Hector stepped up and bowed to the queen, then turned his attention to the other royals, bowing to them.

"I think you are supposed to bow to the king first." Breanna laughed and then offered her hand to Hector.

Sebastian took a deep breath as he watched his wife visibly relax. It was hard not to wish that she smiled at him like that.

"I guess you shall have to school me in royal protocol, Your Highness." Hector winked at the queen, then dipped his head to Sebastian. "Your Highness."

Sebastian nodded, his eyes glued to the playboy who'd dated most of the island's leading men and women. Hector was famous, or infamous, depending on the storyteller, for his parties, his businesses, his life. The man could turn a piece of straw into gold. Then the business got boring for him—at least that was the story—and he sold it.

Started the game over. Never satisfied.

And now he was looking at Breanna as though she was the top prize in the room. Which she was.

"The dance floor is empty, my queen. Can I have this dance?" Hector offered his hand to Breanna.

His wife placed her hand in the playboy's hand and walked with him to the dance floor. Hector pulled her close, and the air evaporated from the room. Breanna was glowing. She was happy. There was no hint of hesitation.

Something the weeks in the palace hadn't granted her. Something he didn't expect to ever be able to fully give her. She had a crown, a title and duty.

Just like him.

"Breathe, brother." Alessio passed the champagne flute to one of the waitstaff. Then took Sebastian's and passed it over too, waving away the offer of more for both of them.

"They are childhood friends." Brie leaned around her husband, her brow raising exactly as his wife's did. "She is trying to get his help with the Leaps for Launch, too. But given his reputation for spinning something up and then selling it, she thinks Beau might be a better spokesman."

"That's nice." Alessio's grin was clearly meant more for Brie than him. "Isn't it, brother?"

"Yes. Nice." Sebastian muttered, trying to ignore what could only be jealousy flowing through his veins as Hector pulled his wife closer, leaned forward and whispered something in her ear.

Breanna laughed.

She was enjoying the moment. He was jealous.

Jealous. Such a dumb emotion considering the union he'd offered her. It might make sense if he'd held her close instead of taking that phone call. But he'd done as he had to and put Celiana first.

Now, he couldn't stop the worm from slinking down his veins. Breathe. He needed to breathe. The dance would be over soon.

Soon.

A few more couples ambled onto the dance floor, and Alessio offered his hand to his princess. "May I have this dance?"

"I thought you'd never ask." Briella placed her hand in her husband's but stopped before Sebastian. "Rather than standing here grumpy, you could always cut in."

"I just might." Sebastian raised his chin, enjoying the challenge in his sister-in-law's features before turning his attention back to his wife.

Breanna was enjoying herself. He wouldn't steal that from her. But he would claim the next dance.

As soon as the song ended, he was by her side. "Do you mind?" He held out his hand, and his wife's fingers locked through his. His breath eased a little as she squeezed them.

"Your Majesty," Hector bent his head, then turned back to his queen. "I told you, Breanna. You owe me." He winked, then headed off the dance floor.

Sebastian tilted his head as his wife stepped into his arms. "Why do you owe him?"

"He bet me that you would interrupt either before the song finished or just after. I told him that was ridiculous, that you probably didn't even notice I was gone." She smiled, but her eyes didn't light up.

"Breanna." His fingers tightened on her back, pulling her a little closer. He bent his head, so his words were only for her. "I watched you the whole time. I knew exactly where you were. I wanted you for the next dance the moment you were on the floor."

And every dance after.

Breanna's smile was almost as bright as it had been for her friend. Almost. "I do hope you're happy. Hector wins a date night—"

"A date night?" The words came out harsher than he'd planned.

"Yes." She chuckled, though her features were not as free as they were with Hector. "Dinner, though, I think we are making dinner? Not sure on the exact idea yet. But it is for a few hours in a couple of weeks or so. Again, the details are still a bit up in the air. I shall have to clear the schedules."

She enunciated the word *schedules* and he tried to find some way to figure out what it meant that his queen was going on a date with one of Celiana's most notorious playboys. The man's dance card was full, but he'd never courted a married woman. At least not openly.

"That will certainly make the headlines."

"I think that is Hector's plan." Breanna sighed as he pulled her a little closer. "The king and queen at his date night extravaganza or whatever he plans to call it."

"The king *and* queen." Sebastian blinked, and his footsteps faltered.

"Careful, you might step on my feet, and the lovely shoes

Olga is crafting aren't here yet." This time her eyes lit up as she grinned at him.

The music slowed, and Sebastian closed the tiny amount of distance between them. "You knew what I was thinking, Your Highness." The sweet scent that was just Breanna infiltrated his nose.

"I did." She laid her head on his shoulder. They'd had one dance like this at their wedding, but his wife hadn't rested on him since. He hadn't known it was possible to miss something so much without realizing it.

The music lilted around them, and for a moment it was just the two of them in the world. His lips found her head. This wasn't what he'd promised her. But right now, he wanted so much more than a dutiful relationship.

"So, date night for some new venture for Hector. I think we can make that work." His lips brushed her hair again.

"I used to give Hector a hard time when we were in school together. Told him he couldn't settle on just one thing. He had to try everything. He skipped the traditional lemonade stand and started by selling a computer code that helped students do their math homework—according to Hector. Help the students cheat, was what our teachers said. That one nearly got him expelled. Then it was 3D printing and..." She shifted in his arms as the words failed to come to her.

He didn't loosen his grip, though if his wife stepped away, he wouldn't stop her.

Instead, she smiled at him. And his heart tripped in his chest.

"I can't remember. There have been so many. Hector has an idea. He chases it, and the rest of the world just seems to follow."

"We are alike in that way." Sebastian kissed the top of her head. He couldn't stop. He was drawn to this woman. A woman whose name he hadn't picked out of a hat. A woman he'd married just days after meeting her. A woman who should want more than him. Deserved more than him.

"No." Breanna pulled back as the music shifted. "Hector has ideas and he grows them into something. We have crowns that turn the eye."

There were no words to cut through that truth. Breanna didn't look sad or unhappy. It was acceptance on her features. Something he should be grateful for.

Instead, all he could think of was that the crown had stolen her ventures. Every single one of them.

The pop beat banged out, and Breanna laughed. Her hair bounced as lights hit her crown, her hips swaying to the beat. "Think you can keep up with these moves, Your Highness?"

"Of course." The heaviness around them parted. The worry retreating to the back of his mind. Pushed away, but never truly gone.

Breanna watched her husband's throat move and wanted to shake him. The man was exhausted. And yet, even here alone with his wife, he was swallowing his yawns. As if the image he presented could keep the exhaustion at bay.

"I might just fall into bed for the rest of the weekend." Breanna laughed as she stood in front of her door, hoping he might agree with her. Smile at her like he had in his office this afternoon or on the dance floor an hour ago.

"If you need a break, we can schedule one. Not several days, but a day here and there."

She didn't bother to try to stop the rolling of her eyes. "Ooh, a whole day to myself. Wow." She put her hand on her chest, mostly to keep from shoving it into his shoulder.

"Breanna—" A yawn interrupted whatever diatribe he wanted to give her on duty.

"You are exhausted. What time do you get up? It seems

to be a guarded secret." No matter who she asked, all she got was a shrug.

"Early." He leaned forward like he was going to drop a kiss on her lips.

Her breath caught. So many times over the last few days, she'd thought he wanted to kiss her. But he never followed through. And he didn't now.

Maybe she was the only one wanting kisses.

She crossed her arms, willing him to let her be a partner in more than just the public-facing activities of the court. Maybe they weren't like Briella and Alessio, but they could be more than strangers. Could be friends, at least. Even if her heart cried that it wanted more.

"I'm fine, Breanna."

"That wasn't the question I asked. And you aren't. You are exhausted. Let me help. It's why you wanted a queen. A partner. A person standing here." *Annie. Not me.* Though he hadn't wanted Annie either. Just a body. A person to stand there.

But she wasn't just going to stand there. "Sebastian…"

He let out a sigh, like he truly believed that this was his life and there was nothing more. "I'm fine." An edge hardened in his tone.

"I'm not sure you'd know if you weren't." Breanna raised her hand, cupping his cheek.

His face softened as he leaned into her. Rested himself on her palm. His breathing slowed, but he didn't let himself hold the position for long.

Far too soon, he raised himself, and the king stood fully before her. The mantle the only thing present now. "I would. I did. Last year. I broke. I lost myself. Alessio and then Briella took the hits. The press—" He cleared his throat, shaking his head and if he was trying to dash away the memories.

"The press was vile to Brie. But you are not responsible for that."

"I am. I was the one who was supposed to marry. It was my father's plan. A marriage, a union to make sure the Celiana royal love story he and my mother presented stayed true in the minds of the people. I refused. I wanted to take time to get to know the bride they'd selected. To try for a real union. Then Father passed, and Alessio stepped up with the princess lottery."

"They are fine now. They love each other." He was in a way responsible for that. If he hadn't refused...

"Just because lightning struck for them does not take away that it should never have happened. I understand now what it means when I break and who it might hurt. Alessio, Brie. You."

"Sebastian."

He ignored her, pressing on, "I promise. I am fine."

It was a lie. But she didn't think he was saying it intentionally. No, her husband believed that he needed to break fully to be less than fine.

"Good night, Breanna. Rest well." Then he bowed and left her at her door.

The handle was cool in her hand as she watched his retreating form.

The Sebastian escorting her to her room was the king. Not the man who'd danced with her on the floor tonight. The man who'd smiled and held her close. The man she'd ached to kiss.

That man deserved freedom from the shackles of the other.

Her own yawn interrupted her thoughts. That was a question for a brain more awake than hers. A question for tomorrow.

There was a solution. Breanna just had to find it.

CHAPTER NINE

Today's agenda is quite full, Your Highness.

LETICIA, HER NEWLY hired assistant, always sent her text to arrive at one minute past midnight. It was the first thing she saw upon awaking. The reminder, as though she needed it, that she was the queen of Celiana.

Sebastian's partner…but only when it was the schedule.

Start time five past nine.

At least she'd managed to keep her schedule start time to nine in the weeks she'd been here. A boundary she'd had no luck getting her husband to follow through on.

Husband.

She'd set her alarm fifteen minutes earlier every day for the week. But even arriving in the kitchen at four fifty yesterday, she'd found only the hints of his presence. A freshly rinsed coffee mug, a note from him about the breakfast fixings he'd left for her in the fridge.

Did the man sleep?

If so, she'd yet to see evidence of it. That wasn't happening today though. They were having breakfast, talking, relaxing, and he wasn't starting his day until nine.

She'd even worked that in with Raul. Probably. Sebastian's assistant had agreed he needed a break and was willing to help. But she'd seen the underlying worry in his face.

So, assuming Raul was willing to follow through on the

promise he'd made to the queen. Assuming she could figure out when he rose. Sebastian was resting today.

But that meant she had to catch him in the kitchen.

She looked at the watch he'd given her. Five past midnight. Blanket and pillow in hand, she was going to the kitchen.

One way or another, the king was going to spend a few hours with her today doing nothing.

"Breanna!"

The call was loud, but her brain was too mushy to truly capture the voice. She wrapped the blanket around her as cold seeped through her. Tired.

"Breanna!"

Kitchen, Sebastian, tired. All three words rattled in her mind before finally syncing. He was in the kitchen.

She popped up, looked at the clock through bleary eyes and groaned. "Three thirty. Three thirty in the morning. What the hell, Sebastian?"

"I don't know what you mean. Why are you on the floor? With a pillow and blanket? How long have you been here?"

"Oh, no," Breanna pushed up on her elbow, stood, then pinched the bridge of her nose. Exhaustion gripped her, but she was not losing her train of thought. "I started the question session, so I get the first answer."

"There is no answer to, *'What the hell, Sebastian?'*"

Not true. There were many answers he might be able to give, if he just thought about it. "I think you know very well what I mean, Your Highness."

"You only call me that when you are frustrated. Do you want a cup of coffee?"

"No. Because it is bedtime. We should be asleep." Coffee at three thirty? *No, thank you.* "*You* should be asleep."

Her husband looked to the coffeepot, his fingers moving like he needed caffeine or he might lie down on the floor with her. "I've started my day at three for as long as I can remember."

That was heartbreaking.

"My father started at the same time. He woke me and we had coffee, then got on with the day." Sebastian started towards the coffeepot, not managing to cover his yawn. The only thing keeping the man running was routine.

"At what age?" She grabbed his hand; he was not going to start the coffeepot. Not right now.

"Huh?" He looked at her hand around his wrist, then back at her. "It's fine, Breanna."

No, it very much was not!

"At what age?" She'd repeat the question as many times as necessary to get an answer.

He started to push a hand through his already done hair, but caught himself. Even at three thirty in the blasted morning, the man didn't want to ruffle the king's appearance. "I don't know. Sometime around ten or eleven, I guess. The crown—"

She tightened her grip on his wrist. "If you are about to say the crown does not rest, I swear..." Her parents were controlling. They believed their daughters belonged to them. It was horrifying. Sebastian's father had convinced him that he belonged to an entire country.

She pulled on his hand. "We are going back to bed."

The words were out, and she heard exactly how they sounded. "Not like that, though!"

"Breanna—" His voice was soft, low, and despite the exhaustion pulling through her, she wanted to lean into him. Kiss away his frowns and make him believe he was worth more than what his title gave him.

The man was her husband. He was also a workaholic and still a near-stranger. "Do not *Breanna* me. You need sleep. *I* need sleep."

"I don't." He used his free hand to cover his mouth as another yawn escaped.

If only there were a way to reach into the afterlife. Because Breanna very much wanted to have a discussion with King Cedric. At least his mother was still within her reach. Because this was ridiculous.

But getting angry right now was not going to solve anything.

"I'll make you a deal. You lie in my bed for fifteen minutes." She grabbed her phone, opened the clock app and put it on a fifteen-minute timer. "I will start this the second your head hits the pillow and you close your eyes. If you are still awake when the alarm goes off, I will not stop you from starting your day when others are stumbling home from the bar."

"You're tired." Sebastian lay his hand over hers on his wrist.

"I *am* exhausted. And I had to sleep on the kitchen floor to even find out what time *my husband* wakes. So yes. I am exhausted and a little furious."

"At me?" For a moment he looked so young. So lost. So much like the boy he must have been when King Cedric dragged him from bed, plied him with coffee and told him his soul belonged to a kingdom.

Breanna stepped close and shook her head. "No. I am furious at your father. But we can discuss that in a few hours. Right now, we are both running on fumes."

"I'm used to it." He grinned, and the twinkle in his eye would have been adorable if she didn't think it was wholly tiredness pulling at him.

"Then lying down for fifteen minutes will not cause a problem."

He looked at the coffeepot. "Let me set it up." He moved fast, his hands flying in an easy motion that he'd done thousands of times.

The drip started. She pulled on him. "Now."

He looked at her and then the coffeepot. "At least the coffee will be here when I get back." He dropped a quick kiss on her nose, surprise dotting his features as he pulled back. "Right. Fifteen minutes, Breanna."

"Fifteen minutes, Sebastian. From the time you close your eyes!"

Bending down, he collected her pillow and blanket and nodded towards the door. "After you, Your Highness." His gaze was bright.

Maybe she was wrong. Maybe he wasn't as exhausted as she thought. Well, then her alarm would go off and she'd find some other way to get the king to relax.

Opening the door to her suite, she took a deep breath as her bed came into view. This was mostly a spontaneous plan. She wanted him to take a break, but she'd not truly expected to find him up so early. And now they were in her bedroom.

Sebastian put the pillow on the bed and crawled in. "The timer starts the moment my head touches the pillow."

"When you close your eyes." She'd been a child who hated bedtime. She knew the tricks to staying awake. And she suspected Sebastian did, too. For very different reasons.

"You coming to bed, too? You're exhausted."

"If I lie down, I will fall asleep. And then the alarm will go off and wake us both."

"I will still be up in fifteen minutes." So sure of himself.

"Then me sitting in this chair doesn't cause a problem." Breanna raised her chin. The king was stubborn, but she could rise to the occasion, too.

"Fine." He lay down, let out a sigh, then closed his eyes.

Breanna started the timer. And shut it off at the four-minute mark when Sebastian's light snores echoed across her chamber.

The man needed rest. And if no one else was going to get it for him, then she would. She sent a quick note to Raul clearing his schedule for the morning. Then Breanna stepped beside the bed.

The lines around his eyes were gone. He looked peaceful. A stray piece of hair fell across his face, but she dared not touch him.

"Good night, Sebastian." Breanna's words were more in her head than spoken. She grabbed a blanket, curled up in the oversized chair, closing her eyes, and let sleep take her, too.

Sebastian knew as he rolled over that the fifteen minutes had passed long ago. He rubbed the back of his hand against his head, then looked at his wrist. His watch was gone.

No. He blinked. He put it on every morning, first thing. It was part of the routine his father had kept. And Sebastian kept. Bed at eleven, up at three. Clothes already set out. Watch on the dresser.

Sitting up, he looked to the window. But the heavy curtains were pulled, giving no indication of the time. How long had he been out? What meetings had he missed? How far behind schedule was he?

Rolling out of bed, Sebastian reached his hands up, stretching. He needed to get moving, but he couldn't argue that he didn't feel great. Apparently, his body craved the nap.

Walking into his wife's study, he wasn't surprised to see her standing next to her workbench. The woman seemed glued to that space when she wasn't on official business.

"Are you feeling rested?" Breanna set her tools down and smiled at him. A full smile. Like the one he'd seen her give Hector. But this was directed at him because she'd won the bet.

It was like winning the lottery. His whole body seemed to sing as her smile radiated over him.

"I am. Feel free to say told you so." Sebastian had earned the call-out. He must have been completely out for her to remove his watch without him noticing.

Her dark curls bounced as she tilted her head. "Why would I say told you so?"

He waited for the laughter, or some other trick. That had been Sam's go-to. A laugh to lighten the mood before a devastating comment. She'd excelled at weaponized words.

Something he'd only realized after their terrible breakup.

Breanna looked at him as he waited for the shoe to fall. Better to get it over with than for it to fall later when he wasn't expecting it. "It's okay. I earned it."

"Why did you earn it?" Such a simple question.

He'd failed today. For the first time in more than a year, he'd missed meetings and caused havoc. All because he couldn't operate as well exhausted.

"Because you were right." His father was always right. And his mother. Hell, even Alessio stepped in after his father's passing when Sebastian had fallen apart and made all the right choices.

King Cedric had made it look easy. His mother was excellent at navigating aristocratic politics, and Alessio had come home from abroad and stepped right into the hole Sebastian had vacated.

He'd been raised for this life. Trained—literally at dawn. Yet he was constantly feeling like he was failing. Living up to his father's legacy was draining.

"It's not about being right. It's about taking care of people."

Taking care of people. That sounded nice. But it was his job. He took care of Celiana. He didn't need anyone looking after him.

"Yes, you do."

Breanna words made his head pop back. "What?"

"You were thinking that you don't need anyone looking after you." She crossed her arms; her bright gaze bore into him. "I can see it written on your face."

"I am the king, and we..." He gestured to the space between them. "We are married, but..."

So many things hung on that *but*.

His wife's stance softened. "Even when the marriage is nothing more than a contract agreement."

She took a deep breath, closing her eyes. Did she want more? Was that even possible? Would hoping for it destroy him if he was wrong?

Yes.

"Breanna." He wasn't sure what to say. No words came to his well-rested mind.

"You slept for nearly twelve hours. Do you know how exhausted you have to be to do that?" She moved around the sewing table and stepped right in front of him.

"Twelve hours?" His brain was firing, but it couldn't seem to calculate everything that meant.

Breanna put her hand on his chest. The motion was soft, but he got the distinct feeling that she'd shove him if he fought her right now. "The entire weight of this country does not rest on you, Sebastian. And even *if* it did, you still deserve some rest."

His hand lay over hers and he leaned his head against hers. This was a lot to take in. There were meetings to reschedule, but right now all he could muster was, "Thank you."

"You're welcome. But, um…" Color traveled up her neck as she pulled back a little. "There is more. I…um…"

"You are saying 'um' a lot." Sebastian let out a chuckle.

"I cleared your schedule for the next two weeks." The words were said so fast he almost didn't catch them.

"That is a funny joke." He laughed, and then the chuckles just kept coming. Two weeks. Tears of mirth started down his cheeks. Two weeks off as the king. Sure.

She might as well as said that they were going to the moon tomorrow. It was as feasible.

"I did." Breanna stepped away, and he ached to pull her back.

"Breanna, two weeks? I'm the king. You are the queen."

"Thanks for the reminder. If we were a normal couple, a two-week honeymoon would be a luxury, but it would raise no eyebrows. This is the same."

"Honeymoon?" The word hit his heart and the simple meaning behind it. Honeymoon. Something nearly every couple took. Something he hadn't even thought of. "I didn't think—"

"Of a honeymoon for us. Yeah. I know." She focused on the fabric on the table, not quite covering her sigh.

Darn it.

He'd hurt her. Not intentionally, but that perception was what mattered, not intent. Rule one you learned in the palace.

"Did you want a honeymoon?" He'd assumed she wanted the crown. Assumed she'd beaten her sister for it. Assumed that he was just an accessory.

Assumed a lot, if he was honest with himself.

"What I want stopped mattering long ago. If it ever did." Breanna grabbed the shears and trimmed an edge.

If it ever did.

"You didn't really want to be queen, did you?" He'd suspected it after their wedding. Worried over it. But he wanted her to say it. Though he had no idea what he'd do with the information.

The scissors in her hand seemed to slip just a bit. "What are you going to do with two weeks off, Your Highness? I suspect it is your first vacation."

Deflecting the question. Breanna was nearly as skilled at shifting the topic as him. But right now, he didn't have time to force the issue.

"I don't know." Right now, he needed to talk to Raul about scheduling their honeymoon. If he had two weeks off, they were not hiding away in the palace. He could at least give his bride a vacation.

CHAPTER TEN

"WHERE ARE YOU going on your honeymoon?" Annie's peppy voice was a good sign. It was the first time she'd sounded like herself since she'd fled their parents' mansion.

"It's just a story for the press, Annie." One she'd cooked up as she'd watched her husband sleep soundly. It had taken her longer to convince Raul to leak the news to the press. The man was as on board with Sebastian taking a rest as her. Maybe more so, but he was also steeled in tradition and protocol.

Only her promise to post it on a piece of paper on the palace wall if that was the only way to accomplish it had caused him to bend. She'd approved the press release from the public relations office then waited…and waited…for Sebastian to wake.

And she'd not seen him since he'd left her room after she told him about the two-week vacation yesterday. Their first fight. Though it didn't have much bite behind it. For fights to matter, you had to matter.

She was a name not drawn out of a hat. A woman to wear the crown. One easily overtaken by a phone call.

Breanna blew out a breath. As much as she'd love to soak up the sun on a beach, read a fun novel and think of nothing, she had no illusion that they'd go anywhere. Though Breanna planned to get to know her husband during this forced isolation period.

If he didn't have work to focus on, then he could focus on her for at least a few minutes. Right? They could have a real conversation. Not one timed to fit into his always busy schedule. Not one easily interrupted by nonsense masquerading as emergency.

"A story, Breanna." The disappointment flowed through the phone connection.

Disappointing her parents was a common thing; disappointing Annie always cut. But letting her sister know how much she wished there was some truth to the story was not an option.

They weren't a real couple, but she wished he wanted to spend time with her. It shouldn't matter. Her family had never spent much time with Breanna. The bonus twin. The one who meant her parents got a two-for-one deal.

She'd survived by pretending, accepting, and finding the silver lining.

And it was going to be her life forever. That was the part that stung. The knowledge that she'd never have the fairy tale. Not that the fairy tale truly existed.

"Well, in your mind you can imagine me in a bikini on the beach, reading a sex-filled romance novel while the sun kisses my skin."

She heard a noise and turned to find her husband standing at her door. His head was bent over his phone. Had he heard her? Probably not. The man was focused on whatever was on the screen, not her.

"I need to go, Annie. I want to see pictures of the changes you made to the apartment when you get a chance." Her sister had cut a deal with the apartment manager. He'd pay for supplies, and she could upgrade her unit and the three empty ones. It would let him raise the price of rent and give her a start on replacing her portfolio. It was a brilliant idea.

And one Annie had come up with on her own. Her sister

was getting her freedom. That was worth everything. Even marriage to a king she still didn't really know after weeks of being his wife.

"Good afternoon, Sebastian." The small line that appeared on his cheek when he was trying to hide a frown stood out. "I suspect you are here about the honeymoon story."

"I admit that it surprised me to find my queen has already managed to get the staff on her side." The words were said with a little bite. Surely he knew the staff was looking out for him, too. They were all worried about him—if only he could see that they cared about him. Not the crown.

Breanna plastered on the smile she'd used at home far too often. "It was a good plan, though. Right?" She was actually pretty proud of the calculation.

"It was." He looked at his watch. "You have thirty minutes to pack."

"Pack?" Breanna laughed. Was he kicking her out? Just for making him take a vacation.

"Yes. Pack. For the beach. Make sure you put the bikini in."

"Bikini?" He had heard her. He wasn't focused elsewhere. Was this a joke? A way to poke fun at a queen who'd overstepped her place?

Sebastian tapped his wrist "Twenty-eight minutes, Breanna."

"Where are we going?" How was she supposed to pack if she didn't know what was expected?

"On a honeymoon." Sebastian winked, then headed for the door. "I need to change something in my bag." He hit his watch one more time. "Twenty-seven minutes," he chuckled as he closed the door.

Checkmate.

His wife had successfully found a way to make him take two weeks off. Releasing the honeymoon statement while he was still deep in the land of Nod was a stroke of genius. And a honeymoon was a good idea.

It wouldn't be traditional. No matter how many times his wife appeared in his dreams, how many times he replayed the kiss on their wedding day. The dances they shared. The laughter in those stolen minutes. The feel of her while she was pressed against him.

He'd sworn to have a marriage of convenience. To give her a life with no expectations of sharing a bed with man who'd chosen her sister's name from a hat.

But they were going on a honeymoon. A long-overdue extended get-to-know-you session. His plans to head to the mountains to ski had changed as soon as he'd heard her chattering with her sister.

"Imagine me in a bikini."

It was all too easy for him to piece together the image. His mouth had watered. Spending two weeks with Breanna on the sand wearing a hopefully skimpy bathing suit would be its own form of torture.

That would have been enough of a reason for him to text Raul to change the location for this trip, but the wistfulness in her voice had stolen away his breath. The hint of wanting something. He knew that sound, the plea only his heart recognized.

She'd said that to the one person she trusted. Her sister.

"What I want stopped mattering long ago—if it ever did."

He loved skiing. The few day trips he'd managed to make as a child and teen were heaven. During his year of rebellion, Sebastian had spent more time on the slopes than at the palace.

But if her first choice was the beach? Well, she was the one who'd plotted this honeymoon out. It should be her choice.

Breanna walked up the hallway with a backpack and a small carry-on rolling bag.

"Where is the rest of your luggage?" His mother went on an overnight with more luggage than Breanna had on her.

She looked at the roller, then back at him. "You said pack for the beach. Bathing suits and shorts don't take up that much room."

His mouth watered, and he had to take a breath before he could answer. Control. His wife was gorgeous, and the idea of spending two weeks with her barely clothed…

Focus.

They could always purchase items if she needed them. The benefits of royal life.

"I do need to stop by a bookstore." Breanna smiled. "I am all out of—"

The pause hung in the air. He'd heard her words to Annie. All of them.

"Sex-filled novels?" Sebastian winked. The idea of his wife reading such novels was its own turn-on.

"Yes." She didn't look away. No color crept up her cheeks. Good. This wasn't something that should embarrass her.

"Do you know what you want?" Sebastian pulled up his phone. They could order whatever she wanted and have it sent to the beach cottage. It would be there, wrapped in nice packaging before they arrived.

Her fingers wrapped around his wrist, and she pulled his phone from his hand. The touch was gone before his mind could fully register it, but the heat it left behind scorched his skin.

"I have my TBR on a website dedicated to books. But that isn't the same as a shop."

"TBR?" Sebastian read occasionally, but he wasn't aware of a specialized lingo in the reading community.

"To be read pile." Breanna shook her head with a vigor that screamed, *How can you not know that?* "Mine is infinitely long, but I will always add to it."

"So, pick a few things off of it." Sebastian started to reach for his phone again but stopped. There was wonder in her eye. A look that was purely Breanna.

Have I ever looked like that? Excited? Free? No thought of the place or the crown.

He knew the answer. And the fact that time would likely steal the excitement from the woman in front of him tore through him.

"The fun of book shopping is the store. Walking down the aisle, picking up something with a fun cover or great title. You don't know what you want until it calls to you from the shelf." Breanna was nearly bouncing. "I know we are royals and everything, but surely there is a way we can stop at a store?"

Now she was bouncing. "You might even find something to keep you busy this week. Something besides work correspondence!" Her face was bright and excited.

And he was about to crush it with reality.

"As you say, we are royals. You are the queen. Stepping into a shop isn't as simple as just stepping into a shop."

Her face shifted, "I understand, but I mean, I am also…" Her voice wobbled. Then she lifted her chin. "We have to have a process for doing so. When you go…"

He watched the wheels turn and the realization cross her face. "I don't go anywhere that isn't preplanned. Everything is controlled, and nothing is ever just for fun. It's to promote a shop or raise awareness of a cause."

"Duty thy name is Sebastian." Breanna pulled at her neck, then reached for her phone. "I guess the TBR list it is." The laugh that fell from her lips wasn't crisp. It wasn't fun or happy.

Resigned.

That was the word for Breanna in this moment. Resigned. No anger. No frustration

She pulled up an app, clearing her throat. "I guess the top five on here are a good start."

He took a screen shot of the top ten and sent it to Raul with instructions for them to be delivered to the beach house before them.

"Wonderful." He pointed to her bag. "Really sure you don't need to add anything else? We're going for two weeks."

"Really."

All right then. He held out a hand, his body relaxing as her hand fit into his. "Time for a honeymoon."

Whatever that means.

The blue bikini was skimpier than she remembered. All of the bathing suits Breanna had brought were skimpier than she remembered. Annie used to joke that Breanna bought as little material as possible as though that would let her soak up more sun.

Which was technically true. And if this was a traditional honeymoon, the bright blue string bikini—well, this would make most people's mouth water.

He'd told her that he'd watched her with Hector. Hector swore Sebastian was jealous. But how could he be?

Breanna was hoping for kisses. Sitting in his lap like a fool, only to have the phone give her husband a reason to be free of her. Oh, he'd offered five minutes, but she hadn't wanted that. No matter how many times she thought he was about to drop his lips to hers, the most he ever did was lightly kiss her head. A sweet motion for those watching, probably.

And on their "honeymoon," they had separate rooms.

"Technically, I don't have anything with more coverage." She looked at her bed and sighed. There was no way she was spending this vacation inside.

In my own room.

She opened the door to her private beach entrance, pushing back the tears that were pulling at her. A private room. A private entrance. All to herself...on a honeymoon.

If she gave herself time to think on that, her heart might break. Silver lining, Breanna. She was on the beach. She was away from the palace. Away from the schedule.

The sun hit her face, and Breanna's heart lifted a little. The beach called to her. She had a book—freshly delivered—and a lounge chair calling her name.

Strolling up to the chairs, she was shocked to find Sebastian already in his. Washboard abs ordinarily hidden by suits and tailored shirts were on full display. He looked like a man who had stepped from the pages of one of her books.

Maybe being around her hot, mostly unclothed husband for two weeks wasn't the best plan.

"It's nice out, but the sun is bright. If you want me to get the umbrella—" Sebastian turned his head, his words stopping as he stared at her.

Guess the bikini was as head-turning as she thought.

"I like the sun. Annie says I crave it." It was one way they were different. Annie liked cloudy, rainy days.

"My parents could always tell us apart in the summer because I had a tan." It was the only time in the year the girls weren't interchangeable.

"Only in the summer?"

Her husband's tone was sharp, but she just shrugged. Mistaking their daughters' names never bothered their parents— if it bothered the girls, then that was their problem.

"Identical twins. Interchangeable and all."

His hand was on hers in an instant. "You are not interchangeable."

"Sure I am. Even on the day you came looking for Annie I was. It's okay." Mostly it was. It was her life.

Sebastian's thumb ran along her wrist, the movement sending little spikes of energy up her arms. "I am glad you were the one who came into that room, Breanna."

Her name rumbled from his lips. Her name. Not her title. His muscles were relaxed, but her eyes couldn't seem to stop from staring. What would it feel like to run her hands down them? Drag her lips across them?

Not like she'd find out in the private room she occupied. He was glad it was her. He was holding her hand, but not pulling her any closer.

Get it together.

Breanna slid onto the chair next to his and pushed her sunglasses back on her head. Time for some sun, and she didn't want to risk tan lines around her eyes with the glasses. That and forcing her eyes closed would make sure she couldn't drool over the physical attributes of her husband.

"Annie is the one who stands out—even looking just like me."

"What is that supposed to mean?" Sebastian shifted beside her. Maybe pushing up on his elbow? If she was sitting on the other side, she could get a great view of his butt. Of course, if her chair was on that side, he would have turned to look at her that way. So, the hypothetical situation where she drooled over his backside was flawed from inception.

She heard him twist again but didn't open her eyes. "It means what it sounds like it means." Breanna wasn't sure what the question was about. And her mind had very little available space for anything more than picturing her hot husband who she'd barely touched during their month together.

Seriously, fantasizing about how to get a glimpse of the Adonis's butt. Yep. There was no way she was daring to open her eyes. At least with the sun's rays dancing on her skin, she could pretend the heat wasn't embarrassment crawling up her body.

Sebastian's hand stroked her arm, and she nearly shot up. Only a lifetime of ignoring her wants kept her in place.

"Breanna." Her name was soft as he rubbed a thumb across her arm.

Goose bumps appeared despite the heat.

"Breanna."

"Yes, Sebastian?"

He waited for a moment. Probably seeing if she'd open her eyes. Nope, not happening.

"Why does Annie stand out?" The words were barely above a whisper.

Why was this the first conversation they were having? It was sunny. They could talk of books. Of places they'd visited. Him for official business. Her for family business trips. They could talk about anything. But no, he wanted to know this.

If she didn't answer, he'd press. She knew that. But right now, it was a soft question. A plea. "Annie was the daughter to secure a good marriage. I was the extra. A two-for-one deal, they liked to say. And she is so talented. She is going to make a name for herself. All for herself."

Sebastian didn't say anything, but the pressure on her hand increased.

She hadn't meant to say anything else, but now that the first words were out, her mouth seemed incapable of controlling itself. She'd never told anyone how it felt to be the extra. How much she wanted a different life.

She'd wanted to teach. To disappear into a classroom. Educate the next generation. Something so small. Meaningless to her parents. So meaningless they'd stymied every attempt she'd made to get into the classroom.

"And you?"

If she opened her eyes, the words would likely stop. She'd lose the ability to form them. But she'd also have to see the pity in Sebastian's eyes.

"My dreams were smaller. A classroom decorated with bright colors and little students who wanted to be in circle time. Or didn't. At that age, sitting still is not a skill most little ones have. My student teaching days were my happiest. But teaching is not a profession for Galanis women. Not when we can marry well, according to my parents."

She laughed, but the lack of humor wasn't lost on her. "Anyways, Annie is brilliant with colors. She has dreams. She's an interior designer. One day everyone on this island will know exactly who she is—for her work—not her name."

"So when I pulled her name from the hat…" Sebastian's whispers chilled her skin.

"She was going to marry you. I saw it. All the work she'd done to get her portfolio ready. Our escape hatch." She cleared her throat. "Anyways, I pointed out that you didn't know her so you couldn't mind if we switched the script. We look the same, after all. And you didn't know us. Which was true."

"Breanna." Her name. The twin he hadn't meant to meet at the altar. Why was this bothering her now? They'd been married a month. A month as his queen. A month of accepting that this was her life.

And she was doing a good job. Or she had been. Until she'd stepped onto this beach.

"I don't say that to make you feel bad. I say it as the truth. Annie has a dream." Breanna sighed as she remembered the first room Annie had ever redecorated. A spare room her mother had no use for. A room designed for failure.

Her parents had only let Annie try because Breanna would not stop pestering. And then the finished product was gorgeous. It was still the room her mother had all the guests sleep in. Not that they'd ever praised Annie.

But others would.

"And your dream was a classroom?"

Rolling over, she opened her eyes, letting the grin swimming in her soul appear freely. "No. My dream was for Annie to get her dream. And she is going to. She has an apartment now. She is decorating it, and the empty units, with her landlord's approval. Maybe it isn't the fancy portfolio our parents stole, but it's something that can't be taken from her."

"But what was *your* dream?" Sebastian's hand gripped hers. Heat bloomed beneath it.

She lifted it, placed a soft kiss on it, then rolled onto her back. "That was my dream. Now my dream is to get some sun." There was no point discussing this. She'd made her choice.

This was her life now. She was a queen. Annie was free.

Maybe this wasn't the life she'd envisioned. She'd never step into the classroom as a teacher. Never see little eyes light up as they learned their letters and numbers. But she'd make the same choice again without question.

CHAPTER ELEVEN

"WANT TO ORDER some lunch?" Breanna stretched on the lounge chair next to him. She'd occupied it nearly every moment since they'd arrived yesterday. Flipping when the timer on her phone went off. Or running into the sea for a quick dip. "Or would you rather cook?"

The sun kissed her skin in ways he could only dream of.

"What would you prefer?" He had a fully stocked kitchen here. Outside of sushi, he could fix up just about anything she requested.

His wife sat up. The pink polka-dot string bikini left so little to the imagination, if he was standing, he might drop to his knees in worship of the beauty beside him. She was delectable.

The blue bikini from yesterday had played the main role in his dreams last night. Today, his fingers ached to travel down her stomach. Circle her belly button, see what sounds she might make if his lips followed the same path.

None of which was going to happen.

"I do not enjoy cooking, so fixing my own food on vacation is not high on my priorities." Breanna moved her hand like she was going to push his shoulder, but he caught it and held it.

Her eyes flicked to their combined fingers, but she didn't pull back. "However, you do enjoy it. And this is your vacation. Do you want to cook?"

She'd put his needs first. Again. It was a pattern that he should have seen faster. One he might have seen if he'd spent more time with his queen. The woman put others first. It was an admirable quality.

But it didn't mean you had to give up everything you wanted. Outside of sewing, did his wife even know what her preferences were? Had she ever had dreams that revolved just around her?

Just because she was an identical twin didn't mean she didn't get to be an individual.

"What is your favorite food? The day after our wedding, you asked about me, but I learned little other than you like a little coffee with your syrup in the morning." Her laughter filled his heart as she swung their combined hands.

"My coffee is not that full of syrup." She stuck her tongue out, then laughed.

His statement wasn't that far from the truth. His wife put at least four squirts of coffee syrup in each mug. He watched her create combinations that he'd never consider. Sometimes it was clear she had a drink she was recreating. Other times it seemed she was just flying by the seat of her sweet tooth.

"What is your favorite food, Breanna? I know you like lemon cake, and I will make that if you like, but one cannot live on dessert alone."

"Not sure that is true." Breanna pulled her hand back, and even though he wanted to reach for it again, Sebastian let it be.

"I can't make it if I don't know it." This was such a simple question. One most people could spout off with no thought.

"I like vegetable lasagna. Our cook used to make it once a week so I had something besides salads for dinner." She rolled her head, shifting in the chair. Discomfort was clear on her features.

This was about food; it wasn't hard. Or it shouldn't be. And the statement's meaning struck him. "Did you not have vegetarian options at dinner?" The Galanis estate was famous for the luxury dinners they served investors. Sebastian had attended more than one event at the estate with his father.

He racked his memory for anything about those events, but they were a blur in a lifetime of service. He wasn't even sure he'd seen Breanna and Annie there. Though they were probably in the sea of people.

"My parents did not support my choice." She stood and walked towards the sea.

He followed.

"That can't be surprising, Sebastian. Unless you and Raul had intervened, I would have eaten very little at my own wedding reception." She strolled into the waves, then turned and splashed him.

Water dripped down his face as she squealed and sent another small wave towards him. He cupped some water and tossed it her way. Her laughter increased.

The moment was fun, and happy. A honeymoon moment—and once more she'd redirected the conversation away from her. He splashed some more water her way, then reached for her waist and pulled her towards him. "What is your favorite food, Breanna? I am not letting you go until you tell me." Sebastian dipped his head and kissed her forehead.

He'd done that many times. It was never thought out, and not what he truly wanted, but he didn't want to push her for more than she'd signed on for. Even if he craved more.

Water slipped off his wife's face, and she didn't pull away from him. Instead, her hips pressed against him as the waves broke around them.

"You plan to hold me until I tell you my favorite food, Sebastian?" His wife moved her head, her lips so close to his. "Not sure that is much of a threat."

The sun's heat had nothing on the flames pouring through him. Steam should have risen from the ocean water as his mind replayed Breanna's comments back to him. "Breanna." His brain seemed incapable of forming any other thought besides his wife's name.

"Sebastian." Her arms wrapped around his neck. "How long do you think we'll just stand here? High tide comes in shortly. Then what?"

"What if I cut you a deal?" He stroked her back, enjoying the feel of her in his arms.

"A deal?" Her arms tightened just a little, and her hips brushed his again. The sun glinted off her dark hair. It was like he was standing with a fairy-tale creature. One he desperately wanted answers from. Though the question was far too simple for a fairy tale.

"Sebastian." Her purr echoed with the waves.

Maintaining his focus was a never-ending battle. "A deal." He cleared his throat, the action doing nothing to clear the thoughts of trailing his lips down her throat. "You tell me your favorite dish; I fix it. Then we spend the night cuddled on the couch. You pick the movie."

"I told you." She pressed her lips to his. The connection lasted barely a second. "Veggie lasagna."

"No. You said the cook made that once a week so you didn't have to eat salads. Not the same thing. And if you shrug that off—"

"You'll what? Kiss me into submission?"

Tempting. Oh, so very tempting. And if he didn't think she was using this to make him try to forget about herself, then he might just offer that. But this was important.

Even if she didn't think so.

"I won't cuddle on the couch." He wasn't sure how they'd slipped from serious conversations to playfulness, but he was embracing it. There was more than one way to get an answer. And sometimes humor worked best of all.

The Sebastian he'd been a year ago bolted from the cage

he'd locked him away in. "Or maybe I will spend the whole movie talking. Just interrupting and asking questions."

"You wouldn't." She threw one hand over her heart in playful surrender, but the other stayed wrapped around his neck.

"I guess I don't know. I ate a lot of salads, so definitely not that. At home it was lasagna though...my college roommate, Binna, used to make this potato dish. It..." She closed her eyes.

This was a moment he recognized. A dish that touched you. That made you feel something. It was something chefs worked for years to achieve. He'd once made a lamb stew that had brought tears to his eyes as the flavors mixed together.

Food had power. It held memories...good and bad.

"Describe it to me." He whispered the words against her ear as the water rose around them, binding them together. His fingers stroked her back. Staying a respectful distance from the top of her bikini bottom.

She brushed her lips against his, again. It was like they were going with the motions. This place was out of time and space. Just for them.

"Breanna." Her name was power. He ached for her to deepen the kiss, but he wasn't going to push this.

"Sebastian." Her lips passed his again. Then she seemed to remember they'd been talking about food.

"Binna used a giant pot with a lid. Not a sauce pot but something she'd brought over from Korea. But you could find it anywhere. She joked with me once that I knew so little about cooking, I thought the pot was something special. She had a name for it, but one of the other roommates called it an oven of some kind."

"A Dutch oven." It wasn't an uncommon method for making a stew. In fact, he'd crafted several in the one he stored in his kitchen.

"Yep. That's it. Binna's dish was called gochujang potato stew. I have no idea what the recipe was, and I wish I'd asked. Unfortunately, we lost touch after graduation. I heard she works at some big pharmaceutical firm in Germany now. The spices were strong, and I remember she was worried the scent would upset people."

"Did it?" Food was home. It was also something people judged. At uni, a young man had talked about how the kids at his school bullied him for the ethnic food his mother packed each day. A reminder of home for her. Something that made him different during a period everyone wanted to fit in.

Now he owned one the most successful restaurants on the island, and people paid a good bit for the Vietnamese cuisine others had judged.

Breanna shook her head. "It drove them to our door, but in a good way. It was so aromatic and yummy. Whenever people smelled it, we'd have them begging for a taste. I think Binna could have funded university by selling the stew."

"Well, I know how to make a gochujang stew, so I just need to see if there is gochujang in the spice cabinet here. I keep it in my kitchen at the palace. I'm not sure I have the exact potatoes Binna used, but it is a fairly standard dish, so we can play around and see if we can recreate it."

"Seriously?" Breanna planted a solid kiss on his lips before pulling back. "Oh."

It looked like all the blood in her body might be running to her face. "You're turning red." Sebastian dropped a playful kiss on her nose. "Don't want my bride getting sunburned."

"It has nothing to do with the sun, Your Highness." Breanna kissed his nose, recreating the movement he'd used.

He held his breath, and when her lips met his this time, there was no hesitation. A strong wave pushed against them, and rather than pull back, she wrapped her legs around his waist.

She opened her mouth, her tongue sweeping his, and the

world melted away. She tasted of the ocean, sun and future. Breanna. His wife. His queen.

The kiss was over far too soon. She dipped her head, then grabbed his hand and pulled him towards the beach. "Let's see if you have the spice."

If perfection ever needed a new descriptor, it could use this moment to build it. He wanted to stop time. Be just Sebastian and Breanna forever.

Spices and ocean air might be her new favorite scent. She had no idea how she'd recreate it, but the spice smell meant she wasn't surprised to find Sebastian standing in the kitchen tossing a few things into the Dutch oven he'd found in the back of a cabinet yesterday.

"I figured we'd eat leftovers today." They had at least enough stew for a second serving. His gochujang potato stew wasn't the same as Binna's, but it was good. And the fact that he'd made something for her, something she wanted...it was a feeling she couldn't describe.

Which was why she'd jumped into his arms yesterday. And kissed him. It was spontaneous. But it felt right. Like she'd been waiting her whole life for a switch that was finally on. He'd kissed her back. Really kissed her.

Maybe he'd finally initiate a kiss. A real one instead of brushes against her forehead and nose. Their relationship was finally shifting.

Relationship. She wanted to laugh at the word. They'd gone from married strangers to people who'd shared a confidence beside the sea. It should feel awkward.

Should feel weird. They were married. Staying in separate rooms. But kissing and touching and...and figuring out what they were. It was certainly a unique way for spouses to play get-to-know-you.

Still, it felt right.

"We can have the stew for lunch. But I'm making some lentil curry for dinner. It will be perfect after cooking all day." Sebastian tilted his head towards the coffee. "I just made a fresh pot."

Just made.

"How long have you been up?" These two weeks were supposed to be about him resting. He couldn't do that if he was rising at three.

Sebastian bent his head.

The sudden focus on a dish she guessed he'd made dozens of times and the rapid spin of the spoon broke her heart. "Sebastian." He'd spent his entire life in service. Even on vacation, he was still serving. Except instead of a country, it was a focus of one. But what about what he wanted? What he needed?

She walked up behind him, wrapping her arms around his waist. She laid her head against shoulder. "What time, honey?"

The endearment slipped out, but she wasn't going to focus on that now. They were helping each other. Giving each other rest. A place away from the lives they'd grown up in. A fresh start, hopefully.

"I managed to stay in bed until five."

Managed...

"Okay. But what time did you wake up?" She was a master of wording, too. One did not grow up in the Galanis household without learning more than a few phrasing tricks.

He chuckled, but there was no humor in the sound. "My wife is keen to my tricks already. I thought that was something that took time to develop in a marriage."

She squeezed him tighter. There was no judgment here. Just concern. "Sebastian."

"Three forty-five." He uttered the time and shrugged against her. "It's like my body needs to be up and going."

His voice was coated in exhaustion and frustration. "Sorry."

"You don't have to be sorry." His body was following the only routine it had ever known. The routine that had been forced onto him as a child. She couldn't get mad at that. At least not at him.

He stirred the dish, but she didn't let go. She was here for him. "During my rebellious year, I used to slip my security early in the morning. It drove Alessio mad. He accused me of trying to get hurt. Brie gave me an exceptionally strong talking-to one day. Told me I was hurting him."

And that would have nearly killed him. Sebastian cared for everyone. Full stop.

"Anyways, even when I was pushing back on the duty I was born for, I couldn't manage to keep myself in bed. What kind of rebellion involves being up before the dawn?"

"Not a very good one." She kissed his shoulder. "Somehow, I can't imagine you as rebellious. I mean, I remember that year. I know you call it failure and other ridiculous things, but please!"

Sebastian turned in her arms, wrapping his arms around her waist. They stood there, in the kitchen. His lips pressed to her head. "And what would you know about rebellion, Breanna?"

"Oh." She pulled back, then kissed his cheek. "I have rebelled a time or two." She laughed and kissed his shoulder again.

"I doubt that, very seriously, *Your Highness*." This time his chuckle had a true lilt of humor.

She pushed on his shoulder, breaking the connection and offering a very fake pout. "How dare you say that." She grabbed a mug of coffee, dropped four pumps of brown sugar cinnamon syrup in it, then hopped on the counter.

Sebastian nodded his head the way she'd watched one of

her uni professors do when about to press an important point. Her husband was getting ready to ask a very deep question. "Tell me one truly rebellious thing you ever did?"

"Hmm." She put her finger on her chin, playfully looking at him. "I need to think about what secrets to give away. Tell me what you did, *Your Highness.*"

Sebastian went to the fridge and pulled out two jars. "Overnight oats made with almond milk and dried fruit."

"Ooh." She grabbed a spoon from the freshly washed rack and opened her container. "So good."

Sebastian took a bite of his, then pointed a spoon at her. "I broke off the relationship with the woman my father wanted me to marry. A year-long affair just..." He snapped his fingers, and a look she worried was wistfulness floated on his features.

A girlfriend. Whoever she was, there'd never been any hint of her in the press.

There was no sign of animosity in his voice. No dismissive tone for a relationship that hadn't worked out. Did he miss her? Was she who he'd really wanted to wear the crown and the reason he'd settled for Breanna?

Words escaped her.

"The night of my first state dinner, I told Samantha that I hated the crown. Hated the responsibility and wished I'd never been born heir to the throne."

He took a deep breath. "And she said she didn't understand that because without it I was a nobody. The crown was the only thing that made me special. Pretty sure it just popped out and she tried to walk it back, but... I could see it was the truth."

That was horrible. "Sebastian." She wasn't sure what else to say. "You—"

"I don't want to talk about Sam. She's gone, and luckily

the nondisclosure agreement my father worked out was iron clad. The man had some good ideas."

His voice was set. But the look on his face broke her heart. His title was such a small part of him. But they'd discuss that another time. "Well, that doesn't count."

"Excuse me." Sebastian stepped between her legs, and she dropped a kiss on his lips, happy that he was grinning.

"You broke off a relationship that didn't work. Sorry, Your Highness, but there is nothing rebellious about that. Very standard stuff, actually."

Her husband's eyes rolled to the ceiling. "Fine. I arrived almost three hours late to my first state dinner. It made Briella the villain in a media narrative that still floats to the surface now and then."

Not anymore.

Breanna knew the articles printed about them were less than congratulatory. More than one op-ed had run about the king so openly agreeing to a marriage of convenience. As though he'd been forced into it, rather than marching into her home after choosing Annie's name from a hat.

Alessio had a lotto bride. King Sebastian had the leftovers. The headlines practically wrote themselves.

"Enough about me. What mischief have you ever gotten up to?"

"I orchestrated my sister's escape."

"Doesn't count." He mimicked her voice, and she couldn't stop the giggle. "I already know that." Sebastian turned the stovetop to Warm, then reached for her hand. "Come one. We can finish breakfast on the patio."

"I told you I changed places with her." Breanna said as she followed him outside. "I didn't tell you that I used a secret fund of money to get her an apartment. That I helped make sure she never has to contact our parents again. Their two-for-one deal is forever outside their reach."

Breanna laughed. "They hadn't fully realized it by the wedding. They refused to talk to her, thinking that would bring her back. Nope. She's gone. Then my husband—the king—ordered them out." She put her hand to her lips and blew a kiss.

No words fell across the small table for what felt like forever. "I think that counts." She scooped the last bits of oats into her mouth and held up the spoon.

"That isn't rebellion, Breanna." Sebastian's words were soft. "It's survival."

Survival. Three syllables; three tiny daggers she didn't want to acknowledge.

"Want to go into town today?" Breanna pointed to the beach. "It's a beautiful day. Though I suspect every day is beautiful here."

"Breanna—"

"Shopping sounds fun." That wasn't really true. She'd never been a fan of shopping. Except for books and in thrift stores. Those places she could spend hours in.

"We can go shopping later in the week. I have to get security set." Sebastian's brow burrowed as he reached his hand across the table, wrapping it through hers. "But I have an idea."

"More talking..." Breanna had wanted to get to know her husband. Wanted to care for him—it was what she did. But him seeing through her own armor...it was exhausting.

"Yes. But about food." Sebastian put his free hand over his heart. "I am making the curry for dinner, but do you want to make bread?"

"Isn't that baking?" She made a playful face. "I was under the impression my husband did not like baking."

He stuck his tongue out. "I like making bread. But yes, I guess, technically, it's baking. But it's a process. A long one. We can make the dough. Knead it, then sit in the sun or play in the sea while it rises. If you think about it, it's the perfect vacation bake."

"I've never made bread." Breanna ran her thumb along his hand, enjoying the connection but wanting to be away from the chairs, where she seemed intent on spilling secrets she didn't even share with herself.

"But sure."

Breanna beat the dough. Her dough had passed the right stage for rising minutes ago. The bread was going to be hard. But this exercise wasn't about perfect bread. Even hard, it would still be good for croutons and dipping in sauces.

She needed to work out her anger towards her parents. Anger she'd not even allowed herself to acknowledge.

He did, too, but his wasn't decades long. Though if Lucas and Matilda Galanis thought they could profit from having a daughter with a crown, they were sorely mistaken. Money bought lots of things. Power, security, influence.

Things a king had, too. And while he couldn't strip the Galanises of power and security, he could limit their influence significantly. At least in the aristocratic circles they craved. His wife was not part of a "two-for-one deal." She was not interchangeable.

She was amazing, and he was lucky she'd switched places with her sister. His wife sacrificed herself for everyone else. Even a husband she barely knew. From this point forward she needed to be herself. Whoever that was.

"How long am I supposed to beat this?"

"The baking term is to knead." Sebastian chuckled. "Though I think what you have done to that bread counts more as beating than kneading."

Breanna looked up, her mouth falling open. "Wait. Did I do this wrong?"

"Not at all." Sebastian grabbed the oiled bowl he'd prepped for the bread to rise in. "Just put it in here."

Breanna gave him a look he couldn't decipher as she dropped the dough in the bowl. "I feel better." She looked at the dough she'd pummeled, then at him. "Thank you."

"I may not like baking, but making bread is a healing process. Not sure why, but it is true." Sebastian shrugged. He'd created many hard loafs in the last few years.

"You know what else is healing?" Breanna tilted her head, and her fun smile reappeared.

"Should I be worried?" Sebastian saw her hand move to pile of flour she'd used for the bread the instant before it landed on his chest.

"Flour fight!" Breanna giggled as another pile hit his pants.

Flour dust filled the air as he reached for a handful. His toss landed on her shoulder, the dusting cloud dropping specks across her nose and cheeks. She squealed, and happiness burst through his body.

When Breanna grabbed the last handful from the counter, he raised his hands, providing her with a full target. "Give it your best shot, wife."

Wife.

A flash passed over her eyes, but she didn't launch the flour. Instead, she sauntered towards him, the flour tight in her hand. "Husband." She wrapped her arms behind his neck and raised her brows. "There are two options as I see it."

Her husky tone triggered goose pimples on his arms. "And those are?"

"I can drop this flour in your hair. See what you will look like when we have been married for decades and you have passed gray and gone on to white hair."

"That would make quite a mess." Sebastian squeezed her waist. He thought he knew what option two was. And he'd choose it over anything else. But if he was wrong, or she chose to dust his hair with flour, that was fine, too.

"You could kiss me." Pink rushed to her cheeks, but Breanna didn't break her gaze. "Really kiss me."

Sebastian pulled her as close to him as possible. "If I get to choose—" he ran his hand up her back, leaning as close to her as possible "—it is the easiest choice of all." He dipped his head, dropping his lips along her jaw. They were coated in flour, but he didn't want to miss this opportunity.

He took a deep breath, then pressed his lips to hers. This wasn't the hesitant kiss they'd shared right before their wedding. It wasn't the passing glance they'd shared over the altar. Or even the flirty fun they'd had in the sea.

This was the future. It was sweet, passionate, and timeless. Everything he'd dreamed of. Sebastian ran his hand across her skin as his tongue danced with hers as though they'd done this hundreds of times.

She pressed her hands to his back. The handful of flour dropping to the floor behind him…and probably splashing across her skin, too. Another thing that didn't matter.

"Sebastian."

His name on her lips, breathless. Desire exploded through him. He wanted to kiss her, everywhere. Spend the rest of his day worshipping her lips, her body, everything.

She slipped a hand under his shirt. The light touch of her fingers set his skin ablaze. He followed her motion, slipped his hand under her shirt, mimicking each of her strokes.

"We are getting flour all over." Breanna's silky voice matched this moment even though her words were the stuff of comedy.

"We are." Sebastian ached to scoop her up. One word from her and he'd take her to bed and spend the next several days learning every inch of her. Memorizing what made her sigh with satisfaction and pant with need.

"We could rinse off in the sea." Her lips slipped along his neck.

He'd never had trouble finding words, but when his wife flirted with him, the synapses refused to fire.

"First one to the water wins." Breanna kissed him, then took off running. She was out the door and onto their private beach before he turned.

There was no way he was winning this race, but each of her giggles felt like a trophy.

CHAPTER TWELVE

SEBASTIAN WASN'T BEHIND HER. At least not yet. That final kiss had thrown him, but her husband would follow soon. Still, the delay was the only reason she had the courage to take on the truly rebellious act of dropping her shorts, T-shirt, and bathing suit before racing into the surf.

He'd said she wasn't rebellious. But she could be. She'd show him.

She planned to carve her own path as queen. And she doubted queens took naked dips in the sea after food fights with their husbands.

Turning to the beach, she saw the moment her husband discovered her pile of clothes by the chair she'd occupied most of this vacation. All the momentum he'd had from running evaporated as he looked from the water to her clothes, then back at Breanna. If he'd been a cartoon character, his eyes would have popped out as the sand flew up around him.

She splashed a little but did not rise far enough up for her breasts to exit the water. The bloom of heat she feared was embarrassment was pushing at her mind. Breanna was not going to give in to it. She'd started this. And she was finishing it.

Maybe a rebellious queen was the exactly what King Sebastian needed.

"Come in, the water is very nice. You can keep your clothes on, if you like." He could, but she wanted him to strip. Wanted to run her hands over all of him. Give in to the emotions she felt every time she was near him. Tame the heat that refused to cool whenever his hands were on hers.

The king looked at the pile again, then pulled his shirt off. His abs gleamed in the sun, and Breanna licked her lips.

No one was ever going to say that King Sebastian of Celiana wasn't the most handsome king to sit on the island's ancient throne. His hands went to his shorts. Then he paused and looked at her.

"You will have me at a disadvantage if you leave your shorts on, but I will understand."

I might die of embarrassment, but I'll understand.

Sebastian smiled, then walked into the water. His bathing shorts still firmly on.

Hell.

As he stepped next to her, she fought back the urge to cover herself with her hands. Rebellion wasn't all that good if you didn't commit.

"How is that for rebellion?" She winked, then slid under the water, running her hands through her hair.

When she surfaced, she raised her hands, patting her soaking hair. "Did I get all the flour out?" Her nipples were just below the surface, but easy to see in the crystal-clear water. And the primary focus of her husband.

He blew out a breath. "Breanna—"

Her name. Only her name left his lips. It was like a meditation as he stared at her.

"Sebastian." She swam a little closer. "You didn't answer my question."

"Question?" He titled his head.

She couldn't stop the giggle. "I *asked* if I got all the flour out of my hair. Aren't you paying attention?"

"I think my wife knows very well exactly what attention she is drawing out of me." The huskiness of his tone sent little waves of desire through her body. She'd never had someone so in thrall to her.

He lifted his head, purposefully looking at her hair. "I don't see any more flour."

"Anywhere?" She twirled, breathing deeply, fearful that her nerve might evaporate any moment.

Sebastian's gargled sound as she spun slowly in the water made her giggle. Power. Excitement. Happiness. In this moment she was simply Breanna. Not one of a pair.

All the emotions swirled in her body as she waited for his answer and met his gaze. "Well?"

His Adam's apple bobbed as he swallowed, then cleared his throat. "No more flour."

She swam close enough that her breasts were nearly touching his chest. "You have a little on your cheek." She dipped her hand in the water, even though it was already wet, then ran her fingers along the streak, wiping it away.

She didn't lower her hand. Instead, she traced her finger along his chin, enjoying the hint of stubble there. "You don't shave as close when you aren't at the palace. I like it."

"Breanna."

There was her name again, followed by nothing else.

"Sebastian." She mimicked his tone. "I like when you kiss me."

His hand was around her waist in an instant. He pulled her close, her body, her naked body, pressed against him. "Your wish, my lady."

She might not have a lot of experience with men—or any—but she understood how the human body worked. Breanna knew how to give herself an orgasm and knew that the bulge on her hip meant her husband was incredibly turned on.

"I think I am going to enjoy having a wife that runs naked into the water. We certainly couldn't do this on a ski slope." Sebastian dipped his head to hers and placed both hands on her butt, lifting her out of the water as his tongue danced with hers.

She wrapped her legs around him. Her body knew what she wanted; her mind would just get in the way.

Waves cradled them as they clung together. Here and now, it was only Breanna and Sebastian. The past, present and future didn't matter.

Nothing mattered except the feel of his lips on hers, the dance of his fingers on her skin.

"Breanna."

Her name sounded different this time. A force rather than a meditation. A breaking. Reality seeping back into their lives.

She pulled back but let her fingers run through his hair. Touching him was a necessity she couldn't understand even as she knew he was about to end whatever was happening here.

"We need to go back inside the cottage." His voice was tight as he pulled back. The moment over.

"Right." She nodded. "The bread is probably ready for the oven."

"I very much doubt the bread is ready for the oven." His lips were so close but not on hers. Not where she wanted them.

Before her brain could muddle through any words, Sebastian continued, "I want you, Breanna. My desire burns. Come to bed with me?"

"Breanna." Sebastian breathed her name against her ear as she clung to him through the waves. For the rest of time, he'd remember the moment he'd stepped into the sea with his naked bride.

The only reason he hadn't fully stripped was that he'd needed some kind of barrier between him and the stunning sea creature waiting for him in the surf.

"I like how you say my name." Breanna ran her fingers along his chin.

She liked the stubble there, too. His father had instructed him to shave multiple times a day. A prince and king must always be presentable. And stubble or a beard...apparently those didn't fit a royal image.

The first morning, he'd held the razor, then put it away. He was on vacation, after all. In the realm of rebellion, it wasn't anywhere near dancing naked into the sea. But it felt nice.

"Breanna." He let the syllables drip off his tongue before he pressed his lips to the top of her ear. Salt, waves and the scent that was simply his wife invaded his senses. His bedroom seemed so far away, but she deserved her first time to be slow. Sensual. Memorable.

Not a romp on the beach.

"Just like that." Her hands dipped to the waistband of his shorts, her thumb running along the top.

"Again, you have me at a disadvantage. You *are* clothed."

"No." He nipped her ear. "It is *you* who has me at a disadvantage, Breanna." She was the only thing he could think of. Her slick body set his ablaze.

He stepped up to the cottage, and Breanna reached over and turned the door handle.

"Teamwork," she whispered as her fingers ran through his hair.

Teamwork.

He liked that.

Moving through the cottage as quickly as his legs would carry them, Sebastian let her open his bedroom door, and he kicked it closed behind him. Capturing her lips, he gently laid her on his bed.

Stunning didn't begin to describe the siren on his bed. Her wet, dark hair splayed across his pillow; her pink lips were swollen from kisses. Her nipples tightened as he twirled a thumb around each.

"Sebastian."

His name. The power behind the sound of it on Breanna's sweet lips nearly sent him to his knees. Letting his fingers dance across her glorious curves, he listened to each hitch of her breath. Studied each movement that made her arch against him.

Greed was the best description for the urge within him. But it wasn't his own release he needed. Sebastian craved the knowledge of Breanna's needs. Her wants. The touches that would make her say his name with such perfection.

Dipping his head, he trailed his lips along the same path his fingers had traveled just moments before. Breanna's hips arched, and he took the offering.

His mouth found the right spot, his fingers trailing along the insides of her thighs.

"Sebastian." The pant was perfection as she crested to completion. "Sebastian. I...want...you."

Every bit of control fled his body.

He stood, stripped, and moved on top of his wife. She wrapped her legs around his waist, and it was only as he was pressing against her that the rational thought of contraception broke through passion's fog.

"I don't have a condom." He kissed her neck. This was supposed to be a honeymoon in name only. Only in his dreams had he allowed himself to contemplate this moment.

Breanna let out a breath. "We *are* married, and I have an IUD." She kissed his lips, then pulled back. "But if you want to wait..."

He did not. "Breanna." Sebastian kissed her, joining them and losing himself in the blissfulness that was his wife.

CHAPTER THIRTEEN

BREANNA STRETCHED IN the kitchen. She'd fallen asleep in Sebastian's arms and stayed there until just after six this morning. Her husband was still snoozing. It was the biggest win.

Maybe having company in his bed was what he needed to stay put. If that was a sacrifice she needed to make, it was the best one the universe had ever asked of her.

She smiled as she fixed a cup of coffee for herself and then another for Sebastian. She'd love to let him sleep, but he'd promised her a trip into town. Breanna grabbed a muffin. The top was a little hard. It was still good, but not as fresh as when it had been delivered a few days ago. But neither she nor Sebastian wanted to bake muffins.

It would work for today, and while they were in town, they could make sure they stopped at a local bakery. She'd enjoyed the last several days alone with him. But she was also looking forward to checking out the local bookstore.

Breanna needed to get moving, or rather get her husband moving. So, she tossed the muffin on a platter she'd found, then headed for the dark room.

"I smell coffee." His words were slow, and his eyes weren't open. The sheet was loosely covering his bottom half.

Her body heated, and the urge to spend the rest of the day right here was nearly overwhelming. But they'd asked security to take them. And a few of the stores in town were planning on their arrival. Inconveniencing others wasn't a good look, especially for royals.

Particularly for such a reason. *Sorry. Can't come, the queen and king are too busy getting busy* wasn't really a statement she wanted anyone to type up.

Sebastian sat up and grabbed the coffee.

He took a deep sip and met her gaze. "I slept in."

"You did." Breanna laughed as he grinned over the mug. "I think we may have found a way to keep your butt in bed."

His eyes sparkled as he looked to her. "I like having your butt in bed." He reached for her, but she pulled back.

"I let you sleep as long as possible, Your Highness!" She tapped the watch he'd given her. "But if I let you touch me..."

She swallowed as he sat up a little straighter. The sheet slipped even further. Her husband, ruffled from a night of good sleep, was sexy as hell.

"If you let me touch you?" His gaze dipped to her breasts.

Her nipples tightened as the memory of him stroking her filled her. "If I let you touch me, you know exactly what will happen."

Sebastian playfully raised his eyebrows twice, then took another sip of his coffee. He was a dream.

"I also brought you a muffin, though it's not super fresh." She held up the platter and tried to remind herself that they had security arriving in less than an hour. That was not enough time to spend in his arms. Though a Sebastian unconcerned about his daily schedule was also hot as hell.

Sebastian leaned forward. His lips met hers, and she melted. Luckily, he pulled back.

"I could get used to my wife bringing me breakfast in bed. Give me one sec." He winked, then slid from the bed, walking to the bathroom.

She didn't look away from his retreating naked form. He was delicious.

Sebastian returned quickly, now wearing a pair of loose slacks, his hair combed but still shirtless. He leaned against the doorframe and looked at the muffin. "I think I'll pass on the three-day-old muffin. We can pick something up in town."

She put the platter on the dresser and wandered to where he was. "Sounds like a plan."

His arms wrapped around her waist, and his mouth found the spot just below her ear that made her knees go weak. "Sebastian."

"I do enjoy when you say my name." His tongue licked the spot, and then he pulled back. "You're right. We can't start this when today's adventures await us. One of them might even include a bookstore."

"Sebastian." She grabbed his hand, pulling him to the front of the room. A bookstore. Something for her.

"Security is here." Sebastian pointed to his watch. Then the door and the knock followed less than a second later.

"Impressive." Breanna smiled at the security guards as they stepped through the door. It was also sad. Sad that he had his life timed down to the minute.

"Nice to see you." Sebastian nodded to the group as they bowed to him. "My wife wants to spend as much time in the bookstore as possible, and we need to get some goodies from the bakery. But what else is on the agenda?"

Breanna saw the subtle tilt of the security staff's heads. Their dark glasses hid the movement of their eyes, but she wondered if several had raised brows. Sebastian was relaxed. Yes, he was talking about agendas, but not with the stiff air he'd had at the palace.

The head of security nodded to them. "Your honeymoon seems to be going well."

Her cheeks were fire as Sebastian slid his arm around her waist. "My wife has proven to me that vacations are a good idea. We'll have to pencil them in each year." He kissed her forehead.

She knew the head of security was outlining the day. Knew he was explaining the adventures and schedules they needed to keep to. But her brain refused to focus on anything other than Sebastian saying they'd have to pencil in vacations.

He was willing to schedule the vacations. Willing to take time off. Yesterday was fantastic, but today felt like she'd truly won a lottery.

"Ooh." Breanna patted his hand as they walked towards the bookstore. Cameras clicked around them, but his wife's eyes did not leave the blue door of the not-so-tiny bookstore. "This is going to be so fun."

"It is." Sebastian leaned over, kissing the top of her head. Touching her was intoxicating, but watching her get excited for herself brought forth an emotion that there was not a descriptor for.

Stepping through the front door, they left the crowds outside.

"Your Highnesses." The owner of the store and her two employees stepped forward. "We are so glad you came in. I am Lila Patri. Welcome to my store."

Breanna reached for Lila's hands, then the workers standing on each side of her, giving each individual attention as she shook their hands. She was so good at this. Like she was built to be a queen.

"You get to work in one of the best places ever!"

The sincerity of her tone seemed to bring tears to Lila's eyes. "This was my dream as a girl. Owning my own shop full of books from wall to wall. It took until I was fifty to see it to fruition. Spent most of my working life as a public relations manager. Now, though..." The woman gestured to the walls of books; her was happiness clear even if she couldn't put everything into words.

"Dreams are important." Breanna nodded to the owner. "What is your favorite thing about owning the shop?"

Lila looked to him, but he just nodded for her to show his wife around. "I am not sure I can pick just one, Your Highness."

"Breanna. Please, call me Breanna."

He stared at his wife and Lila as they wandered around her store. The king he'd been before they'd gone on this honeymoon would have known down to the minute how long they had to be here. After all, there was a plan for this shopping trip. One he'd asked Raul to work out before their arrival. But Breanna was interested, the owner clearly wanted to show off her store, and he needed a minute to process Breanna's words.

Dreams are important.

Such a simple phrase. One he'd murmured hundreds of times at events for students, workers, the general public. It was true.

And his wife had never had a dream for herself. Her dreams were all for others.

"Are we ready, Your Highness?" Lila was standing next to Breanna, holding a pad.

"Ready?" His wife looked at him, and the door. "I thought we were browsing for a while."

"You are." Sebastian swallowed the emotions boiling in his throat. Before she could worry there was something jam-packed into their schedule, he grinned. "This bookstore has a fun activity. When I heard about it, I knew you had to try."

Breanna raised a brow. "Activity?"

"Yes." Lila looked like she might bounce away with joy. "This. This is the favorite thing."

"Today." One of her assistants laughed as she gave her boss a big grin. "She says that about all sorts of things."

"Why don't you explain?" Sebastian nodded. She clearly wanted to, and it was her store and activity. No need for him to step in. Though he had a role to play.

"Oh." Lila clapped. "Thank you. I saw a television show once where everyone ran around with a shopping cart. As a kid, I wanted to do it so bad, but in a bookstore."

"You have shopping carts?" Breanna looked at the aisles. They were tiny and stuffed with books.

"No." She bit her lip and leaned in conspiratorially. "I wanted to do it that way, but there isn't room. It was either less aisles or more books."

"Oh, easy choice! Always more books." His wife chuckled, and he thought Breanna and Lila might have been fast friends if she wasn't queen. In this role, there was always a power imbalance that made true friendship nearly impossible.

"Exactly." She motioned to Sebastian. "So, the king is your cart."

He made a show of pumping his muscles, and everyone laughed. "Not sure that is what I was going for." Sebastian made a playful pouty face as Breanna leaned into him.

"You are fine." She kissed him, lingering for just a second. How a few days alone could change so many things.

"You get to walk around for fifteen minutes. Take stock of what you want then. At the end of the fifteen minutes, you get five minutes to pick out as many as you can. The only catch is that Sebastian must be able to carry them all to the checkout without dropping them. Anything in his stack will be twenty percent off."

"Ready?" Sebastian held up his wrist, tapping on the watch. This would be the best use of it he'd ever had. "Set."

Breanna's eyes roamed the store. She was already breathing fast.

"Go!"

She took off. Not running but moving very quick. She

slowed as she reached the romance section and started to pull a few books forward.

"That might be cheating." He laughed as she stuck out her tongue.

"I listened to the rules of this game. No one said anything about not being able to touch the books while I looked around." She raced down the aisle to the general fiction area.

"True." He chuckled as he kept up with her. "Not sure my muscles are going to be able to handle this."

"Better start stretching!" Breanna giggled as she rushed for the hobby section and pulled a few books on sewing and one on crocheting animals. Then it was on to the education section.

There she pulled a few books on early education and lesson planning.

He stopped to look at those titles.

Build Your Classroom for Student Success
Burned Out and Busted: The Road Back for the Exhausted Educator
Everything You Need to Know About Lesson Planning in the Digital World

The titles made zero sense for a queen. She had a degree in education—one she'd never use.

He looked at the three books she'd pulled. Did she want those? She'd wanted to teach. But that was out of her reach now. The queen couldn't walk into an elementary classroom as a regular instructor. It would cause havoc.

Still, there had to be a way to give her something of her own.

"How much time do I have left on my expedition phase?" Breanna was across the store.

He looked at his watch, but before he could answer, Lila called out. "Two minutes twenty seconds, Your Highness."

"Lovely!" She bounced back over to fiction and grabbed a few more titles there. Then raced to the starting line. "Let's go, Sebastian."

"I think you still have a minute or so left?" He looked at his watch as he walked back towards her.

"I know." She pulled one leg up to her back. Then the other. Stretching. "You ready?"

"Honestly?" He shook his head as his wife readied herself. "I'm a little terrified of you right now. Swear you won't hold it against me if I can't carry everything."

Breanna looked him up and down, and playfully held her hands out, measuring his torso. "I think you will do just fine, Sebastian."

"Promise me." This was the first time he'd seen her do something that was just for her. Something she wanted. And if he couldn't carry the whole load. He didn't want to fail at this. Fail her.

She stepped into his arms and kissed him. Lila and the assistants let out a sigh behind them.

"You are going to do fine." She tapped his nose and looked at Lila. "Let's do this!"

Lila could not have asked for a more excited customer. "All right." She nodded to the queen and held up a stop-watch. "You have five minutes, and the king must be able to carry the books."

"Oh, he will carry the books." Breanna laughed and then ran as Lila shouted *Go.*

Books piled into his arms. It was a flash, and he was staggering behind her, letting her shift the books as she added more. Her ability to stack and add was truly impressive even though his arms were burning when Lila called time.

"I can barely see over the top." Sebastian didn't dare laugh or do anything that might jostle the mountain of books in his arms. His muscles were shaking, and he could barely make out the path to the checkout desk, but he was not going disappoint his wife by dropping her precious cargo.

"You just have to set them on the counter." Lila's voice guided his way, but he could hear the surprise in her tone. She was expecting a catastrophe, too.

Breathe. Step. Breathe. Step.

"Almost there." Breanna stood beside him. Calculating the distance or the likelihood of a topple, he didn't know. And there was no way he was turning his head in any way to upset the delicate balance.

Breathe. Step. Breathe. Step.

"Made it." Breanna clapped as he set the pile on the counter. "Nice job." She squeezed him tight, then moved to the other side of her bounty. "Ready for the picture."

"Oh." Lila made another noncommittal noise. "I was under the impression that you didn't want a picture." The proprietor's eyes cut to Sebastian before landing on Breanna.

Breanna pointed to the wall behind the counter. It was covered in pictures of women, men and children posing next to their bounty. None of it quite as hefty as the queen's, but the smiles all brilliant. "It's part of the process, right? I mean…" His wife's gaze cut to him.

"I think Raul thought you might like privacy on your picks." Sebastian shrugged. "You're the queen, after all."

"I want the books shared. I picked local authors, books I have loved, books I look forward to loving, and nonfiction topics that are important to me. These will sell out if people know the queen bought them. Both in Lila's store and online. The authors will reap so much from the free publicity."

"Were any of them your choices?" His tone was rougher than he meant, and he saw Lila step behind the counter, giving them a little distance. This was a gift for Breanna.

For her. Just her.

"Of course." Breanna pointed to the top book. "This one

is a local author that sells at the booths in our market, next to a stall that sells the cutest purses. I think Brie actually has one of the purses. And this topic—" she pointed to the burn-out book "—is vital for educators."

She pointed lower. "Did you know there are studies that show most teachers leave the field in the first three years?"

But what about books for her?

"Oh." She grabbed a bright blue one with a winged creature on the front cradling what looked like a human woman. "This one is simply a pure delight of gooey sex that everyone should read. It should be a bestseller in its genre but…" Breanna shrugged.

"So yes, I did pick these for me, but there were other thoughts, too. I am the queen. We have a duty. Something you are so fond of repeating. You chose a queen that wanted the title and the duty that came with it." She huffed and looked around him.

She was right. When he'd walked into her parents' mansion weeks ago, he'd wanted someone who wanted the title. Someone who would let her life belong to the country so she could be called queen. Someone who was doing exactly what Breanna was.

"Sorry, Lila. We don't normally argue in front of people." Breanna bit her lip as color traveled up her neck.

"We don't normally argue." Sebastian added.

"Not sure that is true."

His mouth opened, but he didn't know what to say. Luckily his wife was rushing past it, too.

Breanna pointed to the books. "This was a lovely treat. I got to run around a bookstore picking things out. I got to watch you carry them without tripping, and now, I want to finish this. And yes, it will help others, but these are also my choice."

"But you've already read at least that one." He pointed to the book with the winged creature.

"Yes, but it was downstairs when your people gathered my things. So, I need a new copy. I've reread it at least a dozen times. It's like an old friend. You get it, right, Lila?"

"I do." Lila's answer was quick, and he suspected the shop owner would normally chatter on about all the books she also considered old friends. Dissect what made the characters or plot memorable. Make recommendations for future friends.

None of which she did now. The assistants had disappeared to the stock room. Likely sent there by Lila when this disagreement started. He saw the shop owner look in the back and suspected she was considering if she needed to do the same.

He'd instructed the staff to pick up her room and put her belongings in the suites she occupied in the castle. Told them it needed to be exactly as it had been. A ludicrous order.

And she'd never mentioned that they didn't have all of her things. In fact, the only complaints his wife had issued regarding herself were that her feet hurt. And only after she could no longer stand in her shoes.

Duty was his life, and he'd picked the perfect partner for it. Except he could see the life she'd live. The duty that she wouldn't let overwhelm her like it did him. But that would claw at every part of her life.

Because of him. Because of his title and hers.

"Smile and take the picture, please." Breanna's dark gaze was holding back tears. She'd thought of something lovely. Something helpful. Something that would make a difference in many creatives' lives. And he was trampling on it.

"Of course. I am sorry, Breanna." He stepped next to the books and she stood on the other side.

"Smile." Lila stood in front of them, holding her phone up. "I will post it to social media and then print it for the wall."

She looked at the image, swallowed and then pointed to the stack. "Umm...the light isn't quite right. Queen Breanna can you move your head just a little that way?" She gestured for her to turn her face more towards the books.

It was a trick his father had used frequently. One a public relations manager turned bookshop owner would certainly know. A smile that wasn't as bright could be hidden with the right tilt of the head. The right focus.

He'd stolen his wife's smile with his worries over her books. There was no way for him to kick himself, but he'd find a way to make this up to her. Some way.

CHAPTER FOURTEEN

ROLLING OVER IN her bed, she reached for her husband but knew he was already up. They'd returned to the palace three days ago. And he'd risen well before six each day.

At least he wasn't putting anything on his schedule until eight. It was a small win and one she hoped would stick.

"You're awake." Sebastian swooped in with a breakfast tray and a big smile. At least he still looked rested.

"Yup." She looked at the clock then at him. She wasn't going to ask it directly, but if he volunteered the wake-up time…

"Earlier than yesterday but after five." He shrugged, then set the tray in front of her. "The good thing about me waking early is that I can make you breakfast in bed."

He leaned over, brushing his lips against hers. The quick nature of the kiss left her wanting for more. And as happy as she was to have breakfast in bed…again…she'd prefer to wake next to the man she'd married.

"Today's delight is breakfast tacos. Made with flour tortillas, avocado, seasoned tofu and some cheese." He bowed, so pleased with himself. He was cooking. For her. It was nice.

Sweet.

Before their honeymoon, she'd have given anything to have such attention. Now though. It felt off. Like he was worried she might float away.

She wanted him, but the authentic man.

"Thank you." Breanna looked at the tray. "No plate for you?" There hadn't been one for him yesterday either.

"This is just for you." Sebastian smiled as he moved to open the curtains. Bright rays fell across his face. Light bounced off the hints of blond in his dark hair. Mentally she snapped a picture, wishing her creative side leaned towards painting.

"If you wake at five, wake me. I'll come to the kitchen with you. We can cook together." Breanna took a bite of the taco. It was delicious. Like everything else he made in his personal kitchen.

Sebastian nodded as he looked out the window, but she knew that he wouldn't. He'd sneak out, letting her sleep. Then bring her something sweet or savory.

She finished the taco, grabbed the platter, got out of bed, and set it on the dressing table. Then she went to where her husband still stood.

"What are you thinking?" She wrapped her hands around his waist, grateful when his fingers locked with hers.

Sebastian took a deep breath. "Honestly?"

"Of course." She wanted the truth, but the breakfast tacos in her belly seemed to flip. "Tell me." She pressed her head to his shoulder, glad that he was turned away from her so he couldn't see the worry she knew was etched on her face.

"I was wondering what you might have done if you'd gotten to teach." He turned in her arms, pulling her close. "If you'd have used your sewing skills to wear fun outfits to go with the lecture."

"Lecture." She laughed. "I was an early education major. I would never have given lectures." She kissed his nose. "Most days I probably would have come home sticky."

He pulled her closer, like he didn't want any distance between them. "I'm serious, Breanna. You would be getting ready right now. Packing a lunch and probably thinking over how to make sure each student excelled for the day. I bet your classroom would have been bright and colorful."

"Annie would have ensured that color was everywhere." Breanna lifted her head, hoping he'd kiss her. Focus on today, on where they were now. Together.

The life he'd described was never going to be hers. Yes, she'd trained for it. Yes, it was something she'd have enjoyed. Probably excelled at. Yes, her upcycled outfits would have played a role.

In another timeline, in a different place, that Breanna would have been happy.

But this Breanna, the woman she was now in this place, was happy, too.

"I think I'd have enjoyed the classroom. My favorite age was third grade. They are learning to read small chapter books. Still excited to be in school. We'd have painted and sung math songs."

His shoulders slumped.

"But—" she held him tightly "—I am happy here, too." It wasn't hard to say. This wasn't the path she'd have chosen for her life. Maybe that was good.

Life was made from the unexpected. The gifts you didn't know you needed. The people you never expected to fall into your life. To love.

Love.

The word hit her mind, hammering its truth through her. She loved Sebastian. She didn't know how it had happened. How she was so certain that her heart belonged to him.

This wasn't the life she'd asked for. It was better.

"Sebastian." She stepped back and waited for him to turn. "Sebastian."

Finally, he turned, but it was the king standing here now. The shift was subtle. Less movement in the jaw. Eyes hiding emotions.

"I am happy here. Playing a what-if game can be fun." In the right circumstances, she mentally added. "But it gets us nowhere. After all, what if you weren't the king? Would you be a chef? You'd handle the hours well."

Breanna smiled, but the king didn't show any signs of finding fun in the words.

Instead, he adjusted, like the mantle he'd worn since birth was sliding fully into place. "I never had any choices."

"Neither did I." Breanna lifted her hand, running it along his chin. "But we have choices now."

"Do we?"

"Yes." She didn't stamp her foot, though she desperately ached to add emphasis to the moment. "We are the king and queen."

"I know."

"Do you?" She stroked his chin. The five o'clock shadow he'd worn at the beach house had disappeared the morning they'd packed up to return to the palace. "Do you know that you can choose?"

"Breanna."

She laid a finger over his lips, stopping the argument she saw brewing in his eyes. "You can choose if you wear the title of king. Or if it wears you.

"Here and now, with me, we are just Sebastian and Breanna. In these rooms, with no one watching. There is no crown. Okay?"

He nodded, and she let out a sigh of relief before removing her finger from his lips.

She replaced it with her lips. He stood still for a minute, then wrapped his arms around her waist.

Breanna drank him in. These moments were the best moments with Sebastian. Her husband. The man she loved. The man she wanted to be happy. They'd wear crowns the rest of their lives. But in this room, with each other, they'd just be Sebastian and Breanna.

"Starting the day with kisses from my wife is certainly my favorite way to begin the day." His fingers caressed her cheek.

He'd started his day alone in the kitchen, but she had no desire to point that out right now. "It's my favorite way to start the day, too."

"Any idea what we are doing for this date night?" Alessio slapped Sebastian on the shoulder as he stepped up to the table Hector had put Sebastian and Breanna's name plate on.

"Nope." Sebastian looked at the tables, each with the name of a couple. Just their name. No titles. "Breanna agreed to this when they were dancing several weeks ago. I guess he bet her that I'd be jealous."

"Were you?" Alessio's gaze went to his wife, who was laughing with Breanna and Hector over something.

"Yes." There was no need to lie, particularly to Alessio. "I didn't have any reason to be. Not just because there is nothing between Breanna and her friend, but because I didn't really know my wife at the time."

"And now that you know her?" Alessio grinned, his eyes saying there was no need for Sebastian to confirm the feelings.

He looked over to his wife. Annie had joined Hector, Brie and Breanna. The four were in a world all to themselves.

"Quite the group." Beau, Brie's brother, stepped up.

A queen, a princess, the sister of a queen and a party planning entrepreneur. A group bound together by friendship and family. Not titles and rank. Something his wife might have easily had with so many others, if he hadn't marched into her home demanding a bride.

"Any idea what we are doing tonight?" He needed to change the subject. Needed to focus on something, anything other than the feeling that he'd stolen something from Breanna he could never replace.

"Nope." Beau shrugged. "Briella told me to be here. That I was on a 'date' with Breanna's sister, Annie. Whatever Hector has planned is a couple's event, and they needed to round out the numbers. So here I am."

"Brie." Alessio crossed his arms. The nickname was the princess's preferred name and the only one anyone besides her family called her.

Color traveled up Beau's neck as he nodded. "Brie. I know that, and I will get better at it."

Alessio nodded, a man in love with a woman who wanted nothing more than to protect her.

Once more Sebastian's eyes found his bride. She looked over at him, smiled, then waved. The world narrowed to her dark curls, the curve of her lips, the light he knew was dancing in her eyes. All he wanted to do was make sure she had everything.

Was this what Alessio felt when he looked at Brie?

The all-encompassing urge to give her whatever she needed. The desire to make her happy and never let her down.

Love.

He was in love with his wife. With the woman he'd trapped into becoming his queen. A role from which there was no exit.

"You are thinking very deeply." Breanna was beside him, her lips brushing his. "He gets this far-off look when he is worried." She winked at Alessio. "But there are no worries here tonight."

She kissed his cheek and pointed to their table. "Showtime." Her fingers wrapped through his as she pulled him to their table. "This is kind of our first date."

Not kind of. It was their first date. And even in this, she was helping out a friend.

"What are we doing?"

Breanna's face lit up as a group of people, each carrying a box, walked out, depositing the closed boxes on the tables.

"Do not open the boxes until I give the instructions." Hector was standing in the center of the four tables, the ringleader of whatever circus he'd designed.

"You are going to love this." Breanna clapped as Hector gestured to the boxes.

"So, you are in on the activity?" Sebastian put his hand around her waist, enjoying the feel of her laying her head against his shoulder.

"Of course. This is based off some game show he saw a while back. When he told me the plan on the dance floor, I knew we had to be the first to give it a go. There are all sorts of activities, or at least that is his plan, but when he told me about this one—I knew you had to try it." Breanna bumped her hip against his hip. "Now, pay attention."

Hector turned to the table behind him. "Tonight, we cook." He gestured to the three flags on the table. "Sweet. Savory. Spicy. When I say go, one member of your team will run up here and grab a flag. You then have one hour using the items in the box to make a dinner item that is what your flag suggests. Ovens are behind you, and there is a hot plate in the bottom of your box. At the end of the hour, we will judge the dishes, and the winner gets a prize."

Breanna clapped. "This is going to be so much fun. Can I please run?"

"Of course." Sebastian squeezed her tightly. "Try to get anything besides sweet."

"Annie, you and Beau need to get something besides sweet. Otherwise Sebastian will win," Alessio called out. "Unless anyone besides the king is hiding a secret talent for cooking. But the man hates making sweet things."

"Not true." Sebastian stuck his tongue out. "I just don't *like* to make sweet things."

"Not sweet." Breanna stepped beside the table, her knees bent, ready to dash into the fray for him. "Don't worry. I got this."

"Go!"

His wife took off, reaching the table a full second before anyone else. She grabbed the third flag, the savory one, and bounced in front of Alessio, smiling as she headed back to their table.

"May as well pass the trophy to the king and queen now." His brother playfully rolled his eyes as Brie came back holding up the sweet flag with a huge smile for her husband.

Annie had spicy, and she and Beau both looked a little lost as they gazed at the flag and their box.

"Let's do this." Breanna planted the flag and then started pulling things out of the box. "I have no idea what these spices are, but my husband does." She grabbed the chef's hat in the box and placed it on his head. "Tonight, I am your lovely assistant."

His throat closed as the words left her mouth. That was the plan. For her to be his lovely assistant. A queen to get the press off his back. A role anyone could play if they followed the right script. An interchangeable person to give the people of Celiana what they wanted. A lovely assistant.

But she was so much more. So very much more.

"What if you cook tonight?" The words left his mouth before he even knew what he was saying. Lifting the chef's hat, he held it out to her. "You cook, and I will be the lovely assistant."

She looked at the hat, then at him. "You are very handsome, but don't you want to show off your skills?"

"I am here to have a fun date night with my wife. That is all I care about." He kissed her cheek, then set the hat on her head. "That looks good on you. Though everything looks good on you."

She lifted on her toes, pressing a kiss to his ear before whispering, "I think you like it best when I wear nothing at all."

"So true." He leaned toward her, straightening the cap. "Tonight isn't about winning. It's a date night. Just for the two of us."

"I have no idea what I am doing, Sebastian." Breanna held up the rosemary and peppermint. "I mean, I know these are herbs, and this one—" she sniffed the peppermint "—is mint."

"I got you, and you got this." He stepped beside her and looked at the ingredients. "How about a veggie pot pie?"

Breanna looked at the ingredients, too, and then laughed. "I am looking at these like I have any other idea." She gave him a little salute as she giggled. "All right. I'm the cook."

"It almost feels like cheating." Breanna sighed as she sat beside Sebastian on the little couch.

Their pot pie had gone into the oven ten minutes ago. It needed another ten, and then they'd just leave it on warm.

Brie and Alessio were whipping up what looked to be brownie batter with a fancy icing. Annie and Beau hadn't even started whatever they planned to make. Probably not the best sign, but her sister didn't seem overly distressed by whatever was causing their delay.

One of the great things about pot pies was that they only took a few minutes to whip up. Particularly when the host provided a premade pie crust.

"It's hardly cheating." He wrapped his arm around her. She'd done all the work for the pot pie. He'd supervised the steps, but most of the seasoning she'd done to her taste. And watching her realize that there wasn't an exact recipe—that she could just toss in extra rosemary because it tasted good to her—was one of the top five moments of his life.

And with the exception of Alessio returning home, the other moments all revolved around Breanna, too.

"What if they don't like it?" Breanna looked over at the oven, the minutes counting down.

"They will." He squeezed her shoulder and kissed her head. "They will like it."

"And if they don't, they probably won't tell me." Breanna laughed.

"Probably not." Sebastian let out a sigh. "One hardly ever tells the king and queen the truth."

His wife sat up, her eyes wide and hurt. "Sebastian, I meant that our family and friends would spare my feelings. They would ooh and ahh over the dish, as I will for theirs. Not because of their titles."

"Right." Her words made sense, of course. Even if he wasn't sure they were the complete truth. Alessio rarely spared his feelings, but in a group...in a group he'd defer until later. Beau, Annie and Hector. He doubted they'd see more than the crowns that were metaphorically always attached to Breanna and his heads when critique time came around.

"No." Breanna sat up straighter. "No, this isn't a 'right,' moment."

"I like it when you use air quotes." He winked, looking over her shoulder to see if anyone was noticing the disagreement going on. Alessio and Brie now had piping bags out. Annie and Beau were studiously cutting up something at their table with Hector by their side, laughing and trying to break the clear tension between the two of them.

Breanna looked over her shoulder, too, then back at him. "Worried someone might hear us arguing? It's one of the things we do best." She crossed her arms and shook her head. "These are our friends and family. Here, you are Sebastian, not the king."

"I'm always the king, Breanna." He let out a heavy sigh,

hating how he'd soured the evening. "As you are always the queen. And arguing isn't what we do best."

Why did she keep bring up their tendency to spat?

"I said one of the things." Breanna patted his knees. "It's not a bad thing."

"Arguing is bad." It was the definition of the word. His parents had never argued. In fact, he didn't remember seeing any kind of disagreement. They'd lived separate lives, but when they were together, it was not quite peaceful but serene enough.

"No." The timer dinged on the pot pie, but Breanna didn't move. "Arguing is communicating. And when done in a healthy fashion, it's positive. We don't yell at each other. We don't scream. We discuss. We hash things out. That is healthy."

"Somehow I can't imagine the Galanis patriarch and matriarch having solid communication capabilities." The few times he'd seen her parents together, the loathing they had for the other was hardly kept at bay. In fact, he was fairly certain the only thing keeping them together was the mutual desire for more wealth, and probably spite.

"They didn't." Breanna blew out a breath. "I took a family communications class in university. Parents can get miffed when teachers give feedback that their children are less than perfect."

The timer continued sounding. "We need to get the pot pie out."

"We do. But this is more important. You are more than your crown, Sebastian. I don't know why you can't see that. And your wife pointing it out, not fighting but arguing with that belief, is healthy dialogue."

He could see Alessio looking at the oven with the time. Then his brother glanced over at the couch, his eyes widening before turning back to the brownies. "Breanna, we can discuss this at the palace."

"This is family and friends. We aren't fighting. We aren't yelling. We are talking. They aren't listening any more than you are listening to whatever argument Annie and Beau are having right now."

Annie and Beau were working on their own. Neither appeared to be saying anything, and her back was towards them. "They aren't arguing."

"Yes. They are. I can read Annie like Alessio can read you." Breanna stood up. "The people that matter see you. Just you. But if you can't see past your crown, then that is one you." She moved towards the oven.

"Oh. It bubbled over. It will probably still taste good, but it looks a fright."

"So do the brownies!" Brie called, her laugher echoing in the room.

"My cheese dip will *actually* be spicy, but it looks a little like yellow mud," Annie responded, her eyes cutting to Beau.

Alessio held up a brownie that could only be described as a mess. "I don't know. I think this is gorgeous. It could fetch a nice price at the farmer's market."

"Only because you are the heir to the throne." Brie kissed her husband.

It was funny...because it was true.

And forgetting it wasn't an option.

CHAPTER FIFTEEN

"You sure you're okay with Alessio and me going up to the ski slopes today?" Sebastian looked at his calendar.

He wasn't surprised that Breanna had wedged a day off into it, but he was a little shocked at how much he wanted to go.

"Why wouldn't I be?" She kissed his nose as she looked at her calendar. "I have more than enough meetings to keep me busy." She stuck out her tongue and laughed. "Go. You deserve a day on the slopes. And you will have more fun with Alessio than you will with me."

A knock echoed on the chamber door. "That will be your brother."

Alessio stepped in a moment later. "Hey, um, Brie is a little under the weather. We think it's because..." Alessio pulled at the back of his neck, color traveling up his neck.

"Because?" Breanna clapped; she'd seen Brie make a face after smelling Annie's cheese dip the other night. She probably should have warned people that Annie could put fire on her tongue and think it needed a bit more kick. She didn't want to assume, but she thought she knew what Alessio was getting ready to tell them.

"What?" Sebastian looked from Breanna to his brother. "I feel like I am missing something."

"Brie's pregnant."

"Yes!" Breanna danced over to Alessio, gave him a hug,

and then stepped back to let Sebastian have the time with his brother.

"Congratulations. Did you want to stay off the slopes today?"

"No, but since we aren't certain that the illness is pregnancy-related, she wanted me to give you a choice about coming. I think she wants me out of the house. I am a worrier, according to my wife."

"That makes sense. I still want to hit the slopes, if you do. And now we can talk baby things." Sebastian slapped his brother on the back, then came over to her.

He kissed her deeply, "Thank you for setting this up. I—"

For a second, she thought he might say the words she craved hearing. But instead, he pushed a curl behind her ear and kissed her cheek.

"I will see you when I get back."

"I don't think the flu that captured Brie and Alessio is going to spare me." Sebastian let out a sigh as he lay in bed. His wife was snuggled next to him.

"You are burning up." She pressed her lips to his cheek.

"I don't feel hot." It was kind of true. The chills wracking his body refused to take any of the heat pouring over his head. He felt cold...and then hot...and then freezing.

"I think you should accept that you need a sick day." She kissed his forehead, then pulled back. Breanna climbed out of bed and grabbed her phone. She typed something out quickly. "Any chance there is a thermometer in your bathroom?"

Fog coated his brain, trapping words. Plucking them out of the mental ether was exhausting. "Why would I have a thermometer?"

Breanna clucked her tongue and muttered something under her breath.

"All right. I've canceled your engagements for the next two days. Do not argue with me."

Even if he wanted to, there was no charge in his battery. Maybe he could still manage some correspondence from bed.

A knock sounded at the door, and Breanna stepped to it. "Raul, is that you?"

"Yes, Your Highness."

"Did you bring the thermometer?" She still hadn't opened the door.

"Yes. And the other things you requested."

He wanted to ask what else she'd requested, but his eyes were so heavy. A short nap and then he'd text Raul to bring any papers he needed.

"Thank you. Please leave them at the door and back away. I've already been exposed, but no sense having the staff take more risk than necessary." She waited a moment, then opened the door.

He heard her say something about schedules and thought he heard his mother's voice. But then the nap won.

Breanna kissed her husband's forehead, thankful that he was cool. Day three of their lock-in and he was finally turning a corner. Sebastian's fever had broken last night. But he was still exhausted.

He was rounding the cusp, as she tried to ignore the tickle in the back of her throat and the sweat at her temple that she knew meant the virus was on her heels now.

Smoothing the dress she'd asked Raul to bring her, she stepped into the king's suite. Which now had her sewing machine and her latest project to help her pass the time.

She checked herself in the small mirror and smiled. It was a silly alphabet dress that she'd made when she was student teaching. The ABCs were splayed in no real pattern. A few pencils and apples were sprinkled in for good measure.

One did not put it on unless you were a teacher. The kids she'd taught as a student teacher had loved this dress. And the others she'd made. It was cliché, but she enjoyed dressing up for her class. At least as queen she could reuse the outfits when she did outings for small children.

She'd been scheduled to attend a primary school today. The students were putting on a poetry reading they'd worked for weeks on. Seven-and eight-year-olds took their writing as seriously as any national poet. She was to be the exalted guest. The kids were excited to read to a queen.

But there was no way she was risking little bodies with what the doctor had confirmed was influenza. Particularly since she was fighting her own battle with it now.

Still, she'd asked Raul to check with the teacher to see if there was a way for her to attend virtually. The woman was apparently very open to it, but as soon as the virtual call was over, Breanna was crawling into bed.

"Good morning, class." The teacher's voice echoed over the computer.

She'd been instructed to keep her computer screen off until she was announced since the kids thought she'd had to cancel. A good plan in case she'd been too busy taking care of Sebastian. Or too sick herself.

"Today we are reading our poems, and I have a special surprise." The teacher clapped, and the squeals her students let out on the word *silence* stopped. A well-run classroom.

"Remember how the queen was supposed to come?"

A chorus of yeses echoed through the speaker. Little voices that brought an immediate smile to Breanna's face. She'd have enjoyed the life of teaching.

"Well, she is taking care of the king, who has the flu, but..." The teacher did a little drumroll on her desk, and the students followed.

At the top of the roll, Breanna started her camera and then

waved to the room full of excited kids. A cough built in her throat, but she smiled through it.

Was this what Sebastian always did? Probably.

"So, we are going to read our poems for the queen after all." The teacher looked at the camera, bowed her head. "Who wants to go first?"

Most of the room's hands shot up. The teacher laughed, walked to her desk, and picked up what looked to be a decorated tin can with popsicle sticks. "You know the rules. If I call your name, you can pass, but you don't get another chance to go until everyone else has gone."

She drew the first name, and a little girl with pigtails and a blue dress stood up. She read a devotion to her cat—Pickles.

After that was a funny poem about a little brother that the boy didn't want but was learning to love. And then another poem about a pet, a rabbit this time.

The afternoon wore on. It was fun and great, but the throbbing in her head, the pain in her throat, the aches in her bones grew with each passing second. But her smile never dropped.

When the final child rose to give her reading, Breanna was taking strategic breaths through her nose to keep the coughing fit at bay.

A few more minutes. A few more minutes. Hang on. Do not interrupt this child's experience. She gets the same as her classmates. A few more minutes.

The mantra repeated in her mind as she kept the smile on her face. When it was finally over, she waved one last time, knowing that if she said anything, it would be covered by coughs.

Shutting off the camera, she let out a shudder, and then the coughs erupted. Her body rocked as she tried to gain any semblance of control, but the coughs refused to abate.

"Honey." Sebastian's arms wrapped around her shoulders, gently lifting her up.

All of a sudden, there was no way to ignore the ache in her bones. She let out a little cry, but Breanna was pretty sure the coughs covered it.

"Into bed. I'll get you some lemon tea, but rest is what you need." Sebastian guided her to his room.

"Do you want me to go back to my room?" The words were garbled. The brain fog her husband had talked about seemed to leap from his brain to hers. She honestly wasn't certain she'd make it down the hall.

"You are in your room. Our room." He kissed the top of her cheek as her head traced the pillow. "You really pushed yourself for those kids."

"I needed to." They'd worked so hard. They'd been promised a royal, and... Words evaporated, and she wasn't even sure she'd gotten them all out.

"Uh-huh. I get it." His voice was far away. Dreamlike words. "And now you do, too."

Sebastian's lips were cool on her burning forehead. There were words she needed to say. A thought she wanted to get out. But no matter how hard she tried to grasp at it, the darkness pushed it farther away.

CHAPTER SIXTEEN

SHE WASN'T SURE how long she'd lain in this bed, but Breanna did know that she had no desire to spend another moment in it. Pulling off the coverings, she gave herself a shake. There were three things she wanted to do. Find her husband. Take a shower. And put on new clothes.

Preferably in that order, but at this moment, she didn't particularly care.

Stepping into the study, she wasn't surprised to find Sebastian at the desk she'd pushed out of the way for her sewing machine and fabrics back in its rightful spot. The mountain of paperwork was disheartening but not unexpected, either. "Did you take any time for yourself while I've been under the weather?"

Sebastian's head popped up. His hand moved too quickly, and the bottle of ink he was using to sign documents tipped.

"And that is why you need to put the lid back on if you insist on using a fountain pen dipped in ink." Breanna didn't laugh—her chuckle was too likely to bring on a cough—but she smiled so her husband knew she meant it as a joke.

Sebastian was at her side, ignoring the spill and the other documents it would wreck.

"Your desk will get stained." Breanna looked over his shoulder, but he just raised his hand to her forehead and let out a sigh.

"No fever." Laying his head against hers, he pulled her

close. "And the desk has a hundred years' worth of stains on it." He kissed her head. "Want a shower?"

"Do I stink that bad?" She laughed, and a small cough followed, but at least it no longer wracked her body.

"You are gorgeous, even minutes past your sickbed, but the first thing I wanted when I got up was to see you and then to shower."

To see you.

She'd felt the exact same thing.

I love you.

The words were on the tip of her tongue, waiting to drop. Still, she held back.

Why?

Maybe because she didn't want to say it while she still looked a fright from her own flu battle. Maybe...

Sebastian gazed at her, like he, too, had words that wouldn't fall.

Shower—then—then it was time to tell her husband how she felt.

Sebastian stood in what until yesterday was his reading room and desperately tried to control the anxious wobbles in his soul. This had seemed like such a good idea after the headlines regarding Breanna's "choice of outfit" for the poetry reading. The fashion columns had critiqued the ABC dress no end. The reviews online were mostly positive. But the main headlines discussed the reviews that weren't. Plastered them up front before pointing out that even the fashion icons who claimed to hate the dress admitted that it was a good option for a children's poetry event.

The cut. The tailoring. Everything she'd worked on had been pulled apart.

Because he'd fallen ill, she was sitting in the palace rather than in the classroom. Maybe if she'd attended in person, she'd have been spared most of the comments regarding her attire.

But that wasn't the only thing they'd discussed. A few podcast interviews had dissected her look on the camera. How she'd seemed focused elsewhere. Things that should have stopped the moment the palace announced she was under the weather.

Instead, the news had buzzed that the palace was crafting that narrative to give her peace after she'd looked "bored" with the children.

The thing she loved most, along with her love for children, tarnished because he'd taken a day off at the ski slopes.

He'd had to do something.

The buzz around the dress, and the fact that no one knew his wife's talent, spurred this room. She could use it to create and maybe…just maybe to teach, too. At least online. A little piece of the dream she'd once wanted, even if she hadn't put it into words for herself.

He'd put out a statement regarding the dress and the fact that the queen had made it. That most of her garments, even her wedding dress, were crafted on machines with love by her own hands.

That had sent the news cycle into a spiral. And stopped the news about her appearance at the school. Glowing articles about a queen making her own wardrobe. Creating her own custom pieces. The negative statements had eased away. And now one of the articles praising her was framed and hanging on the wall, next to a ring light and recording equipment.

She was too talented to hide this. Too special to let this gift go unnoticed. This could have been her dream. If she'd just allowed herself to have one.

He couldn't undo the crown on her head. But he could give her a dream that was for her. Show her this and then tell her how much he loved her. How lucky he was that she was his queen.

"What?" Breanna's voice hit his back. "Your reading room—"

"Never got used anyway. So..." He spun, showing off the racks of fabric the staff had carefully shifted from her old rooms. "And don't worry, they all came through the outside door. No one else got the flu."

That was an impressive feat. One he never would have thought of. But his wife had jumped into action, keeping everyone away to protect them and care for him. The woman never thought of herself. So, this was for her. Something that was Breanna's.

She looked at the machines, each in a separate area. One of the staff was into fabric works and was able to help the team understand why aesthetics weren't as important as function, with each machine having a designated place and role to play.

"Wow." Breanna's hand covered her mouth. "This. This is..." Whatever she planned to say dropped away as her eyes found the framed article and ring light.

Time slowed as she stepped towards it, shaking her head. "Breanna—"

"Why is there an article about my sewing? You framed it?"

Tears coated her eyes, but he couldn't understand why. Her skill. Her creativity. Those were worthy of praise. So much more than just the crown on her head. "People were writing articles about the queen looking upset at the poetry event. Bored. And there was a lot of focus on the ABC dress. The headlines before I told them about this were rather unflattering."

"Unflattering to the crown." Her words were soft, broken.

This was not how this was supposed to go. "I'm proud of the work my queen does. I want the world to know that the queen is talented." This was Breanna.

"My queen." Breanna let out a breath. "That is all I am, isn't it?"

"We had to answer, Breanna. Make them understand the queen—"

"No, we didn't." Breanna bit her lip, shaking her head. "And *we* didn't answer. You answered. Without talking to me."

Okay. That was a fair assessment. And one he'd worried over—apparently with good cause. "You were ill. The headlines…"

"Right. The headlines. The king and queen must respond. It is our duty to be available. Always available. Everything we do belongs to the country."

"I was proud of you. Your work is so impressive, and you were ill but smiled through it." Wrong words.

"What I meant was—"

"I know what you meant. I finally stepped fully into the role, right? The all-encompassing crown, serving even when I was far too ill." His wife crossed her arms and looked down at the ring light. "Lighting for me to show off on what, the palace social media? Or do I have to run my own video streams now, so that everyone can see what *the queen* can do?"

How had this gone downhill so fast? This was a gift. A surprise.

"No. You don't have to *do* anything. But the country—"

"The country comes first. Everything is for Celiana. Even the one thing I told you was for me. Mine. The thing I didn't share."

Sebastian pointed to the article. "Do you know what they were running before this piece? They were breaking down the cut. Discussing the neckline and why you would choose such a silly design."

"Who cares?" Breanna damp curls bounced as her bottom lip quivered. "I asked—no—I told you that this was mine. Weeks ago. Before I…" She bit her lip so hard, he worried blood was coating her tongue.

"We have an image. A duty. This humanizes you. It gives..."

"I don't care. In these rooms, I told you I just wanted to be Sebastian and Breanna. Just us." Brenna wiped a tear from her eye. "This is my job. It is not who I am."

It wasn't that simple. It would be nice if it was. But they were the king and queen everywhere. Even when they didn't want to be. Everything was tinted with the golden hue of their crowns. "You are the queen. You married the king. This is your life. We are the king and queen. It is all we are."

She'd done so well the other day. Hiding her illness to make the students happy. It was what a queen did. What a royal did. She'd truly become the queen that day.

Breanna turned, looking at the image on the wall. The article he'd been so proud of now destroying the gift he'd wanted to give.

"You're right. This is my life. I am the queen." She sucked in a breath.

Words he'd ached for her to say. Words he wanted her to believe, but her tone, the resignation in it, destroyed him.

"It's a role anyone could play, if they knew the script."

"Breanna—"

"I am going back to my rooms, Your Highness." There was no emotion in her tone. No fire. No spirit.

"Because you want to?"

"What I want doesn't matter. It's all for the crown. You showed that." Breanna pressed her hand to his shoulder as she started past him. "For what it is worth, until just now, you were never just the king, in my eyes."

Her words nearly broke him. But he needed her to understand. "I still am more than the king for you. But wanting more, a life outside the crown, that only leads to heartache, Breanna. We are royal. We are—"

"The king and queen of Celiana. I know." Her words were soft, and then she was gone.

CHAPTER SEVENTEEN

"THANK YOU FOR complimenting my dress. I didn't make it. It is the work of a young man named Mathias who is apprenticing at Ophelia's. Yes, he does amazing work. One day everyone will know his name." The queen's voice carried next to him as she shook hands with another guest who was hoping she'd made the stunning purple floor-length gown.

His eyes had bounced out of his head the moment she'd stepped into the room tonight. The first time he'd seen her all day. A common occurrence over the last week. Breanna was never late to her appointments.

As queen, she sparkled. Shining far brighter than he ever did. But the sparkle was fake. The smile plastered in place. Others might not be able to tell, or maybe they could and didn't care.

Her sewing equipment, or was it tools…crafting lingo was foreign to him…whatever they were, were still in his suite. She hadn't touched them all week.

Breanna had become the ghost he'd promised she could be when she took the crown. Separate lives. And he was dying inside.

"If you'll excuse me, my dear. I need to get a drink. Do you want to come?" A soft shake of her head was all she gave him.

Barely an acknowledgment. It stung. A week ago, he'd have leaned in and kissed her. Flitted her away for a break.

Now…a wall of his construction stood between them. "I shall bring one back for you, too."

Breanna nodded, but she never turned her attention away from the guest in front of her.

"She plays the role well." His mother slipped her hand through his arm, walking in step as they headed to the refreshment stand.

Role. The thing he'd wanted Breanna for. What a fool he'd been walking into that compound. A name from a hat. The wrong name. "She shouldn't have to play a role."

"All humans play roles." His mother's voice was soft as she took the glass from the waiter and then lifted it to her lips before looking around. "The question is, do we play the role we want or the one expected of us."

Sebastian didn't bother to hide his chuckle. "We." He downed the drink. "*We* don't get a choice."

His mother tilted her head, her eyes landing on the other side of the room. Alessio and Brie were chatting with someone. Her hand was protectively over the bundle of joy they'd shared with the palace but not the world yet. And the flu that had crippled them had done no harm to the precious little prince or princess arriving in seven or so months.

"They chose." His mother squeezed his hand. "The plan for them was to have a marriage of convenience. A fake love story, just like your father and me. But they chose a different path. A better path." Sadness passed over her eyes but no tears.

"Did you want more with father?" King Cedric only cared about Celiana. It was his greatest trait. And largest failing.

The dowager queen looked at the couples on the dance floor and sighed. "I didn't know there was more to want. But there is, Sebastian. You will always be the king to the country. To the world."

"But." He wanted there to be a but so badly. Needed a but.

His mother's eyebrows lifted. "But?"

Sebastian's ears rang, and heat cascaded over his face. "But in the palace, with the people I love, I get to choose."

Such a simple statement. One his wife had told him over and over again. And then he'd stolen the thing she was keeping for herself. Given it to the country, while she was sick and unable to voice her wants.

Her wants.

Her family had refused to let her have her chosen career field. Her chosen spouse. And she'd stayed happy. Chosen happiness for her sister. Chosen happiness with the husband who'd pulled a name out of a hat.

Been something different in a world that just wanted to see her as a cookie-cutter image. She'd been different, too. Until he'd turned her into what she was now.

"I messed up. God, that doesn't even cover it. I screwed up." Castigating himself might feel good. But it didn't do any good.

He was going to make this up to her. And tell her what he should have told her a week ago. He loved her. Loved Breanna, not the queen. Just her.

"I am stealing my sister." Annie grabbed Breanna's hand as she led her from the never-ending receiving line. "Go dance!" her sister yelled to the gathered and flabbergasted crowd.

Breanna was glad for the reprieve and shocked by the deliverer. "Annie."

"Don't look so surprised. You needed saving."

"And no one else was going to do it." Breanna bit her lip as the bitter words welled up. She'd played the queen all week. The perfect attendant. The person her husband had married her to be.

She'd spent her life looking for the bright side. Grasping

at every silver lining. A week of this was killing her. What would a lifetime look like?

"Sebastian offered you a break."

Breanna shrugged. That was true. Maybe. But being in his presence hurt too much. The man was the king first. He'd made that clear. And she was the queen. Trapped in a life of her own making. She'd make the same choice again, for Annie.

But she'd guard her heart. Some way.

"The king is back in the receiving line."

Back right after I left.

That didn't hurt. It didn't.

Maybe one day it wouldn't, but right now… "That is his job. His purpose."

"And what is yours?" Annie squeezed her hand.

"What?" Her giggle was nerves, but the question landed in her heart. "What?"

"You already said that." Annie led them through the garden. "Repeating it doesn't change my question. What do *you* want? And you can't say anything about my safety or security. You can't say something about your husband. Or a friend. What do you, Breanna, want?"

"I don't understand the question."

"Yes, you do. You're scared of the answer maybe, but you know what you want. Just like I know that Mathias helped with that dress, but it is your design. Your fabric—its reclaimed from a piece you found after the high school dance season. If the young woman who'd worn the original design knew it was on the queen, she'd squeal with delight."

Breanna ran her hand over the fabric. The original gown was a ball gown with so much tulle Mathias and Ophelia had used it to create two wedding veils. "This is mine. Something that is just mine. No one can take—"

The words were out, and Annie hugged her as a sob wracked her body.

"Sebastian wasn't taking it." Breanna squeezed her eyes shut, the truth shaking her. He was trying to give her something. Something she would not have reached for for herself.

"No. He was bragging on you. A weird feeling when no one has ever done it." Annie pushed a tear away from Breanna's cheek. "It's a good thing you have waterproof mascara."

"He should have talked to me." Breanna was grasping. She knew that. She'd have told him no. Told him that he couldn't. Even if part of her wanted the world to know. To display the benefits of sustainability in a world focused on consumerism.

"Yes, but would you have listened?" Annie was always good at knowing her sister's internal thoughts.

So much so that Breanna didn't even pretend to give an answer other than sticking her tongue out.

"That is what I thought." Annie hooked her arm through Breanna's. "Another thought, if you'll allow it."

"Do I have a choice? You didn't used to be so pushy." Breanna squeezed her sister. This was a good thing.

"My sister gave me wings," Annie beamed as she guided them back to the ball room. "But that isn't my thought. It's this: If you didn't love him, would it have hurt? You don't have to answer to anyone but yourself. But our parents can snipe at each other, then push through their next big project as a team because they don't care about each other. They care about themselves and found a partner willing to go along."

"I never said I loved him." Breanna had kept that realization to herself. Even if part of her wanted to shout it to the entire world.

"It is clear to anyone who looks. You love him. He loves you. You've hurt each other. You have two choices now. Live in this role bitter and alone. The country will be fine and most probably won't notice that you two ache being near each other. You will know. Always."

Breanna shuddered. "Or we carve our own paths together."

Annie smiled and pushed her into the room. The receiving line was longer now than it had been when she left. How was that possible? How did so many people want to spend so much time in line rather than enjoying themselves at a party?

Sebastian caught her gaze before she got to her place. She saw more than a few heads turn as he walked past the line he always stood in until the last person arrived. When he'd asked if she'd wanted a drink, she'd purposefully said no to try to get through this faster.

"Breanna." Her name was soft on his lips.

The room was watching, but all she could see was the man before her. The dark circles under his eyes. Her hand went to his cheek. "You don't look like you're sleeping."

"I'm not." He placed his hand over hers. "Dance with me?"

"The line…"

"Dance with me, please?" Sebastian asked again.

"All right." She placed her hand in his.

He squeezed it tightly. "The queen and I are dancing. The receiving line is over. Come join us on the floor. Let's have a good time."

"Over?" Breanna couldn't help the laugh. "Really, Your Highness. I thought that was our duty."

"Breanna, we have roles to play, but I never want to be anyone but Sebastian to you. As for duty, we have been in that line for almost two hours. I want to dance with my wife. Hold her. Tell her how sorry I am. This isn't the right place. I know that. But I can't wait. I don't want to."

Her mouth was open. There were words she should say. But her mind was firing too fast to find any.

"I should have waited to ask about the sewing. I am just so damn proud of you. And I wanted to show you off for something that had nothing to do with the crown. And yet I made it about the crown. I—"

She laid a finger on his lips. "I know. It took me time to

see it, and one very pushy twin sister. But I know. I've hidden all my life. Worried that others just see me as an interchangeable twin. But I don't want to hide anymore. I'm the queen, but so much more."

"And I am the king and so much more."

Her lungs exploded as she cried, "Yes." Several heads turned towards them. Alessio and Brie were watching and grinning.

"In these walls and together, we play the role we want. And I want to play the role of a man who loves his wife. Crown or no crown." Sebastian ran one hand over her cheek as he pulled her closer with the other.

"I love you, too. Just you. Just Sebastian. You could throw away the crown, the palace, everything, and I would still love you."

His head lay against hers. "I love you. I love you. I will never tire of saying that."

"I certainly hope not." Breanna let him spin her around the room. "I love you, too."

EPILOGUE

"As you can see, needing to rip out a stitch happens to everyone. Even those of us who have created more garments than they can count." Breanna laughed as she held up the seam ripper to the video conference she was running from the sewing room next to their suite.

She hosted one of these monthly and had worked with Ophelia and Matthias to train a few teachers on the art of upcycling. And then worked with thrift stores to ensure that they didn't drive up the cost of their clothes just because more people were thrifting now.

It was amazing to watch her emerge from the protective shell she'd kept herself in.

"Oh, Sebastian is here, do you want to say hello?" Breanna stepped aside as he moved to where the group could see him.

A few members of the class raised their heads to wave, but most kept the focus on their projects. The aura of the throne had diminished in the last year as the people came to see the king and queen more as people than fairy-tale creatures.

Now there was a deeper connection with the populace and a palace that finally felt like a home. All because of the woman beside him—who the class really wanted to see.

"All right. Work your projects, reach out to the mentors if you have questions, and I will see everyone next month." Breanna waved and then clicked off. "One woman found that she doesn't like sewing nearly as much as knitting. So she is taking apart knitted sweaters and reusing the yarn. I didn't even know that was possible. It's really cool; she was talking about it at class when she explained this would be her last one. I need to reach out to Raul and see if he can get her contact information. I bet there are other yarn workers who would be interested in learning her technique."

"I bet there would be." Breanna's drive and care for others was invigorating, "But I didn't barge into my wife's studio on our day off to talk about projects. Well, not true, I came to talk one project in particular."

"You never barge in. You are always welcome." Breanna kissed his cheek. "What project?"

"Our anniversary is coming up, one year." The best year of his life.

She glanced at him as he looked over the fabric. "Our wedding day wasn't the best." He kept his tone upbeat, but he'd always regret that she hadn't gotten the day she deserved.

"Wasn't the worst. We had a good time."

His wife, ready with the silver lining. "I thought maybe you'd like a do-over. A vow renewal, just with our family and friends. To say all the things I wish I could have said at the altar the first time. With a dress and suit made by you?"

"I already have a dress. I think wearing the same one would be a nice touch. But as for a suit…" She bounced as she grabbed her tape measure. "I have the perfect idea. Ooh!" She danced around him, wrapping his body with the tape measure, taking notes.

Sebastian grabbed for her wrists as the tape measure slid up his thigh and her fingers wandered with it. "Still taking measurements?"

Breanna's eyes lit up as she dropped the tape. "I think this would be easier with your pants off."

"My queen." He bent, capturing her lips, then lifting her off her feet. "We have all afternoon free, and I plan to spend it with you."

"In bed?"

"Your wish is my command."

* * * * *

MODERN

Glamour. Power. Passion.

Available Next Month

Greek's Enemy Bride Caitlin Crews

....

The Heir Dilemma Abby Green

....

Snowbound Then Pregnant Cathy Williams

....

The Twins That Bind Jackie Ashenden

....

Queen's Winter Wedding Charade Heidi Rice

....

Deception At The Altar Emmy Grayson

....

Italian Wife Wanted Lela May Wight

....

Boss's Plus-One Demand Louise Fuller

....

Amore

Jet-Set Escape With Her Billionaire Boss Andrea Bolter
Consequence Of Their Parisian Night Michele Renae

Keep reading for an excerpt of a new title
from the Modern series,
SHE WILL BE QUEEN by Carol Marinelli

PROLOGUE

'SLOW DOWN, SAHIR...'

Sahir turned. He'd been a little relieved that the ancient steps carved in the bedrock were so narrow that there could be no conversation, and Mother was some considerable distance behind.

Queen Anousheh of Janana was unsuitably dressed for a rugged walk.

The wind was blowing her black hair into her eyes and her elegant robe was clearly a hindrance. Naturally, his delightfully eccentric mother was in full make-up. Even her footwear was jewelled.

It didn't usually slow her down, though.

Sahir retraced his steps and offered his hand for the steepest incline. 'Why are you wearing palace slippers?'

'They are my walking shoes.' She smiled.

Sahir had not been looking forward to this. It wasn't just that at thirteen he felt a little old for the annual picnic his mother insisted upon. It was more the fact that when they eventually got to the top there was an awkward conversation to be had.

Sahir, much like his younger brother and sister, had grown up vaguely aware that their mother had a *confidant*—whatever that meant.

As heir to the Janana throne, Sahir spent his summers being tutored in protocol and Janana's intricate laws—and a few years ago he had discovered that their mother had a lover!

Sahir had kept that knowledge to himself, but this particular summer their mother's disinhibition had meant his younger siblings had worked things out for themselves.

Something *had* to be said.

'It has to be you,' Ibrahim had said, always happy to avoid a task and volunteering Sahir. 'You're going to be King one day.'

'Mama's going to leave Papa!' Jasmine had sobbed dramatically. 'Oh, poor Papa.'

'She is not going to leave him.' Sahir was firm with his sister. Even if he was cross with Mother, he felt defensive towards her. 'As Queen, she's done nothing wrong—the law states that she can take a confidant—and anyway, Father might have—'

He'd halted abruptly, deciding not to reveal that the King was allowed a *haẓiyya*, or second wife. Not only would Sahir prefer not to deal with more drama from Jasmine, he could not begin to fathom his austere father invoking such a rule.

'Papa should be kinder.' Ibrahim had been indignant. 'He's miserable and always cross…'

'He has a lot on his mind,' Sahir had reminded him sharply. 'These are troubled times. The King has to focus on peace for our land—not dramas within the palace walls.'

Growing up, they'd all heard their mother taunting the King whenever she felt she was being ignored—telling him that she would take it up with her confidant…saying that at least *he* listened to her, at least *he* noticed what she wore…

It had all come to a head this summer.

Ibrahim had seen her one night, all dressed up in lipstick and jewels, and their mother had urgently warned him not to tell.

And Jasmine, after a bad dream, had tried to get to her mother's bedroom. But the entrance to the *syn* wing had been locked…

'There were no maidens and she took for ever to answer,' Jasmine had sobbed to Sahir. 'Then she wouldn't let me in… just sent me back to bed…'

More worryingly for Sahir, he had seen the sour expression on Aadil's face when a lavish delivery had arrived for the Queen.

Aadil was Sahir's protection officer, but Aadil's father was the King's senior advisor, and if this reached the King's ears there would be trouble.

Sahir knew every rule, and he knew that while a confidant was allowed, all parties *must* be discreet.

Increasingly, Queen Anousheh of Janana was not.

'Oh, Sahir...' Mother was breathless as she reached the top. 'Give me a moment.' She caught her breath as Sahir spread out the rug and blankets he had brought up earlier. 'It looks wonderful.' She smiled. 'Look at all the treats you have brought. It is good for you to learn to do this without servants...'

'I make my own bed at school,' he said, opening the hamper he had carried up the cliff steps and pouring her some iced tea. 'Here.'

'Thank you.' She drank it thirstily. 'What I am saying is that it is good to know these special places.'

Sahir resisted rolling his eyes. Last year they had climbed dusty palace stairwells, the year before they had explored caves... 'The places you take me to are practically inaccessible.'

'Exactly.' Mother smiled. 'So you can do things without others always knowing. You might want a little privacy one day...'

Mother was a fine one to talk about privacy, Sahir thought as they sat drinking iced tea and eating the delicacies Sahir had sourced while they made small talk. Or rather, while Mother attempted to squeeze conversation from her thirteen-year-old son, talking about his life in London and his school subjects, trying to find out about his friends.

'It's a shame Carter didn't come this year.'

'He's spending the summer in Borneo with his grandfather.'

'Poor Carter. To lose all his family like that...' She gave a pensive sigh. 'Does he speak of them?'

'No.' Sahir shook his head. 'He never has.'

Years ago, his friend Carter's mother and baby brother had been killed in a crocodile attack—his father had perished attempting to save them. Sahir only knew what had been said at school or in the press. His friend had never discussed it. Not even once.

'Sometimes it's as if he's forgotten them.'

'He hasn't,' Mother said with certainty. 'Be there for him, Sahir. Always invite him to join us for holidays and celebrations. Speak their names...'

'I've tried.'

'You'll know when the time is right.'

The desert was like an orange fire behind the palace, and the ocean was pounding on the rocks below. Sahir looked to the city skyline beyond.

Janana was a land of contrasts...beautiful and fierce, delicate and wild, mighty yet conversely fragile.

Sahir knew his history, and even if his father was distant and remote he was fiercely proud of him. King Babek of Janana had fought long and hard to have a thriving capital and CBD, with state-of-the-art hospitals, hotels and designer shops, even though the elders and council had been strongly opposed.

For his mother, Queen Anousheh, it was the ancient city and the desert that were her passion.

They both gazed towards the palace, taking in the magnificence of the ancient citadel. From this vantage point the *setarah*—star structure—was evident, but not so the hidden passages and stairs that led to the unroofed centre tower—outwardly bland, glorious within—with its view of the night sky the jewel.

The palace, though a sight to behold, bore the scars of history. Centuries ago an earthquake had devastated Janana, razing buildings, wiping out villages. The fracture had stretched to the palace, where an entire wing had been reduced to rubble, killing the then Queen as well as many palace staff.

Shortly after the earthquake the King had taken his own

life, throwing the beleaguered country into further chaos and turmoil. In consequence the lineage had changed, and so had some of the marital laws. New legislation had been put in place to ensure such a tragedy could never befall the country again. Any future king or queen must have but one passion—the Kingdom of Janana.

Love was for commoners, not their rulers.

'It is such an eyesore,' Mother said, following Sahir's gaze to the destroyed wing.

'It serves as a reminder,' Sahir responded, repeating his teachings. 'A ruler's heart can belong only to his country.'

'Well, once your father brokers peace I am going to fight to have the wing rebuilt and the palace returned to its former glory.'

Mother always had grand plans.

'Sahir,' she ventured, perhaps attempting a gentler approach with her very self-contained son. 'I know that love is forbidden for a monarch, but I do believe that a heart is for sharing.'

'Yes,' he agreed. 'A king's heart is divided equally amongst his subjects.'

'I want you to listen to me.' Mother put down her refreshments to speak. 'Just because you are going to be King, that doesn't mean you have to agree with everything the elders—'

'I don't always agree,' Sahir interrupted.

This topic was one he wrestled with himself. He knew his mother must be lonely, even if she smiled and laughed. And yet he could understand the demands placed upon his father.

'I am learning, and not yet King,' he said. 'Until that time I shall abide by all the teachings.' He turned to face her. 'You do!' At thirteen he had not quite mastered being as aloof as his father. 'Especially the ones that suit you.'

'Pardon?' She blinked.

It had to be said, and it fell to him. 'Your discretion is lacking.'

'Sahir...?' Her head was cocked to the side, her hazel eyes

curious. Perhaps she was unsure about the warning being given. 'What are you saying?'

Sahir held her gaze and refused to blush. Nor did he allow a glimpse of his agony at having this conversation. His voice was deep, that of a man, and he held on to his trust that it would remain steady now.

'There is no place in the palace for an imprudent confidant.'

To his surprise, she laughed. 'Oh, Sahir.' She laughed so much she wiped tears from her eyes. 'You can be so staid at times—just like your father.'

'He is King!'

'Yes…yes.' She took a breath, pressed her lips together and composed her face. 'You are right.'

'Mother, please…' Now his voice croaked…now fear surfaced. Sahir had done his best to reassure Jasmine, but he too was scared of what might happen. 'Be more careful.'

'Sahir…' She held his chin. 'You were right to speak to me. It will be addressed. Now, let's enjoy the rest of our picnic. Tomorrow you fly to London, and soon you'll be back at school.'

Sahir nodded, but then frowned. 'Mother?' There was a trickle of blood coming from her nostril. 'You're bleeding.'

'It's the climb,' she said, reaching for a napkin. 'Is there any ice in the hamper?'

'Of course.' He felt dreadful, even if it was quickly sorted. 'I should not have said anything.'

'Sahir,' she reassured him. 'I'm fine.' She put her arm around his tense shoulders, as if she knew how much this conversation had killed him. 'I know it took courage to discuss this with me.'

'You'll be more careful?'

She nodded. 'Everything shall be fine.'

Three weeks later he was summoned from class and told his mother was gravely ill.

Mid-flight home, Sahir was informed that Queen Anousheh was dead.